Florida Justice

a Novel of Sexy Florida Suspense

by

Emma "Freeway" Lincoln

(originally titled *Retribution*)

Florida Justice

Copyright 2000 Emma "Freeway" Lincoln
Originally published as "Retribution"

Published 2011 by Awesome Book Publishing
P.O. Box 1157
Roseland, FL 32957

ISBN # 978-0-9840538-1-0

This book is dedicated to my gorgeous husband, Ray, who always believes in me.

Chapter 1

Lee County, Florida
November 1994

"This suspect is dangerous," Kelsey Reed told the police officers. She rode in the back seat, leaning forward to be heard as they sped along the county road to their destination in the Florida Everglades, the Three Pines Trailer Court.

Kelsey, an investigator for the State Attorney's Office, had considered this her case from the very beginning. Dave Daniels, the man they were going to arrest tonight based on her work, was an identity thief who also happened to be enormously fat. Daniels had not only used other people's credit to purchase tens of thousands of dollars worth of merchandise- he had also bought weapons.

"I really think we should wait for backup," Kelsey again tried to persuade the middle-aged deputies, raising her voice over the noise of the wind that came in the open windows, along with the scent of marsh. "I know Daniels has a house full of guns!"

Deputy Frank Ryan, a Florida native with a relaxed accent that seemed at odds with his tight muscular body, glanced back at Kelsey from the passenger seat and patted the holster on his side. "I'm not worried," he told her. "We're going to do this real easy."

Neither Ryan, nor his partner, Doug Pierce, showed much emotion. They had told Kelsey earlier that they'd been to the Three Pines Trailer Court hundreds of times, often on cases more serious than this one and Kelsey understood that they planned to handle this their own way. Unfortunately, she had no official say in it.

The squad car turned in over a dirt culvert, with the headlights illuminating the park sign, and then the shapes of rusted and battered trailers came into view one after another, alternating with trash and overgrown shrubbery. Only one or two dim lights showed in windows across the park.

Officer Pierce slowed the car down, and the squint lines around his eyes deepened with tension as he cocked his head to indicate the trailer on his left. "This is it, number one-eighty-one. There doesn't seem to be anybody up."

Kelsey stared as they pulled into a cul-de-sac with several units and she noticed that the trailer Pierce indicated was relatively well kept. It was a large single-wide with fake wood trim and a high redwood deck and Kelsey caught a glimpse of a child's swing set and toys in the yard, all looking brand-new. The sight of this trailer made Kelsey feel angry, the fact that the fat and uneducated Daniels could perpetrate the largest credit-card scam in this county's history and then go to ground in this pathetic place.

They pulled up right in front of the trailer and came to a stop; the breeze pushed Kelsey's long hair into her mouth and she impatiently swatted it away.

"Okay, we're doing it," Ryan said.

The two big men stepped out of the car, adjusting their gun belts, and Kelsey opened her door and stepped out with them.

"I'm going with you," she asserted.

Ryan just shrugged inside his uniform, with his back to her. She had been expressly forbidden to go inside when the Joint Task Force had planned the arrest, but now the deputies were in a hurry, and taking time to argue might get someone killed. Kelsey had counted on this. She wanted badly to see Daniels for herself and she had persuaded the Sheriff's Department to let her ride along for the arrest, based on all the work she had done on the case. In addition to her curiosity was the fact that Kelsey thought she could help. She didn't want to leave these cops to go in alone when she thought she had a better idea of the nature of the suspect. She also had a registered .32 caliber automatic in her purse, and she was prepared to use it if she had to.

The deck shuddered and shook with their footsteps, all going up the front way. Kelsey thought this approach unwise and she kept one foot on the ground, prepared to run around back to cover the rear of the trailer, if necessary. With brand new jeans accentuating lean muscles, Kelsey was in the best shape of her life and she felt like she was up for anything she might be faced with.

Officer Pierce pounded on the metal door and yelled in a loud voice. "Police. Open up!"

Then, speaking to Ryan, he said, "The other windows are too small for Daniels to go anywhere. Looks like we're going to be seeing him face to face."

Ryan pushed Kelsey against the wall, protecting her, and told her, "Stay back!"

Two heartbeats went by. Pierce yelled again, "Police, open the door!"

Then Ryan said firmly, "Let's do it!"

He slipped something quickly into the metal door, and pried it open with a pop.

They were inside. One of the deputies flicked on a light, a dim incandescent that showed shabby furniture and newer electronics crammed into a small living room, and the poverty in the trailer contrasted with the brand new Chevy Tahoe parked outside. The living area smelled faintly of trapped heat and rotting wood, with knickknacks and junk everywhere, and the policemen's large bodies seemed to crowd the room.

A piercing cry, a young child's scream, came from the closer of the back rooms and the deputies turned in that direction. The two men tripped over a giant, furry calico cat that hurried out of their way, hissing in protest, as they rushed toward the room where a light burned.

Now Kelsey heard a woman's voice, yelling and cracking as the men pushed back into the narrow hallway and she assumed this was Allison Hart, Daniels' common-law wife.

"Get out! Get out of here!" the young woman screamed and Kelsey could see the top of her blond head over the men's shoulders.

Kelsey shivered. She kept checking behind her, looking towards the empty living room and the banging front door to make sure that no one else was coming in.

Deputy Pierce followed the woman into the room while Ryan advanced down the corridor, moving along the walls. Kelsey stood on her tiptoes behind the first cop's back and saw the woman in the lighted room bend protectively over a screaming curly-haired child. Children's pictures covered the walls of the tiny bedroom, the kid looked healthy and angry and his big blue eyes stared at the men defiantly. His mother looked towards them with the same blue eyes, but hers looked pleading and confused.

"Don't do anything; don't hurt him," she cried and Kelsey wondered if she was referring to her child or to the young man in the room behind them.

Kelsey examined the woman for only a split second, noticing something blowsy and indolent about Allison Hart, but also something elemental, like this is what it meant to be just getting up from sex. The woman wore a T-shirt with a fishing logo on it bunched up on two rolls of belly fat and her large breasts hung loosely as she bent over her child. She walked around with bare feet and her calves and legs looked muscular, despite her being overweight. Her face was puffy, her blond hair was going dark at the roots and she looked ten years older than her actual age, which Kelsey knew was twenty-five. Kelsey knew Allison Hart ought to be ashamed of her appearance. She herself felt ashamed just looking at her, because once this woman might have been pretty.

The young woman and the whole scene seemed so different from anything Kelsey had known in the past. It all felt so embarrassingly real. Although this wasn't a house in the sense she understood, in other ways, it *was* a home and there was something very private here.

Kelsey momentarily felt like a violator as Allison Hart briefly met her eyes. Deputy Pierce tried to turn the woman's breasty body around while Allison struggled with him, but it looked like the struggle was just on principle. The woman was crying and submissive yet she didn't want to let go of her child. Pierce gently maneuvered mother and child, trying to slip on handcuffs.

"He'll be fine," Pierce said, referring to the boy. "I just need to do this for everyone's safety. We know there're some firearms in the house."

The deputy was trying to get the handcuffs onto the woman, moving her arms like they were in some strange dance together while she twisted. "Let's just set your son back down on this bed," Pierce said, "so he'll be okay. What's his name now?"

This question seemed to be the charm. The woman stopped crying and spoke. "Brandon," she said. "His name is Brandon."

The officer got the handcuffs onto the woman's plump wrists, guided her to sit down on the bed and then moved to follow his partner. But Kelsey was in his way. She moved quickly ahead of him down a hallway so narrow that her hips brushed against the walls. She and the deputy entered the master bedroom that was lit only by moonlight and Kelsey heard Deputy Ryan talking to someone, but his body in front of the doorway blocked her view.

4

Ryan's voice was quiet and conversational, but Kelsey immediately picked up the tension and fear in it. "Put the gun down, David," Ryan said. "It's not gonna do you any good. It's just the two of us deputies here and we're not hurting anybody. We're doing this nice and easy. No one is going to get killed."

Kelsey stood between Ryan and his partner, but she still couldn't see anything over Deputy Ryan's back.

Ryan flicked the briefest of glances over his shoulder to Pierce and then spoke calmly. "Don't do anything, Doug. He's got an assault rifle in here."

"The kid's back in the other room," Deputy Pierce said, speaking deliberately loud enough so that Daniels could hear. "And the lady's fine."

Kelsey was stunned. *They were all going to die here.* These guys had refused to wait for backup! She had *told* them there were guns in this house, so why did they think this guy was so harmless? She felt terror all through her body, suddenly picturing her belly being torn apart with gunfire.

Kelsey wanted to get a look at Dave Daniels and she wanted to take her own chance. She stepped to the older cop's side in the bluish light and now she stared at Daniels, the suspect she had been investigating for months. The fat young man crouched in his bed, half-nude, among the rumbled sheets, holding the short black rifle aimed at Deputy Ryan. A thread of fresh air came in from the two low louvered windows and Kelsey thought she could smell body heat escaping from the side of bed the woman had just left.

Daniels' mean eyes glowed at Kelsey from behind the gun sight as though he was an animal, hurt and furious. She had expected him to be fat; she knew that he was from his driver's license photo in her case file. But now the bluish rolls of his flesh lit by moonlight struck her, how astonishingly ugly he was, how anticlimactic it would be if he killed her.

"I'm the one you want," Kelsey said to him. "I'm Kelsey Reed, from the State Attorney's Office. If you're David, then I'm the one you spoke to on the phone a few months ago. Don't let any innocent people die because of this."

Deputy Ryan tried to push Kelsey away but it was too late. The young man began moving towards them.

Ryan's voice sounded broken. "We never should have brought her here," he said to his partner.

Daniels had slid to the end of the bed. He looked up at them with darkly glowing eyes. "No, I'm glad you did bring her, guys. If it weren't for her, you wouldn't be here, right?" he asked, sarcastically.

Kelsey spoke up. "There are innocent victims of your crimes. Did you think it didn't matter? There are families out there who are going to lose their houses because you messed with their credit. You didn't think of that, did you?"

She stared at the angry, unrepentant, obese young man whose lifestyle was nothing more than what she saw in this trailer. All the things he had taken from others, he had made into this.

"Call off your dog!" Daniels said to the deputies. He glared up into their faces, with a fringe of ill-cut brown hair hiding his eyes. Kelsey could see the sheen of sweat over his rolls of fat.

Daniels gestured with the automatic rifle across their midsections.

Kelsey noticed how Ryan steadily held out his own gun aimed at Daniels. Ryan held a .45 caliber pistol, which she supposed was equally deadly at this range. But it didn't matter. Deputy Pierce had an arm on hers, steadying her, and she sensed that she was the explosive element in this situation.

She looked over at the peach and blue covers bunched on the floor, the everyday items arranged on the bedside table and the new, frosty blue area rug. The room felt too snug crowded with Kelsey and the two police officers. Their increased body heat gave off strong smells of stale cologne and deodorant. Seeing the artifacts of the young couple living in this room, she felt some regret being here. But she couldn't turn back.

"I'll blow you all to hell!" Daniels ranted, swinging the gun in an arc, back and forth.

Then he glared up at Kelsey, with his thick wet lips curling in a smirk. "You're a stupid bitch," he said. "None of those people lose anything. They just have to report it."

Was that what he thought? Breathless, she opened her mouth to debate with him because she had the facts and he was wrong. Hardworking people's lives could be ruined because of what he had done to their credit. Then Kelsey appreciated the emptiness and loneliness here, tasting the night air. Lives might be lost because of someone's error in judgment. She chose not to speak.

In the silence they could hear sobs coming from the room behind them. Daniels' girlfriend alternately cried and comforted the little boy. As the woman realized the others were being quiet, she called out in a ragged voice, "Davie, please don't do anything. Put down the gun, please!"

Then she returned to sobbing in that torn, helpless voice.

Daniels had moisture on his face and Kelsey couldn't be sure if it was from tears or sweat.

"Allison's not part of this," he said to the three of them. "Leave her out of it!"

Ryan glanced toward Kelsey, questioning, because it was her investigation. The State Attorney's Office might not have been able to prosecute any of this without the thoroughness of the research she had done, devoting herself to the case for four months.

Kelsey addressed her comments to the police officer, avoiding Daniels, even though he was watching her. "We don't really have anything on her," Kelsey confirmed. "There's no reason she has to be involved."

Deputy Pierce was still pressing down on Kelsey's arm as he spoke to the young man. "But we still need to take Allison in for questioning. You've got to understand that..."

Daniels bit his lip, seeming torn. "If anything happens..." he said.

The cops were quiet. It was as though Kelsey and Daniels were the only ones on the same wavelength in this room, the only ones feeling anger.

Daniels paused, seeming to think over the consequences for a moment, and then he suddenly lunged to his feet and pressed his assault rifle into Deputy Ryan's stomach. The deputy stumbled back against Kelsey and then caught his balance. He grabbed Daniels by the back of the head and shoved his own gun against Daniels' jowly throat.

Kelsey reached for her purse, thinking she would kill Daniels if she had to.

But Pierce steadied her hand and mouthed, "No!"

Allison wailed from the other room, like some sixth sense told her what was happening. "Don't do it, Davie. Give up!"

No one shot. The cat came in and wound itself a few times around Kelsey's and Pierce's legs. They had gone so far here. They had judged things so wrong. No one would have a career anymore if this terrible thing went down.

"Daniels..." Kelsey said.

Daniels looked to Pierce instead. "I'm not doing jail time," he said. "I'll take your partner with me..."

In another situation, it probably would have been Frank Ryan who did the negotiating. Now all Ryan could do was hold still, braced against the deadly weapon pressed into his tight stomach. His muscular body visibly shook. Kelsey could smell the slight ammonia smell of urine in the air. It was the officer's, she suspected, not Daniels'.

"Look, Davie," Deputy Pierce said, "you're probably not looking at any hard time for your credit cards."

This, Kelsey knew, was a lie. Some of the fraud charges carried mandatory federal time and then there would be serious charges stemming from tonight.

Pierce went on, persuasively. "... But if you kill anyone here, you're going to the electric chair. You know what state you're in, Davie. You know the laws in Florida and you know I'm not lying. You do want to see that kid back there again, don't you?"

Pierce reached out his hand, all the way towards Daniels. He approached, crouched, stretching out his hand for the weapon.

Kelsey stepped back out of the way, leaning against a low curtain, and she felt glad she had come here, after all.

Daniels surrendered the gun.

Allison had come to stand in the doorway. The little boy was behind her, clutching his mother's fingers, which extended out of the cuffs. Allison breathed raggedly, hyperventilating, staring at her lover while the cops pushed his arms into handcuffs.

"There you go, Davie," Pierce said, "safe and sound."

Daniels' body was exposed now. It was unmanly, pear shaped, with broad hips and a huge belly hanging over cotton shorts that were the match to Allison's shirt. Rather than pectoral muscles, his chest stuck out like breasts. The hard nipples brushed against Kelsey as Pierce pushed him through the narrow doorway. Kelsey looked at her suspect disdainfully. She was wearing high boots and it made her his height or a little taller. Obviously, in an attempt to make up for his personal deficiencies, the young man had stolen identities and ruined innocent lives. She was glad they were taking him in.

As Daniels passed, the heavy blonde's eyes met her lover's and they stretched toward each other to exchange a kiss.

"I love you, Davie," Allison said.

Daniels glanced down at his child. Then he looked away, letting the policeman push him into the corridor.

In the bedroom, Deputy Ryan was bent over double, breathing hard and laughing to himself. "Man," he said, "*that* was a close call. Hey, Pierce, I peed myself! That little punk made me pee myself!" He reeled towards the small bathroom to wash up.

His partner laughed heartily while pushing the prisoner forward. With no real malice, he said to Daniels, "You got him so scared he pissed his pants. That's no joke! A guy like you shouldn't be allowed to have a gun."

The child followed the line of adults into the living area and Pierce guided Allison and Daniels to sit on kitchen chairs while he made a call from their telephone.

Kelsey sensed that this was real, as real as it got. This case *had* been something big. Dave Daniels *had* been a menace to be out on the streets. He had proven that tonight.

When Deputy Ryan got back, he pulled Kelsey aside into the living room to talk to her. "You were right," he told her. "Daniels was dangerous. I guess he would have blown, sooner or later. It seems a shame, though. He's not really a bad guy."

Kelsey didn't see it that way. This was a crime. It had its consequences.

Cars were pulling up now, the backup that the two officers had refused to wait for before.

Deputy Ryan leaned out the doorway and Kelsey relished the gust of fresh air he let in. "I need a policewoman in here," Ryan called out into the night. A few minutes later a solidly built policewoman came jogging up the steps.

The young couple in handcuffs leaned across the table and kissed each other again. Kelsey noticed the blue veins in the young woman's legs and the milky flesh of the young man in the harsh fluorescent light somebody had turned on.

The cat ran out the door.

Now the room was crowded with busy personnel. The lady cop talked to the little boy who kept turning away from her and rubbing at his eyes. There were two officers standing beside his mother; they had been directed there by Deputy Ryan. "Please take this lady out of here," he said. "It'll make it easier."

Allison began crying again and her two-tone hair fell into her face. There was moisture all over, tears and drool mixed, and she didn't seem to care. "I can't do this," she cried. "Davie, I love you. I can't do this alone!"

Deputy Pierce leaned down over her. "Calm it down, now. You've got to go with these officers. Let us do what we have to here so that we can read Davie his rights."

"My baby, why can't I stay with him?"

She was referring to Brandon. The policewoman had picked up the small blond child and was holding him tight.

"You should be home tonight, Allison," Pierce said. "Shouldn't she?" he asked the female officer, who shook her head like she didn't know.

Pierce continued, "Okay, Allison, no promises. But come on, you gotta go."

Daniels' girlfriend cried like she'd never stop. Daniels looked up at her, with his body steady and calm, as though he was sitting at the table by choice. "I'll take care of things, Babe. I promise," he said, as they finally pulled Allison out onto the porch.

The police led Allison away, with four men in uniforms struggling with her buxom, sweaty body. She kept turning back to try to see her boyfriend. She was barefoot and still in underwear.

From Kelsey's vantage point at the doorway, she watched them hustle the blonde towards a marked cruiser. Someone had placed a police jacket over Allison's shoulders. A group of neighbors stood outside, talking to some of the officers, and red and blue lights bathed the cul-de-sac.

Ryan and Pierce brought their prisoner to his feet, telling him his rights while he gritted his teeth, with most of his face hidden by unruly hair. His belly jutted out, huge and pale. His genitals hung loosely in the little white and green shorts, which were almost hidden by his excess flesh. He breathed loudly. The two officers didn't seem bothered by his physicality or the fact that he had earlier tried to kill them.

Kelsey shuddered with understanding, grateful for the cool wind from the door, which contrasted with the heat inside the trailer. What she had seen tonight in the two police officers was true bravery and she wished that she could someday live up to it herself. That is why she dreamed of becoming a prosecutor.

Glancing over at the living room, at stacked milk crates filled with music CD's, she saw the last evidence of Dave Daniels, evidence of who he, in particular, was. She had stood up to him tonight, she realized, rather than backing down, and she had stood still when the officers did, rather than trying to run away. Probably not too many people would have had the nerve to stand there like she did. Kelsey was only twenty-two-years old, still a girl in her own mind, yet tonight, in that room, she had faced death along with the other participants.

The police brought Daniels right up by her, facing her in the doorway, with his bulk filling up the space. At the moment Kelsey felt righteous and confident, with her slim body and form-fitting jeans, and not like him at all.

"Hold it a minute," Deputy Pierce said. "Let's get some more bracelets on you." He ducked down by the young man's feet to adjust leg irons. A cleaned-up Deputy Ryan, looking a little older after the stress of tonight, held Daniels firmly by his arm. The suspect ignored them.

Dave Daniels breathed in and out, staring at Kelsey with a lower lip roughly grasped in his teeth. He waited for her to seek out his eyes under the mess of hair. Involuntarily, though she didn't want to look at him, her eyes flickered there. She really couldn't see him, but he could see her.

Daniels leaned in close and then, in a quiet voice, he asked her, "This is personal, Kelsey. Isn't it?"

Chapter 2

"WHAT GOES AROUND COMES AROUND, KELSEY," read the anonymous message on Kelsey's email at work.

But there was no way Kelsey was backing out of her plans for tonight. At ten-o-clock, she cranked up dance music so that it thudded through her condo and she and her best friend Miranda bumped hips trying to share her bathroom mirror before going out dancing.

"I should have bought the other dress." Kelsey pouted as she cocked her head at the image of herself in her new burgundy cocktail dress.

"No way!" Miranda exclaimed. She gave a throaty laugh and shook out her big head of red curls, a distinctive gesture since they'd been friends as little girls. Then she leaned forward to slick on her usual bright red lipstick.

Kelsey also leaned towards the mirror, examining her face as though it could answer some of the questions she'd had about her life lately. Currently, she wore her dark brown hair long and straight, with chunky layers starting at the chin and curving inward. The currently popular hairstyle happened to complement her heart-shaped face. Kelsey had large brown eyes, a small mouth and slightly strong, dark eyebrows. Her face might be called a *gamine*-looking if you were being complimentary, elfin if you were not.

"Did I tell you," she asked Miranda, "that, when Paul broke up with me two weeks ago, he actually asked me if I would still want to go with him to *business functions*? Like I was just a *convenience?*"

Miranda's eyes widened and then her wide lips slid into a jaded smile.

"That's why we go out to the clubs," she advised, "and why I dress like a disco slut from hell- so we don't have to feel so vulnerable."

Kelsey controlled a smile. "You've been dressing in platforms and minis since junior high, Miranda. It suits your personality!"

Miranda directed her green eyes, half lined in smoky shadow, down at her friend. "So, do I have to remind you that the way you dress so perfect is something special, too?"

Kelsey did like staying current with fashion. It was one thing she felt she could control. She sighed, and leaned against the counter, stalling for a moment in her preparations. "I don't think going out to clubs since Paul dumped me has helped, Miranda. Maybe I can't do this."

Kelsey watched her friend process the information. Miranda was tall and very thin, with hollowed shadows under her cheekbones, and long red curls parted down either side of her chest. Her angular features could sometimes look mean even when she was being pleasant. "Do this or die," she said, referring to the club scene. "It's this or the sound of that lonely night wind."

"Well, why bother?" Kelsey asked. "All I ever wanted to be was a hero, enforcing the law. Now I feel like I'm accomplishing nothing in criminal justice just working as a private investigator..."

Miranda pointedly ignored her. "I'm feeling kind of dirty tonight," she commented, "so, why don't we go to Creamsicles? Hey- look what I bought!"

They stepped into the bedroom, where Miranda leaned over her capacious leather pocketbook she had thrown on Kelsey's bed. She brought out a handful of condoms in colorful wrappers and held them up triumphantly.

"You're so bad!" Kelsey admonished. Yet she felt a familiar excitement build as she stepped into her strappy high heels. Her new satin dress felt cool on her skin, and she allowed Miranda to fasten a perfectly matched garnet choker around her neck. Kelsey felt fully in the moment now, with the odd threat on her email this morning temporarily forgotten.

It didn't matter that she hadn't gone to law school yet or that she worked for a marginal firm like Confidential Investigations, rather than for the good guys at the State Attorney's Office. At the moment, she *did* yearn for something to happen tonight.

Perhaps she could meet a decent guy; maybe they'd start dating. She caught a glimpse of herself in the full-length mirror on the back of the door and saw that she looked tall in her high heels, and almost beautiful in the dusky light.

"Fine," she told Miranda, "I'll meet someone. I'll rock some poor guy's world tonight."

Miranda stood beside her and smiled.

Then the friends hurried through the apartment, shutting off lights. They grabbed last sips of white wine off the kitchen counter and set their glasses back on the tile surface, where Kelsey's tomcat, Mr. Cooper, sat up on the counter with his short gray coat blending into the dimness of the room. He looked up and he mewed at Kelsey, as if to beg, "Don't go."

Kelsey acknowledged him, giving his chin one brief affectionate rub. "Hush, Baby", she told him. "Mommy's gotta go out."

As soon as they got into her car, Miranda cranked down the window and lit up a cigarette. Kelsey leaned forward and played with the radio until she found a top-forties station, while Miranda gunned the ratty black Sunfire out of the condo complex and onto the back streets, heading for Hillsboro Boulevard. Six-lane Hillsboro would take them to crowded Interstate 95, where Miranda would do the dance of traffic seven exits south.

Riding with Miranda was always a nerve-wracking experience and Kelsey preferred driving herself, whenever possible. Unlike her friend, she had what she considered a real car, a two-and-a-half year old red Dodge Avenger. Kelsey's sporty car had a powerful engine and good handling, while her girlfriend's car was not fit to be on the road. Kelsey felt she was always taking her life in her hands as the other girl tested her limits in the small unsound vehicle. It was as though Miranda had a death wish.

As they merged onto the highway, Kelsey's hair blew all over her face and she got sparks from Miranda's cigarette. Miranda deliberately changed the radio station back to club music, which overwhelmed the noisy pounding of the wind.

"When are you going to get air conditioning?" Kelsey yelled. "And when are you going to get a new car?"

Miranda pretended not to hear her. "Your friend Jerry's kinda sexy," she yelled. "Too bad he thinks he might be gay."

Kelsey's coworker and close friend, Jerry Klein, *was* attractive, with his slim, graceful body, flirty ways and sophisticated sense of humor. He also had an enduring crush on Kelsey that they always joked about, and he made it clear that he'd like to be her serious boyfriend if she ever wanted it. But it was Kelsey's nature to be uncomfortable with anything not black and white. Even though she knew Jerry had never been physically intimate with a man, his sexual preferences seemed somewhat ambiguous, so she had just left the relationship at friendship.

Right now she felt a bit out-of-control, yet also giddy, as her girlfriend's car tilted in its lane at eighty miles-an-hour. Miranda suddenly yanked the car left, cutting off an eighteen-wheeler that honked at them with its gigantic, low-pitched horn. She was attempting to get closer to a white Jaguar convertible with two young men inside.

"Hey!" the driver yelled when he saw them, and he swerved closer to their car. "Where are you ladies heading?"

"Creamsicles," Miranda screeched, climbing halfway out the window to be heard. "It's on Oakland Park, west, past Turnpike."

The guys fishtailed off and Miranda sat back, slowing down abruptly in a satisfied, dreamy mode. "The driver looked nice," she said. "Do you think we might go home with them tonight?"

The huge truck Miranda had cut off bore down angrily behind them and it finally passed them on the right.

"Miranda, why do you take chances like that?" Kelsey demanded.

"You mean one-night-stands?" she asked. "Those guys? Because I'm horny and it's safe sex..."

"No," Kelsey said, turning in her seat to look at her friend, "the truck back there. He almost hit us."

"Look, Kelsey," Miranda said. "I know that you drive like a traffic cop and you're precise about everything. But still, you go out interviewing criminals for your job, and that's something even I'd be afraid to do."

Kelsey attempted to contradict her friend about her job, even though she *had* gotten in a lot deeper than she intended. "Confidential specializes in problems with employees. It's nothing really high-risk..."

"So how about that cocaine smuggling case at Port Everglades that you and Jerry have been undercover on? Aren't a bunch of guys going to trial?"

Kelsey felt a bit queasy. Not only had there been the threat on her email today, which she felt probably involved defendants in the drug case, but she was also concerned about the morality of the work she did. She knew if she and Jerry *did* uncover anything questionable about employees on the yacht that carried the drugs, they'd only turn their information over to the shipping company, not the police, as she would have wished.

16

Kelsey already knew she wanted to leave Confidential Investigations; her dream was to become a prosecutor. She had an application in to Nova University's Graduate Law Program and, as soon as she received an acceptance, which could come within a few months, she planned to quit the job. If Nova's grad school ended up rejecting her, then she'd leave Florida, not take the option to buy her condo and move back home to New York State. In fact, she and Miranda planned to move back together. Her girlfriend was only waiting for Kelsey to say the word.

"Miranda, you know I want to leave that job," Kelsey said. "In a few more months I'll be out of there one way or another. Just don't mention it to my coworkers yet, okay?"

Ten minutes later, at Creamsicles' parking lot, Kelsey caught sight of Jerry Klein already waiting in line. He stood beside the new girl from work, a young blonde named Wendy Pedersen.

"Girlfriends!" Jerry exclaimed, and he and Miranda acted all huggy and kissy.

Then Jerry made a big deal of introducing Kelsey to the new girl. He reeled Kelsey in, wrapping an arm tight around her and kissing her on the lips. "This is the love of my life," he boasted to Wendy.

Kelsey brushed Jerry off, mortified by the idea that the other girl might get a totally wrong idea about their relationship. As the group stepped forward, Kelsey realized that she recognized the bouncer, a big man named Lou that Miranda had a brief sexual fling with when she first came down to join Kelsey in Fort Lauderdale.

"Kelsey, Miranda," Lou asked with pitiful eagerness, "why don't I ever see you here anymore?"

"We don't like all the losers," Miranda teased.

"I hear you," Lou agreed. "But that's all the owner's doing, not mine. We can party afterward if you want to, though. I've got some coke..."

Miranda shrugged and she whispered, giggling, in Kelsey's ear, "Been there, done that! Let's just get inside!"

"Sorry, we've gotta go!" Kelsey told the bouncer, backing her girlfriend up.

The burly man just looked down, seeming depressed, as they walked away. Kelsey wondered idly what would happen if her bold best friend ever made one of these guys really mad, the way she sometimes teased them.

Thinking about how Lou, or someone like him, could get violent with Miranda, made Kelsey think back to the threat she'd received at work and the fact that she'd felt jumpy a lot lately, as though someone might possibly be following her. Threatening messages were not uncommon at Confidential, but this one had been aimed at her personally. What if one of the guys *she'd* slept with had sent her the *"goes around, comes around"* email, rather than someone involved with the drug case? Yet that didn't make much sense, since she and the young men she'd seen had always parted on good terms.

With her chest constricted with her concerns, Kelsey didn't suppose she matched up much with her festive dress. But men in the club still looked at her body as she edged along the catwalk behind her friends. This bar had an incredibly tacky atmosphere, with milky orange cement walls decorated with paintings of giant ice-cream pops. Kelsey and Miranda only came to this "meat market" when they were desperate to pick someone up.

Her friend, Jerry, leaned in to Kelsey as they tread carefully down to the bar. "Lovely place," he commented. "This theme is like, so *phallic!*"

She laughed and put her arms around his neck. "You're my savior, Jerry, you know that?"

Kelsey knew she needed a drink and Miranda seemed to read her mind as she presented a big iced concoction in a plastic glass. "Strawberry daiquiri, on me, Baby," she offered. Kelsey thanked her, then ducked her lips down into the cold drink, sipping it fast.

A while later Miranda stood up, looking suddenly alert, and pushed at Kelsey's arm. Kelsey turned in the direction Miranda indicated and immediately noticed the two young men walking across the dance floor. The nicer-looking, dark-haired guy was obviously into bodybuilding. His extremely broad chest and back and his massive arm muscles bulged in his tight polo shirt.

Kelsey smiled. "Yeah, I see," she said.

Muscles were Kelsey's biggest weakness and she found it difficult to ignore the way every cut in this young man's massive upper body showed up. He and his friend had dark tans and wore noticeably flashy jewelry and watches. They looked like tourists, yet there was something vaguely familiar about them.

"It's the guys from before," Miranda pointed out, "the ones from the Jaguar on I-95."

Miranda watched the men make the circuit. Then she brushed back her heavy hair, looking kind of tired. "I like the one with the expensive watch," she said. "What do you think?" she asked Kelsey.

Miranda had picked the smaller guy for herself, the one who had been driving, and Kelsey couldn't help but be intrigued by his friend

18

with the large muscles. The pair finally approached the girls, immediately invading personal distance with the scents of cologne and fresh gum.

The one Miranda had picked had narrower features and inquisitive eyes along with light brown hair. He glanced around edgily, snapped his gum and grinned.

"Does the music always suck like this?" he asked.

The bigger guy just stared at Kelsey, with soulful dark eyes. "Don't mind my friend," he apologized, "he's from Jersey". He gazed at Kelsey, as though just the glimpse of her in the car had been enough to make him like her. "I was hoping you'd be here," he said.

"My name's Marshall Sawyer," his friend broke in rudely. He reached his hand out for both girls to shake. "And this is Joe Carpenito. My best buddy in the world. He's showing me the town, and we're going into business together."

"Nice car," Miranda commented, cynically.

Marshall threw back his head with laughter. Then he tucked a proprietary hand on the back of the tall redhead's neck.

"It's a fuckin' rental. We just got it to impress the chicks," he admitted. Then he held up his arm to show off his gold Rolex watch. "But the watch is real!"

Miranda seemed to appreciate the fact that he could laugh at himself. She grinned at Kelsey and then went off with her new find. The couple found a spot on the dance floor and immediately leaned into each other in a sensual dance.

Kelsey thought that Joe Carpenito had a sweet earnest face, different from his friend's. And he didn't seem the type to casually pick up girls in bars. "Let me get you a drink," he offered her.

He bought Kelsey a sex-on-the-beach and she drank it, surprised that she had lost count of how many drinks she'd already had tonight. Then Joe got right up in her face, capturing her attention.

"I've been thinking about you all night," he said. "Don't think I'm the same as Marshall. I'm looking for a girl I can really care about."

Joe stepped closer, checking her reaction, and Kelsey felt a bit shy. Yet, like a cuddly bear, Joe seemed big and protective to her.

"I sell cellular phones," he boasted. "It's our own company, mine and Marshall's. I used to work construction but I invested all my money into his business. I think it will be really good."

He showed her a cell phone that he pulled out of his tight pants' pocket, a tiny flimsy thing. Yet this big man's heart seemed all wrapped up in it. Kelsey watched his friend feeling up Miranda's backside on the dance floor and she swayed on her heels, too tipsy to focus on Joe's little gadget. Didn't he know Florida ate people like him alive?

"Stupid, isn't it?" he asked, noticing how she looked at his phone. He gave a dry, self-disparaging laugh. Then he took her in his arms, leading her to the throbbing poor-quality music, and they stayed silent for a while as they danced.

"I work as a private investigator," Kelsey said, eventually. "My company is right here in Fort Lauderdale."

Joe seemed to perk up. "That is really cool," he said. "I really respect that. I could tell you were a smart girl!"

They pulled toward each other and he met her lips in a kiss.

Her friend, Jerry, came over at some point and tapped Kelsey on the shoulder. "We're going home," he told her. Then he leaned over and said, for her ears only, "But if you don't trust this guy, I'll hang around..."

She must have said no because Jerry left. Then she danced with Joe for a long time, allowing him to kiss her and caress her body as he bought her drink after drink. Towards closing, Miranda and Marshall came back and put their arms around Kelsey's and Joe's shoulders, locking the four in a group hug.

"Marshall's got some cocaine," Miranda whispered to Kelsey. "You want to go in the bathroom and do it?"

Kelsey shook her head. Even buzzed as she was, she wouldn't mess with drugs and she didn't like her girlfriend doing it either. Joe gave her an apologetic kiss on the forehead before he walked off with the others. And then Kelsey was left alone. She looked around blearily, feeling abruptly exposed and off-balance standing here holding a drink that was too large for her clutches.

The club's strobe lights blinded her momentarily and suddenly she felt a cold feeling, as though someone had laid a hand on her back. It was the same feeling as she'd had earlier today after she'd gotten the email. Kelsey felt sure someone was watching her.

With all the liquor she'd consumed tonight, she was in no shape to evaluate the situation as rationally as she would like to. She set her drink down and tried to get her bearings. Looking around her, she confirmed that she was alone on the catwalk and the club looked like it usually did this time of night. She didn't see anything or anyone out of place and, eventually, the adrenaline feeling started to pass.

The Watcher had brushed by so close that he could have touched Kelsey. He could have steadied her as she stumbled; in fact, he had almost wanted to.

In this game of mirrors, he definitely had the advantage. Kelsey was drinking tonight, letting herself be blinded by disappointments in love life and career. He, on the other hand, had nothing to lose. Kelsey Reed had seen to that long ago.

There were days, before he tracked her down, that he used to picture Kelsey's face obscured by a sheen of his own red rage. There were nights that his hate made it difficult for him to breathe as he thought about hurting her. But the Lord had replaced his disabling anger with coldness.

From behind, he could have simply snapped Kelsey's neck here in the club. But, instead, he wanted to play it out, to make Kelsey suffer like he had.

The Watcher took a step back into the crowd and he let another man approach her.

Someone touched Kelsey. She spun and roughly squeezed the man's arm, applying pressure.

Then she looked into his face and knew immediately she had nothing to fear. Embarrassed, she released the young man's slender arm, and he smiled, rubbing at the spot where she had hurt him. She recognized the guy from earlier, when he'd been dancing with a group of four girls. He was tall and thin, he wore nerdy wire-rimmed glasses and his hair was close shorn and bleached neon yellow in constrast with his dark skin.

"Sorry," the young man said to Kelsey. Then he reached out a delicate hand to touch her silky hair, assessing it. "It's just that you look so pretty," he said. "And this is such a striking dress. My friends and I were just commenting that you look like Jennifer Anniston..."

Kelsey breathed out a rush of air, again aware of herself and her pretty dress. "Thank you," she told him.

When Joe came back, a few steps behind Miranda and Marshall, he seemed to read the whole situation totally wrong. He didn't even notice that the guy talking to Kelsey was openly effeminate, and he seemed to puff up, acting pissed off and jealous.

He immediately put a proprietary arm around Kelsey's shoulders. "Let's go," he said and he pulled her away from the other man, steering her towards the exit.

"He said I was pretty," Kelsey mumbled, unable to explain the relief she felt. She had been so sure someone menacing was watching her just

21

now when, in fact, it had only been a harmless individual who wanted to play with her hair.

"Why do you get all the weirdos?" Miranda laughed. And Kelsey laughed with her, determined that no one, ever, would have her running scared.

Joe Carpenito's condo was located on Pompano Beach, on the third floor of a large building on the west side of A1A. Kelsey felt disappointed to find the apartment cold and bare, obviously a short-term rental, and Joe seemed a little ashamed. He moved awkwardly in the inadequately lighted atmosphere.

"Would you like a drink?" he asked her. "Soda?" When she said yes, he retrieved two cans of coke out of a basically empty refrigerator.

The only decorations in the room, aside from standard hotel room stuff, were Joe's business things- an open briefcase on a sideboard full of electronics. The one other item was a framed photograph of a pretty dark-haired girl.

"That's my ex," he said, when he caught Kelsey looking. "Her name is Tracy." He sat down beside her on the couch and sipped his soda. The big man still smelled of nice cologne and sexy pheromones, yet there was a disturbed feeling coming off of him now, as well.

"Tracy left me," he said. "She didn't trust in anything I did. I still hurt because of her..."

Joe's raw hurt and anger put Kelsey off a little. At some other time, she would have wanted no part of it. But, at the moment, she felt she related to his pain because of what her ex-boyfriend, Paul, had just put her through.

"I know," she said to Joe. "I felt maybe you were hurt by someone. So was I..."

Joe reached for her with the same intensity he had earlier. "Well, let's show them!" he said.

He climbed on top of her with his heavy body and started kissing her and pumping against her. Momentarily, Kelsey wondered if she should be doing this. But the way Joe covered her took away the thoughts of all her disappointments. Next to him, Kelsey felt small and petite, and she felt proud of her trim hips as he lifted her up off the couch, pushing up her dress.

Joe panted loudly, tensing all his muscles as he pushed against her, and he was built very big and thick. Kelsey gasped when she finally took him in her hand, surprised at how big he really was.

But Joe gave her no time. He pushed at her with his powerful hard-on that was already wet with pre-ejaculate, pushing aside her panties while he dominated her mouth with his tongue. Then she was suddenly drenched by his climax.

Joe kissed Kelsey's face all over. He whispered in her ear, "We'll do it again. I'm gonna make love to you again; you're so sweet."

Kelsey stood up, reeling from the alcohol and the intensity of the experience. She'd gone on dates with questionable men before, but never quite like this. She wished now she had just faced up to the problems with her career and life, rather than looking for comfort in a man like Joe.

"I have to go to the bathroom," she said, just to wanting to be alone for a minute. Joe acted very attentive. He helped her fix her dress, then he led the way to the bathroom and kissed her on her shoulder.

"Come into the bedroom," he called out from the other side of the door, "I'll do you again."

There were no personal effects in this bathroom; nothing for Kelsey to look at except her own face in the hotel-style mirror. Her face seemed swollen and flushed from the making out, with all her makeup eaten off. She gazed into her eyes inquisitively, noticing that the two little fires that usually seemed to burn inside were distant, almost hidden. Kelsey bent down and drank some water from the faucet. Then she headed back to the bedroom, and to Joe, in a way wanting to get this night over with. She'd been hopeful earlier, but now she suspected she'd never actually go out with this guy.

In the darkened bedroom, the red glow of a digital clock cast a warm sheen over Joe's large naked body. He came to the edge of the bed and slid Kelsey's dress off, then kissed her hungrily on her nipples and her belly. Then he ducked his head and licked between her legs. Behind her, the air conditioner clicked loudly to life.

"Come for me, Baby," Joe encouraged.

"I don't know," Kelsey said. She felt overwhelmed and she knew she wouldn't climax, no matter what. She never had yet, with any man.

Joe pulled her down beside him on the bed; then he climbed on top and started working his fat penis into her. But he was just too big. He thrust all the way in and Kelsey gave a whimper. His muscular body had seemed so exciting earlier, yet now he was hurting her.

Kelsey pulled away from Joe's kisses, trying to breathe, while his giant erection filled her, pushing around her insides. "I really like you," he panted.

Kelsey tried to squirm away. She murmured, "Slow it down," but her partner didn't get it.

Then he climaxed again, inside her, and Kelsey thought about how she was only protected from pregnancy, but not from disease.

Joe rolled Kelsey to her side. He cuddled her and talked weirdly about how he wanted to be her long-term boyfriend. This all seemed to be moving way too fast and Kelsey felt something shivery in her stomach. Maybe there was something wrong about Joe psychologically. If his body hadn't been so spectacular, she probably would have noticed his failings immediately.

Joe put her hand over his penis and held it there, using it to stroke himself to another erection. Kelsey tried to hold him off.

"Maybe," she suggested, "we should use a condom, for HIV..."

Joe pulled off of her abruptly and his voice got mean- defensive and incredulous.

"What is this?" he demanded. "I sleep with only one other woman the past five years and you think I've got AIDS? Is that all this is to you, a one night stand?"

Kelsey tried to struggle to a sitting position. She tried to argue, but Joe easily pushed her back, with his overdeveloped muscles flaring.

"Is this a game to you?" he yelled. "I'll show you a game!"

This was one time when being slim was not an advantage to Kelsey. It meant that Joe could keep her completely pinned by the weight and size of his body alone, while he straddled her, inching up closer to her face. His penis reeked with the smell of his juices mixed with hers, and the air in the room seemed close.

It occurred to Kelsey that this man might possibly try to hurt her and she wished she'd carried her gun tonight. For all she knew, Joe could even be the enemy who had sent the threat on her computer.

Now he pushed his penis into her mouth and started pumping. Because of the angle, he cracked her lip and she bled, tasting her own sweet blood along with his musty ejaculate.

After he climaxed, Joe suddenly began to sob.

Kelsey had been trained in self-defense. And her mind was quite clear now. But, before she could do anything, Joe would have to shift position. Then she'd have to judge his intentions. She determined to fight only if there was no choice, because fighting him could possibly put her in worse danger, even though she would have liked to fight him.

The oral sex had taken place in silence except for Joe's rough breath and his quiet crying, and Kelsey let her mind distance itself. For some reason, her memories retreated back to shadowy places in her past, times when she was a little girl and felt helpless. She tried to guide her mind back to times of comfort, when she had felt safe. But the more Joe was rough with her, the further away her mind took her, pulling her at breathtaking speed through a childhood that existed as mostly a blur for her.

Miranda had always been there to fill in the memories. Whenever Kelsey had a question about the past, she used to just ask her best friend.

A feeling of betrayal almost choked Kelsey with tears. Where was Miranda tonight when this was happening to her? She had gone off with Marshall in the Jaguar, with just a wave good-bye.

Joe inched his body down Kelsey's, but she didn't use force against him yet. She had hardly been able to get any air in before; now his lips replaced his penis on her mouth. There seemed no real threat, she just felt suffocated.

"You're bleeding," he said, "I'm sorry."

But he already had his hand inside her, twirling around painfully in circles.

"This is rape!" Kelsey exclaimed, now that she had her mouth free momentarily.

Joe chuckled and looked her in the eye, and she vaguely remembered the friendly face she had first been attracted to. He pushed his penis back into her, but not painfully; now he took his time.

With a smug attitude, he said, "No, this isn't rape. You and your gold-digger friend thought it would be cool to pick up a couple of guys and mess with them. And you're just so frigid! I'm sorry, but it's true."

Lately things had descended into madness for Kelsey and tonight seemed proof of it. At least any danger seemed to be past, although Joe still moved inside her, bucking her whole slim body each time he thrust. And she was actually arguing with him.

"I don't know what I wanted. And I'm *not* frigid; it's not usually like this..."

She just wanted out of this place. She hated Joe so badly. Yet a small part of her blamed herself for her problems with sex.

"C'mon, move with me," Joe commanded abruptly. And Kelsey actually did move, lifting her hips gently to him and speeding up his climax.

When he finished, she slid out from under him.

"I'm going," she said firmly.

Joe reached for her, but she could feel the extreme tiredness in his body. When she pulled away, his arm fell back down limply on the bed.

Kelsey got back into her dress, shaking and weak. She listened to an emergency vehicle speeding down A1A and realized that it was already sunrise now- and the room was getting light. As she put on her strappy silver heels, it somehow felt weird to be leaving. It seemed so sleepy in here now, with all the tension gone.

"Stay, please," Joe begged her, sensing her indecision. "You really are a special girl. I want us to go out together... We could go to dinner tonight."

Kelsey shook her head with her hair flicking around her face. If she had spoken, she might have cried.

The young man in the bed didn't move. But then he yelled out to her as she started to walk away, "Don't think this is the last you're going to hear of me!"

His threat caught her attention and, for a moment, Kelsey turned back. In a softer tone, Joe pleaded, "At least let me drive you home..."

Kelsey turned again and walked quickly away from him, just wanting to get out of the oppressive condominium.

Chapter 3

In the fluorescent-lit elevator of Joe's building, she noticed an enormous dark spot all along the stomach of her burgundy satin dress. A pair of old people in shiny jogging suits glanced at her with curious faces, and she curled in on herself, tucking in her stomach and dying of shame.

Looking for a boyfriend like this was going to have to stop. If she couldn't find a decent guy in Florida, she'd have to go back to New York and stop punishing herself. After all, Joe could've had any kind of diseases. She had to hope he was telling the truth about only one partner.

For a moment, Kelsey seriously considered reporting Joe Carpenito to the police. But she quickly dismissed the idea. Even if the State Attorney's Office took the case seriously, people would laugh at her when they heard the details of the incident, and the injury to her pride would be worse than anything Joe had done to her body.

She just needed to find a way home. She'd have to find a telephone and hope that Miranda was there to take her call.

On the side of the road, a group of landscape workers stopped work to stare at her and Kelsey snapped at them, "Leave me the heck alone!"

She found a telephone at a shabby 7-Eleven and tried Miranda's number several times, but got no answer. There was nothing for her to do right now but go to the beach and kill time while waiting to reach Miranda at her job in a few hours. But getting on the beach wasn't as easy as Kelsey would have thought. Most of the beach accesses were through large high-rise condos and hotels that blocked almost all of the beach view. And everything was spaced according to vast distances meant for cars.

Kelsey finally found a walkover and made her way over it to the beach. She noticed how, this early in the morning, the beach seemed to be filled with misty glare, and the air tasted uniquely effervescent. Other people might find this appealing but, to Kelsey, it seemed vaguely unpleasant.

She had always liked being a northern girl. She'd only moved here for the promising job she had scored on the west coast of Florida three years earlier. For a few months, she had loved working for the Fraud Task Force in Lee County. Then the funding had been pulled and the Task Force disbanded. Kelsey moved east to Fort Lauderdale, to work for the private investigation firm while applying to grad schools. Eventually, she was offered the lease option on her condo and it seemed too good to pass up.

But Kelsey had never liked Florida for a moment. The enormity of the beaches and the ocean tended to scare her. She didn't really like the oppressive heat, or all the coastal development, or even the irritating tingle of the sea air that seemed to push at you insistently, without any freshness.

"Okay, ocean," she said now, determined to kill four or five hours dwelling with her own thoughts and watching the four-foot waves. She noticed a few other people out this early- several surf fishermen, and one elderly couple who were obviously intoxicated with each other. The frail man and woman could hardly keep their balance in the damp sand, yet they held hands. Kelsey sat down on a wooden lounge chair and watched the pair.

Despite her bad luck with recent relationships, she still held a deep belief that she could be part of a couple like that someday. But she knew her life the way it was now wouldn't bring her to her goals. Statistics said that two-thirds of people who came to Florida from northern states went back to their home states within a few years. Good weather was the main reason they came here, and lack of community was the main reason they left.

Kelsey thought that maybe she should decide to go home to New York State. First, she'd have to tell the couple that owned her condo that she didn't want to take the option to buy that was coming up within the next few months.

Suddenly, Kelsey felt a chill, a breeze that seemed to come from the wrong direction. She spun around and felt her heart race to life. She felt like she was being watched again. She looked all around her and saw only the same people from before, but she still felt disturbed. There had definitely been some change in the natural noises. Maybe it was that the birds in the sea grapes behind her had stopped twittering, or maybe the dune grass had rustled, parted by human hands.

Her watcher almost laughed, or almost cried, when he saw her spin around, looking in his general direction, but not seeing him. You think you are so tough, Kelsey, when really you are weak, he thought. No, that wasn't it, he corrected himself, while he felt the morning sun settle comfortably on his skin as he kneeled behind a little dune.

The problem was that the world handed power to people like Kelsey Reed, empty young women that didn't know how to use it right. If justice came bottled at some trendy shop in the mall, then maybe someone like Kelsey Reed would buy it.

Otherwise, he would have to show it to her.

Joe Carpenito could be standing behind the dunes watching her, Kelsey thought. He could have taken the time to get dressed and then followed her here to the beach.

She hated people like Joe. If he really had followed her now, after what he'd already done, she'd have to turn him in to the police. Why couldn't he just let her go?

She stood up and scanned the area several times, but the only people she saw were the strollers and the fishermen, and all of them at a distance. It was possible someone had stood on the walkover and watched her from there, and then ducked back out of sight behind one of the small dunes when she had turned. And there was an enormous bank of windows behind her, in a high-rise hotel. All she could see were reflections in those windows, so someone could be standing at any one of them.

Joe could be there, or maybe one of the suspects from the drug case. Glancing around her, Kelsey realized how little protection she really had here on the beach. Even though it was broad daylight, nobody was looking in this direction and she knew that the crashing noise of the ocean would cover any calls for help.

Kelsey turned toward shore. She walked over the wooden crossover with no one coming near her, and the oppressive feeling of being followed began to lift as she approached Highway A1A. It was possible she was just manufacturing the feeling of being watched because things were so wrong in other areas of her life. Maybe all her fears meant was that she needed to get out of Florida.

Kelsey walked briskly further north on A1A. Her first stop was a tiny ladies' room in the back of an ice cream parlor, where her once-pretty dress filled the little room with the smell of old semen and sweat, making her feel nauseous. She bought a shorts' set at the tourist boutique next door and then hurried back to the ice cream parlor bathroom to change.

When she was done, she stepped out and pushed the soiled burgundy dress into the mouth of a tall metal wastebasket that felt cool to the touch and smelled like fresh cream.

Miranda picked Kelsey up several hours later and seemed upset when she heard the story about Joe. "Why not come to the gym with me later?" she suggested. "Let me buy you dinner at the snack bar and we can laugh about those two losers."

But Kelsey didn't want to face the gym at a time like this. She was so shaky she couldn't even find her keys as they stood outside her condo and Miranda had to let her in with an extra set of keys that she kept for cat feeding emergencies.

"Go to bed," she advised. She gave her friend a quick, sympathetic hug before heading back to work.

When Kelsey stepped inside, Mr. Cooper was nowhere to be found. But she knew her cat had a tendency to act spiteful when she stayed away too long. He'd hide under the bed, pretending he didn't care that she was finally home.

But this was too much. He'd knocked a few rolls of undeveloped film from the tile countertop onto the linoleum, where they had rolled in all directions. Kelsey had to crawl around to retrieve all of the canisters, which were evidence for a case at work. Then she noticed that Cooper had dragged one of her brand new cross-trainer sneakers into the living room, where he had apparently spent the long night shredding it. It looked like a large puppy had totaled the sneaker, and not a medium sized cat.

"Cooper!" Kelsey yelled out, annoyed. "Why did you have to ruin my sneaker? I never even wore it to the stupid gym!" Her voice trailed off because it was really herself she was reprimanding, more than the animal.

Mr. Cooper finally came to her and she cuddled his pliant gray body against her neck while she went to the refrigerator to get a glass of wine. Then she retrieved three messages from her machine, the first from her mother, asking her if she might come home to New York for the holidays. The second was from her boss, apologizing for calling so early on a Sunday, but asking if she would work today.

"Oh well," she said to herself, amused that her day would have been ruined no matter what.

The last call was an enigmatic message from her ex-boyfriend, Paul, asking if she and Miranda would go on some boating thing for his brokerage company next weekend.

"Bastard," Kelsey said, and her cat gave her a questioning look with his translucent green eyes. Kelsey felt sad more than anything else. She didn't hate Paul; in fact she missed how he had been so totally seamless.

She opened the refrigerator to get the meal she had been planning for this morning; fresh sliced strawberries in a glass bowl, enough for a family, and the other makings for a smoothie.

When she opened the refrigerator door, Mr. Cooper hopped down from the counter onto the floor, and he cried to her pitifully. Kelsey finally forked chilled cat food into his bowl, because she couldn't stand listening to the sound of his wails today while waiting for his food to warm. As soon as she filled his dish, her cat ate crazily, snorting and sneezing on the food and spilling it onto his Garfield place mat.

Kelsey started the blender and, while she waited, she leaned forward to observe the comings and goings in the parking lot through the little window over the sink. There was rarely anything to see at her complex, at the moment just some old man helping his wife into their Lincoln Continental. In fact, almost all her neighbors were senior citizens, but Kelsey was endlessly curious.

As soon as the smoothie was ready, she locked up the front door and went in to shower, stuffing the shorts' set into the hamper until she could figure out what to do with it. All she wanted was to get clean and get to bed.

She finished her smoothie in the bedroom, leaving the glass on top of her white wicker bedside table, and she curled into bed with the covers not even up all the way. She fell immediately and deeply asleep, all night going in and out of uneasy dreams that went back to some dangerous place in childhood for which she had only shrouded memories.

The next morning, in the shower, Kelsey discovered that someone must have been in her condo- because two of her shampoos had been switched in their bottles!

When she poured out her favorite twenty-dollar salon shampoo, she was surprised to see it come out pink and creamy. The problem was, the salon shampoo was supposed to be white, with tiny electric-blue shimmers and a subtle herbal scent. Her store-brand shampoo was supposed to be pink and scented like flowers- and it *had* been when she used it yesterday afternoon! Now Kelsey reached for the bright pink bottle with trembling fingers and she found it filled with scented white shampoo with blue crystals, just as she had feared.

Someone must have switched the shampoos while she was sleeping! She felt the same sick feeling in her stomach that she'd been trying to shake yesterday. For a moment, she stood naked with the water slapping down around her, unsure of what to do.

But she knew she had to check the condo- because someone could still be here.

Kelsey stepped out of the tub without drying off and she pulled on her robe, ignoring the water that pooled on the tile floor. She forced herself to peer around the door and saw that no one was there. And the corridor was empty as well.

Kelsey edged out of the bathroom, then padded silently through her sun-drenched condo, heading first for her bedroom, where she retrieved the cordless telephone and her handgun. She slipped the telephone into the pocket of her robe and held the gun in a police officer's stance as she explored every corner of the apartment.

She felt a bit more confident with each room and closet she checked. She found no one in her condo and, when she checked the windows, found them all locked and undisturbed.

There was no evidence of forced entry and Kelsey hadn't really expected to find any. She couldn't imagine that a stranger could have come in here during the night without her awakening. She would have at least had some feeling that the space had been violated. And her condo felt the same as it always did to Kelsey; it felt safe despite the fact that she *knew* someone must have been here.

There was no sense calling the police. They would need evidence, which she didn't have. But the horrible prank of the two shampoos switched, coupled with the email threat and the feeling she'd had recently of being watched, was proof enough for Kelsey that someone really was trying to terrorize her. She just didn't know why.

She sat down at the kitchen island with the gun still near, trying to figure out who might have done these things. She knew whoever had come into the condo had to have a key, or access to one. That probably left Joe Carpenito out. He'd only known her one night, he had no access to her key and, even if he'd followed her and Miranda here yesterday, Kelsey doubted he could have come in quietly enough not to wake her. Even if he did, Joe was such a pervert he'd surely have headed for her bed rather than her bathtub!

As for the suspects from the cocaine smuggling case, the three previously convicted felons were now free on bond. Kelsey was pretty sure these dangerous men, or their unsavory associates, would have torn apart the entire condo if they ever got in. Or they might have even brutally attacked her when they found her sleeping.

The only person in the world who'd know how much something as seemingly petty as switching shampoos would bother Kelsey was Miranda. And Miranda was also the only person with a key to the condo. But that would mean Miranda had also left the threatening email on Kelsey's computer at work. And it was hard for Kelsey to believe something like that about her lifelong best friend.

Yes, Miranda could do some strange things. And Kelsey sometimes thought that her less successful girlfriend might resent or envy her. Kelsey also knew that it would be a crushing disappointment to Miranda if she decided to purchase the condo, attend college at Nova and remain in Florida. She knew Miranda's hopes were pinned on their leaving Florida together soon.

But Miranda could never do anything to actually hurt her, Kelsey was sure. Perhaps her friend had decided to sneak in to take a shower and then had switched the shampoos by accident, or as a joke. In that case, Kelsey still had to figure out who sent her the email that hinted at vengeance. *And what was the wrong that person felt she had done to them?*

When she knew that, she'd also know the person's identity. Then she just had to get some kind of evidence on them to get them sent to jail. In fact, the person probably feared and hated Kelsey to begin with because of her capabilities as an investigator.

Kelsey hurried back into the bathroom to quickly wash her hair in the sink. But she did it with soap. She ziploc-bagged the two bottles of shampoo to bring them to her office to send out for fingerprints.

When she got to her desk at work, she immediately began opening files on her computer. She planned to look not only at the individuals involved in the cocaine smuggling case, but at the principals in all of her cases, dating back almost three years, to when she first began working at Confidential Investigations.

On Wednesday evening, Miranda talked Kelsey into driving her to the gym so they could try out a new aerobics class. Kelsey actually didn't mind, because there was something she'd been planning to ask her friend.

"Miranda," she asked, in what she hoped was a casual-sounding tone. "That night after I had the run-in with Joe Carpenito, you didn't happen to let yourself into my condo, did you? And take a shower?"

Miranda's big eyes widened and her full lips dropped.

"Huh?"

"Did you switch the shampoos from bottle to bottle? You know, like an accident?"

Now Miranda's brow scrunched and her green eyes twinkled like she *knew* her friend had gone crazy.

"I don't *think* so!" she teased, with her voice inflected with laughter.

At the gym, along with thirty other young working women, Kelsey and Miranda laughed and sweat in an advanced aerobics class. They did some of the steps wrong and bumped into each other and laughed even more. Then they filed out with the others at eight-o-clock.

One of their friends from the class, a girl named Ty, who had a very pretty Asian face and a near-perfect body, suggested that she, Miranda and Kelsey go upstairs to the weight room.

"Some of the personal trainers go up there to do their own workouts after most people go home. And they're so animalistic!" Ty laughed and made an exaggerated facial expression, pretending to growl. "We can work out on the ab machines and watch their male bonding."

"Oh shit, yeah!" Miranda said, and she dragged Kelsey along with them to the weight room. "*I'd* like to see those guys!"

Kelsey had to admit that the four bodybuilders looked sweet. They were big, sexy young men with enormous muscles and they clanged around gigantic free weights and joked with each other in an elevated area next to the windows. The gym was almost empty now, with some of the lights dimmed, and the presence of the four men seemed to completely dominate the large space.

Kelsey felt foolish lying on her back on a bench, with Miranda hovering over her.

"Check the big guy out!" Miranda whispered, "His name's Juan Reyes, and he works here as a personal trainer- he also does competition bodybuilding, and I get faint just looking at his body!"

Kelsey suddenly stopped paying attention to her girlfriend. A streetlight shone in from outside and, in its glare, Kelsey noticed one of the four men get up from a weight bench and walk to the window. She only saw the young man in silhouette, yet she was shocked at how he presented the perfect male form, with astonishing proportions of arms and chest to the rest of his body. Each gigantic muscle looked intricately carved, and his body gleamed under the sheen of his sweat touched by the yellow light. He had trendy, close-shorn platinum blond hair, and he stood with his huge back to her, seeming intent on looking out the window, and not realizing she was there.

Kelsey gasped at the sight of this young man and all of her past days' fears went away. Now she felt only hope. She sensed that this was what a man was meant to be, and she wanted to know him. She didn't care what had gone wrong in her life previously.

He definitely had the most perfect male body Kelsey had ever seen. Yet it was the young man's way of moving, more than his incredible size that completely captured Kelsey's attention. The blond bodybuilder hadn't just *moved* to his feet, he had *glided*, Then, as he stood there by the window, he remained utterly still. Kelsey had learned that warriors trained in the martial arts were supposed to have this kind of discipline, yet men of her generation never seemed able to do it. They always seemed fidgety and impatient. But this young man was different; she thought she observed something classic about him, and something timeless.

Miranda and Ty disgraced themselves making all sorts of provocative moves in their workouts to catch the attention of the other three men. But Kelsey took no notice. She sat up, completely riveted, watching the mesmerizing rise and fall of breath inside the enormous chest of the young man by the window.

She felt so odd about her sudden, visceral response to the young man's body that she didn't discuss it with the other girls. She didn't want them to think it was the same thing as when she usually panted over muscle-bound guys. Kelsey had felt an immediate respect for the character she sensed to be inside this particular young man. She really wanted to know him in every sense and the intensity of the feeling couldn't be easily explained.

Kelsey didn't mention what she felt when they were told the gym was closing and they had to gather up their gear. She didn't say anything as Miranda and Ty went on about how sexy the bodybuilders were and plotted what they could do next time to meet them. It was only later, when she and her best friend stood in the parking lot so Miranda could finish a cigarette before getting into the car, that Kelsey spoke.

"It's him," she said to Miranda when she saw the handsome bodybuilder walking across the parking lot to a motorcycle parked on the grass in the shadows. "He's so gorgeous," Kelsey whispered. "And he's different from the other men I've known. I sense this could be completely different."

The next day at work, Kelsey found that someone had permanently deleted all her files from her computer. It wasn't just the recent files from the Port Everglades drug case, although those were the first thing she found missing. She'd also lost every single bit of information from every case she had worked on since being at Confidential. The loss also included email messages she'd saved, her favorite Internet sites, lists of business contacts that she frequently used and every conceivable type of research she had done over the years. Anything saved electronically was gone.

She couldn't believe what she was seeing as she searched for her most important files and found them gone. The pattern of what was still available and what was missing indicated that this was definitely aimed at her. Files her coworkers had saved were still available in the system; only the cases she had worked on had been targeted. There could be no doubt that someone was after her now, and it was probably someone whose information was in one of those deleted files.

Either this person didn't want Kelsey looking deeper in the files, or else they wanted revenge for something they perceived she had done to them in the past. And, apparently, they would go pretty far, if they had done this and also gotten into her condo to switch her shampoos.

Now Kelsey faced her empty computer screen and talked to the invisible person who had done this to her. "You can't keep doing this!" she said. "I *will* find you!"

She wandered over to the glass front door of her office on the chance that there was someone out there still watching her and she could get a glimpse. But the only face she saw was that of Confidential's owner, Joel Lester. Her middle-aged boss was accompanied by a young man with messy red hair contrasted with pale skin and a silver piercing in the side of his lip. This young man wore a faded black T-shirt with some dot.com logo on it, and he practically reeled away from Kelsey when he had to brush by her in the doorway. But then he started sneaking furtive and intense glances at every part of her body as soon as he thought she didn't notice. Perhaps *he* was the one who had done this to her computer, she thought cynically- he seemed demented enough and, obviously, computers were his thing.

"Kelsey," her boss said, "this is our new computer expert, Michael Cole. He'll be doing work for us whenever our system needs a major overhaul."

The young computer expert took a nervous lick at his lip piercing and then reached out a sweaty hand to shake with Kelsey. "I hope we'll be working together *a lot*," he said.

Kelsey tried to detect if he was trying to sound menacing, or if he was just being an idiot. Either way, it was assured she would be spending more time with him than she would like.

Mr. Lester did admonish Kelsey for not backing up her files. But he also seemed curious about how a person could get past their office's extensive security precautions.

"Obviously, Kelsey," Joel Lester said, "someone didn't want the facts in one of your files coming to light. You'll need to find out who that person is and what those particular facts are. But first you'll have to replace everything in those files or this office can't function!"

The next week was miserable. Shadowed by Michael Cole, with the two of them alone in the office after hours every night, Kelsey labored to replace the lost files, typing in information from paper files, handwritten notes and what she remembered about each case.

"The most likely scenario is that someone pulled the trick with your files remotely," the computer consultant told her, when she pressed him. "Unfortunately, I can't track down the specific source."

Kelsey again felt frustrated and angry.

One of the businesses Confidential regularly worked with was a "spy shop" down in North Miami. On a Sunday, she visited the shop.

"I have a client who's being stalked," she told the older man she usually did business with, not wanting to reveal her own vulnerability. "I want to catch the person on camera without them suspecting they're being watched."

She ended up purchasing two miniature cameras, the kind that were used as "nanny cams" because they could be hidden anywhere. Her office already had several cameras mounted in visible locations, but she wanted these to be a surprise to her enemy if they ever chose to visit in person.

Kelsey hid one of the cameras amongst books on top of a file cabinet at work and she pointed it straight at her desk. The other she took home and camouflaged in a basket on her kitchen counter, making sure it gave her a view of the front door.

"There!" she said, with satisfaction. "Now you won't be taking anybody by surprise..."

The loss of control was the worst part of the situation for Kelsey. But another thing that hurt her was the way it took away from her personal life. She was afraid that she was losing out on any chance of meeting the gorgeous bodybuilder she had seen at the gym. After seeing him that Wednesday night, she had planned to go back and look for him the next day.

Instead, she had been forced to spend five nights in a row at her office, only getting to leave after the gym was long closed. She knew that, to other people, it might be considered a petty concern. But to

Kelsey, meeting a good man at this point in her life was vitally important. She felt that her loneliness and profound lack of love could kill her as surely as any stalker could.

Chapter 4

Kelsey was amazed at her intense feelings for the handsome bodybuilder, even in the midst of the crisis she was dealing with at work.

She remembered the young man's facial features had been small and perfect, fiercely handsome like a model's or a movie star's. He wasn't just cute; he was heart-stoppingly gorgeous, with looks that were totally out of her league. People who looked like he did usually ran with an elite crowd. But, even though she knew this, Kelsey felt desire.

She had talked to Miranda about her crush on the bodybuilder but Miranda hadn't really encouraged her. All Miranda said was that she'd talk to the personal trainer, Juan Reyes, the next time she went to the gym, and she'd ask him if the blond guy was a friend of his. Kelsey went back to the gym on her own the next few nights, not even lying to herself about why she was there. But the object of her desire still didn't show. Unlike Juan, her guy was not employed at the health club, so he had the power to come and go as he pleased, and he might not even come back at all.

But Kelsey was used to stakeouts in her work and her instinct told her he would be back eventually if she was just patient. Kelsey dressed in her favorite workout outfit on a Saturday and she washed her hair with a new bottle of Pure Silk Shampoo. She had gotten up very early that day and, even though she wasted time driving thirty miles to Davie to pick up Miranda, she still had to fight with her friend to get her up out of bed and out the door.Kelsey had been right about the bodybuilder returning to the gym. He was there when they walked through the door, standing right at the front desk, as though waiting for her. Ashley, the tall, rangy young woman who did the registrations had turned all the way around talking to him, apparently getting him to help her with something. Ashley had hiked her skirt almost all the way to her crotch and extended her long legs all the way out so he could get a view.

Meanwhile, the switchboard was going crazy and the answering machine was taking all her calls.

The bodybuilder appeared not to notice. He chewed on a protein bar while looking over Ashley's shoulders at a printout, and he seemed bored. Kelsey stared directly at him and he looked up at her momentarily.

Now she saw clearly how frighteningly handsome he really was. In his facial features the young bodybuilder resembled the actor Brad Pitt, with his bleached blond hair, small velvety features and lush lips. He also had the same sexy insouciance. Right at the moment, Brad Pitt was considered the sexiest man alive in the world, but Kelsey knew the actor *wasn't* the sexiest man alive, because this man standing negligently in front of her was.

Meanwhile, Ashley was going crazy trying to snag the guy for herself. Miranda asked something about when Juan was working and the young man answered, with his voice so sexy and intimate that Kelsey could imagine she was alone in bed with him, rather than standing in a busy health club. And, even though Miranda was flirting and so was Ashley, it was Kelsey that the bodybuilder glanced at, lazily lifting his eyes to meet hers for a small moment of time.

The look was blank, as though he was dumb and not intense at all, but Kelsey sensed that this wasn't true. His eyes were an illuminated light brown color that seemed to bring the sun indoors. They could be seen as laughing eyes but also melancholy eyes. Eyes that left you awash in emotion that you could not easily understand, eyes that could stare at you curiously, totally unashamed. Sex was not really Kelsey's strongest point and sex would never be equal to all she was feeling for this guy. He looked back down to his printout and Kelsey thought about how she might happily watch him forever.

She spent a little time on the treadmill, peeking through the glass wall to see when the young man would return to his weights and she felt no sensation of her body walking as she focused on him like a huntress. Eventually he did go back to the weights and he worked on a few machines and he looked happy to be doing it, like he was absolutely content to be working out in a gym. For the next hour, all of the prettiest girls took their turns approaching and flirting so blatantly with him that Kelsey could read it from their body language alone. Her bodybuilder turned each of them away in the oddest way she had ever seen. He would patiently wait each girl out, just staring at each in a friendly but blank way until she got bored and walked away. Then he'd shake his head and return to working out.

Kelsey watched every part of his body. She watched his silky determined movements for hours while he pushed against the machines and she wondered if he could feel that he was being watched. There was a chance he had noticed and was just trying to wait her out like he had the others.

But that strategy wouldn't work with her. Kelsey went into the weight section and she spent the next hour working her body against machines she had never tried before until her upper body felt all hard and pumped. She was slipping on her own sweat and hurting muscles that had never been used before, but her full concentration remained on the young man. She felt she could wait forever if she had to.

Her bodybuilder wore two gold hoop earrings like many other hip young guys and this careless slacker style seemed so incongruous with his glossy enormously muscled body that it made Kelsey crazy. Other guys who looked as good as he did would come here to show off, but it seemed this guy was here only to work, Kelsey realized, not to play games or attract attention. She watched him quietly punishing his own body, gently pushing it each time as though analyzing his own capabilities.

She had inched over to the stomach curl machine and now he definitely had to see her because she was the closest person to the free weight area. Sitting on a weight bench directly in front of her, the guy lifted what looked like a fifty-pound dumbbell and settled it into his hand. And then he lovingly curled it up in a bicep almost the size of Kelsey's waist. He watched his own muscles while she did, moving the weight up and down, and working each arm for what seemed a very long time. Then he shook off in front of the window, gazing down briefly at the parking lot. He turned back around and sipped out of a bottle with a plastic straw. And he looked blankly over at Kelsey.

Next he roamed around and selected a bench and weight. Kelsey was actually frightened when she realized what he intended to do. He loaded the bar balanced on the rack with four enormous weights on each end and he clipped the weights down. The full barbell looked like the kind powerlifters used in cartoons. It must have equaled four hundred pounds. The young man then crawled underneath, staring the whole time at the weight. He obviously intended to bench-press it.

Kelsey really looked at the man now, with his seductive young face and the tanned chest muscles that twitched under a flimsy string of tank top as he readied himself for the lift. And it looked as though he would

41

be able to do the lift, as though he had done this sort of thing many times before. It didn't seem like his judgment would lead him to attempt something he couldn't complete.

While he was occupied in staring at the weight, the trainer, Juan Reyes, who was of similar bulk, approached to stand behind him.

"Let me spot you with that, Buddy," he said.

The other man took a moment to give his friend a funny look. "In life, there's no one to spot you, man," he said. "Just let me do this mother."

Juan backed off to a respectable distance, which was surprising since as an employee of the gym, he probably wasn't supposed to let people attempt reckless things like this. But this group of men apparently had their own code. Juan stood there, possibly watching for his friend to be killed in front of him.

Silly top-forties music pumped through the speakers and, in the other room girls in bright clothes worked noisily on the aerobics machines while televisions blared. And Kelsey saw how men like these would be distracted by none of it.

The young man grasped the bar and slightly extended his arms. Muscles stood out as he pulled the weight off the bar. His chest heaved out, accommodating, and his biceps bulged as he centered the weight over himself. Gently, he lowered it, his eyes staring and going glassy. And then more muscles stood out, epically beautiful chest muscles. Cuts Kelsey had never seen on a man emerged, as she watched the weight gradually lifted up straight.

"Go, Jayson!" Juan urged. "You can do it, Buddy."

Other big guys who were standing in the area stopped working to watch the lift. Apparently, the blond bodybuilder's name was Jayson.

Sweat broke out all over Jayson's body, sweat that made him look golden. He had lifted the enormous weight and it hovered above him. Now would be the time to put it back on its rack.

But instead he lowered it gently back down towards his pumped chest. He was going to work with it! Everyone watching seemed like they were shocked. But Kelsey understood. He would not have lifted a weight like that to show off. He was intending all along to work with it. He pushed the weight up again and she saw the incredible strain. But he was able to count to himself through clenched teeth.

"Two, three…"

He moved the weight slowly up and down with perfect form, taking the strain all in the chest and not going sway-backed like others guys benching enormous weight. Of course he was not going to hurt himself.

He was some kind of power lifter, probably, and the fact of his perfectly symmetrical form was just some lucky accident of genetics. He was here for the weight itself, to challenge himself against the weight. His movie-star looks were nothing. You would have had to watch him for hours like this to understand. This guy was for real.

He did five repetitions with the weight.

Juan hovered near his friend as Jayson slipped the weight back onto the stand. Jayson looked glowing and transformed after the lift. Again, he looked at her and through her. Then Jayson laughed at himself to Juan.

"Okay," he said. "Maybe next time I'll go a little lighter." Looking tired, he went back to dismantle the weight. No one else would likely be using it for a while.

Jayson was drenched with sweat as he walked off alone to the locker room. Kelsey felt a renegade feeling like love for him and it frightened her. How could she love him? How could she even know him? She was aware she had never felt real love for a man before- and right now she felt comfortable admitting it to herself. Nothing in the past had ever come near working out, and nothing had ever felt like this. Kelsey needed love, and a true bond, so badly. So could true love be this brand new obsessive determination that seemed so glorious, and yet so powerful and ugly that it could destroy anything rational in its path? The second Jayson left the room Kelsey's life felt over. But meanwhile she ached for the pathos she was sure she had seen in his aloneness. She knew she truly cared for him even though she didn't know him. Surely none of the other women who flirted with him had seen or felt that.

That day was the start of Kelsey going to the gym to watch Jayson. Whether or not there was any hope of Jayson ever going out with her or even talking to her didn't matter. It energized her just to see him.

She began resenting going to work, especially because she was still assigned on this drug case. Her boss had her going to the different marinas with Jerry Klein posing as a couple wanting to rent a boat. Then they were supposed to ask if the crew would let them bring drugs aboard. Kelsey thought the plan was stupid and too obvious. But rather than argue with her boss, she just went through the motions of the stakeout unenthusiastically. She spent all day waiting for the afternoons to come so that she could return to the gym and look at the perfection of the guy named Jayson.

Jayson must know what she was up to because they worked side by side every day, but he still never said anything to her. She supposed he might have talked to her if she had started the conversation; he certainly talked to enough other girls. But Kelsey was content with watching him for now. What she wanted was for him to be really near her, to really know her. If she couldn't have that, then she would just watch him and know him that way

Kelsey didn't lie to herself about how much she wanted Jayson. She had never wanted anything in her life quite this way. The only things that had ever come close were some things in her career and that had been a while ago. Her desire for Jayson felt like the prominent thing in her life now; it even came above nailing the person who was tormenting her at work. Maybe all that person had wanted were the files they had erased, because there hadn't been any additional problems, and Kelsey felt free to concentrate on her feelings for this man.

The next Saturday could have been a good day but instead it turned out frustrating and dark for Kelsey. Jayson had come down one step to do part of his workout on the machines near her rather than on the free weights. She thought she noticed some kind of awareness on his part that she was there next to him, a nod or almost a nod. An hour or so went by and Kelsey was killing herself on a chest machine, not even liking the changes that were being wrought in her body by all the weights.

Then a girl walked over to Jayson, approaching with unusual confidence. The girl had a pink gym bag and sneakers slung over her shoulder. She wore her hair in bleached blond curls and was about a size one, just the kind of girl Kelsey hated for their impossible weight. She herself would have loved to be really thin like a model, and often she berated herself for not having quite enough self discipline to starve off those last pounds that would put her under a size five. Even though Kelsey was unusually trim and looked great in body-conscious clothes by everyday standards, she never took that last step and relinquished her health to make herself look even better. And yet, from adolescence, she had despised fat and revered the really skinny girls who she thought in some way were better, more disciplined, and perhaps more worthy of love than she was. And now this size one girl was talking to Jayson as if she had known him forever, making plans about some restaurant!

"Maybe you ought to wear something warmer," Jayson said to the girl, "because the place is on the Intracoastal and there may be a breeze." He was taking this girl out on a date! They were making plans!

They talked more as Jayson finished up on the machine. But Kelsey could hardly hear what was being said. Blood thudded loudly in her ears from her own anger. Why this girl? Why couldn't it be her? He was going on a date with this girl. It seemed like it was the easiest thing in the world. He was probably going to sleep with her!

Jayson left the gym with the thin blonde, cutting short his usual workout by hours, and Kelsey felt an emptiness rush into her that felt different from any emptiness or lonliness she had ever known.

"What's the matter?" Miranda asked her when they met in the locker room. "You look like you just saw a ghost."

"I'd like to go out tonight," Kelsey said. "Can we do that?"

When they went out, Miranda was again talking about using cocaine and this was unusual for her. Miranda tended to go in phases, accepting coke when she was with a certain crowd like Marshall Sawyer, the cellular phone salesman and then forgetting about it, but not ever seeking it like she seemed to be now. Miranda was determined to go to Creamsicles rather than another bar because their friend the bouncer was supposed to have some coke that he wanted to share. And then she'd probably end up sleeping with him.

Kelsey thought that her girlfriend might be getting herself in a little deep here and Kelsey did not approve of hard drugs at all. But now was not a time that she could concern herself with anyone else's morals or their problems. She just needed to find an outlet for her own irrational anger about Jayson and the girl and the feeling of shame that went along with it. There were also all the other negative things that had been happening to her lately, starting with the threat on her email and the destruction of her files. For the moment, she wanted to be free of all the thoughts that played in her head with no resolution.

She and Miranda danced at Creamsicles that night and men approached them. But thoughts of Jayson- frenzied, jealous thoughts- occupied her mind and she could not ever recall feeling anything this intensely. She felt like she had entered a realm of feeling where her friends and her previous knowledge of relationships might not be able to help her at all.

Miranda had gone off with someone to take a ride and get high and Kelsey was left alone with her brooding thoughts. And then a man was leaning his face on her shoulder. She felt the tingle of his breath and it felt warm and comforting. Kelsey turned and spoke warmly as she recognized her coworker, Jerry Klein.

"Jerry, what are you doing here?" she asked. Kelsey was so incredibly glad to see him at the moment. It was as though she was being welcomed back to a gentle earth, being forgiven her dark fantasies.

Jerry smiled very warmly, he was flushed and his eyes were twinkling. He looked so focused on her. "Actually, I was looking for you," he said. For some strange reason, the statement was enough to get

Kelsey excited and put her in devilish mood. And Jerry seemed on the same page.

"Wendy brought me out," he said, "because I told her I was feeling like I just wanted to fit in somewhere. She wanted me to meet a woman; and you're the most beautiful woman that I know of. And you're always hanging out in this sad singles bar, so I thought why not come looking for you? And now I've found you!" He took her under his arm. "So, what do you want to do first, dance or tell me what's been bothering you?"

Kelsey cuddled under his arm and let her friend and coworker lead her out onto the dance floor. They danced to slow songs, a little too intimately. Then Jerry bought her drinks and they huddled together as she confessed her lustful feelings for Jayson. It meant something to her how Jerry was so totally focused on her and how he could be so sympathetic. Right now, he was the only man in the world she was sure really cared about her.

Then she asked Jerry something she never would have sober because it revealed too much of her deep insecurities. "Jerry, am I really pretty at all? Is there anything special about me?"

"Honey," he said earnestly, "you are nothing but special. I look into your big brown eyes and I can see all the warmth in you, all of the honesty." Then he laughed. "And I can even see that unique spark in you of your curiosity, which I might add is not always good for you."

Kelsey was laughing with him but, at the moment, her curiosity was about to get her into another mess. She looked directly into her friend's lively eyes and asked, "How about you? Aren't you ever curious?"

Miranda surprised Kelsey and Jerry staggering to the parking lot together. Kelsey was sure the fact they planned to be together tonight was already sealed in their furtive glances and that her friend could probably see it. All Miranda did was to offer to cover for them with Wendy and to ask Jerry to do the driving.

"Kelsey's drunk," Miranda said, "and she hasn't been herself lately."

Instead of being offended, Kelsey actually liked the feeling of being taken care of by both of them like this. Usually she was the one in control, but tonight she felt different; she felt she needed something to make her secure.

Jerry brought Kelsey back to his apartment and she was impressed by the place. It was the first time she had seen it although, at work, Jerry often talked about this or that piece of art he had saved up to buy for the apartment. They joked around together and Kelsey complimented how the rooms were decorated; she really loved so many of the items he had selected. Jerry showed off a new set of gold-rimmed dishes that he intended to use for the holiday party he and his roommates were going to host.

Her friend's concerns seemed so effeminate, yet Kelsey couldn't deny that his body felt warm and masculine to her. They sat down, leaning near each other on his plush sofa, and Jerry talked with her for a long time about his dreams, things he said he didn't usually discuss with his other friends from work. He shared how, from the time he was a little boy, he'd always fantasized about creating something truly special in this world, something people could react to and feel they'd grown. Jerry told her how, as a preteen, he used to sit in his parents' golfside home in an up-and-coming suburb of Chicago.

"Our house was all white inside, you know, with lots of vaulted ceilings and skylights and unforgiving light streaming in everywhere from off the golf course. I don't think I can even remember any of the rooms specifically- I think all the houses in that community looked basically the same. But what I do remember was the art on the walls. A few of the pieces were original- brightly colored things that my mom picked up at local craft fairs. But what sticks in my mind most, so that I don't think I'll ever lose the image of it, was the painting my mother had over the mantle for a while. It was Matisse's "The Dance". I guess it was just a cheap print- you could buy it for twenty dollars. But that painting was able to reach across the years and totally rock my world! It made me feel like my surroundings were insignificant. When I looked at it, I felt sure that there was a better world out there- one that could be full of passion and promise. Do I sound silly?" Jerry asked, dropping his head a little.

"No," Kelsey reassured. She put a gentle hand on his shoulder, reaching her fingers up to absently play with a strand of his curly hair. "It's not silly at all. In fact I understand. I sometimes think I could feel that way about decorating and it feels good to be able to share that with you, because I don't tell most people. But, for now, my passion is fighting crime. That's why I persist working at Confidential- even if it *is* a lousy job."

Kelsey giggled and Jerry laughed with her in sympathy. He then drew her closer against him and caught her attention with his eyes. Jerry told her that the mark he wanted to make on the world could be though art, or it could even be through a daring and beautiful relationship like the one he hoped to have with her.

Kelsey went willingly into her friend's arms and she made love with him in his comfortable bed, which smelled slightly of his familiar tasteful cologne. With Jerry, she didn't feel any danger at all, like she'd felt with

Joe or some of the other men she'd been with lately. There was just a beautiful feeling of safety. In the soft lighting of her dear friend's bedroom, where time seemed to be suspended for a while, it even felt possible to get caught up in his dreams.

Kelsey didn't feel used after making love to Jerry and she didn't regret what she'd done. In fact, she felt very well and energized. Miranda stopped by at Kelsey's condo the next day and she immediately noticed how great her girlfriend was feeling.

With a playful smirk on her face, she teased, "So, I bet you're not feeling the need to hang out at the gym today!"

And this was true. After her night with Jerry, and because of her own feelings of betrayal and pride, Kelsey was able to avoid the gym, and the bodybuilder named Jayson, for a while.

What she wasn't able to do was to start up a relationship with Jerry, and she didn't even feel able talk to him about what had happened between them. She had a sense of still having some unfinished business. Jerry called her at home each day to chat, but he was wise enough not to put her on the spot about the fact they'd slept together- he appeared able to sense that she needed space.

Thanksgiving came around and Kelsey and Miranda went to eat at Jerry's instead of going home. Miranda couldn't go home to her family because she didn't have the money, and Kelsey couldn't go home because of new work demands. She'd been so preoccupied with the young man at the gym, she hadn't even returned her mother's calls until days before the holiday. She confided in Miranda and Jerry. "You know, I feel really sad about this, really empty, like there's something important that I'm going to miss by not going home, even though I've been down here in Florida like this for three years."

Kelsey looked to Miranda, who knew so much of her family situation, for advice. "I feel so much like there is something so heartbreakingly sad, like I love my parents, but I don't even know them..."

"Maybe you'll get away for Christmas, after all," Miranda said, "if you and Jerry wrap up your case at work. I know I'm going home."

It was odd how Miranda thought. She was deeply in debt and her car was dying. Yet she planned to jeopardize her job by taking off for the Christmas holiday, even though it would be the busiest time of year at the cosmetics counter, and the department store had told her she needed to stay. Perhaps Miranda was loosening her ties with Florida and didn't care if she got fired. Kelsey knew how badly Miranda wanted to leave and go back to New York for good.

Kelsey had come from a perfect family and Miranda from an abusive one; yet it was Miranda who kept a passionately close relationship with family, and Kelsey envied it. In Kelsey's family, everything had been given to her, except for real warmth. She had been the overachiever, while her older sister Sarah was always failing at things and often acted sullen and rebellious. Yet now Sarah was with Kelsey's parents every day, doing the holiday things, while Kelsey was alone, challenging this bright, but empty, city.

"Don't get depressed," Miranda told Kelsey. "Come to the mall with me. We're both off work and today has the best sales of the year. I know I have all kinds of shopping to do if I'm going up to New York!"

It felt a little odd to Kelsey, buying gifts for people who she would not get to see, gifts that Miranda, who was like another sister in Kelsey's family, would deliver. Miranda might be spending more time with Kelsey's family than she would with her own. And Kelsey could only let the money that she invested in gifts for her family show how much she cared about them. But logic won out. Sarah's children would be expecting nice presents from their aunt and wouldn't understand the sudden depression and weirdness that she was going through this year.

Kelsey and Miranda drove to the mall and found a spot in the parking garage near the elevator. There was bright sunshine outside but Kelsey felt intuitively that she was going to spend all day going wild in the dimness of the mall. She felt a pressure building inside herself and she knew that it could be released here. It felt weirdly exciting as she clutched her credit card in hand, poised to buy something before they were even inside.

"Oh, my God!" Miranda exclaimed about one of the perfume gift sets in the first department store they hit. Kelsey decided that she would make another trip and buy this gift set for her friend. Ironically, the set that they both liked best contained a gilded angel. "It's not really for us lately," Miranda smirked.

"You know," Kelsey said to her girlfriend as they walked into an open corridor teeming with well dressed shoppers who were already loaded with bags, "I'm not really proud of what I did with Jerry. I mean, I care for him and all, but lately I feel like such a tramp, as though all I do is sleep with men. And you know that isn't me. I just fooled around with Jerry because of Jayson, and even Jerry knows that. The problem is, I still feel so empty."

Kelsey bought some toys from the science shop for her niece and nephew: dinosaur models, a book, and a little constellation of glow in the dark stars that they could stick on their bedroom walls. She also bought some computer games that her mother had written the kids wanted. And then she dragged Miranda into Gap Kids.

"Wonderful," her tall striking friend said. "Everyone is going to think that we both have a couple of rugrats at home. Look at that poor women," she whispered. She was being snide about a fashionable young blonde fighting with two kids. Like Kelsey, Miranda probably felt jealous about how good the woman actually looked.

Kelsey bought her sister's children outfits that were going to put her credit card up to the limit. Everything else she bought would have to be on a personal check, but she wanted to do something nice for the kids. Her sister didn't have much money, and these might really be the children's only decent clothes this year. Kelsey's parents had always dressed Kelsey and Sarah in very nice clothes and had gone without other things themselves, but Sarah's priorities weren't the same. And Kelsey loved to spend on her niece and nephew whenever she could.

Miranda had shopped more casually and cheaply and she was now satisfied with her full bags. She was ready to go outside to smoke when she noticed Kelsey still hovering.

"What is it?" she asked, and then said, "oh, I get it, you want to go into the grown-up Gap for yourself."

They walked next door to the regular Gap store and Kelsey felt a sort of strain. Buying clothing she always felt okay, because she thought of it as necessary, but she wanted to treat herself today, to Gap Dream cologne. She had smelled it in a magazine strip and she had wanted it for months. Now, as she roamed around the display, which included wire soap dishes and translucent blue soaps and candles, she felt the desire build.

"I really want this," she said, as much to herself as anyone. She tried a spritz of the light cologne and it felt tingly and good. For a moment, she didn't feel her loneliness as badly. She looked up to Miranda as though for permission. "It smells really nice..."

Of course, Miranda would approve of any expenditure of money as long as it was on impulse, so she encouraged her friend. Kelsey got out her checkbook and bought the cologne. At the moment she felt excited, like a little girl.

The Gap was on the second floor and when Kelsey and Miranda came out, they stood momentarily at the Plexiglas railing, which was topped by round, white plastic edging. The young women leaned over on it, watching the Christmas shoppers walk by underneath them. Kelsey unwrapped the new cologne to share a spritz with Miranda and, suddenly, her sadness came back. Watching all of those people below them walking so confidently toward their own destinations made Kelsey feel like she had always been sad and alone. It made her feel all she had ever achieved was never enough to grant her a sure place with anyone. She didn't even know why she should be feeling this way and she didn't know why the holidays always made her so sad.

Kelsey had tried a new haircut, and now, as she bent over the railing, a big wave of hair hung down, and she turned her face into it, attempting to hide what she feared were going to be big messy tears.

Different strains of Christmas music played and the shopping mall was decorated in reds and greens and big tinsel snowflakes. Some shoppers almost tripped over themselves in their hurry. Few of them met the eyes of the young man, and those who did pulled away, strangely disturbed. The Watcher stood a few steps inside a Kaybee Toys Superstore, partially disguised, as he had planned, by what he was holding. Ironically, the prop was a very conspicuous thing, very Christmasy- a huge, white, stuffed bear, dressed up in a bright red Santa suit.

The Watcher kept the bear close to his face. He looked out from beside its fat belly while sucking slowly on the big red lollipop that had come with it, a lollipop which said, in white sugar letters, "Have a Beary Merry Christmas."

The lollipop went in and out of the Watcher's mouth while he held the bear steady, intoxicated by his own thoughts. He was positioned directly across from the girls, but he was on the lower level. He looked up at them as they awkwardly passed the cologne, almost losing their bundles. He felt as though he could almost smell it from here, that unmistakable scent of Gap Dream. He'd gotten a whiff of it as he had watched Kelsey inside the store, indecisive about treating herself, even after buying so much for others. Her body language told him so very much.

Later, he would return to The Gap, to touch all the items she had touched, and to memorize that "Generation X" scent, intended to seem practical, yet ethereal. Kelsey's choice of scent told him so much about what his enemy was trying to be.

He smiled up towards her, grimly, seeing how lost she looked when she hung her head. Her loneliness communicated itself to his gut. Little did she know that she was not as alone as she thought. The other shoppers seemed so frightened by their lives and so wound up in their own materialism. The young man thoughtfully sucked the lollipop and an occasional shopper smiled at him, people who didn't notice the look in his eyes, but only his pleasant face and the garish toy he clutched so strongly.

"You're mine," he whispered, looking in Kelsey's direction. He knew as she looked down, that she'd only notice the bear with its perky black nose and red snow hat, and that it would remind her nostalgically of her own wintry New York home. He knew that, out of everything in this whole mall, she would respond most wistfully when her eyes rested here, on this display he was creating, looking at it, but not able to make him out.

The Watcher observed the slender, overly polished girl dispassionately, noting how her trendy haircut with a single blond streak defeated the intensity of her eyes and noticing how weary and lost she looked amongst all the others. Gently finishing the lollipop, and with an odd light in his eyes, he spoke in her direction. "That's all over now, Kelsey. Now it's time to come to Papa."

Chapter 5

Nothing out of place had happened to Kelsey since the incident with her files and her miniature video cameras had picked up nothing out of the ordinary so she tended to agree with her boss that the files were probably what the person had wanted. But she still remained alert, especially when dealing with the drug case.

On a pleasantly cool afternoon, she and Jerry worked at one of the smaller marinas, watching boats. They sat on plastic chairs, finishing up juice drinks purchased at the snack bar. Kelsey swung her crossed leg, feeling bored after a whole day of this. And Jerry looked worn and tired. He leaned forward in his chair, impatiently pushing his dark curly hair out of his eyes every time the breeze messed it up.

"We've got to talk about things," he said. Kelsey knew he was referring to their relationship but she was in no better a position to tell him anything now than she had been the past few days. Her brain felt feverish with the presence of Jayson in her life. It didn't seem to her that what she felt for Jayson could be just about his looks. There was this feeling that there was a larger connection, although she could not make out what it was yet. She needed time to think.

Watching her foot move in a new sandal that she had bought to wear to work today, a bright orange thong with a four inch platform heel, she said something too direct and abrupt, and it came out sounding mean. "Jerry, I thought you weren't sure about your sexuality."

She felt bad once she said it, but Jerry just acknowledged it with a half-smile and gazed at her warmly. "I'm sure about what I feel for you," he said.

This was a non sequitur. It was at this moment that a small yacht slowly motored up the Intracoastal Waterway toward the marina. Kelsey grabbed Jerry's arm and got up, saying, "Come on," even though she wasn't too happy to be hurrying toward this particular boat. "It's the *Ascension*!"

The new-looking yacht that moved slowly into dock was one of the boats owned by the company they were investigating; a sister ship of the one found carrying the drugs. Kelsey knew that the same crew who were taken off the other boat were now manning this one; so this would be an ideal chance for them to approach some crew members and see if their trap worked.

As they hurried toward the boat, Kelsey was excited despite herself. Even though this particular case was probably the one that was putting her in danger, her investigative instincts still prevailed and she was tremendously curious about what was being carried aboard that yacht. She wanted to believe that her boss's plan of them posing as a couple who wanted to rent the boat would work. She couldn't wait to be allowed aboard the boat so she could start to nose around.

Not that she was tremendously disappointed when the captain told her it would be at least a month before they could rent the boat. He took their deposit, wrote them down on his schedule and at least this was some progress. Plus, this was something she could tell her boss.

Kelsey finally chose to go back to the health club on a Sunday. She was ready to face Jayson and his blank stare, which she felt was almost certainly deliberate since it was not as though she made her interest in him that secret. If he felt she was a woman up to his standards, then he would have at least smiled at her by now. Kelsey understood how the game was played. His never even looking at her was a way of letting her down easy. She had done it to enough loser guys herself. But Kelsey felt that Jayson should at least speak to her so she would know if the deeper connection she suspected had any basis in reality.

On this Sunday Kelsey had a strong conviction that today could be the day she would talk to the bodybuilder. She was dismayed when she realized that she had nothing clean to wear. She had used up every one of her newer workout outfits in the past weeks' frenzy of going to the gym every day and she hadn't bothered to do laundry because none of her other clothes had gotten dirty at the same rate. Then, when she was angry with Jayson, she hadn't thought she would be going back to the gym for a long time.

Kelsey pulled on something that she would not ordinarily be proud wearing: spandex shorts and an oversized top that she still had from when she was a member of an all ladies' gym back in New York. At that time she had been into aerobics and bright colors. The shorts were a shade of pink that never faded, the top had a flower pattern and an inspirational saying that matched the color of the shorts. This was actually Kelsey's taste when she was at college at SUNY-Oneonta, in upstate New York and a lot of the girls dressed cutesy like that at that time and place. Wearing the outfit from her past boosted her in a way. It seemed to say to the handsome young man, this is who I am at my truest and least cool and, if you cannot accept me, too bad, because I am still here.

At the gym, Kelsey strode over to the weight machines on the regular level, noticing, without much emotion, that Jayson was there. The two of them pretty much had the floor of weight machines to themselves. Most people who went to this gym did not care to get up this early on a Sunday morning. Kelsey heard the occasional yells from downstairs. Some women, mostly moms who could only get away at this time, were punishing themselves in an early aerobics class.

At the moment Kelsey felt very far away from that. She sat down at a shoulder machine and let out a "huff" as muscles that she had built, and then ignored, took on the weight. Her arms felt very painful, shaking and weakened, and she had to strain to get herself back into this.

For a while her concentration was on herself and the machines. She had let many of the obsessive thoughts about Jayson go and she felt she would let fate take this over. She would still watch him but would not give him the power to take away her strength.

After a while, Kelsey moved over to the more interior of the bench-press machines, planning on going for seventy pounds today, which was higher than anything she had ever done. She supposed that, if the gorgeous guy had a problem with coming this close to her, he would just delay this part of his workout; he had the whole rest of the gym to himself, after all.

Unexpectedly, he did come over. He came slinking over, with his muscles rolling. She thought maybe she saw an ironic amusement in his eyes as he noticed her, with her legs spread and every muscle in her body straining against the weight above her.

Jayson's cropped blond hair was glistening, freshly washed. He wore a faded rose-colored tank top and smelled faintly of soap and carried with him his usual sport bottle filled up heavily with some liquid. Kelsey guessed that it must be something cold, because the length of the bottle was covered in droplets. He set the bottle down carefully next to him and he adjusted himself on the bench, also carefully, as though maybe he had a rough night and was taking this workout easy.

Kelsey breathed out with a whoosh, tired after the first set of her own strenuous workout. Immediately, the electricity was there. It felt like it was pulling her with it, a whole tingling fabric of it, pulling her irrationally toward Jayson and the feeling overpowered her. Kelsey noted it with interest because it was something so amazing, something she had never felt before.

This is when Jayson looked at her, with eyes slightly slanted as though to avoid the sun or wind. He lazily twisted his body along the bench and he looked her full in the face and he just kept looking at her.

Of course, this is how it had to be, all along leading up to this. Kelsey knew that she was in a place where her previous experience, or the experience of her friends, would be of no benefit. It had all been leading up to this. All along the young man had teased her by not looking at her. Now when the moment came, it all made sense because, when he did finally did look at her, it was intense like this. It was the way an animal would look at you, or the way an innocent child would look at you, with total honest contemplation and unflinching focus.

Kelsey got to see into Jayson's eyes now, which were extraordinary. From a distance they were a light golden tone, seeming to pick up the light from outside, even though he was facing in the wrong direction. His eyes had this incredible lucidity. Kelsey felt refreshed and transformed in being able to meet his gaze. And, although the shape of his eyes spoke of compassion and that childlike freshness and innocence, there was something knowing and sophisticated there as well, something that made her feel completely undressed down to her soul.

The young man gave away no facial expression other than the unflinching gaze, which simply confirmed that he knew she was looking at him and was calling her on it. But in some way Kelsey also sensed something like a humorous smirk as he slowly turned away back into his workout. None of the other women who came around the gym wanting him would believe the way that Kelsey had just seen him; it wouldn't even pay for her to try to explain.

She felt energy within her, a totally burning energy and empowerment. Kelsey knew that he was saying that the next move would have to be hers. And if he really meant that much to her, then it made a kind of sense that she would have to put herself out there.

Kelsey got to her feet. It was as though something deep within herself powered her, some hormone left over from animal times, which allowed her to move with a deep sense of calm and absolutely no awareness of what was going on around her, just the focus on her destination. Her movements toward him were graceful and economical. Kelsey thought that even Jayson seemed momentarily surprised by what she was actually doing.

She came to stand over this gorgeous guy as he lay on the weight bench. It would have probably looked ridiculous if anyone had looked over this way. But no one did. It seemed as though the two of them had the entire gym to themselves, except for the incongruous presence of the loud, insistent music.

Jayson pushed under the bar. Rather than watching his chest muscles move with the exercise, Kelsey was completely focused on the stretching of the taut stomach muscles where his loose tank top had ridden up. He had the hardest stomach muscles Kelsey had ever seen in real life. She found herself actually salivating as she watched the repetitive movement of those muscles. She knew this wasn't good. It felt like it could only go one way.

Jayson looked up at her with a pouty sensual glance, following her eyes as they moved over his body. Then, unexpectedly, while her attention was riveted, he bunched his hand together in the well-worn fabric and he ripped his shirt. He held her gaze as the shreds of fabric fell open, revealing the whole glistening eight-pack of abdominal muscles. Then he slowly worked them for Kelsey's benefit, manipulating how he moved the barbell to target the stomach muscles enough that she could have her show.

He then rested the weight back in its brackets, his arms still held up and partly behind his head, so that his body was exposed to her. His face still looked like Brad Pitt's, his handsomeness was astonishing in that way. But Jayson had slightly stronger and more impressive features. And, of course, there was his awe-inspiring body.

Kelsey could hear the sound of her own shallow panting breathing. But she didn't care; there was only the moment. She met Jayson's eyes again and he gave her that languorous somewhat amused look he managed to convey without using any facial muscles except his eyes. Now he allowed the slightest smile, looking at her looking at his stomach.

"Is there something you want?" he asked.

It seemed like she was going to be with Jayson. At the same time she thought that it couldn't possibly happen. Kelsey didn't feel nervous at all. Rather, she was deadly calm. Her whole body felt very tight. She felt like a different girl than she had started out as this morning.

She leaned down and she boldly picked up Jayson's sport bottle. The bottle filled her hand, it was cool and moist and it triggered her with a jolt of energy. There was no going back.

Jayson watched her sleepily as she raised the bottle and tilted it to drink. Another jolt was felt as she put her lips on it, then she was sucking down the cool fluid. It tasted of apricot and exotic fruit. She was aware of her own lips and the movement of her throat. She sucked the liquid down strongly as Jayson watched. Drops of it slipped suddenly from where the plastic straw was inserted and made a mess on her arm, a few drops falling down onto Jayson's stomach.

What Kelsey craved to do was sick; she had never done it with anyone before, not even lovers. And this was a stranger in a gym. And people were around. Yet both their glances were locked down there where the drops had fallen on his body. Jayson probably knew what Kelsey wanted and was daring her to do it. Looking into his eyes and trying to match his sleepy grin, Kelsey bent forward to where one of the droplets lay quivering in a hollow of stomach muscle. Jayson's body tensed as she reached for him, his abdominal muscles trembling minutely, and she saw a bulge start to rise in his surfer shorts.

This was the sexiest thing Kelsey had ever done or even fantasized doing. She ran her finger over the surface of his moist skin as though she had done this with him many times before. Then she lifted the droplet of juice with her finger and she raised it to her mouth. Jayson had relaxed his arms off of the weight and now he was just watching her as she raised the droplet to her lips.

Kelsey knew the show she made with the light from the window on her, she hoped that her lips looked moist and full. She sucked at her finger, actually tasting the sweetness of the juice mixed with the watery taste of Jayson's sweat. Kelsey felt intoxicated and raised to a new level, feeling it not so much because it was this man, but because of the strange powerful thing that she herself had done.

Jayson looked inquisitively at her lips, and then licked his own briefly. Her heart was pounding with the message she was giving. He appeared to think and to make a decision and he spoke to her in a low, slightly husky voice.

"You're sure that you want to do this?" he asked.

Kelsey knew he meant sex. He wasn't even speaking to her before. Now he was challenging her. Her feelings for him were more complex than sex and he was putting her on the spot. She felt he was unfair for doing this. She had the impression that he didn't even like her very much at the moment. Yet she felt such safety and completeness within the circle of his personal distance. And he was demanding an answer.

"Yes," she said truthfully, "I do want to." She would have done or tried anything with him and, being honest with herself, she knew it.

Again, the man did the unexpected. Having been passive and lazy for so long, it was strange for him to show these sudden assertive movements, alarming and out of character. But as soon as Kelsey answered, Jayson climbed to his feet, standing on powerfully bulging legs. He took Kelsey immediately by the arm and started leading her across the carpeted floor. It didn't seem that there was going to be any more talking. Kelsey glanced up, surprised that this movie-star cute young guy was doing this roughly assertive thing. But yes, it was the same face, set blankly as she had known it the previous weeks.

Kelsey thought about the outfit she was wearing, not liking that Jayson was taking control away from her while she was in these weird tasteless clothes. If he was going to make out with her today it wouldn't be right, it wouldn't be the way she had imagined it. And then the moment would be over. She pulled back against him but he kept going.

And now he was leaning his shoulder into the pink door of the ladies locker room. Kelsey looked up to protest and Jayson glanced at her, with his lips just inches from hers.

"Don't even talk," he said. "Don't even talk now."

Weird feelings warred inside Kelsey, the feeling of being overwhelmed by the love that she had for him, like she truly belonged right here forever in his grasp, mixed with a feeling of prickly nervousness and panic. Jayson swung her around a few times as he got his bearings in the unfamiliar space and she had a suspicion of what he intended to do right here in the locker room.

He stepped forward to the next row of lockers. All around was the gilded, fake marble pattern of the wallpaper and the smell of new glue and carpeting. There was also a slight mustiness and a loud water drip coming from the shower area. Jayson paused to listen, probably checking that there was no one in there. He had his head up like a dog checking all around.

Kelsey remembered that he had a hard-on and now it seemed like he intended to use it on her in the locker room. There was something so brutal, so unfeeling; this wasn't the same thing as if he had taken her to the parking lot for a quickie. There, she would have easily given in to him, with the way she was feeling today. But this was obscene because of the shame she would feel if anyone walked in here. It wouldn't be right to them, it would shame them and violate their own sanctity as women.

Kelsey tried to argue but Jayson pushed her back further into the row that held her own locker, that pink and gold claustrophobic space.

There was a glass block wall here, chest high, with a pink Formica surface; it stood very near the main entrance. Jayson wrestled her behind the wall, standing in back of her and running one hand over her buttocks. She felt oddly like laughing, because this was all so strange, with the sound of the constant pounding music, the silly girly songs, making it all the more grisly.

"Jayson," she said, "we can't do this here. If somebody walks in..."

He whispered in her ear and the feel of his breath made her vaginal juices gush between her legs. "But we are doing this. I'm going to fuck you now, Kelsey. Which is what you wanted."

It didn't even sound obscene as he said it. He put his body very close to hers; she felt the safety and the complete immobility wedged between his steely muscles and the rough cement between the cold glass blocks. Jayson lifted the ugly big shirt and pulled her shorts partway down over Kelsey's butt, along with her thong underwear.

It couldn't be happening like this, suddenly and degradingly. Kelsey felt like crying for how this was being spoiled. And yet her body was meeting the hard, yet silky, head of his penis and swallowing him into her. Jayson rested his head on her back and gave a little grunt. Despite what he was doing, there felt like something gentle and right in how he held her. Kelsey was very tight, as usual and Jayson had to move his whole body for each movement deeper inside her. He filled her comfortably though and she felt a warm languidness inside as he moved. She felt like silk inside, so wet, not scratchy and dry like she sometimes felt.

And then a woman walked briskly in. She had keys on a little elastic jingling on her wrist. She didn't even appear to see them.

Kelsey felt sick inside; she wriggled in Jayson's grasp, but he held her firmly and worked the whole time they heard the woman moving around and finally starting a shower.

"Stop," Kelsey said in a quiet, sob-like voice that didn't carry any conviction. Jayson moved in her in circles, she felt his hard legs and chest against her and she dreaded the moment when the touch would be over.

Jayson's face was near hers, pressed against her hair. She saw his eyes from the side. His breathing was a little labored but he was trying to be quiet. "I'll come," he whispered, "unless you want to come first."

She shook her head, feeling shamed by him again.

Now his body moved in jerks. He held onto her tighter, as she was anchored against the wall. Jayson started panting more loudly now, while a song mounted to a frenzy on the PA system. And then Kelsey felt the hot explosions inside her body.

Jayson's next movements came suddenly and Kelsey almost fell as she lost her support. He slid out of her abruptly. In the same movement, he slipped a hand under her big hanging shirt, grasped her delicate lace bra by the front and ripped.

The bra slipped out instantly and then Jayson pulled her shorts and underwear back up over her damp throbbing body. Confused, she spun to look at him and there was nothing reachable in those eyes. Her body still yearned out to his warmth. She couldn't believe this was over. Jayson tucked her bra into his waistband and, with his eyes locked on hers, he reached his hand up and pulled off the gold chain and medallion that he always wore. He literally threw the necklace towards her curious face.

"Souvenir," he said. "Now you know what it's like to be with me."

Then he left. Two seconds later, the whole aerobics class full of women started coming through the door. Kelsey pulled back from the wall, with her hair bedraggled and still intoxicated from the excitement of the sex with Jayson. She felt unworthy, a million miles from the other women's cleanliness and ordinariness. Maybe Jayson intended her to feel like this. She sensed that it would be a long time before she even contemplated what had happened here, let alone analyzed his motives. She slunk back and curled onto a bench, feeling both less powerful, and infinitely more powerful, than the other women. If Jayson had been trying to turn her off her crush on him, he had certainly succeeded.

She laughed to herself, sounding a bit crazy, and put her head all the way down in her hands. She supposed she looked like she was crying, because one of the women approached her and asked her, "Are you okay? Is there anything I can do to help?"

Chapter 6

"Guess what. I found out the dirt on your mystery man," Miranda said on the other end of the phone.

Kelsey was holding a basket of laundry to take downstairs. She was just getting out of the gloomy mood she had been in since the episode in the locker room this past Sunday and was now sorry she had ever picked up the phone on her way out the door. Calls to Miranda had been Kelsey's lifeline since the girls were six years old, and Kelsey had never knowingly hidden anything from her friend until this week, when she had neglected to tell Miranda what had happened with Jayson in the locker room.

She hadn't meant to deceive Miranda in any way, and it wasn't just her own shame that had kept her from telling. It was just that Kelsey was still so confused and hurting about how she had been with Jayson. She didn't want to let her friend near the subject until she came to terms with it herself.

Now it appeared she was going to be paying for the secretiveness. No matter what Miranda was going to say about Jayson, Kelsey wouldn't be able to bring up the subject of what had happened in the locker room. It wasn't exactly the kind of thing she could say she forgot to mention the last few times she and Miranda had talked.

Miranda sounded breathless and giddy. "I can't believe you weren't there yesterday," she said, "and I couldn't get you on the phone. I swear to God, I couldn't figure out what happened to you, and here I am finally talking to these two guys, and I'm, like, running to the pay phone every two minutes trying to call you..."

Kelsey's stomach clenched. "You talked to Jayson?" she asked.

"Yes, Jayson and Juan. I talked to them for two hours at the gym. Then they wanted to go out to some diner for coffee and I went with them." Kelsey had the thought that maybe the guys were mad rapists, wanting to score off Miranda the way Jayson already had with her. But what her friend said next eliminated that possibility. "I told them that I wanted you to come out and meet them." Miranda said. "That's why they suggested the diner. The gym was closing and I was so sure that I'd get you on the phone any minute."

"So, you mentioned me?" Kelsey asked.

"Yeah. Don't worry, though. I didn't say anything about you liking Jayson."

Kelsey thought to herself that it might be a little late to worry about that. "Did he say anything about me at all?" she asked.

"Jayson? Not really. He did mention that he knew who you were from the gym and that you seemed like a nice girl."

Kelsey had this bitter taste in her mouth, amused in a way at Jayson's irony in turning a phrase. But she knew she had deserved everything she got for trying to play in the big leagues. Jayson had simply showed her that if she wanted to play games, there were others who played them harder. When Kelsey had seen him at the gym after that day, he hadn't ignored her. Working out with his hardbody friends, he had simply glanced at her and nodded pleasantly, like he might do with any friend or acquaintance. She had to face the fact that, even at this time with other things going so badly in her life, she was still going to be left all alone to deal with everything. Someone like Jayson was not going to care about her; she had been stupid to think that he would.

Now Miranda said to her, "You know, Jayson's not at all like we thought he was. You're going to be amazed. He and Juan are two of the nicest guys I've ever met. It doesn't matter how he looks, Jayson's not stuck up at all; he's the type who'll sit there and listen to all your problems. Juan says that he's actually kind of shy..."

Oh, yeah, Kelsey thought, I know all about that.

Miranda went on, excitedly. "Anyway, I got all the dirt you wanted on him. He and Juan came over together from Gold's Gym. They've been friends for a while. Juan is into competition bodybuilding and Jayson helps him out. Jayson doesn't compete; he just works out for himself. His last name is Carter, by the way. He's twenty-five years old and he came here from San Diego. He went to college there but he didn't graduate, so now he's going to college here in Boca Raton. And he works also..."

Miranda was breathless. "... I don't know why you didn't just ask him all of this yourself. Those two guys are so easy to talk to that it's embarrassing the way we went on about them before. And they don't even want anything. Juan told me that Jayson is definitely not into flings; he just got out of a long-term relationship and he's basically just looking for friendship..."

"Miranda, I don't know if you should trust this guy," Kelsey said.

"Why?" Miranda asked, incredulously. "You mean you don't want to go out with him now?"

"Not really," Kelsey said, feeling sad but feeling that she was telling the truth. "I met him at the gym and I just don't feel the same way about him."

"What?"

"I can't say more about it than that, but that's how I feel. I really don't have that same kind of interest in him anymore..."

Miranda sighed, sounding crushed, like she was the one about to cry. Kelsey regretted so badly that she hadn't told her friend the truth the day when the sexual encounter happened. But she felt so vulnerable and wounded after the incident with him coming after what had been happening to her at work. She hadn't wanted to reveal her weakness to her best friend.

Miranda persisted. "You wouldn't mind just hanging out with Jayson and Juan as friends, though, would you? I went ahead and I made plans for this weekend... And I was so happy... We were all supposed to hang out on Fort Lauderdale Beach: the two of us, those two guys, and Jerry. I was supposed to pick Jayson up because he lives on Hollywood Beach and his motorcycle is broken down. I thought you'd be dying of excitement when you heard this."

"Us with them at the beach?" Kelsey sounded completely incredulous.

"Yes, I'm telling you, these guys are wholesome! They're not like the club crawlers we usually meet. I thought we could get a tan and have a good time. Really have a good time, with nothing to prove..."

"And you mentioned me in reference to this beach thing and Jayson had no problem with it?" Kelsey asked.

"No, why should he have a problem? He sounded happy about the whole thing. I thought you'd be happy, too, Kelsey. I thought I was doing something nice for you. Lately, it seems I've just been screwing things up..."

"Okay," Kelsey said, stepping back one step further from her own emotions, "I'll go".

That Saturday, Kelsey dressed in a bright orange string-bikini that complemented her light tan with a native-print sundress over it. She wore her funky, high-heeled orange thongs and carried a brand new orange towel. It was an outfit that would, ordinarily, make her mood soar, especially on a day like this, when the water was as calm as it usually was in the summer combined with the refreshing wintertime breeze.

Kelsey wasn't much of a swimmer, and Miranda usually had to act as her personal lifeguard. Usually she wouldn't swim this late in the season. But on an unusually warm and calm day like today, with low tide in the afternoon she would feel confident enough to get in the water, lie back on her inflatable raft and just let her troubles float away somewhere on the emerald horizon.

But today, other than dream weather, Kelsey wasn't expecting much. She was first of their group to arrive at the beachside parking lot. She sat inside her red Avenger with the door open and the radio on, fiddling with tying on a leather ankle-bracelet, while other vehicles crowded the parking lot and her black upholstery started to gather heat.

Jerry got there next and he helped her out of her car with her towel and raft and chair. "So, where are the musclemen?" he asked sarcastically and his tone made Kelsey feel somewhat better.

But, when Juan pulled in driving a metallic green pickup truck, the first thing Kelsey saw was his big friendly smile. A genuine smile like that was so rare amongst the young people in South Florida and even rarer for someone with his physique. Kelsey knew, immediately that Juan had no attitude and that Miranda had been right, at least about him.

The big dark-haired man, in his brand new clothing, looked embarrassed as he got out of the truck. "Would you believe that this is only my second time on this beach since I've been in Fort Lauderdale? I didn't know where the parking lot was and I got caught going all the way down the one way and then I had to double back around..."

He reached out and gently took Kelsey's hand. "Hey, Kelsey, how are you?" Then he shook with Jerry, with hands held up, like men who are good friends, "Jerry, good to meet you. I'm Juan Reyes, Miranda's friend."

The familiarity worked, and Kelsey saw that the big personal trainer made her friend feel at ease. "Don't worry," Jerry said with a smile. "With Miranda responsible for the driving, those guys won't be here for a while. It's, like, one-o'clock now, so she should just be getting up!"

Jerry helped Juan get a big insulated cooler down from the back of his truck and then they stood around debating whether to go onto the beach without the others.

They waited a few minutes and then, as predicted, Miranda and Jayson spun into the parking lot late, with the swollen tires of the little black Sunfire sliding on the slight coating of sand and music throbbing through the open windows. Jayson got out, with his muscles hidden under an oversized lace-up shirt and he shook his head, as if dizzy, while grinning at the others.

He spoke to Kelsey first. In addition to showing that he had impeccable manners, just like his friend did, his words also expressed that, no matter what had happened, there was no enmity between them, and he was not going to reveal anything she didn't want him to.

"Next time," he joked with Kelsey, "you drive."

They all laughed together, the ice broken. Miranda put her arm around her friend's shoulders and the two women led the way onto the beach with the men behind them, carrying the supplies. The beach was very crowded and usually Kelsey would be complaining about all the other girls' bodies with envy. But that would be ridiculous today, considering the men she and Miranda had with them.

Today, they were the ones being stared at with envy. Other young women looked up from their magazines wide-mouthed and nudged their friends. Kelsey was grateful when the men selected a spot a little further down the beach from the young crowd, somewhat more private.

"This is what I want to do," Miranda declared, revealing a big bottle of baby oil that she planned to smear all over her long exposed body. "I intend to fry. I envy all of you guys 'cause you're all so dark skinned." She squinted her eyes, "except maybe Jayson and he's from California so he's tan anyway."

They all laughed and drank beers together. A pair of young girls with silicone breasts and disproportionately tiny bodies kept strolling by Juan and Jayson, obviously trying to get the men's attention. The two men leaned into each other to shake their heads, even as Kelsey and Miranda whispered to each other, verbally tearing the girls apart.

Jerry, never one to mince words, asked straight out, "Does it bother you guys to have girls constantly after you like that?"

Juan thought about it a while. "Well, you know, my body is my living. As a competition bodybuilder, I have to be brutally hard on myself each time out, or I'm never gonna get the opportunity to compete again. Same for my work at the gym; I have to consistently set an example. It doesn't really flatter me to have a girl tell me I'm the greatest when, among other guys I know, I'm not."

"Jayson?" Jerry asked and Kelsey cringed, knowing of her friend's dislike for his rival.

"Well," Jayson said, smiling at the smaller man, "it's going to sound ridiculous, but I'll say it and hope you all don't go home and laugh at me- to me weightlifting is a part of Zen. There is no right and wrong and no one body being any better than another, there's only process and awareness. Get it?"

For that one second, with his face squinted up and in shadow, Jayson did not look so incredibly handsome, and his thoughtful words were the dominant thing. Kelsey tended to believe him about what he said about bodybuilding.

Maybe it was the beer, but she felt herself getting mellow. Miranda ran into the gentle surf, and Kelsey followed her more carefully. The tall redhead ran out too far, as usual, and she dove in and swam out to where some of the waves were breaking. Kelsey just stood in the tingly waist-deep water watching her friend, and she checked that there was a lifeguard in the tower paying attention. She wasn't going to lower herself in to swim until her friend was safely back onshore.

Miranda soon came back, running out of the surf with a broad smile and flinging herself back on her lawn chair, and then Kelsey retrieved her raft and took it into the water. It was a small struggle as the ocean hissed and whooshed around her. But finally she was on top of the raft, paddling gently to stay in place and watching the blue and turquoise of water and sky. Kelsey heard Jayson and Juan walking in the surf behind her, talking in the deep boasting voices of men bullshitting with each other, and she caught a glimpse of Miranda, sprawled on a sand chair and glistening with her oil, and all felt right with the world.

When Kelsey came to join Miranda and Jerry at the sand chairs, Jayson and Juan were up and getting physical, throwing a Nerf football to each other at the edge of the surf. In their baggy trunks, jumping around and half drenched by water, they looked so happy and playful like two teenagers. But Jerry was giving them a bad look, as though he felt left out, like they knew he wasn't masculine like they were.

And then Jayson yelled out, "Heads up," and he threw the football to Jerry so that Jerry had to catch it. "Take my place, dude," Jayson said, "I need to go get something to eat."

Again, everything was right with the world, as he put Jerry at ease. Jayson wanted to know if anyone wanted to go across the street with him and Miranda decided to answer for Kelsey. "Kelsey needs to go pee but she refuses to go on her own and I can't get up because of all this oil..."

"Kelsey?" he asked.

Kelsey went with Jayson, but she moved stonily. She felt hard inside and she knew that she would not show the weakness of talking about what happened between them. Jayson also seemed neutral, walking at a distance from her, as she preferred. The sidewalks along the curvy whitewashed wall were crowded with strolling tourists and the two lanes of traffic on highway A1A, where the road was one-way, were unbroken. Most of the cars were filled with young men and women cruising up and down to see what hot people were walking the strip or sitting at the sidewalk cafes. Many of the strollers were dressed up in designer beachwear and music throbbed from live musicians performing island music in one of the new restaurants.

Kelsey must have been distracted because, suddenly, she felt Jayson's arm on her body, roughly pushing her back. As they attempted to cross the road, she had stepped thoughtlessly into traffic and she stumbled on her high loose shoe, while a white Mustang was speeding up at the break in traffic, rapidly bearing down on her.

"Hey," Jayson said, and he looked briefly at her with concern in his eyes. "Don't do that!"

This time he helped her across the road, with his arm through hers, and then he let it go when they were on the opposite side.

"I'm starving," he said. "Those guys want to wait to have dinner later at one of these restaurants. But I want some dinner now!" He laughed at himself. "And then I can eat again later. That's one thing about me, Kelsey- for my bodybuilding, I eat all day long."

They smiled together. In a way it felt great to be around Jayson. If Kelsey could forget that he was breathtakingly gorgeous and that a few days ago he had fucked her in a totally degrading way, she could think that she was with a friend. Out of all of the hip, and not-so-hip strangers brushing against them, she was sure that none was quite so natural and instinctively kind.

They chose an open-air bar with six-foot-high parrots painted in bright primary colors on the walls and the ubiquitous "Wasting Away Again in Margaritaville" playing on the stereo. Kelsey went to the ladies' room and when she came back onto the street, Jayson was lifting the edge on a full take-out container that he had bought. He took out some round fried item and he reached it towards Kelsey's mouth; it smelled spicy and its warmth tickled her lips. Jayson smiled so kindly that she couldn't reconcile it with what happened the other day. Today he really seemed to like her.

He made it obvious that he wouldn't push the food on her if she really didn't want it, and maybe this was symbolic. "It's a conch fritter," he offered, "it's spicy but it's good. I love any kind of spicy food. Maybe we can all go for Jamaican one of these days..."

Kelsey bit gently into the conch fritter, pulling it out of Jayson's hand in the process and holding it in her own. Jayson was already eating as well, ravenously. Then they walked back across the street and sat on the low concrete wall, which, at nighttime, would be all lit up with a multicolored neon strip. They faced the cafes and shops on the other side of the street and looked out at all the cars while Jayson pulled the food out.

"I hope you don't mind," Jayson said, "I kind of wanted to be alone for a while and not hurry back onto the beach."

There was no sense wondering what he meant by that. It was amazing how Kelsey's schoolgirl crush had gone away, replaced by wariness and an honest attention on what it was like being with him. Just being. Together, they finished off the food and they sat on the wall for a while before going back on the beach.

Two hours later they came back up to street with Miranda, Jerry and Juan. They stowed their beach gear in the vehicles, fed the master parking meter more money and then had dinner at the same restaurant where Jayson and Kelsey had the snack. But, when darkness had fallen and the others said they were going to continue on to a dance club at the beach, Kelsey felt an invisible line drawn inside herself. She did not feel right putting herself in a situation where she might be seen as Jayson's date. So she declined the offer, saying she wanted to get back home and do some leftover paperwork from her job.

When the group walked Kelsey back to the parking lot, Jayson looked almost saddened, as if he knew that her not going out with them was his fault. Miranda leaned forward to kiss Kelsey and Jayson looked as though maybe he'd feel right doing that himself. But she and Jayson were both conspiring in keeping the problem between them a secret. He squeezed her hand and said, "Thank you for coming, Kelsey."

It was only after her group vanished into the pedestrian traffic a ways down the sidewalk that Kelsey was aware of what her twisted pride had done. The others were all going off together to party where it was safe, while she would be returning alone to a dark apartment where she had felt edgy since the incident with the shampoos. Even if she was totally safe there and no stranger had ever been inside, her vacant condo would still be horribly lonely at this time on a Saturday night.

The next morning she woke up early and prepared to do some work. She had papers spread all over her coffee table, reports from the forensic lab. She was good at picking out details that might be pertinent to her cases as well as those cases assigned to the other staff, so Mr. Lester always let her take care of these reports for the entire office and she didn't mind doing it. She appreciated the quiet time she would have to work on the reports today.

At ten in the morning her portable phone rang and, when she answered, she heard an elderly male voice. "Kelsey, Mr. Eisenberg here. How are you?"

She was wondering why her landlord would be calling right now. "I'm fine," she said. "How are you? How's your wife?" she asked.

"Well, I don't like to be calling with bad news, but Edna's taken a turn for the worse. We're going to have a personal care aide come in. We may not even get down to Florida at all this year. I know you wanted some extra time to decide about whether you're going to buy the condo but I'm afraid we're going to need a final decision right away." He sounded painfully apologetic.

When Kelsey took the option to buy two years ago she had been sure she would want to purchase the condo. Now the time had rolled around too soon. Money was not the problem. Kelsey was waiting for a decision from Nova University, which might not come for several more months. If she said no to buying the condo, she could lose the over twenty thousand dollars in equity that she had already paid as rent. But if she did buy the condo, and then the Nova University law program turned her down, she could end up stuck in Florida when she might have had a chance to go free.

There was also the matter of the person who had been stalking and harassing her. Her enemy hadn't done anything in a while, but it was hard to forget the possibility that the person might once have been here, inside her condo, even if her only evidence was the crazy episode of the shampoos.

"Mr. Eisenberg," Kelsey said, "I'm really sorry about your wife. I hope she'll feel better. I'm just so shocked about having to make this decision right now. If there was any way possible, could I maybe wait until after the first of the year to give you my decision? Then we could do a really quick closing by, say, the fifteenth if I do want to buy it?"

"Sure Kelsey, that would be fine," Mr. Eisenberg agreed. "We hate to be putting you in this position just during the holidays..."

Just then Kelsey's call waiting went off and, as soon as Kelsey switched lines, a breathless female voice spoke immediately with no introduction. "You're not going to believe what happened."

Kelsey was shocked and irritated. "Miranda, I've got my landlord on the other line long distance. He's telling me I'm going to have to buy the condo right now. Can we talk about whatever this is later?"

"Just guess!" Miranda persisted.

Kelsey asked, a little testily, "You slept with Jayson, right?"

"No Hon, not quite," Miranda said. "But he asked me out on a date!"

Kelsey seemed to feel her soul spiraling down away from her. "Look, hold on a minute." Practical as always, Kelsey felt the need to take care of business matters before she fell apart, and she switched back to finalize her plans with Mr. Eisenberg.

When she got back on the line, Miranda said, "I don't see how you can buy that condo. I thought we were going to get out of here and move back up to New York State. Why would you tie yourself down?"

"So, what happened last night?" Kelsey asked, without replying to what Miranda said.

"This is going to be entirely up to you, Kelsey," Miranda told her. "Jayson wants me to go with him to some dinner with clients for his firm. It's just a friendship thing but, if it bothers you even the tiniest amount, I would never go. I'm no man stealer."

"He's not my man," Kelsey said. "And I've already told you that I'm not going to go out with him. I think he knows that, too. So, do whatever makes you comfortable; I'll be okay with it."

"It's ironic," Miranda said, "You wouldn't picture Jayson as a stockbroker, would you, but that's what he does for a living. Doesn't that remind you of Paul?"

Jayson was nothing like her ex-boyfriend Paul and, even now, he was so much more important to Kelsey than Paul had ever been. Yet Kelsey felt a lassitude. All that was happening seemed inevitable and she felt a numbing distance from it.

Chapter 7

After her first evening out with him, Miranda reported to Kelsey that Jayson had been a total gentleman. It then became a habit for Jayson and Miranda to spend a lot of time together, although Miranda kept insisting that there was nothing sexual going on. It seemed to Kelsey that Jayson enjoyed bringing Miranda to work engagements with him. He worked for a small brokerage firm that tended to entertain lavishly to get clients to invest with them and there were constant holiday parties. It also seemed like Jayson was protective of Miranda. He would go to clubs and hang out with her late nights to keep her out of trouble, especially the kind involving drugs.

Kelsey saw Jayson practically every day between the early December day at the beach and Christmas Eve night. This was because the four of them usually hung out as a group: the two girls, Jayson and Juan. They would meet in the evenings after work for cocktails and dinner at some of the mid-priced places on the pretty Intracoastal Waterway or they'd stroll along the sidewalk on crowded Fort Lauderdale beach on the weekends. Jayson's face became a familiar and expected feature across a restaurant table, to the point where Kelsey was even losing some of her distrust of him and starting to take him at face value as a friend.

There was so much socializing because of the holiday season and their new acquaintance with the guys that Kelsey almost lost herself in it. She even didn't have to worry about her feelings about Jayson because, at the moment, everything just felt comfortable and good. He was there when she needed to talk to him and she was getting to know him this way.

She also didn't have to worry about the person who had been stalking her. Nothing had happened since before Thanksgiving, and it was logical to assume that the person was content now that they had eliminated whatever evidence there was on them by eliminating her computer files. The two hidden cameras had showed nothing, although she checked them every day, and Kelsey was starting to let her guard down overall. She was also starting to feel somewhat more positive about buying the condo since it seemed to be totally safe and it felt like home again.

Christmas Eve was particularly tough for Kelsey, though. It had always been a special time for her immediate family. On Christmas Eve, she, her parents and her sister would open one gift each and sing carols together before going to Midnight Mass. This year Kelsey would be spending the early part of the evening at an elaborate supper hosted by Jerry and his roommates at their apartment and then the later part of the evening totally alone.

Juan had left days earlier to stay with his close-knit family who lived in Miami; Jerry, who was Jewish, was preparing to leave on Christmas Day for a week-long visit with his family in Chicago and Miranda, as usual, was doing things her own unique way. The only flight out that she was able to afford was one nine o-clock on Christmas Eve. Connections wouldn't get her home to Endicott, New York until two in the morning.

But at least she was going home, while Kelsey could not leave at all. She had known for months that if she had to stay in Fort Lauderdale because of work, she would spend Christmas Eve at Jerry's party. Now Jerry also took pity on Jayson, who could not go home to California, and invited him along as Miranda's escort. Jayson would also act as Miranda's chauffeur to the airport, meaning that the others would not have to leave the party early.

Jerry had said that he wanted to make the evening magical for his friends, and he almost succeeded. There was a strong wind coming from off the ocean; it lashed the palm fronds against the windows of the apartment just west of the beach on Bayview Drive but the group felt sheltered inside in the circle of their laughter. Jerry's roommates' Christmas tree was covered in gold and silver balls and, as promised, the friends ate off fancy dishes and drank champagne out of slender handblown glasses with gold rims.

But then Kelsey went home to loneliness. Even the normally busy Hillsboro Boulevard was desolate, with the wind driving empty plastic bags across six dark empty lanes. Kelsey's condo complex had the same desolate feel. Only several of the doors in the four-building complex were decorated with lights. Most of the residents here were Jewish, some were extremely elderly and infirm and others had gone away to visit their families for Christmas. Most of the windows in the complex were darkened and others showed only the blue light of television.

Approaching from her car, Kelsey saw the shape of her cat waiting at her own open window. She hurried to get upstairs but then the clean cool scent of her condo only emphasized the emptiness. It was such a contrast compared to the smells of cooking that had filled Jerry's apartment earlier. Kelsey was reluctant to turn on a light. She crossed the living room to stand at the glass patio doors and look down at the pool. The condo management had made a desultory attempt to decorate by throwing ropes of red lights loosely over shrubbery and palm fronds. Now the lights swayed crazily in the strong breeze. Kelsey thought for a moment about going downstairs and swimming but it was cold and she didn't want to make a spectacle of herself down there.

Finally, she went to stand by the small kitchen window and she stroked Mr. Cooper, who had jumped up to be with her. She watched the parking lot even though there was no activity there.

At about eleven-o-clock she watched Miranda's black Sunfire pull in, driving more steadily than usual. This was no surprise to Kelsey. The plan had been that she would watch her girlfriend's car while Miranda was away and Jayson had left his motorcycle here earlier so that he could make the switch.

Kelsey had thought he would leave as soon as he changed vehicles. Instead, she was surprised several minutes later when she heard the scuffing of boots coming up the stairs outside her condo. Jayson, carrying two paper grocery sacks, walked right by the window she was standing by and he rang her front bell.

Kelsey took a moment to get there. When she opened the door Jayson looked lit up, like he was tired but exhilarated. His grocery sacks smelled strongly of something spicy, like Indian curry, and she wondered where he had managed to buy anything at this time of night.

Jayson grinned at her. "Well," he said, "her Highness is safely dropped off at the airport. And I didn't think that anyone should be alone on Christmas Eve. Do you?" He looked at Kelsey directly and gently. "I hope you'll let me come in."

There seemed to be something so genuine in him and she knew that he was as alone as she was tonight. And she could tell that whatever this was had nothing to do with what happened between them in the locker room that awful day.

She didn't answer him directly but she switched on the light and lifted one of the bags and carried it inside, so that Jayson would follow.

"Your condo is beautiful, Kelsey," he said as he walked over the threshold. "This place is truly beautiful." He said it with respect and interest. Jayson was the first person that seemed to really get it when they first walked in, how this place was a reflection of Kelsey and how important decorating actually was to her.

Jayson walked around for a long while, just looking at her things and thoughtfully brushing his fingers over certain items. Then he came back to stand near Kelsey by the breakfast bar. They both spoke at the same time; she, to ask where he'd gotten the groceries and he, to ask if it would be all right if he took off his jacket. Tonight the normally confident Jayson actually seemed shy and unsure.

Kelsey took his leather jacket and hung it with her own in the living room closet then she helped him unpack the bags. One bag had nothing but food: a jar of popcorn, premium ice cream, Kahlua liqueur, hot-cocoa mix and fresh-ground gourmet coffee. Kelsey couldn't help but smile as all the stuff emerged. "What did you do here?" she asked.

"I thought we could make something festive with the coffee and the liquor," he said. "And I just sort of took you for a gourmet coffee drinker."

Kelsey pointed to the cappachino maker in a recess of her counter and she indicated the coffee beans Jayson had chosen, which were a simple vanilla flavor. "Well, you're right about me and coffee, and this is a good choice, nothing too exotic."

"I've got good taste," Jayson said, looking at Kelsey a little too closely.

Then he glanced down at the cat that was sniffing around at the hem of his pressed jeans. This was unusual, Kelsey thought. Cooper would usually hide out if she had any male visitor. Sometimes, if he thought the man was a threat to Kelsey, the cat had been known to dash out abruptly and bite the guy.

"You, know," Kelsey asked, "would Miranda have a problem with you being here?"

Jayson eyed her strangely, probably wondering at her concern for her friend's feelings, knowing her own feelings for him and the fact that Miranda had moved in on what should have been Kelsey's territory. But Kelsey's concern for her girlfriend was genuine. Her friendship with Miranda would be forever and she was worried about the type of emotional damage this guy could cause. She knew that under the tough shell her girlfriend was fragile. Unlike herself, Miranda might not bounce back from the same kind of encounter with Jayson that Kelsey had in the gym.

Yet the feeling was so powerful tonight that it was Kelsey, not Miranda, he actually wanted to be with.

"You really care about her, don't you?" he asked.

"I'd lay down my life for her," Kelsey said truly.

"Okay, maybe I haven't always been known to be the most correct guy in what I do..." he said, and she knew that he was referring to the incident in the gym. "...But I wouldn't hurt Miranda. I know that she'd have no problem with me coming here. Anyway, we're just sort of seeing each other socially. I just like to be in her life right now because she's going through a lot of things at the moment."

"Oh," said Kelsey and they looked at each other with some amusement because, at the moment, the feeling was so strong that they ought to be the two dating.

Kelsey reached into the second bag. "What's in here?" she asked.

Then she pulled out several boxes of Christmas lights- the multi-colored kind, which were her favorites. "Oh, my God!" she squealed. "Why did you do this?" She was so excited she couldn't hide her pleasure, even though she was trying to be cold to Jayson.

"Do you like them?" Jayson asked, smiling also.

"Yes, yes, I do," she said.

She glanced at her little Christmas tree that sat forlornly by the patio doors. It was too small, so she looked around for someplace she could put the heavy lights.

"Don't worry," Jayson said. "That's why I brought these."

He took out a brand new hammer and a box of nails and he headed assuredly for the patio doors, with Mr. Cooper following at his heels.

One moment Kelsey felt so light and happy but, the next, it was as though some dark creature had moved into her line of vision, blocking out the light. It was the memories again, her childhood memories, rushing in for some reason tonight on the holiday. There was something about when Jayson climbed up to hammer in the Christmas lights that made her start remembering. The memories were very dark and uncomfortable, very weird. They seemed to come from a time in her life that she was usually unable to remember. She knew the memories came from a time before she met Miranda, so it must have been before her sixth birthday. Kelsey now felt like she was being swept away by something that she didn't even recognize. She felt like she was going to cry in front of her guest.

She put her hands up in front of her face and she ran for the bedroom, praying that Jayson wouldn't notice. Then she crawled under her covers in the dark, shivering and hoping that this episode, like the others she'd had in the past month, would just pass. She didn't know how much time had gone by, but soon Jayson's bulky silhouette was blocking the doorway.

"Is this about me?" he asked. "Would you like me to leave?"

Kelsey shook her head and Jayson came over by her. He selected the bedside lamp that was a huge conch shell, and flicked it on. Although kitschy, the lamp gave off the most beautifully serene light, an orangey pink light like the color inside the shell. Jayson examined her face in this soft light.

"Well, what is it that upset you?"

"I don't know," she said, honestly. "It must be something to do with the holiday. These terrible feelings just sort of exploded out of me." She tried to laugh.

Jayson lay down on the bed next to her outside the covers. He checked the view of the parking lot behind the wicker headboard before settling. This was also one of Kelsey's habits. Most of her guests didn't even realize there was a window behind the gauzey curtains.

"Is it memories from your childhood?" he asked, "bad memories?"

"I wish I knew," she said. "I had this picture perfect childhood. I have the most traditional family and my childhood was great. I don't know why I keep getting these flashbacks lately. Maybe it's just homesickness; I've been overwhelmed by homesickness lately. I've been here in Florida over three years but I'm only really feeling it now."

They lay for a while in silence.

Then Jayson said, "I'm here, if you ever need to talk. My friendship is here if you want it."

He seemed hesitant to look into her eyes. When he did, she really saw the humanity in him and his extraordinary looks were secondary. Maybe that was what the harsh lesson in the gym was all about. She didn't even feel uncomfortable lying next to him now with her clothes and hair messed up.

"Jayson," she said surprising herself with what she was discussing, "two years ago I rented this condo with an option to buy, and now the option's coming due. I have to decide by New Year's Day whether to buy it or not. The problem is, I might want to move. If I don't get accepted to Nova University next fall, then there's nothing holding me. Florida isn't my kind of place and I'd like to go home... Miranda knows about this

78

and she would move back with me if I left. She definitely doesn't want me to buy the condo."

Jayson answered assertively, with no hesitation. "Go ahead and buy the condo, Kelsey," he said. "You have to. You love this place, right? I can see that. So when you make your decision, you have to go with your heart. Later, you could always leave, but this condo is your heart. You can't betray that."

He got up to go back to the other room. "I hope it's not a problem me putting holes in your walls?"

Kelsey's concern as a hostess won out. She got up and went back into the living area to make them cappachinos well spiked with liquor and the room filled with an intoxicating odor. Jayson finished stringing the colored lights.

Kelsey put the popcorn in the microwave and she said, excitedly, "You know what else I could make us if you wanted to hang around? I could bake cookies!" She showed him what her other friends had rejected, a roll of Pillsbury Holiday Cookie Dough. "They've got Christmas Tree patterns that bake into them. Miranda and Jerry thought it was stupid, but maybe you'd be into it."

Jayson jumped down off the chair and he hurried to her; the Christmas lights had come to life.

"Sure," he said, "make the cookies, but first look at the other stuff I bought you." Out of one of the paper bags, he pulled a plastic one and he gave Kelsey the store-wrapped box inside. "I was at the mall waiting for Miranda and I saw this and thought about you."

For a moment she had this thought that it could be sexy underwear or something horrible and then she tore the gift open anyway, feeling like she needed something good to happen to her tonight. Nestled in the paper was something simple, a beige cotton camisole, with delicate lace embroidery at the neckline and a tiny golden ornament at the vee. Kelsey picked up the camisole and it felt buttery and pleasant to the touch, it was something she would definitely wear. She looked toward him inquisitively.

Jayson actually blushed. "I don't know why I got it. It just seemed like it could be so sweet on you."

Kelsey fingered the metal charm, a tiny gold angel sewed on the shirt. "How did you know I liked angels?" she asked.

"Miranda told me," he said. "Look, look what else..."

Kelsey laughed as she pulled a little plastic snow scene out of the bag. It wasn't the flamingo or palm tree kind they sold here in Florida as souvenirs, but the real thing, with a Santa Claus in it. Kelsey was bubbling over. She reached around Jayson's neck with one arm and gave him an impulsive hug.

"Thank you. Thank you for all of this," she said.

"No, thank you," he told her, "because no one else would have appreciated my gestures in this way. They would think I was silly and excessive, whether I have a cute face or not..."

Kelsey realized that he was probably right. "Jayson, this is an emotional time for you, too, isn't it? You have some sadness of your own, don't you?"

"Maybe," he said, dismissing the subject. He dug into a handful of popcorn. "Why don't you put on your present? The oven's making it hot in here."

Jayson was wearing a baggy white cotton shirt and, thankfully, he made no move to remove it. Kelsey didn't want the moment to feel drenched in sexuality, which was what exposing those muscles would mean. She suspected Jayson felt the same way and she wondered what it would be like in the camisole without a bra and her breasts and nipples standing out. But, if she could wear that type of thing in public, she thought she could in her own home. Jayson didn't strike her as a man who couldn't control his own desires, despite what happened in the gym. And he had made it clear that tonight he was here as a friend. Anyway, the sweater she had on was scratchy and the metallic pants were uncomfortable. She went to the bedroom and changed in the dark, into the camisole and a pair of knit pants and the shirt felt like she had owned it for years.

She found Jayson on the couch with her big gray cat weaving back and forth over his splayed legs as he expertly scratched his back. "I never even knew you had a cat," he said. "If I had known, I would have picked up something for him, too."

He seemed happily mesmerized, stroking Mr. Cooper. Kelsey busied herself in the kitchen, putting in the second batch of cookies and improvising her own decorations on the first. She then made them more drinks. This kind of domesticity suited her. Other guys had let her play at it but it always felt phony. Jayson, however, stayed patiently away from the kitchen, although she suspected he was as competent there as anywhere else.

"You know, Mr. Cooper doesn't like most people," Kelsey said. "Most guys come over here and they don't even know I have a cat, he hides so effectively. He watches them coming when they're still in the parking lot."

"Well, I have a sort of bond with cats." Jayson looked into the distance dreamily and Cooper gave him a gentle nip on the hand to get his attention. "I had a cat when I was younger," he said, "this really big hairball kind of cat. His name was Scruffy."

Kelsey lowered herself onto the sofa next to them and she waited for her cat to remember her long enough to give her a kiss. "Well, Mr. Cooper is an excellent judge of character. Sometimes he even bites guys. I think it's kind of funny. He's so protective of me." She was laughing, remembering, and Jayson laughed with her.

"Seriously, though," she said, "I know why he's that way. Cooper is a shelter cat. I got him when he was already full-grown. And he had been badly abused. Apparently, the people at the shelter healed him physically, but they doubted he would ever trust anyone again. He wouldn't even look at people at that time. I came in to get a kitten and they told me not to attempt it with this cat. But I just thought I saw this earnestness in his eyes."

The gray tomcat looked directly into Kelsey's face and mewed.

"Yeah, baby. I know," she said. "Anyway, you see him now. He's so healthy and happy. But he only likes select people and never men. You should be honored."

Jayson nodded. "I bet he must dislike Miranda, even though she's probably over here every day."

Kelsey smiled. "You're right. She's too wild and he doesn't like her perfume."

They giggled together; Miranda was always good for a laugh. "So," Jayson said, "you don't let her smoke in here, do you?" He went to the stereo to look for Christmas music.

"How do you know that I don't let her smoke in here?"

"I would have smelled it; it lingers."

"You're observant," Kelsey said, watching him crouch down and play with the stations. "Did you ever think about being a cop or an investigator or something like that?"

"No." Jayson laughed. "No. Not me. Why, do you really like what you do?"

Kelsey actually felt comfortable sitting near him with her nipples standing up in the delicate camisole. There was no tension between them.

"You know," she said, "my job used to mean very much to me, because I had this version of an ideal society. I was born with this observant quality and I have an eye for details, and I hoped that my talent would be useful in this world, to sort out the truth from lies.

"I lived in Naples, on the West Coast of Florida, for about nine months and I worked on this special task force for the State Attorney's office. It was very good; we dealt with some very big fraud cases and we helped a lot of people. The problem was, it was an experimental program, and we lost the funding. At least that type of work made sense to me. But now, in the work I do, we collect evidence against people but in civil trials, it's all about money, not about right and wrong.

"I always knew I never wanted to be a defense attorney. My dream was to be a prosecutor. But now I see that in this business, there are no absolutes. Justice seems to be in shades of gray. I still want to go to law school but maybe I'd go into some other branch of the law, not criminal. It's ironic; I also used to want to be a cop. Maybe I should have done that; I'm so tenacious with my work."

"That's something I noticed about you, even at the gym," Jayson said, "how observant you are. I liked that about you. Me, I'm also observant, but in a philosophical way. I could never be a cop, because at times I do see in shades of gray. In San Diego, I went to college for business administration. My father wanted that because he deals in commercial real estate out there. But I had no real interest in that type of business. Right now, I'm going to Florida Atlantic University for Public Administration but it's basically just to finish my bachelor's degree. Then I'll decide what I want to do. The job I have now is good because the schedule is so flexible. It lets me go to college and do my workouts, but it also means I'm traveling a lot. And I feel a little old for that."

Kelsey smiled at him, at the thought of him feeling old when he was only twenty-five. But, when she thought about it, there did seem something very mature, even wise, about him.

"Florida wasn't what I expected," she told him. "I thought it would be this exciting fast-paced lifestyle and I would show what I was made of. I guess I wanted to prove something to my parents. But the irony is, my sister can always be a failure and she still gets more attention than I do, no matter what I accomplish. I'm even a little resentful right now because they're all at church together and I can't even call."

"That reminds me," Jayson said. "Could I use your phone for a quick long-distance call before we get occupied with other things? I'll pay for it."

"Go ahead," Kelsey said. "You don't need to pay."

Jayson went to the phone and, in a minute, she heard him speak.

"Hi, Pop, it's Jayson. Yeah, how are you? I just figured I'd call to say Merry Christmas. Actually..." he shot a look over his shoulder, "...I'm at a girl's house right now, a really beautiful woman."

He got off the phone a few minutes later and took his drink from Kelsey, who was crouched by her little tree. "My Dad says hi," he told her, lowering himself to sit beside her.

"Look at some of these ornaments," Kelsey said, indicating antique ornaments on her tree. "These are some of the ones I brought from home."

They looked at each ornament together, and then they went back to the couch and Kelsey turned out the lights. The display of winking colored lights at the patio was beautiful. It washed them with color as they ate their popcorn and cookies. Kelsey felt pleasantly buzzed by the liquor, and she stayed silent, transported by all the traditional Christmas songs playing on the radio, and, finally, the heartbreaking Ave Maria.

Kelsey and Jayson smiled at each other when the song was over.

"This is about as good as it gets," she said. "Did any of the women you went out with ever tell you were wonderful as a boyfriend?"

"I've been told I'm the best, that it doesn't get any better," he said. "At the same time I look back and, in retrospect, I see some pretty major errors and flaws. Maybe this next time I'll put it all together right. Who knows?"

Kelsey wondered if possibly the next time was meant to be with her.

It had just turned midnight when Jayson made a very odd request. "Kelsey," he said, "this was the night when the Lord Jesus was born. I believe, very strongly, that it really is the holiest of all nights. Would you get down on your knees with me and sing this song?"

The song that was just beginning was "Silent Night"; a single, pure, female voice sang it on the stereo. Kelsey had been brought up to be very religious and she recognized the earnestness in Jayson's request. They took each other's hands and they knelt down in front of the Christmas tree, looking out to the blinking lights and the night beyond. Unselfconsciously, they sang together. Kelsey felt as though maybe their song really was an offering to the baby Jesus because, for the moment, it rejected cynicism and sophistication and spoke of innocence and hope.

Chapter 8

When Kelsey returned to work the day after Christmas, there was another email on her computer. The subject line said, "Hello, Kelsey" and she opened it naively, thinking it was from one of her friends. She was chilled when she saw the message, which said, simply, "PAYBACK IS HELL." So, it wasn't over. Someone really was after her and they hadn't stopped. This person had managed to take her by surprise again and this message filled her with much more dread than the last one had. This one made her even more sure that this was not just a random thing that could have been aimed at anyone in her office.

It was also clear that the computer files hadn't been what this person wanted from her. The terrible truth that Kelsey was now just realizing, even though she had sensed it all along, was that this person was very angry with her for some reason and they wanted her to know it. She didn't really think they wanted to protect themself as much as they wanted revenge.

Kelsey wouldn't let herself panic, even though she felt like whimpering at the unfairness of the threats. She didn't even know what she was supposed to have done that had so enraged this person. She suspected they were going to want to let her know, but on their timetable. They obviously had some kind of aggression in mind. But Kelsey couldn't wait around for this like she was okay with it happening. She had to take some action.

She stood up to go after the videotape in her hidden camera to see if anything had been recorded but then she stopped, indecisive. It was probably more important to get this email saved on hard storage before someone tried to erase it like they got to her files last time. The cameras could wait.

Kelsey quickly hit the save button for the computer's hard drive but she knew that this kind of saving wouldn't be enough. It hadn't been the last time. She rushed into the front room and leaned into one of Wendy's storage drawers, fishing around for disks and meanwhile panicking and cursing at the disorganization. She knew she had to hurry before her enemy did something to the evidence. Two minutes later she straightened up with a floppy disk in her hand and she ran back to her desk in the other room.

But when she looked back at her computer, she found the email message gone, like she feared it would be. In its place was a screen full of fragmented letters and symbols, with all the text broken into jagged, unreadable pieces. When Kelsey tried to use her mouse, the screen remained frozen, with no change. Somehow, remotely, her whole computer had been destroyed while she was searching for the disk, as if the stalker had been watching her and knew what she planned to do.

Kelsey rubbed a hand over her face to stop herself from crying and she rapidly punched out Miranda's phone number. "I need your help right now," she said to Miranda's answering machine. "I just need to be with someone".

This time, unlike the last when she had received a threat, Kelsey didn't even bother to look outside the front door of her office. She sat by her desk in a depressed pose, with the arm that still held the phone flopped over the desk. Thoughts moved through her brain, but slowly, as the office filled up with the other staff.

They were all here this morning- Mr. Lester, Wendy, Margaret and the consultant, Michael Cole. No one said anything to Kelsey. They just walked around her, after finding her sitting there staring like that with the fragmented screen in front of her, and they went about their business like nothing was wrong. These people were usually constant chatterers but today they moved around silently, like everything was happening in a dream. And this got Kelsey to thinking, how much could she really trust anyone? Why had no one here said anything about the broken computer screen that was sitting right up in front of her for all the world to see?

Did one of them already know what had happened? None of them had been in the office when the email came. Kelsey had been totally alone even though it had been nine-o'clock when business was supposed to have started. Any one of them could have done it if they had the expertise. Why hadn't Michael Cole come to hang over her like he usually did and greet her with his usual greeting of "how's the computer doing?" she wondered. The young computer expert was now sitting in a corner looking sullen and spacey. When he noticed Kelsey looking, he gave her a dark look and then he went back to playing with his fingernails.

Someone hated her, Kelsey was sure, but she didn't understand why. In the cases she had dealt with here at Confidential, people had often gotten fired or lost some money as a result of what her investigating turned up but nothing really serious had happened to them. Many times, the employers threatened to have the employees prosecuted but, as far as Kelsey knew, none of them had ever done it. And most of her cases were situations like petty theft, sexual harassment or routine background checks. They just didn't seem to represent situations that people would want to get violent about.

Then there were the employees who worked for the shipping company in the drug case she was now working on and the owners themselves, as well as the defendants who were going to go to trial in several months. Maybe there really was something much bigger in this case than she imagined and maybe she was getting too close without realizing it yet.

In her gut, she doubted all of this. It felt to her like the person who was doing these things was laughing at her. And it felt like it was someone who knew her.

Kelsey sat most of the morning in front of the ruined computer. Miranda had called back and said she would meet Kelsey that evening on Hollywood Beach and Kelsey knew she needed the human contact. In the meantime, she'd have to check the tape in the hidden camera and she'd have to inform Mr. Lester of what had happened here. Finally, at eleven thirty, she got to her feet to head into her boss's office.

Both the threats were long gone from her computer screen but they were still in Kelsey's head. "WHAT GOES AROUND, COMES AROUND, KELSEY" and "PAYBACK IS HELL". It felt like there was nowhere she could go where the words wouldn't follow her, demanding she understand who was after her before it was too late.

Miranda took Kelsey in her arms as soon as she saw her that night and she gave her a big consoling hug. Then her friend pulled away and looked Kelsey in the face.

"You'll be all right, girl" she said, "I know that you will."

After only four days up north Miranda looked wan and edgy. She said she had decided to go chasing after some cocaine before meeting the rest of their group at Hollywood Beach and it was obvious that she was high. Kelsey had arrived first and she was annoyed with her friend.

Miranda had agreed to get there early so that they could talk. Now they only had five minutes before they spotted Jayson and Juan ambling up the Broadwalk. Jayson's good mood was apparent, even from a distance. He was horsing around and bumping into his friend, until the taller Juan caught him in a playful headlock and dragged him toward the girls, with Jayson yelling and squealing.

"Look, don't say anything to those guys, okay?" she told Miranda, before the guys came into in hearing distance. "I don't want their pity."

Miranda shrugged and then went into Jayson's arms as he came up to greet her. He gave Miranda a big hug and a gentle kiss on her forehead before disengaging and then he glanced over at Kelsey.

"What's wrong?" he asked immediately, looking at her with concern. When Juan tried to wrestle with him again, Jayson pushed him off, concentrating on Kelsey. "I can see that something's bothering you."

Kelsey shook her head. "Nothing," she said, "nothing that concerns you."

Then Jerry and Wendy arrived, hurrying from the direction of the public parking garage. Wendy practically fell apart when she got to speak to Juan and Jayson; she was wriggling like a friendly puppy under the amused stares of the two gorgeous guys. Then there was a lot of noise and giggling as the group all settled into a stroll down the beach and Kelsey was able to forget her concerns for a while like she had wanted to.

Later, they all ate ice cream sitting in the bleachers by the bandstand and they watched all the French Canadian tourists strolling happily in front of them. Often, on weekday nights, there were free concerts and dancing under the stars but no band was playing tonight, so the group continued down the Broadwalk, looking for something to do. Miranda's arms were linked with both Juan's and Jayson's and Kelsey walked behind them talking with Jerry and Wendy.

Jayson selected a popular bar that the guys usually went to whenever Juan visited him. The bar was open to the beach and a reggae band was playing tonight. Juan and Jayson immediately went up to the bar to get beers and then they stayed there amongst a crowd of sunburned big guys who looked like they had spent the day fishing.

The other four grabbed a table that was crowded in amongst other groups. Jerry asked Miranda and Kelsey to come dance with him but she and Kelsey brushed him aside, wanting to stay at the table and talk to each other. He put his hand on Wendy's waist and led her onto the dance floor instead. Miranda fiercely blew out smoke.

"She's already got a crush on Jayson," she said, tilting her head to indicate Wendy. "That's why she was so eager to come out with us tonight." Miranda let out a rumbling laugh.

"I'm just worried about you," Kelsey said to her friend. "Are you happy with Jayson? And all this coke you're doing..."

"Yeah, Jayson's after me about that too. I'll stop. I'm sure I'll stop soon. As for Jayson..." she said.

Kelsey thought she actually saw her friend blush.

"I mean," Miranda continued, "he's so incredibly attractive and the way he teases me makes me crazy. But in ways he's much too slick for me, too perfect. It's Juan I wanted at first. He's more down to earth, he's a good person and he's attractive in a very masculine kind of way. I think we're all kind of tangled up here."

She indicated Jerry and Wendy dancing in the middle of older couples. Those tourists were making fools of themselves, drunk and trying to be sexy, while the young couple glided amongst them. Jerry really knew how to move to the reggae beat as he dirty-danced with Wendy. This fluidity of movement reminded Kelsey of why she had found Jerry attractive to begin with and why, physically, she and Jerry had clicked so well in bed. Among other things, they moved well together.

Miranda was filling Kelsey in about the latest news on Kelsey's family. The news was that her mother had been hurt that Kelsey hadn't made it up to visit and her father had been pissed. Kelsey's father was also frustrated with his own life. He had been forced into retirement recently because of a heart attack and Kelsey's mom had to spend all her time fighting with him to keep him from doing heavy work around the property. And, according to Miranda, Kelsey's sister Sarah was a self-centered bitch who didn't care about anything but her own problems.

Kelsey took a swallow of beer. "I can't take listening to this," she said. "Let's go dance."

At first Jayson and Juan wouldn't be budged. "We don't dance," Juan said, apologizing to Kelsey with a boyish, embarrassed smile. "We really can't." Then the two men went back to drinking.

Kelsey and Miranda joined Jerry and Wendy on the floor and they danced for a while in a group, just like in the old days. Then Wendy took the opportunity to separate herself from their group. She went to talk to Jayson and persuaded him to dance with her and the couple came back to dance near the rest of their group.

Now Kelsey saw why Jayson had declined their offer to dance earlier. Trying to dance to the reggae beat, his big body looked stiff and ungainly, not comfortable with this kind of movement. Juan came to join Miranda and it was the same sad story there.

Jerry and Kelsey were left together and they hung onto each other, trembling with laughter, drunk and careless and washed by the warm, salty breeze.

"Those two are so beautiful," Kelsey said to Jerry, "but they look like big dancing bears!"

"So, let's show them how it's done, girlfriend!"

Jerry whipped Kelsey's body around and they started undulating together, so that other couples noticed and backed off, giving them more room. Kelsey felt frenzied and wicked but she was proud to be showing off something she did well. She was wearing stretch jeans tonight and her body felt tight and limber in them.

"You go, girl," Miranda yelled, cheering her on. Juan was laughing at his own ineptitude at dancing and Miranda shrugged and threw her arms around the big man and started happily doing something that looked like a tango.

Despite the way Wendy was gazing admiringly at him, Jayson did not look happy. He kept looking at how Jerry suggestively twined his body around Kelsey's and then he'd look back at his own clumsy feet.

Jayson narrowed his eyes in concentration and placed his hands gently over his partner's hips. Amidst all the laughter and whirling middle-aged bodies, every move of Jayson's seemed to be in slow motion. With his eyes fixed on Kelsey and Jerry, he began to work his muscle-bound body in the unfamiliar movements of the dance.

At first it was subtle, with him just starting to find the beat, then, imitating Jerry, he worked his body around and under his partner's. Wendy's eyes closed in rapture as he used those powerful abdominal muscles to pump like not even Jerry could. Kelsey was actually thrilled at watching Jayson learn something. The determination he showed was uncanny and, once again, she found herself inspired by him.

Later, the band started playing slow tunes. Their group left the floor to go cool off out by the sidewalk and drink beers and look at the ocean. Kelsey noticed Jayson briefly go back in, step up on stage and whisper something to one of the band members. Then he came back with drinks for the three women.

Miranda seemed totally occupied with teasing Juan about his dancing and she was obviously flirting. She had her hands all over Juan's muscle-bound body and she kept whispering in his ear so that a flush came up under his dark skin. But Jayson seemed to have little problem with this.

90

He approached behind Kelsey, speaking softly so that the others weren't disturbed.

"I requested a song and it will be coming any minute now," he told her. "It's an old song, one that means something to me, and I'd like you to dance with me." It was amazing how Jayson could go unnoticed when he wanted to. The others just continued their loud joshing talk, never turning to see Jayson lead Kelsey to a dark corner of the dance floor in the very back of the bar.

Kelsey went awkwardly into his arms at first, shy about having him touch her body. But then the warmth was overpowering, as though they had needed to hold each other like this forever. She so badly needed his comfort tonight and she was sure he could sense it.

"I've wanted to dance with you for so long," Jayson said. "I don't know what it is that's bothering you tonight, but I wanted you to know that I'm here for you."

His words meant so much to Kelsey right now. She was sure that if she told him all that had been happening to her with the threats, he really would care. And that meant a lot to her.

They held each other tightly, moving to the music, then Jayson squeezed her and said, "This is it; I'm dedicating this song to you."

Kelsey had never heard this song before but immediately it thrilled her, with the lyrics speaking directly to the depths of her loneliness and bringing her fully to attention. The song was called "Help Me Make it Through the Night" and the lead singer sang it in a deep haunting, yet lulling, voice. The words hit her hard because they reminded her just how great her own need was, and how immediate.

She and Jayson pulled back to look into each other's eyes smiling with understanding and then they went back into the tight embrace. She felt cradled by the song.

By the time the next tune began, Jayson's mouth was right on Kelsey's ear, he just had to breathe for her to hear him.

"So," he asked. "Are you ever going to bring up what happened at the gym?"

He held her so tightly that she could feel his body vibrate with amusement.

"I tried to wait you out," he said, "but I just couldn't. It's been looking like you'd *never* talk about it."

Kelsey felt tremendous emotion, realizing that he was probably going to ask her to go out with him right now. She felt overwhelmed by how much she wanted to be with him, but she was still feeling the hurt and confusion from before.

"Well, maybe I got your message," she said with a bitter edge to her voice.

"And what was that?" Jayson asked softly. "I don't even know why I did what I did."

"I guess you wanted me to see that you weren't just an object..."

"So...?"

"I know you're not," she said.

They were speaking softly now, almost in a whisper while their bodies brushed each other and flowed against each other in time to the music. Their corner was almost in darkness. Kelsey blinked drowsily at the other dancers. Jayson's warmth was so intoxicating that it made her forget her surroundings.

Dancing near them were a tourist couple, drunk out of their minds. The woman was stocky with shorn blond hair and her overripe breasts threatened to fall out of an old style tube-top. The man worked at the woman's chest with his stubbly chin, attempting to push the tube-top lower while she bent back in their uninhibited dance.

"I'll take care of you like that," Jayson whispered huskily to Kelsey. He pressed his aroused body harder against hers and angled her to better see the couple. "I'll do it right here. I'll suck on you like he's doing her."

He slid Kelsey's hand under his loose shirt so she could feel his muscles.

"You know that we're meant to be together," he said. "We can start tonight, I can take you to my room and we can make love tonight. And it's not going to be like that other time. It'll last all night long. And I'll kiss you all night long. You want me to kiss you?"

Kelsey felt she could hardly breathe. She and Jayson already felt as though they were fused together. It was beautiful how inevitable this all felt.

"You're serious?" Kelsey asked, pulling back a little to see his eyes.

"As a heart attack," he said and winked at her. "There's just one thing..." He took her back into the tight hug so that he could rest his head on her shoulder and speak into her ear. "There's one thing you'll need to do. Say three words."

Jayson waited patiently for Kelsey to pull back and stare at him. He allowed her to disengage from the embrace into a looser, more formal hold. Her emotions were all twisted up. It wouldn't be that hard to say she loved him. It could be true if she did say it. But things just didn't happen this way. Her eyes were wide as she examined him, looking for clues that he really meant this.

"What words?" she asked, trembling.

His face was blank and his wicked smile didn't extend to his eyes as they swung into a faster dance. He looked so amused.

"Take your time, Kelsey. And the words aren't, 'I want you' or 'screw me, Jayson'. I'll give you my cellular number. You call me when you're ready."

Apprehension and an outraged sense of propriety warred inside her, forcing out an odd smile. "You're kidding, right?" Kelsey giggled nervously.

Jayson shook his head. "I'm not kidding."

They had stopped dancing and the band had stopped playing for the night. Kelsey and Jayson walked hand in hand, returning to their friends and the open air of the beach.

It just didn't seem fair. She did want him so badly, but he was asking her to do something mind-boggling, to say "I love you" out of nowhere to someone she hardly even knew.

"Why would you ask this of me, Jayson?" she asked before they reached the others. "You don't ask anything of anybody else." She heard herself practically whining.

"You can feel what's between us," he answered and then he stepped away from her to go join Juan and Miranda.

The next day at work, Kelsey kept returning to the irony that she had gone home alone, while Miranda went with Jayson. But pride was a strong thing in Kelsey. She could not be forced into saying those words. This couldn't happen his way.

Kelsey worked at the front office computer all day, entering lab data and daydreaming about being with Jayson at the bar last night. She didn't have any plans at the moment about what to do about the person who was harassing her. Her mind was occupied with other matters.

At around five-o'clock her boss, Mr. Lester, came by and leaned over her computer. "Kelsey, you're doing so good with this, how'd you like some overtime?"

Like on many other nights, Kelsey was the only one in the office to agree to work late. It took her two hours to finish the reports he had piled on her desk. At around seven she hurried down to the parking lot, thinking that she could get an antipasto salad from the deli and still get to the gym tonight, possibly in time to catch the last aerobics class or at least get on a treadmill.

She strode across the parking lot and then she stopped abruptly. Something looked funny about her car.

The Avenger's red finish gleamed under the streetlight like it always did. But the car looked short, somehow too low to the ground. Kelsey cocked her head, not immediately recognizing what she was seeing. Then she realized that all four of the tires were flat.

It hit Kelsey with an almost physical shock. She did not even want to step close. It felt creepy under the buzzing vapor light. Exposed.

Kelsey glanced around all directions and saw no one. She had keys in hand. But the car would be useless.

Her mind started bouncing around improbable connections. Maybe the person who did this also had been the one who had come into her condo and switched those shampoos back in October. She didn't know how likely that was, but it was obvious that this had been done by the person who had been sending her the emails, and now she could be sure that the threats weren't just words.

She bent down and observed the slashes in her tires. They were big violent cuts, obviously made with a large knife. This was proof that the person who was doing this was violent and dangerous and now she knew for sure that they weren't afraid to take action against her.

The most likely explanation was that these attacks on her had to do with the drug case and the boat she and Jerry had reserved before Christmas. The case was about to go to trial and Kelsey had never felt safe working it from the beginning. They were due to charter the Ascension later this month and maybe someone wanted to prevent them from doing that. But, of course, she was intelligent enough to know that the person doing this to her could be anyone at all and no one could be considered really safe until she knew.

Kelsey walked backwards, sweeping the area in front of her with her eyes. She tried not to get distracted worrying about what it would cost to replace the tires, four Eagle GT's, which cost one-hundred and thirty dollars apiece when she bought them this past summer. First, she needed to get behind a locked door. Then she could call her boss and call a garage. And then she would call the police.

Chapter 9

Kelsey hadn't told Miranda about the incident with her tires immediately. She was too busy dealing with the police, the auto insurance company and her job. Basically, none of these people did anything for her. The police took a report but they didn't seem too optimistic. They kept making references to her job. Kelsey already knew that the local police considered Confidential Investigations to be unsavory, but now her office's reputation was working against her. The local cops seemed to feel that when you messed with the kind of characters her office did without adequately preparing for the consequences, you were going to get into trouble.

The older of the two police officers did try to be nice. He had asked if she had a ride home and he encouraged her to get out of the dark parking lot and wait inside until her boss got there. "And don't sweat it," he had comforted.

The insurance company was even less helpful than the police were. They informed her that tires were not covered under her policy, even though what had happened to them was an act of vandalism. Meanwhile the tire place that had given her a warranty said that, because the damage was vandalism, they wouldn't pay for the replacement of the tires either.

The only one willing to help at all was Mr. Lester. He suggested that they could expand the hours of the security service that patrolled the parking lot for the entire plaza, and he would do it at Confidential's expense, if he had to. "You're a valuable worker," he said to Kelsey. "I don't want anything to happen to you."

It was touch and go on whether she would have a car for work the next day. She depleted her checking account buying tires and then she had to spend hours at the tire place the next morning. Back at the office, she had to work with Michael Cole setting up a brand new computer at her workstation. It was a few days before she even saw Miranda. There was just too much else she had to get settled.

She went to Miranda's apartment the afternoon of New Year's Eve to help her friend get ready for a big banquet she was going to that night with Jayson. Kelsey handed her friend a submarine sandwich that was intended so Miranda wouldn't pig out at the ritzy party, and then she told Miranda the whole story of the tires.

Miranda talked around a mouthful of food. "It's that scummy job," she said. "Can't you see that it's time to get out?"

"My boss is extending the security service so that the guards will get there exactly at five, not at midnight like they used to," Kelsey said. "And the police know what happened. They're watching one of the guys from the drug case. The guy's got some prior felonies and he's out on bond now. They said they won't stop tailing him until the trial is over."

Kelsey was also looking into the drug suspect's background on her own. She wanted to check for herself if he or any of his associates had a history of this kind of stalking. She was also putting together a file on any cases she'd handled since she started at Confidential where the people might possibly have a grudge against her. And this new file she was making was a paper file; she didn't want any chance that her stalker could get into it.

What Kelsey would not mention to her friend was what had happened with her shampoo back in October, the day after she had slept with Joe. No way would the kind of men who smuggled drugs and slashed tires with what the police said was a ten inch blade go into someone's home and switch shampoos from one bottle to another. That was more a female kind of crime.

Unfortunately, Miranda was Kelsey's only plausible suspect. Her friend had the key to the condo and, with all the drugs she had been using lately, she had been acting pretty bizarre. But accusing Miranda now would do no good. Miranda had already said she hadn't been in Kelsey's condo alone since the last time she had come to feed Mr. Cooper, months before. Kelsey had asked her that time in the car, a few days after the incident. So, the switching of the shampoos remained a mystery. Despite how wild and out of control her friend might seem to other people, Kelsey was inclined to take her at her word.

Miranda looked beautiful today. Kelsey smiled at her own handiwork as she created Miranda's look for the banquet. She had helped her friend with some of the products Miranda got free from work- an Italian Mud pack, then a healing soak for the tub. The expensive products had taken away the last vestiges of damaged skin from the sunburn from the day at the beach, and Miranda's skin was back to its usual creamy white. Now Kelsey worked meticulously, styling Miranda's thick red curls into an updo held by a pearl clasp.

"You think I'll look all right?" Miranda fretted. "Jayson told me that there are going to be dignitaries from all over the world at this event. Maybe I'll meet an Arab prince or something."

The beautiful young woman looked so out of place with her surroundings. Kelsey had always found Miranda's one-bedroom apartment depressing. A glaring light came through the windows, falling across the bare kitchen counters and linoleum floor. Other than beauty products, and hair scrunchies in every color, Miranda had no personal effects around. The only decorations were overflowing ashtrays in every room, which looked unemptied since she had come to live here. The building itself was impersonal, a brick garden apartment style, with children playing below in the bare parking lot. But this was the only place that would accept her with her tarnished credit history.

"Here's the dress I told you about," Miranda said, speaking almost reverently, as she pulled it from its package.

Kelsey gasped when she saw the dress. It was an evening gown, a fluid, blue velvet column with a frosty sheen. The dress slipped over the sharp contours of Miranda's body when she held it up in front of her and it made everything look right.

"What do you think?" Miranda asked, proudly.

"It's beautiful," Kelsey stammered. "You're going to look like royalty, like all your dreams could come true tonight. But how could you afford it?"

To Kelsey, it looked like a six or eight hundred dollar designer dress. She herself had never bought anything in that price range. And she knew, for a fact, that Miranda didn't have that kind of money. In fact, at the moment, Miranda didn't have any money at all left in her bank account, as far as Kelsey knew.

The dress, held up next to her face, brought out the glow in the redhead's eyes. Kelsey had to admit Miranda really did look special.

"I wrote a bad check for it," Miranda said. "I figured they won't find anything out until at least the second of the month. By then maybe I can bring the dress back..."

Kelsey raised her voice at her friend. "You could be arrested if they catch you! Some counties take that stuff very seriously. I used to investigate those cases."

"This is a once in a lifetime chance for me," Miranda said, "to go to a party like this. And Jayson is doing it for me. I couldn't disrespect that."

Miranda was so earnest. It seemed odd that there were depths to her friend, and sadnesses, that Kelsey never knew about. It surprised her to know how unworthy Miranda must sometimes feel. It was true that, even though Miranda tended to be the leader, it was Kelsey who was the more perfect. She had been the high-school cheerleader and she had gone to college while Miranda stayed home, working in retail. Miranda probably doubted that she had the class for this party.

"I just don't want to screw anything up for Jayson with his work," Miranda said. "He's supposed to finalize some million dollar deal with an executive from Japan at this party. I can just see myself saying something wrong and making a fool of us both..."

Kelsey felt so tender towards her friend and also toward Jayson for understanding what this would mean to her. She stretched up and kissed Miranda on the cheek, forgiving her about writing the bad check like she always forgave her everything else.

"Don't worry," Kelsey said, "you'll be the most beautiful women there."

The focus tonight was totally on Miranda. Kelsey dressed quickly, feeling insignificant in the dress she had picked out for her own party. It was a big work-related party that Miranda was originally going to attend with her. Kelsey's dress was short and close fitting, made of silver-threaded brocade with a baroque neckline. It was also a fairly expensive dress and, when they picked it out together, Miranda had told Kelsey it made her look like a fairy princess.

Kelsey had bought a pair of silver platform shoes to give the dress a slightly funky edge and she had been excited about wearing the outfit for New Year's Eve. Now she just felt tired. She was only going to the party for Jerry's sake and would have been just as content sitting here alone in her girlfriend's bare apartment, reading out-of-date fashion magazines.

Jayson arrived for Miranda right on time. He was an odd sight wearing his tuxedo on the motorcycle. Both women rushed to the window to see it. Then Jayson looked so handsome when he came in. He gave not a glance at the ugliness of the small apartment, just gazed at his date in her gown.

"You're magnificent, Miranda," he said, and he kissed her very long and sweetly on the lips, in a way that made Kelsey's heart ache.

"I bought you something," he told Miranda and he handed her a jewelry box. Inside was a delicate glass ornament on a chain, a tiny ballerina with a pink tutu. Jayson helped Miranda hook it around her neck because her hands trembled too much for her to do it herself.

Kelsey had never seen a man make her friend feel delicate and feminine like this; Miranda had always been so jaded.

Kelsey thought with shame of the remnant of Jayson that she had hidden in a dresser drawer, the gold medallion on the broken chain. Why did she get the tawdry, sexual stuff with him while he treated her friend so graciously?

Maybe it was because he actually felt closer to her in some way and he expected more of her. Jayson took Kelsey's hand and squeezed it. "You look very beautiful tonight, Kelsey. You have a good time at the Ramada. I'll take care of your friend."

Like a couple from a modern day Cinderella story, with Jayson coldly handsome in his black tux and Miranda tall and regal in the amazing gown, they got into her dirty black car and rode off with the muffler roaring. It was amazing how Jayson, who had grown up in the jet-set, was able to move so comfortably in Miranda's pathetic blue-collar world and to make it look beautiful.

It was also amazing for Kelsey to think about what he had said to her the other night when they were dancing. He did want to be her boyfriend, like she had suspected. If she told him three little words, suddenly all of this could change. Her whole life could change.

She and Jerry went to the party at the Ramada. In the ballroom, they drank champagne and laughed with other people, most of whom were older and involved with law enforcement. A huge blazing chandelier hanging from the vaulted ceiling filled the air with divinely glittering light. But Kelsey couldn't escape a feeling of wrongness. The feeling pursued her all evening, making her jump nervously whenever anybody touched her.

Kelsey knew what was bothering her. Although she had pushed so hard for some kind of commitment with Paul and other boyfriends, in reality she was very afraid of real commitment, the kind that Jayson demanded. In her modern world, girls her age expected to marry and then divorce. There was always that out.

But Kelsey suspected it would not be that way with Jayson. He would want them to stay together and she would have that gorgeous intense face looking into her eyes forever. She didn't know if she could live up to that kind of scrutiny, she didn't know if she could live up to loving him that way. It had never been so hard for her to make the choice to want to be with someone. It seemed that Jayson had deliberately made it that way so that she must take responsibility if she wanted to have him.

Kelsey danced, tilting her head back to stare at a thousand glaring crystal icicles on the chandelier. These spiraling pieces of light seemed to fall down towards her like rain and, without words, they were all saying, "Jayson"; everything was telling her "Jayson".

Kelsey took a breath so she could hurry. She had a whole ballroom to cross to get to the phone. In her high shoes, she ran amazingly fast, moving through groups of people like they weren't there. When she got to the vestibule, she yanked at the telephone receiver, breathing hard as she put her call through, praying against the odds that Jayson had his cellular switched on.

"Jayson Carter," he answered.

"I love you," Kelsey breathed.

She recognized the familiar deadpan tone he used when he was teasing her. "Who's calling?" he asked.

"Don't even, Jayson!" she snapped at him. "I said it. What now?"

She could hear him chuckling at her.

"Your timing is impeccable," he said. "Were you afraid I'd screw Miranda in the coatroom while the diplomats were doing their thing?" Kelsey could hear subdued voices and orchestral music in the background. "This is a four-hundred-dollar a plate dinner..."

Despite the reprimand he was speaking to her kindly and she wanted him so badly she could hardly breathe. She just kept quiet.

"Can you drive, Kelsey? Are you okay to drive?" he asked her.

"Yeah, I can," she answered, breathlessly.

"Okay," he said. "Give me a few moments to find somebody trustworthy to escort Miranda home. I don't want to totally ruin her night. Then I'll meet you at your place. I'll try to make it there by midnight, but no promises."

"Okay," she said. Her emotions were raw. "Thank you."

"And Kelsey..." Jayson said.

"Yes?"

"... Don't take off the dress."

When she got home, Kelsey left the windows open, smelling the unusually sweet scent of the air and breathing it in big lungfuls as she paced. Then there was a sound of an engine downstairs that she was not familiar with. She opened the door to see Jayson in his tuxedo getting out of a yellow cab. He glanced up and looked momentarily unnerved to see her waiting, like he had become the shy one now.

When he came to the door, Kelsey just stared for a moment at the perfect contours of his face. She felt the wind blowing her hair around her own face. The cat sprang towards Jayson and Jayson caught him in his arms instinctively and then stroked his fur.

"So, you want us to be boyfriend and girlfriend?" Kelsey asked.

"Yes," he said. "And I want us to be exclusive. Do you want that?" He seemed to shine in his handsomness.

"I don't know if I can handle it," Kelsey said. "You're too good looking. It frightens me."

"I can't help how I look," Jayson said. "Anyway, would you have even looked at me if I was ugly?"

Still intimidated by his looks, which were so glittering and cool, Kelsey tried to sort out her own thoughts.

"I guess not," she said. "I wouldn't have looked at you at first if you had been ugly. But I would now. Knowing you like I do, I absolutely would."

"*Why?*" he demanded, like maybe he didn't believe her, but it was important that he could. Cooper jumped down because Jayson had stopped scratching.

"I think," Kelsey said, "it's because there's something so natural and at peace about you. Being around you, even just one second in your presence, makes a person feel totally comfortable, like they're the person they were meant to be. I'd feel this about you even if you were ugly."

"You would...?" he persisted.

"What about me?" Kelsey asked. "Why would you be attracted to me? You could go out with girls so much better looking."

Jayson stepped closer and cupped a hand gently on her hip, looking into her face from only a few inches away.

"There is no better," he said. "There's only you. What I noticed about you when you first looked at me at the gym was your alertness and intelligence. That's something I could go a lifetime and never get tired of seeing."

He centered himself over her so that she tasted his breath, which was surprisingly sweet and milky. "It's almost midnight, Kelsey," he said. "And I want you."

"I want you, too," she told him.

And then he lowered his lips onto hers. All she felt was the warmth. Then there were spinning hallucinatory images dancing under her closed eyelids and a feeling rising up from the depths of her body, a feeling she had never known. She was no longer Kelsey but was transported by the kiss. Jayson's tongue stroked and teased her insistently until wetness gushed between her legs.

After a while, some awareness returned to her. Kelsey remembered her surroundings and what had brought them here. She peeked her eyes open and saw slanted topaz-colored ones watching her back. This man was the best. Kelsey had probably made out with well over a hundred guys in her lifetime, and Jayson was definitely the best. He was the most skillful, in addition to being the most attractive. He had obviously been playing a game that day at the gym, trying to make her think that sex with him was mechanical and boring, to see if she would still want him.

Now, she worked her tongue on his to show the roughness of her love, how unashamed and practical it could be. Kelsey had never kissed like this. She heard a growl of triumph rise in her throat when she felt her kisses make Jayson's erection rise against her. She grinned wickedly when he finally pulled back and she swallowed in the taste of him.

"This is what it's about, isn't it?" she asked. "The stuff I did with any of the men before you, that wasn't even sex, was it? This is so powerful..." she said, with awe. "I can feel that there's no turning back from this."

Kelsey looked at her new boyfriend and the night beyond, recognizing the intensity in not just the man, but in all the physical surroundings.

"Happy New Year, Baby!" Jayson said, lifting her with a hand under her butt cheeks and bringing her inside.

When he set her down and she was standing before him in her dress, Kelsey felt self-conscious. "I'm so insecure about my body," she confessed to him. "I know it sounds stupid..."

Jayson sat down on the couch with his white shirt open, revealing rounded pectoral muscles and his massive legs were spread casually as he looked her over. She watched as his eyes moved over her too-small cleavage, her small, but still slightly rounded, belly and her unfeminine hips and thighs. She'd always felt there was something disproportionate and unwholesome about her body, something creepy. It made it difficult for her to stand straight in front of him.

"That's okay with me if you're insecure," he said and his voice was so sexy it was hypnotic.

Kelsey felt silly standing before him in her sparkly dress. "You're not kidding, are you?" she asked.

Jayson shook his head as he dimmed the light. "You're beautiful, Kelsey. I want to show you how beautiful you are."

He led her to the bedroom and he opened the bathroom door for her to see herself in the full-length mirror. Then he backed off. Kelsey gazed at herself in the mirror, with her trim youthful figure, her straight chestnut hair framing her oval face and the gems in her necklace sparkling in the half-light from the other room.

"Look at yourself and see that you're beautiful," Jayson commanded her.

She did look and she saw some beauty, maybe not in herself but in the moment. Jayson sat on her bed, never taking his intense gaze from her body. She went to him and looked down at him warmly.

"I'll try," she said.

Tentatively, she reached out and stroked the side of his face. Jayson turned his head and kissed the inside of her cupped fingers.

"We don't have to make love tonight," he told her. "We'll have all our lives for that."

"You scare me," Kelsey said.

But, at the moment, he really didn't scare her. She wanted all her life to be like this.

With his eyes still fastened on hers, Jayson reached behind her and pulled down her zipper. Then he edged back toward the top of the covers while stripping off his own clothes. He crawled under the comforter before she could see him fully naked.

"This is going to feel so good," he gloated, "like we've been doing it forever. I'm going to love waking up in this bed."

Kelsey stepped up but Jayson stopped her. "Take off the dress," he said, "slowly. I want to look at you."

Kelsey let her dress slip to the floor, feeling the whisper of fabric over her hips and she knew that her life would never be the same after this. She'd never had this level of awareness. Jayson observed her as she slowly removed her burgundy lace bra, then the matching underwear and then the chunky silver shoes. Kelsey's eyes became misted over with tears, although she wasn't sad at all.

Jayson's gaze moved up and down her nude body, with his eyes slanted thoughtfully as he looked over each inch of her. They both seemed to listen to Kelsey's breathing. There was no other sound in the room.

Finally, Kelsey went to him and, with open arms, Jayson drew her onto his lap.

Immediately and unexpectedly, he slid his erection all the way into her and he was buried deep inside her body. Jayson held onto Kelsey's waist as she pulled back slightly to look at his face. They stared at each other, both looking surprised and then they both started to laugh.

"I didn't mean to,' he said. "I was going to tease you."

"I'm not usually like this..." Kelsey said, shocked that she could be so wet and open with him. With all the other guys, she had been so tight that it had always been a struggle for them to get inside her. She was discovering her own body in ways that she had never known.

"We're good together," Jayson affirmed, giving her a friendly kiss. Then he settled her into a gentle rhythm riding him. He kept one hand on her back and he stroked around her hard nipples with the other.

The passion and warmth went all through Kelsey. She draped her arms over Jayson's neck and felt delivered. Here, in his arms, was the place she had always needed to be. Jayson worked his erection inside her while they kissed deliciously, pausing each few moments to look into each other's eyes. For the first time in her life, Kelsey actually liked having sex. It was a completely different experience. She understood the meaning in it, the intimacy, where before she hadn't.

Then a powerful feeling came from her inside her and swelled through her entire body. Kelsey started trembling and she grabbed onto Jayson's big hard arms, scratching into them with her nails until she pierced the skin.

"I'm scared," she whispered. "I don't know what I'm feeling..."

He laughed and embraced her more tightly. "You're coming. That's what's happening," he said. "Just feel it. Come for me, Baby!"

Kelsey let herself go as he wanted her to and she experienced the incredible orgasm. She felt herself spasm insistently on Jayson, again and again while her body and mind reeled with the pleasure. She felt lost, felt transported to another place, and she let her body relax with total abandon.

Without freeing her from the connection, Jayson rolled Kelsey's limp body onto her side and continued making love to her from that angle. He moved inside her once or twice, taking his own climax while kissing her sweetly. Kelsey murmured in satisfaction, enjoying the incredible warmth and sweetness of his body, and then tiredness overwhelmed her and she could feel herself spiraling gently into sleep.

Jayson's mesmerizing eyes were the first thing Kelsey saw when she woke up. He had spent the night inside her, never pulling out. Now, with a few moves of his hips, he became hard again, stroking inside her body where she was still wet from last night. Instinctively, Kelsey reached her open mouth for his and mellowly joined her desire with his. They climaxed together, effortlessly and gently.

Jayson lay back and he looked dreamily up at Kelsey. "I didn't even expect it to be this good," he said with a mischievous, boldly assessing look in his eye.

Then he rolled her underneath, so that she was looking up at him. "How about you? Don't you like it? Aren't you amazed by it?"

Kelsey thought about how her whole world and all her priorities had changed after last night. The day felt opened up, light seemed to spill out of it like it was the first day the world opened up. She was finally and fully awake.

"Jayson," she said, "with what you've made me feel, if you ever wanted to hurt me, I'd have no defense at all."

It wouldn't be just the feeling of a boyfriend abandoning her, if he left, it would mean that this whole new insight on the world would be taken away.

Jayson settled back on one arm and rested a hand in the middle of Kelsey's chest over her heart. He watched her for a very long while, looking very serious. Finally, he said, "If I ever wanted to hurt you, I'd just have to walk through that door."

"Would you leave?" she asked, genuinely curious to know. There was a lot she didn't understand about Jayson, why she had pursued him so hard before and he had fought it and, now, why he seemed to want her as powerfully as she wanted him. She did know that her efforts to control him at the beginning hadn't worked.

He snuggled down more comfortably into her covers. "No, Kelsey, I'm not going to leave. I just hope that you don't start to dislike my intensity. It's possible that you would."

His gigantic muscles gleamed in delectable curves. His deeply tanned skin looked incredibly tight in the golden sheen of morning. Each facial feature was tight and perfect and his light brown eyes shimmered with the daylight in an almost spiritual way that tugged at her heart. Jayson's thick luscious pink lips curled in an enigmatic smile, mocking the excess of her desire. When all she could think of was having him again, he was suggesting that she might tire of him just because of his specialness. Kelsey narrowed her eyes at him, intrigued by the things he got her to think about and realize. She was just coming to know him and she was starting to suspect that his extraordinary looks were only the tip of the iceberg. She thrilled to the idea that she might be a fitting partner for a man as complex as Jayson Carter, thrilled that she had the chance to try to be.

"Possibly," she told Jayson, "there was always an intense part of me and, by choosing to be with you, I'm also choosing to be an intense person myself. Maybe that quality you have is actually a quality of total honesty. And I guess that frightens most people."

Jayson played thoughtfully with her pointed breasts. "And you?" he asked. "Does total honesty frighten you?"

The look he gave her was very seductive and Kelsey opened her eyes wide and met it brazenly with her own look. She caressed Jayson's massive shoulders and chest and his hard silky stomach while he touched her. She paid total attention to how each inch of him felt.

"No," she said. "Honesty doesn't scare me now."

Jayson's body was so beautifully golden in the morning light. Kelsey let her lips brush over him, moving from his ankles to his forehead and then back down to kiss and lick his rock-hard abdomen, finally now getting to feel him. His skin felt satiny under her light touch and she breathed in his sweet clean scent, which was the same even after the sex. Jayson received her attentions lazily and unselfconsciously.

Then he reached up to grab the cordless phone and he handed it to her.

"Here," he said, "it's time to get on the phone and start telling your friends that you're in love."

Kelsey tried to put the phone back.

"It's seven -o'clock," she protested.

Jayson took the phone and rolled away defensively while tapping out Miranda's number. When it started ringing, he gave it to Kelsey, grinning wickedly.

"Yeah." Miranda's deeply sleepy voice came on the phone.

Kelsey's own voice sounded bubbly like it had never been before in her life. She could hardly get the words out to her friend without giggling. So, this was the new her. It seemed like there must have been a weight on her all her life.

"Miranda!" she said. "I'm in love!"

She checked Jayson's reaction and he was nodding approvingly.

"It's Jayson. He and I are going out. This is all too weird, how it happened but, like, we're together. Not even like me and Paul. This is kind of serious..."

"Very," Jayson mouthed and Kelsey amended, "very serious. He's like demanding I call everyone and break the news."

Miranda laughed and then had a coughing fit. "That would be typical of Jayson," she said, "to do everything in a big way. I'm happy for you, though. He told me last night that he was going to see you."

"How about you, Miranda, are you okay?"

"Me? Jayson hooked me up with a Brazilian commodities trader that does business with his company. The guy sent me home in a limo and he had one of his employees drive my car. I'm fine! Now, could you let me get some sleep?"

Kelsey got off the phone and she called Jerry, who also didn't sound incredibly surprised to be woken or to be told the news. Although not a late riser, he also sounded weary, but he wished her good luck. As soon as she was done, Jayson asked her if he could borrow her car to run to the convenience store on the corner of nearby Hillsboro Boulevard. Kelsey immediately hesitated, feeling weird about loaning out her car, even to him. Unlike Miranda, Kelsey was very protective of her things and she felt that even this man would have to earn her trust.

"I can go," she said. It sounded pretty weak, because it was obvious she would prefer to stay in bed.

Jayson looked at her as though critically thinking about how her mind worked. "That's all right." He smiled ironically. "I can always call another eighty dollar cab to get us groceries."

And he laughed out loud. Kelsey didn't mind his mocking her. Her distrust of him had been so pitifully disguised. And she knew he liked the truth. He tilted his head quizzically.

"Someone must have done such a number on you," he said. "Someone really fucked with you, didn't they?" Then he let the subject go.

Kelsey ended up running them to the convenience store wearing shorts and T-shirt and she was a little annoyed that Jayson had needed food so early. She hadn't gotten the chance to shower and she could smell the residual odor of their lovemaking. Of course, Jayson smelled fresh and looked clean and perfect. He seemed not at all uncomfortable walking into the mini mart in last night's dress clothes.

As soon as they walked back in the door of her condo, Kelsey headed for the shower. And after eating breakfast, Jayson joined her. He climbed into the shower and washed her and then he asked her to wash him. The light caught the spray of the water as Jayson teased her and she thought about how beautiful their bodies probably looked together.

"Let's go to the Keys today," Jayson suggested, out of nowhere.

Kelsey was shocked. She was not used to impulsively driving one hundred and sixty miles on a whim.

Seeing her hesitation, he said, "We can make love all night tonight, I promise. It's just that I have to leave tomorrow on business until the end of the week and I'd like us to do something special today."

They had gotten back in bed and were snuggling and Kelsey struggled to a sitting position. Laughing, she said, "You know, I was planning on us staying in bed all day. Let me just make a phone call. I need to call Mr. Eisenberg about the condo."

Today was the deadline for her decision and Kelsey no longer had any doubt about what she wanted to do. She called her landlord and told him that she did want to buy the condo and she told him to go ahead and send her the papers.

An hour later they were following U.S. Highway 1 south on Jayson's motorcycle, heading for Key West. The road to the Keys was different from any place Kelsey had seen in Florida. In some spots the highway was so narrow you could see water glimmering on both sides through the mangroves, tangled bushlike trees that stood in the water that Jayson had identified for her.

In Key Largo, at the very upper end of the Keys, they passed dive shops and shell merchants and stopped at a restaurant for lunch. Then they stopped at a particularly funky looking souvenir shop and Kelsey bought Jayson a shark tooth necklace on a leather thong and adjusted it lovingly on his neck. It was her first present to him.

They next passed through the centrally located Islamorada, with its locally flavored hotels and restaurants, and Kelsey thought it was very pretty. Next was the larger town of Marathon, which was more developed and resembled places along US 1 in other parts of Florida.

They came out again into the open for the last leg of their journey. It felt a little scary clinging to Jayson on the back of the motorcycle with the wind whipping around them in all the immense spaces.

Jayson yelled to Kelsey over his shoulder, "This is called the Seven Mile Bridge. They built it in the nineteen-thirties to connect the Upper and Lower Keys after a hurricane destroyed the railroad. That bridge the people are fishing off, the one next to us is the original bridge."

As he spoke, the Seven-Mile Bridge opened before them, a long causeway extending over shimmering ocean, a bridge bigger than any she had ever seen. Riding over it felt wonderful with the air washing over her body and the sight of the shimmering sea around them in all directions. Being here today thrilled Kelsey and she was glad now that Jayson had brought her.

The funky party town of Key West was supposed to be another Greenwich Village. But Kelsey found that it was actually a little more upscale and many of the stores were more accessible to her taste. She wandered the streets in a happy daze, pulled up close against Jayson's side and smiling at the other young couples who passed them in the opposite direction. Jayson was like a tour guide, leading her onto the side streets to show her historic buildings with lattice decorated porches and big shady banana trees in the yards. He talked about history and ran scorching kisses up and down her neck.

They ate dinner at an outdoor table of some rowdy restaurant. This place also had some historic significance and Jayson told her that the classical writer, Ernest Hemmingway, used to come here all the time. It seemed wonderful, this small island at the very tip of the country. The whole colorful town seemed to bask in the heat of their love. The intensity of the locale, and the intensity of their love, was all that Kelsey knew that day. It filled her completely. She supposed she could sort out the details later.

After dinner Jayson pulled her by the hand. "The sunset at Mallory Square," he said.

They walked to a small paved area at the edge of the water, where other people were gathering as well. Amongst the relaxed group of tourists and locals gathered to watch the sunset at the southernmost tip of the country, Jayson and Kelsey sat with their legs dangling over the water. Boats moved lazily over the smooth pink ocean, while an old man played the blues, singing in a deep voice that ebbed and flowed hypnotically, like the water. Other performers could be heard further down the pier. Jayson caressed Kelsey's back in time to the music and then kissed her on the top of her head.

"I'm so happy that we're doing this together," he said.

Happy tears slipped out of Kelsey's eyes.

Later, it gave her an exciting, yet almost eerie, feeling riding home in the complete blackness on the back of the motorcycle, with only the glow of the reflectors on the road to keep them grounded. She couldn't see a thing in the complete blackness. In places, it must have been ocean all around them. It felt at times like they were flying, with all that mysterious space around them, and the smell of the ocean battering around her on all sides. Clinging tighter to Jayson's broad back, feeling his faint heat through the leather jacket, she had to remember that now they were together; now she was safe.

They got back very late and Jayson asked if she preferred to spend the night at his room on Hollywood Beach and leave for work from there. Kelsey was curious to finally see the inside of his place. He had a small efficiency but the room got an incredible sultry breeze off the ocean. The set of four louvered windows faced east so that, if you kept the lights off, you could sit on the bed and watch the few late night strollers on the Broadwalk. If you stood up, or sat at the dinette table by the windows, you could watch the restless waves all night.

Kelsey and Jayson made love missionary style, with their movements accompanied by the rhythmic whoosh of the ocean. As Kelsey fell asleep she noticed how cozy it was in her new boyfriend's bed. The blanket was warm and weighty and the sheets had a tangy smell, like salt water. Jayson probably went swimming in the ocean every night and then crawled directly into bed.

The next morning Jayson did something that made Kelsey look like a fool for not trusting him about loaning the car yesterday. He got up and dressed very early and woke her on his way out the door.

"I've got to go to Tampa, Kelsey," he said. "You can use anything you want in the room, make yourself breakfast. And stay as long as you like. Just lock up when you go."

Kelsey didn't feel comfortable staying in the room too long. She didn't want to invade Jayson's personal space although she was immensely curious about him. She immediately noticed several photos. One was of a group of young men in front of what looked like a college building. They all had that young "slacker" look, like Jayson, who stood grinning in the center of the snapshot. The other photo showed Jayson walking up from the ocean with a beautiful blonde with long hair riding on his shoulders. The girl was tall and gorgeous, with that flashy California look. This was Jayson's ex-girlfriend, Kelsey suspected, the one who had supposedly turned him off on other women. It was not hard for Kelsey to understand him wanting a girl like this when the girl looked just like a fashion model.

Kelsey prowled around, seeing what else she could find that could tell her something about the man she was going out with. Jayson's room was quite stark, containing the furniture that came with it and not much else. The kitchen and bathroom were immaculately clean and the refrigerator was well stocked. A few cheerful colored dishes were mixed in with the cheap ones from the hotel. There was a collection of shells on the table. Several pairs of wet swim trunks were hung up to dry. There were two newspapers for today, a *Sentinel*, from here in Broward County, and the more cosmopolitan *Miami Herald*. There was a CD boom box with a small collection of CDs, all alternative groups. And there was the laptop computer that Jayson had taken with him when he left for his business trip this morning.

Kelsey didn't know what she expected to see on the walls. But what she did see gave the room a melancholy, almost monastic, feel. There was an actual crucifix, a delicate wood carving of Jesus bleeding on the cross, at the head of Jayson's bed. On the other wall along the side of the bed was a vintage map of Florida. The only other decoration, one that Jayson had obviously chosen to leave up, was a hotel print of two pathetic-looking baby owls.

The only extravagant thing in the room was a whole wicker stand packed with his books. There were paperbacks and ragged hardcovers, including books on Eastern philosophy, a Bible and classics that Kelsey hadn't seen since college.

A person's environment told you so such about them. Kelsey could usually get the full picture on most people within moments of walking into their home. It would take her a lot longer to figure Jayson out. She was already tremendously intrigued by the person he seemed to be.

Kelsey took a shower in the tiny bathroom, drank a quick glass of water and ate one olive, ignoring the rest of the food. She felt invigorated by the sea air as she walked to her car and she felt special because he had allowed her to stay here in his home like this, when she hadn't even trusted him to drive her car one block down the road.

The first time Miranda saw her friend after Kelsey had started going out with Jayson, she shook her head with pleasant astonishment.

"You're a different girl!" she exclaimed.

Kelsey walked to her mirror to look at herself. It was true, her face looked more refined and her dark eyes looked riveting; the fires within were burning steadily now.

"It's all coming together," Kelsey said. Even her voice sounded more upbeat and assertive. "The closing on the condo is coming up on the fifteenth and I've been dealing with lawyers and going crazy trying to get the rest of the cash together, but I'm feeling pretty competent. As for Jayson, I have no doubts there. In fact, he makes me sure about everything else. Every other relationship I've had was play-acting compared to this. I feel so sorry that I wasted your time all the years making you listen to me agonize about all the other guys."

Miranda scowled. "You know," she said, "you're going to end up like your mom who got married at eighteen and devoted her whole life to one man."

Kelsey heard the warning, but she couldn't see any problem with the closeness she had with Jayson. In fact, she felt stronger all the time. Her body radiated health. At times she felt she couldn't move fast enough, she was that wired.

Two days later, Kelsey walked out of her office feeling full of energy. Her legs stretched the hem of her tight cotton dress as she strode out to her car at exactly five-o'clock, heading into the bright sunshine. She had on high heels but she still outdistanced the guard, a hefty man who got out of breath following her. Kelsey was in a hurry because she'd promised Jayson she'd meet him at the gym where they could grab some time together before he had to go to night class. But she wanted to first stop at home to check her mail to see if her copy of the signed contract was there, then feed Mr. Cooper, change clothes and maybe get a snack herself.

Kelsey looked over her car and all looked well so she waved to the guard to indicate that all was okay. "I'll see you tomorrow," she said.

"Have a good one," he said to her, turned, and walked back towards the building.

Kelsey pressed the remote, then swung open the door and cheerfully hopped into her car, adjusting her dress and seat belt around her. It took her a moment before she noticed the item on the dashboard. With the sun behind the thing, she saw it first in silhouette. It was some kind of rag doll with its head leaning back against the windshield and its feet dangling over the dash. Her very first thought was that it was something pleasant, maybe something left by a coworker as a joke. Then she leaned forward to see the thing better and she let out a scream from deep within her throat.

"Nooooo!" She backed away instinctively from the thing in the car.

The doll was wearing a burgundy, satin slip dress. The material was roughly sewn but the resemblance to the dress she used to own was horrifyingly clear. Kelsey had to force herself to reach out and touch the voodoo doll; her natural abhorrence of it was so strong. She rubbed the fabric between her fingers, thinking as she did that the odor still wafted from it, the odor of sex with Joe on the night he date raped her. It was the same fabric, the fabric of her dress that she had thrown away in the ice-cream parlor after running from him that morning.

Kelsey glanced all around her but there was no one to be seen. She held the doll in her hands now and she saw its odd shape. The body was made of brown burlap. The doll had a wedge-shaped head, crazily staring eyes and crusty brown yarn for hair. Instinct told her what type of doll she was holding- voodoo, Santeria. Someone was trying to hurt her, trying to put some sort of spell on her. Kelsey was horrified and sickened to see that there was a straight pin stuck through the stomach of the Kelsey doll.

She knew she shouldn't let this get to her. With this type of thing it was only the victim's belief that could make the black magic work. And Kelsey did not believe in any kind of magic. The important thing was to find out who was doing these things to her, and why. Some of the people involved in the drug smuggling case were originally from the Caribbean. But why would someone like them follow her on a one-night stand? How horrible! The thought of someone following behind her that day and pulling the soiled dress from out of the trash receptacle, that tall, white metal can that smelled of ice cream, was too much for Kelsey to face.

She had to get the thing away from her. Forgetting all about safety, she jumped out of her car and ran with the doll to a big trash can in front of her plaza. She threw it in violently and then, shaking, she had to reach back in again. She grabbed the doll and pulled the pin out of its stomach, flinging the long pin across the parking lot and letting the doll drop back into the trash can. She was not saving this for evidence. The thing had to be gone. Her word on its existence would have to be enough when, and if, she told anyone.

She kept shaking the whole way driving home. This was just so horrible. She always knew that in her line of work she could be in physical danger. But she hadn't expected something like this. This was unimaginable. Kelsey had to fight to concentrate on the rush-hour traffic on I-95 and not weave into somebody's lane or rear-end someone who had stopped abruptly.

She got off one exit early and cruised around back streets and several parking lots, assuring herself that all was clear behind her before she dared head home. She still felt nervous in her parking lot and on her steps and she kept checking around her to make sure that there was no one watching. Her hands trembled with the keys to her door. Inside, she didn't check messages and just paced the kitchen with different thoughts rushing around in her mind. How did whoever it was get past her car's alarm system? Then she thought about how right she had been with her feelings when she was convinced she was being followed that day at the beach after she had left Joe's apartment. Someone *was* definitely stalking her and they had been following her even then.

Kelsey was shaking badly still and she felt that she needed something to eat. She opened the refrigerator and reached for the skim milk, which she always bought from the neighborhood convenience store in a glass bottle. One of her bad habits, being single, was to drink directly from these bottles without using a cup. This is what she did now. She held the bottle up to take a gulp. Next thing, there was a bitter taste in her mouth, a taste that kept intensifying even as she flung the bottle aside and it smashed against the side of the stove.

The taste was huge and so bad it felt like it was going to blow the top of her head off. Her stomach heaved, feeling like it was going to take all of her intestines with it. Then hot vomit gushed up through her mouth and wetted the front of her dress. Kelsey reeled around her kitchen, basically beyond thought, but still trying to reach for the telephone. Vomit exploded out of her, landing all around the kitchen, while her whole abdomen heaved violently. Then one of her shoes buckled under her and she fell to the floor. She was in fetal position now and the vomiting kept wracking her body. Poison, she thought, fighting for consciousness and a plan for how she could get up and get to the phone.

Chapter 10

Kelsey felt strong hands feeling for her pulse, then she heard Jayson yelling at her, "Where are your car keys?"

The next time she woke they were riding and she was wrapped in a blanket in the passenger seat of her car.

"What happened?" he asked her. "Are you sick?"

She heard her own voice rasp out an answer.

"I might be poisoned. At work, someone left a voodoo doll in my car and there was a pin in its stomach. Then I came home and I drank the milk..."

She didn't recognize the hospital Jayson brought her to, but it must have been the one closest to her home. Jayson rushed in, carrying her in the blanket, pushing past everyone. People crowded the hallways, poor people, bleeding all over so that it seemed like an inner-city emergency room. The doctors and orderlies who ran around looked sloppy and out of control. Kelsey kept going in and out of consciousness. She heard Jayson advocating for her while he placed her on a bed and the nurses tried to argue.

"She's possibly been poisoned!" he yelled at them. "She's projectile vomiting and there's blood in it."

"We're going to have to put a tube down your stomach..." the nurse in charge told Kelsey brusquely.

While another nurse hooked up an EKG, the head nurse unwrapped a tube from a sterile plastic sheath.

"Get toxicology on my stomach contents!" Kelsey insisted. She called out, "Jayson, make sure they do that." She wanted to know what her stalker had done to her, what particular poison he, or she, had used. She still didn't believe in voodoo curses.

The staff led Jayson out to registration. As they shoved the painful tube down Kelsey's nostril, raising their voices at her and forcing her to swallow as they pushed it down, she heard Jayson arguing with them out front, then starting to yell. "I don't care if she doesn't have insurance; you're obligated by law to treat her!"

This was a nightmare, Kelsey thought. Even if she survived this, she would never be able to pay this bill. The nurses pushed a thick, black sludge into Kelsey's stomach through the tube. Jayson came back and she took his hand gratefully.

"I shouldn't be here," she said. "This bill is going to be so high."

Someone drowned her out, screaming behind one of the closed drapes.

"I couldn't take a chance on you dying," Jayson said. His eyes looked almost teary. "What about that job of yours?" he asked. "Is it true that you don't have any health insurance?"

"It's true," she said. "They consider us independent contractors. Not giving us insurance is another way they save money."

She reached out to touch the shark tooth that lay in the hollow of Jayson's throat over sculpted pectoral muscles that bulged out of his loose tank.

"My necklace looks good on you," she said. "And look at me, with this thing hanging out of my nose."

Jayson brought his eyes right up to hers. "You're still beautiful," he said, and he slid two fingers under her hospital gown to grasp her nipple. Just then a woman with a dingy white lab coat and long unruly hair walked in and stepped up to Kelsey.

"Have you been under a lot of stress at work lately?" the women in the white coat asked her, without bothering to introduce herself. "There seems to be some concern that maybe you tried to hurt yourself today," she said in a patronizing tone.

Kelsey went from feeling weak to being furious. This woman, who was accusing her, must be her doctor.

"Someone tried to poison me," Kelsey snapped. "Did you get the toxicology report yet?"

"Not yet," the doctor said, "but..."

Jayson interrupted. "Doctor, I'm sure you don't believe she'd hurt herself," he said. "I know that she didn't."

He was still playing with Kelsey's nipple under her blanket and gown, but he turned slightly to give the other woman a view of his white smile and pumped-up chest.

The doctor flushed and she flung her messy hair over one shoulder.

"No, I'm sure you wouldn't think that," she said breathlessly, and then continued. "May I ask, do you go to a gym around here? I've been looking for one for myself but I don't know where to go."

Shamelessly, the incompetent doctor flirted with her boyfriend while Kelsey swallowed reflexively around the tube, meanwhile squirming under Jayson's agile fingers.

When the doctor left Kelsey said, "I guess I should thank you for defending me. They were probably going to lock me up. Maybe it does seem paranoid, what I'm saying about the voodoo doll and being poisoned. But it's true."

Jayson had a hand under the gown, touching the silky skin of Kelsey's inner thigh. He leaned forward. "Baby, tell me who you think did this to you. Do you think it has something to do with your job?"

"I don't know," she said. Her mind had been whirling around on the subject since she'd regained consciousness. "Someone has been stalking me for a while. I just can't ignore it anymore. They slashed my tires at work a few weeks ago, before we started going out and there have been threats on my email."

"Why didn't you tell me!" Jayson seemed shaken and angry.

"It's my job," Kelsey said, "I'm trained to take care of myself in this type of situation. But I've decided that I will get myself taken off the one case, the big drug case Jerry and I have been working on. The police think one of those guys is responsible for my tires and some threats on my computer. The same person probably did this, too."

"Why don't you just quit the job altogether?" Jayson asked her.

Kelsey hesitated. "There's someone else it might be." She hated having to expose herself this way to Jayson, who seemed so pure and unblemished, and who was now waiting, patiently, for her to explain. Finally, Kelsey told Jayson what she hadn't ever wanted to tell him.

"I had a one-night-stand right before I met you," she said. "Whoever put the doll there knows about it, because that doll was made out of the dress I was wearing that night. I think it might be the guy I slept with. He could be responsible for all this stuff that's happening to me. The whole thing with him was kind of sordid. I was into it at first but then I wanted to stop and he date-raped me."

Jayson's cheeks got two dark red spots on them. "Show me this guy and I'll take care of the problem." he said.

"I need to find out if he's the one stalking me first."

Kelsey's mind worked methodically. Her biggest concern, above all, was finding out who her enemy was and what their motive was. She didn't want Jayson going after Joe if Joe wasn't the one responsible.

This is when the doctor walked in and she had a strange look on her face. "Ms. Reed," she said, "the only things that we found in your tox report were baking soda and syrup of ipecac. If you're not familiar with that…" she raised an eyebrow, sardonically, "…it's a common over-the-counter preparation used to induce vomiting in cases of poisoning. I've seen girls who were bulimic use it to deliberately make themselves throw up." Again, she gave Kelsey that suspicious look. It was frightening to think that, without Jayson speaking up for her, she might have ended up committed to the psycho ward tonight. Everyone seemed to think that she had taken this stuff herself, perhaps to try to kill herself.

The doctor went on. "Usually it's a pretty harmless substance, although it can be powerful. It seems like whoever administered this might have misjudged the dosage slightly. And, by mixing it with the baking soda this way, it was going to cause a lot of pain and there was the potential for some real damage. It's a good thing that your boyfriend brought you in here when he did…"

The doctor told Kelsey that she was all right but she was still badly dehydrated and would have to stay a few hours longer to get some IV fluids.

When the doctor left the room Jayson burrowed his face against Kelsey. "Please let me protect you against whoever did this," he begged her. "I can't believe I almost lost you."

Now that the doctor had told her what substance had been used, Kelsey felt she needed to share with Jayson her most bizarre suspicion. "Jayson," she said, "there's even a possibility that Miranda could be involved. She has the key to my condo and the doll, and the syrup of ipecac, have the tone of something a woman would do."

"But why would Miranda do something like that?"

Kelsey sighed. "Well, I know it's farfetched, but Miranda moved to Florida two years ago to be with me, because I was so lonely. Recently, we were talking about moving back home to New York together and she seemed to be depending on that. Now I made the decision about buying the condo and I got involved with you. Maybe Miranda would want to do something to scare me off Florida so I would leave and she wouldn't be forced to stay here. I can't even predict what she would do lately, she's been so crazy with all the cocaine." Kelsey reached for him. "Jayson, if you could just be there while I get things sorted out."

He hugged her to him. "I'm here for you, Baby."

Kelsey was very tired. She had thoughts of going back to work but Jayson wouldn't let her.

"You might have to talk to the police tomorrow," he said, "but other than that, you're not going anywhere. Stay out of work until Monday. I'll tell them I can't go in to my job and I'll stay with you. We can spend three days in bed."

Kelsey cuddled against his big chest. She was getting used to him being here, and it was a relief not to have to face work immediately to tell her boss that she was taking herself off the drug case. She had a feeling that he was not going to be too happy with her, even though she was the victim of all this.

It was around four in the morning when they got back to Kelsey's condo. The place no longer had the safe welcoming feeling it used to. In fact, being here was terrifying. It got Kelsey shaking. She sniffed back a tear. It had been her idea to come back tonight. She thought it was like getting back on a horse after a fall. If she wasn't going to associate her home with violence, then she couldn't let herself stay away from it out of fear.

The first thing Kelsey did was go to the basket on her counter to check her hidden camera. If ever there was a moment for the video camera it was now. She could have caught the stalker on tape while they planted the poison and she would finally know their identity. But Kelsey's video camera was gone, totally vanished. The stalker had filled the basket with extra groceries to take its place. Kelsey choked back a sob as she looked around her condo helplessly.

She hadn't anticipated the sick reek coming from the dried vomit or the fact that the door had been ripped off the hinges, leaving her possessions unprotected the whole time they had been gone. Jayson explained that he had done it when he saw her through the window, lying on the kitchen floor. He shielded her from the sight of the blood-tinged vomit that was dried all over the kitchen appliances and he steered her to the shower.

"What about that door?" she asked. "How safe is it going to be?"

"I think we'll be all right with me here tonight," Jayson said. "And you've got a gun, right?"

Kelsey nodded.

"That's good" he said, "but if I could do that to your door, somebody else could, too."

"Tomorrow," Kelsey said, "I'm changing all the locks. And I can get some better hardware. And then I want to go looking for that guy, Joe, the one I was with that night."

Jayson's face took on a harsh look; obviously even hearing the guy mentioned upset him.

Kelsey slept while Jayson cleaned up the condo. She held her sleepy cat against her and thought about what would have happened if Jayson hadn't found her and she had died here tonight. It felt strange to her to be loved. Paul and her two other serious boyfriends had said they loved her but, truthfully, they could barely tolerate her near them or tolerate any irregularities in her. This boyfriend, who was so unusually gorgeous and so remote in his personality, the one she had expected the least of, had been there for her every minute. Even in the hospital, or here, cleaning up puke, there was no sign that he was impatient with her or that he wanted to be somewhere else.

It was scary to think that she was accepting somebody's love. Yet it felt so good to hear him moving around out there.

Something woke her toward morning, she thought she heard the squeak of the refrigerator door. "Jayson," she called out, "don't eat any of the food in that refrigerator. Or cabinets. It could poison you! I have to get it checked."

Jayson had overestimated the police. He kept encouraging her to go to them. But, when the couple went to the police station the next day, all the local cops could say was that they would continue surveillance on the main defendant in the drug case, the one who was out on bail. They laughed about the samples of food Kelsey brought in ziploc bags.

"Miss Reed," the lieutenant said, "you're the first one to know we don't have the resources for something like this."

"Okay," Kelsey said as she walked briskly out to the car that Jayson was now driving. "This is not the end of it. I'm going to approach the lab we use at work with this food and I'll pay for the analysis myself."

The locksmith was another bill she had to pay in cash, making her start to fear that she couldn't meet the closing costs on the condo. And then there was the creepy feeling that, since someone had invaded her condo, she didn't even want to buy it, didn't even want to stay here. But of course, until the stalker was found and taken out of the picture, they would be able to find her anywhere. And this place was no worse than anywhere else was.

Jayson wasn't willing to go looking for Joe that first day, because he said that the visit to the police station had been stress enough for Kelsey.

He even got this brilliant idea to have Juan baby-sit for her while he ran to the store to replace the groceries.

The big, dark-haired bodybuilder sat there staring at her with compassionate eyes and making small talk for a while, deliberately avoiding subjects that might upset her, as Jayson had probably instructed him to do. Finally they both broke down and laughed.

"He's in love with you, you know," Juan said to Kelsey.

"He told you that?" she asked eagerly.

"He didn't have to," Juan said. "Jayson's not one to talk about his feelings, but his actions show them so clearly. I know my best friend. I have three brothers of my own, but I trust Jayson more than any of them. I've learned that so much of bodybuilding is being able to have control of your mind, as well, and I'm trying to learn that discipline. One thing I really respect about Jayson is that, when he commits to something, it's absolute. And I sense that's the way he feels about you."

The plan was for Jayson and Kelsey to stay in the apartment and have a five-day sex-fest but now, for some reason, Kelsey felt uncomfortable and shy. The locks had been replaced, she had checked the door and the patio and the windows multiple times and the police had been reported to. She had talked to her boss on the phone and told him assertively that she was off the drug case. Miranda had come over right after Juan when Kelsey called her with news of the psychopath. Then they'd all eaten a fresh dinner cooked by Jayson and there was a lot of laughter and reassurance. But, when Kelsey and Jayson got into bed together and he reached up under her nightshirt, she actually pushed him off.

"Are you still scared?" he asked.

"No, not about that," Kelsey said, "It's myself. How I feel about my body. After what happened, somehow I don't feel right. Someone is trying to punish me, Jayson. How could you understand about how I hate my body and how easily I feel it can be torn down? Lying on the floor like that when I was poisoned, my dignity was gone along with everything else. You don't know what it's like to hate your body…"

"No," he said, "possibly I don't. But all I want is to try to understand you."

Kelsey slept on the other side of the bed, curled away from her new lover. She was awake and she got to hear him tossing and turning restlessly, obviously frustrated at them not sleeping cuddled close together. It was easier for Kelsey to turn away from closeness than it probably was for Jayson. She was the one more suspicious of love.

The night before, still sick, she had slept deeply. But tonight, she kept having flashbacks of the doll, and of herself drinking the milk and vomiting, bent over, with her stomach heaving and the vomit flying three feet out of her mouth, flashbacks of herself falling to the floor. Before she passed out, her last thought was that she was dying and yet she wasn't even tough enough to get to the phone to save herself.

The worst part was that, in reality, it had all been a cruel, mocking joke. Someone was standing back and laughing at her and she couldn't even get to face her adversary. Kelsey had a sense that whoever it was hated her very, very deeply. Only the victim of what had happened to her could understand the malice that went behind it. Of course, she would fight this in every way. But it felt deeply disconcerting to know that there was someone waiting to try and destroy you, maybe waiting to kill you, someone who seemed to have nothing but time.

Thursday morning Kelsey and Jayson went to Pompano Beach, searching for Joe.

"Why do you have these one-night-stands, Kelsey?" Jayson preached, while he drove. "You come off, on first meeting, like you have so much self esteem. But in your personal life, it all falls apart. What happens?"

"I don't know," she told him. "It's not like I even enjoy one-night-stands. I couldn't even come," she added, bitterly. "You know, that was my first time having an orgasm the first night with you. I guess I went with the other guys because I wanted to feel pretty and feel loved. It always happened after someone had broken up with me or rejected me."

"Someday you're going to have to look yourself in the face," Jayson said, "and you'll have to come to terms with yourself."

"I know," Kelsey said. "I want to do that. With you in my life, I want to start learning the truth about myself. Other things that used to be important aren't as important any more."

Jayson gave her a supportive kiss on the cheek when they got out of the car in front of Joe's building. The place hadn't been hard to find; it was the only seven-story monstrosity a half-mile south of the Seven Eleven.

"I might have to tell some white lies," Kelsey warned Jayson.

First, she buzzed the condo she had been in that night with Joe. An elderly lady answered, saying that she had lived there since November 15th and there was no young man there.

Their next step was at the manager's office. The manager himself was like a caricature, fat and cigar smoking. Kelsey didn't hesitate.

"We're from the State Attorney's office," she said. "We're looking for a young man named Joe Carpenito. He was at this address in October."

"Well," the fat man said, "all I can tell you is that he ain't here now. The kid rents his place on a six-month lease for the summer, then decides to clear out before season even starts. Kinda weird guy, real big, but he had these jumpy eyes..."

"We'd like to see his rental application." Kelsey said.

"That's confidential information. I can't show you that," the man protested.

Kelsey handed a fifty from her cupped palm to his and, without further protest, he went off to get them the rental app. Jayson gave Kelsey a dirty look.

"This is about my life," she said to him. "It's worth some money."

The copy of the application they took home could be valuable to her. Even if Joe couldn't be traced to a previous address, at least Kelsey had information like his social security number, information that the police could use if they had to. Kelsey couldn't wait to get home, get on the telephone and start delving into Joe's life.

She made several calls and she found that the previous address in Patterson, New Jersey was no good. Jayson watched, looking fascinated, as Kelsey went about doing what she did all day for a living, doing it as calmly and efficiently as though it concerned a client and not herself.

Kelsey called Joe's mother, who seemed surprised she was looking for Joe, since he was living right there and was just out at work.

"Did he ever leave New Jersey," Kelsey asked, "for a day or a half day, unaccounted for? Any time he could have come back to Florida for a day?"

The mother's voice rose. "I don't know what you're getting at or who you are, but let me tell you, Joe had a lot of problems down there in Florida! He lost his business because a friend cheated him. He's been here every day and he's not going back! He's got no reason to. Joe's got a nice girlfriend here. If you're one of those girls he was seeing in Florida..."

Kelsey gently hung up, while the mother was still yelling insults and threats.

"He lied to me," she mumbled to Jayson, thinking about the mother's mention of many girlfriends, when Joe had told her there had only been one. "But if his mother was telling the truth, Joe Carpenito wasn't down here when these things happened to me. Maybe I can check with Miranda and see if she ever got a phone number for Joe's friend Marshall. I could confirm it with him."

Kelsey called Miranda and got a phone number, which was the number of Marshall's company. It took her about a hundred tries to get Marshall himself on the phone, rather than the answering machine.

Late that afternoon, he finally answered, "South Florida Budget Cellular!" in that nerve-jangling, falsely upbeat voice she remembered.

"Hi, Marshall," she said. "My name is Kelsey. My friend, Miranda, and I met you and your friend, Joe, a few months ago in Fort Lauderdale. She's the redhead..."

"Yeah, I remember," he said. "I never forget a face." His voice took on a sarcastic tone, ratty, like she remembered. "You were the stuck-up one. I heard you spent some night with Big Joe." He started laughing at her. "You're the one who doesn't like to give blow-jobs!"

"Where is Joe now?" Kelsey demanded, assertively, sickened by Marshall's attitude but wanting to get this accomplished.

"The loser took off back to Jersey!" Marshall said. "That doesn't bother me, though. He left his investment. It's more for me."

"Is there any chance," Kelsey asked, "that he could have come back here one or two times?"

"If you want to be with him, you're out of luck," Marshall laughed. "He went running home to mommy. There's no chance he's coming back."

Kelsey was ready to say good-bye when Marshall said, "Why don't you tell Miranda to call me? That offer of a job still stands. Even yourself, we could get together, have dinner sometime..."

"Look, you scum," another male voice broke in, threateningly. It was Jayson, on the kitchen extension. "I'm her boyfriend. If you or your faggot friend have any more problems, you bring them up with me, anytime, anyplace. Don't you ever have anything to do with Kelsey again!"

Kelsey's feelings were mixed, glad that Jayson was protecting her but ashamed at what he had heard. She went to talk to him in the kitchen, after hanging up. He embraced her and rubbed her back.

"Charming people," he said.

"I don't think Joe did it," Kelsey said, wearily. In a way, she wished Joe had been the person stalking her. At least it would have made some sense.

"So where do we go from here?" Jayson asked.

Kelsey shook her head and sighed. She was standing at the counter and knew that she should make dinner. But she was afraid. The flashback of the poisoning came back each time she thought about opening the refrigerator.

"I'm so scared of making dinner," she said. "It's irrational. I've always been strong. Three years ago I was able to face down a guy with an assault rifle without feeling fear, and now I'm afraid to open the refrigerator. I don't like myself this way, afraid of everything, not knowing the real danger."

Jayson sat at the dinette, organizing Kelsey's unopened mail into several neat piles. "You're human, Kelsey, that's all. Now what happened with that guy with the rifle?"

"I hope you don't mind Healthy Choice for dinner," she said and he shook his head. While making the frozen dinners in the microwave, she told him the story of the raid on Dave Daniels' trailer outside of Naples.

"Shit," Jayson said after hearing the story. "I can't believe some of the things they have you doing. But going there that night was of your own choice, wasn't it? Were you trying to be a hero?"

Kelsey blushed; it was as though Jayson understood her so well. In the way other girls dreamed of being an actress or a ballerina, Kelsey had dreamed of bringing criminals to justice.

"It wasn't just that," she said. "I did get a rush out of solving the case because this guy was clever. He had fooled three or four different law enforcement agencies and he was right there under their noses. Then I went in and basically worked eighteen hours a day unraveling the mess he had left with all the credit card purchases and false ID's. But, that night, I think I really went along because of the guns. I had records of purchases of several guns he had bought. No one would listen to me. Maybe I thought, since I was more alert, I could save somebody. He ended up almost shooting all of us."

A nagging thought was in Kelsey's mind as she told the story, a vague thought that someone like Daniels could be her stalker now.

"What happened to the guy?" Jayson asked.

Kelsey still felt troubled, trying to think. "They actually sentenced him to twenty years in prison. The cops on the case thought that was pretty harsh and, in a way, I agreed. But they had all the federal stuff, like mail fraud, weapons charges and the stuff from that night- assault and battery on a LEO. The funny thing is, I found out Daniels did go to prison but then he got out on an appeal after only eighteen months. So I guess it worked out fairly for everybody."

Jayson looked up at her, eyes narrowed, thoughtfully. "Could this guy, this guy with the guns, be the one who's after you?" he asked.

"I was thinking that myself," Kelsey said. "But it doesn't make much sense. Over a year ago, when he first got out of prison, I had some concern, because he had said something about it being personal the night we first arrested him. One of the deputies involved in the case had even called me to warn me that he was out. But I never heard anything more about him. Anyway, he was just a young punk. When he got free he was probably just glad to get back to his wife and kid..."

Chapter 11

The next day Kelsey came out of the shower and she was overwhelmed by the sound of her stereo playing very loud. Jayson was sitting on her bed, listening to a haunting and bitter song by the group Matchbox 20. Kelsey had heard the song before but never listened to the words. She paused, with her toothbrush in her mouth when the song finished playing, and then she listened attentively while he played it once again.

Kelsey became caught up in the stirring but disturbing lyrics as the song was played over and over. The song was about a bad girlfriend/boyfriend relationship. As Kelsey listened she looked at her own face in the mirror. She looked different these days, pretty and careless with her chestnut hair hanging in sexy loose chunks around her face. She quietly padded out of the bathroom and then stood by the door watching Jayson.

He leaned back on a bunch of pillows propped against the headboard, holding one knee up. His naked, sculptured body was bathed in the pure morning light. In this diffused light, his sexiness was so profound that it struck Kelsey as almost angelic. Jayson held the stereo remote as he sang along with the song. She heard his gentle voice blend with the singer's rougher one. His body was totally still, like it was on the first day she saw him, and his light brown eyes remained fixed on the far distance.

It took a long time until he focused on Kelsey. Then he killed the music, sighed, and watched her blandly. Her cat rolled in a puddle of sun on the carpet, reminding her of Jayson.

"What are you doing?" she accused, "brooding on your miserable song and planning how you're going to leave me?"

Quietly, Jayson said, "I was just getting used to sleeping next to somebody again and it bothers me that you don't seem to want to do that." He sounded very sad.

Kelsey was rocked by the pathos in what he said. She thought about the way she had turned away from him two nights in a row, and how he had tossed and turned, unable to sleep because of it. Jayson's eyes gave no clue what he was feeling, except that there was some very deep hurt.

Kelsey went to him and he stroked her cheek under the loose hair.

"What if something had really happened to you?" he asked.

It was as if he was asking himself as well.

Kelsey understood that this relationship was about being truly in unity with another person. To have that unity, she knew she would have to give up some of her own control, and that thought was very frightening. She knew Jayson wouldn't love her for what he saw on the outside or any image she could manipulate. He would see those internal things, the real Kelsey, which she herself was afraid to see.

"Jayson, I'm not going anywhere," she said. "I wouldn't leave you." She had thought about this and realized it was the truth. "I guess, the past few nights, I was feeling very bad about my body and very vulnerable. That's why I've been pulling away from you. I'm afraid you'll end up getting me to love you and then you'll walk away. It'll all be a big joke."

Jayson's serious gaze told her there were no jokes. "You'd leave me first" he said, quietly. "You're the heartless one here. I suspect all your relationships were only skin deep and you got out when the guys stopped playing by your rules."

Jayson happened to be right; no one else had ever taken the time to see her in a harsh, true light like this.

"Jayson," she asked, "what happened with your ex-girlfriend?"

"She left me," he said. He seemed to have some trouble speaking the words, shielding his eyes momentarily.

"What was she like?" Kelsey asked.

Jayson didn't answer.

Kelsey pushed him, recalling the photo she had seen in his room of the gorgeous model type, with her legs wrapped snugly around his neck. "She was blond, wasn't she? Beautiful?"

"She was blond," he said, "and extremely beautiful."

Even though Jayson could be very good at hiding his feelings, Kelsey was able to see the enormous pain inside him. Instinctively, she moved closer to him, feeling his pain with him, yet also painfully searching out the truth in his eyes.

"She was better than I am, wasn't she?" Kelsey asked. "How can you even look at me?" She curled her trim legs closer to her body, hugged her arms across her chest, and let her hair fall in front of her, hiding her face.

Jayson smiled sardonically, then he shifted position in order to turn her body underneath him. Kelsey was wearing the camisole he had given her for Christmas with lacy beige panties and her legs and belly felt very exposed as he looked her over.

"It's all about looks to you, isn't it?" he asked. "You're able to love my body so much, but yet you hate your own."

"I'm insecure," Kelsey said, as she squirmed under his hand.

Jayson thoughtfully stroked her nipples to hardness through her shirt, then moved down, kneading her tanned slightly rounded belly and rubbing in circles into and around her belly button.

"This is what you hate the most, isn't it?" he asked, "this little tummy?" He was tormenting her, but also exciting her. She understood he was just mocking her own screwed-up priorities.

"You envy my stomach," he said "and you wonder why, no matter what you do, you can't make yours go away." He lowered his head, and licked and sucked the flesh on her belly. Kelsey locked her thighs around his shoulders and pushed, trying to get him off.

Instead, he went lower and she felt his words as breath on her most sensitive skin. "What you need to do, Baby, is a thousand crunches a day, like I do. Discipline yourself."

His laughter tickled her skin, and she went crazy, arching her back and giggling helplessly.

Jayson peeled down her lace underwear with his teeth. Then he glanced at how her pubic hair was shaved, with the bikini wax leaving only a neatly groomed brown patch. Jayson played with this with one finger, seeming fascinated. "You're so neat and perfect," he said, "everything about you, even down to your little pussy. Do you like it when guys lick you down there, Kelsey? Does having the hair gone like this make you feel it better?"

Shame and pride swelled within Kelsey as he finally dipped his tongue into her. There was something about the way he noticed every little thing that made her feel violated, but in a good way.

Now that working toward orgasm was no longer a problem for her, Kelsey's thoughts could go anywhere she wished while they fooled around. Jayson had somehow reached the stereo remote while he was licking her. He turned on an R&B station and her bedroom filled with a

129

sexy Marvin Gaye tune that made her move her hips in languid circles under Jayson's mouth.

"It feels so good, Jayson," she sighed. "How can you possibly be this good at sex?"

He lifted up on his arms, leaving her wet down there, and smiled at her as he crawled up and held his chest above hers.

"We all have one thing that we're best at," he said. Then, scrutinizing her body, he told her, "take off the shirt."

Kelsey peeled the camisole up, feeling self-conscious about her breasts, yet wanting to hear his opinion. Kelsey's breasts were B-cup and pointed, characterized by perky dark nipples and dark areolas that stood way out, like the tops on baby bottles. They were the kind of breasts that didn't really need a bra. Adolescent breasts, Miranda had called them when she had gotten a rare glimpse. Kelsey was usually as shy around her female friends as she was around guys.

"What do you think?" she asked him. "Do you really like big breasts better?"

Jayson thought about it while twirling one painfully hard nipple around his tongue.

"What I love about yours," he said, "is the way they can't be ignored. Your nipples always stand out like you're horny, and meanwhile you try to be all businesslike and serious. So, where else are you shaved?"

Kelsey blushed. Every minute with Jayson was like true confessions, like he wanted to know every single thing that made her tick.

"My legs, okay, and my upper lip."

Jayson looked at her strangely until she began to giggle. Meanwhile he slid his hard-on softly inside her while he hovered around her upper lip with his face, alternately putting his lips and mouth very close, and then pulling them away from the area she had confessed to removing hair from.

"Do you think that you have to do stuff like that to have somebody care about you?" he asked while he made love to her. "You're a naturally darker skinned girl. You think that if your lip got hairy I wouldn't care about you anymore?"

"Jayson," she said seriously, comfortable now talking while they had sex, while she used to stay silent. "No, I really didn't believe men would love me for me. My boyfriends didn't. No matter what was said, there was never really any love there. I didn't love them, either, not really. I've become a different girl since I met you."

Jayson made love to her in slow, beautiful circles, making her whole insides happily mold to him. She had slept with sixteen men in her life, but none had made love anything like this. And none of the men any of her friends had talked about made love anything like this, either. Kelsey knew that the responsiveness she had discovered in herself was not so much about her as it was about Jayson's particular skill. If he ever left she knew that her incredible responsiveness would be gone, too.

As if reading her mind, Jayson asked, "Why, do you think you would love me if it weren't for these muscles and the way I move inside you?"

He moved abruptly and strongly, banging his pelvic bone directly on her clitoris so that Kelsey climaxed long before she should have. And then he watched her eyes as she recovered her breath.

"Is this relationship about more than sex to you?" he asked. "Do you actually love me?"

Kelsey took time to think. She saw what Jayson meant. She couldn't ignore the constant rush of his extraordinary looks or his sexiness. Every second with him she was drenched in the passion that his looks brought her. But he had also become her life. All of a sudden he had become her best friend and confidant as well as her lover.

Jayson's honesty had given Kelsey's life another dimension, a reality that had never been there before. She had recently been confronted with some maniac trying to kill her. And she realized that now life really mattered to her, like it never had before. Now she had someone who cared about her, someone she could talk to, someone whom she could pour her heart out to. Before, she hadn't even known she had a heart.

"Jayson," she said. "I really do love you." It felt difficult for her to say this to him. "At the beginning, I waited to say the words because I had to be sure," she said. "I wanted so badly to be your girlfriend, but somehow I felt I owed you the truth. I couldn't say the words to you until I was sure they were true."

She caressed his face, no longer afraid to reach out and touch his handsomness like she had been in the beginning.

"No matter how you looked," Kelsey told him, "I'd still love you. I'd love you for your soul. You were right about me. I grew up thinking that appearances and society's rules were everything. Maybe in the past I might not have been able to see what's inside you because you're so cute. But now I need what's inside you. I need you in my world."

Jayson caressed her face, looking dreamily at her and holding onto her chin so that she could not escape his gaze. "Kelsey," he said, almost surprised, "You're such an honest person. It's not a trait many girls have. I appreciate that in you."

If Jayson didn't love her, Kelsey couldn't understand it, because it felt so strongly like he did. Just like her own focus in this world was down to one person, she knew that his was also and she was that person. Obviously, she was the most important thing in his life. She wondered why he still wouldn't say the three words.

Jayson lifted Kelsey's hips, kneading her butt cheeks and exciting her again, as he dreamily moved toward his own climax. Kelsey interrupted him.

"Why won't you say the words?" she asked, truly mystified. "Why won't you say that you love me?"

Jayson grunted, with his pleasure seeming to be disturbed by the question.

"I'm setting a different standard for myself for saying those words," he answered. "But you know what you can feel. I wouldn't worry."

It was the oddest statement Kelsey had heard from a boyfriend, yet she still felt totally secure with him. Now he asked something else odd as he slid out of her, still hard.

"Do you have a problem with your own come, putting it in your mouth?"

Kelsey gave him a dumb look because she had a problem with anything sexual, tending to think many things were dirty even though she had done them at one time or another when she was drunk enough. She was totally repelled by giving any blowjob, especially the thought of tasting her own juices on someone's penis.

Jayson chuckled, maneuvering her so she could lie on his chest.

"What am I saying here? Of course you'd have a problem." He smiled. He was mocking her, but it was with love. Like a breath of fresh air, it took her fears away. Jayson would never make demands on her other than for her to try to be herself and not be afraid to look at herself.

She inched down his chest, licking delicately at the smooth humps of pectoral muscles, until he groaned.

"I might surprise you," she said, wickedly, "I might just do it." She checked his eyes for a response, then she licked down lower, and more sloppily, licking and sucking the "thousand crunches a day" abdominal muscles, and feeling a tightness inside her like she wanted to come. Then she humped Jayson's big hard leg, grasping it tightly between both thighs.

He was laughing at her and he had one hand gently on her head, messing up her hair. Now she brought her face down to look at his cock. Like all of him, it was perfect, silky and straight, larger than average but not obscenely large. It throbbed at her and glistened with wetness that

132

she knew had come from her own body. Jayson arched his back with frustration. His cock looked beautiful to her and she wanted to suck on it. With a little sobbing sound, Kelsey eased her lips around it.

"Ohh," Jayson said, like this was the unexpected and he was really letting go. "Kelsey," he whispered, "do it just like this, slowly like this. I can feel you thinking about what you're doing."

He seemed lost in the ecstasy of her slow careful blowjob, the first one she hadn't gagged giving. She darted up her eyes and saw his eyes glazed over, looking around the room lost and dreamy.

"One fantasy I always had," he said, "was to have someone blow me like this, someone who didn't really want to do it, but would do it anyway. And you move so nice and slow. I'm pretending that I'm in the ocean, just floating, and you hold the power to make me feel like that, as long as you keep doing what you're doing."

Jayson's perfect muscular body was floating before her, and she had all the power. She narrowed her eyes, lost in the dream with him. Then she swallowed the hot stream of come that he gave her just on her lips, allowing her to choose to take it or not.

He pulled her up to him, roughly licking the inside of her cheeks clean in consideration, then gently kissing her as she watched him with wide eyes.

"How do you know everything I'm feeling?" she asked.

She felt like her heart was right out there for him, totally bare.

"I just pay attention to you, Kelsey. Hasn't anyone else ever done that for you?" he asked.

They played with each other's bodies, stroking and kissing gently and coming down from the experience they had just shared. Jayson commented on the diamond pendant that Kelsey usually wore in the hollow of her throat, asking where she got it.

"That makes me sad," she said. "It was a gift I got for myself during that time I was working in Naples. I tried to do so many things at that time to make myself feel better..."

"It sounds like that was the low point of your life every time you talk about it," Jayson said.

Something was nibbling at Kelsey's mind but she couldn't get it.

"It was. It sounds horrible, but that's when I realized there was really no hope in adulthood. I was totally alone. That's what it had all been building up to. Miranda coming here, me going out with Paul, that was all a reprieve. But I think that time in Naples told me something about my life, about the darkness that could really be at bottom of it."

"And now?" he asked.

"Now I really want to live, Jayson. This attack on me by whoever's been stalking me has made me see that. I don't just want to protect my life out of stubbornness like I would have done then. I really want to find out what living means."

Kelsey meant every word she said.

Jayson stretched, then got up and padded around the bedroom. "So, where's that necklace I threw at you in the locker room?" he asked her.

Kelsey indicated the dresser and that it was okay for him to go into it. Jayson dug the chain out of the top drawer, examined it, then shook his head because it was not repairable. Then he stroked the surface of the dresser which was a much buffed, glowing light oak. The dresser had cost Kelsey three hundred dollars, but was worth a lot more. Jayson's eyes drifted around the room, taking in everything; the fluffy covers, which were white with blue and green swirls and the groups of big translucent pillar candles in both corners.

There were also two prints by Vincent Van Gogh. One was the familiar "Cafe at Night", which expressed the artist's loneliness and the other, a more delicate painting, was of a branch of almond blossoms. It looked almost Oriental.

"Van Gogh?" Jayson asked, "Both of them?"

Kelsey was surprised Jayson had picked up about the second painting being a Van Gogh also because it looked so different than the artist's usual style. She nodded enthusiastically.

"I relate a lot to Van Gogh," she said. "I think, underneath it all, he had good intentions. He just wanted to believe that certain things *should* work out. But, in real life, you can't make people react predictably- even to great achievement."

Jayson grinned. "Even though you're so perfectly left-brained, Kelsey, I can see how you'd appreciate his unlimited talent. And you also have your special creative side. Your talent shows with your decorating. But it's subtle, so it's not the kind of thing that jumps out at people."

Her naked boyfriend had noticed a hidden- yet meaningful- part of her that most people didn't see at all, because her romantic bent didn't clearly mesh with her usual determined pragmatism. But Kelsey's artistic side also represented hope to her.

"You're right." She nodded happily. "Creative expression does mean a lot to me. It's hard to explain. But it's another way I believe in making a better world."

Jayson padded over and looked more carefully at the bed than he had before. The white wicker headboard was crown-shaped, bent decoratively on both sides and open otherwise. The two bedside tables matched the headboard and Kelsey had the glass cut specially for their tops. Extremely trendy and stylish, the set was also over one hundred years old.

"Your bed's an antique, isn't it?" Jayson asked, "just like that dresser is."

Naked, but partially shielded by the covers, Kelsey swelled with pride.

"That's right, most of the stuff in this apartment is antique. I basically know the history on every item, even that lamp with the shell that you like. On first glance the things appear modern. I deliberately pick things like that, things that are just as striking today as they were a hundred years ago. It's my own little passion."

"It's different," he said. "For a girl your age to appreciate something like that."

Kelsey knew he was implying that she seemed too trendy and shallow to go in for something so stuffy and uncool. But she wasn't bothered by it. When she cared about something, nothing could sway her from it.

"I love antiques," she said, "because there's something more to them than just the object itself. The objects were made to make a difficult life better, to make beauty go along with function."

Jayson hugged Kelsey to him while she untangled her legs to get them around him. "You're really special, Kelsey," he said. "And there's always more to you once someone gets to know you. You're a little girl. But you're solid all the way through. I don't know why no one ever saw that in you before and why you never believed it about yourself."

They went down to the swimming pool later. As Jayson swam laps underwater, Kelsey debated whether she should go ahead with the closing on Wednesday. She loved the condo so. But now her life in it felt threatened. Jayson said he would protect her but Kelsey knew how these stalkers could be. If this was some career criminal with a grudge, they could wait her out until she was unprotected and then strike.

Kelsey remained at the pool, just thinking, while Jayson made a quick run to the gym, leaving her guarded by her senior citizen neighbors, who were all out basking in the glorious weather. She ran upstairs once and retrieved the files she had brought from her office. Then she sat by the pool and studied them in an almost meditative state.

When Jayson got back, he didn't disturb her. He knew what she was trying to figure out. While she remained downstairs he cooked them a spicy stir-fry for dinner. After eating, Kelsey picked up the files again and Jayson went to the living room bookcase, looking for something to read. He chuckled looking over Kelsey's collection of books, which included all the law novels by John Grisham as well as many detective novels.

"Kind of legally oriented, aren't you?" Jayson teased.

He selected a book, took Mr. Cooper onto his lap and read for a while. He finally fell asleep on top of the covers. Kelsey was still at her notes. She had made the decision to stand her ground in the condo. What she needed to do was to use her mind to put together the pieces and understand who was after her. And when she knew the face of the enemy, she would know what to do.

They met at Kelsey's real estate attorney's office in Miramar to complete the closing on the condo. Herself, her attorney and Jayson sat across from another real estate lawyer representing the Eisenbergs. Kelsey was happy to be doing this and she felt highly energized. When the closing was completed they walked out into the sunshine, Kelsey in her close-fitting, pinstriped gray suit and Jayson in dress slacks and a buttery colored shirt, tailored perfectly for him. He took Kelsey out to lunch to celebrate and then she had to go back to work for the afternoon.

This was on Wednesday. Kelsey had been back at her job for two days, although she was no longer on the drug case. Jayson had also returned to his work and his college classes and, so far, things have been fine, at least in the sense that the person stalking Kelsey had made no move.

But things were troubled in another sense at her job. When Kelsey had walked into the office on Monday several pairs of eyes had glanced up at her with guarded looks, as though she had somehow brought the troubles onto herself, and also onto them.

"The police have been here, talking to us," Michael Cole, the computer expert told her, leaning in close to whisper softly, as he walked with her toward the back of the office. "I'm also working on a program to trace all the incoming email," he confided.

It was almost as though someone had told him not to give her this information and he was doing her some kind of favor by informing her. They stopped by her desk and Michael still hovered, looking to her for some kind of reaction.

Then Kelsey discovered the problem; Wendy was sitting there at Kelsey's desk and all of Wendy's junk, including a full mini coffeepot, was cluttering its normally immaculate surface. It looked to Kelsey like they were already giving her job away. Wendy responded to Kelsey's dirty look by bending to retrieve a pair of her sneakers from under the desk, gathering her clutter as best she could and carrying her stuff back towards the front office. Kelsey's boss, Joel Lester, came out of his office, hurrying to explain.

"Kelsey, I just moved Wendy over here while you were gone so she could use your printer." He came to stand by Kelsey as she got settled at her desk. "I'm going to keep you off the road for a while," he said. "There's a case I want you to start on, some receipts for an office supply store not adding up properly and they think one of the employees is going home with some of the cash. The files are already downloaded. You just need to review them."

Kelsey got the distinct vibe that she was no longer wanted at this office. Since she was too scared to stick with the drug case, then it seemed they would give her the least important case they handled. It obviously didn't matter that for almost three years she had been their most dedicated and gutsy employee. Possibly her boss took the stalker seriously and thought Kelsey might not be around long enough to complete anything, or else maybe he thought the attacks on her were her imagination and she could not be trusted.

Her friend, Jerry, came in from the parking lot. When he saw Kelsey he hurried to her and lifted her off the ground to give her a big, tight hug.

"I'm so glad you're back," he said, "so glad you're okay. And you did the right thing in dumping that case."

He said this last in a whisper. He was the only one of her friends who even bothered to say hello.

Later, over lunch at a café near the beach, Jerry explained that the police had been in here asking a lot of questions about how their office did their work. He told Kelsey that the police did not seem happy about Confidential Investigations getting paid for work that should have been police work and then running back to them for protection. The office was on shaky ground already financially, as all the employees knew, and they could not afford this antagonism with the police right now.

"Joel Lester's not going to do anything to protect you, Kelsey," Jerry warned. "He's over his head right now himself. He's scared. Everybody's scared with this one."

"But why me?" Kelsey asked. "If it's the guy from this drug case doing this, why pick on me in particular?"

Jerry just shook his head.

Kelsey completed her retail files and moved on to the next boring case. In her downtime, while Mr. Lester was out of the office, she also made copies of the remainder of files that she had worked on since being at Confidential. She took these home with her to review. There was the possibility that the stalker was not the drug suspect, but rather someone else that she had gotten in trouble a long time ago and who now had a grudge. It could be someone she might not even remember.

Friday afternoon, before Kelsey left for the weekend, she found another message on her Email.

"KELSEY," it read. "PREPARE FOR REPARATION."

Chapter 12

Kelsey was not able to save the message before it vanished, and Michael Cole was not there in time to see it. Apparently his special program was not doing its job. She told Michael and Jerry about this third message but did not even bother telling the others at work.

Kelsey's plans for the weekend involved going with Jayson, Miranda and Juan to a big party at Juan's relatives' home in Miami. She wondered if the stalker would be so brave as to follow her all the way there. It gave her a creepy feeling to consider it, but it did not really ruin her time at the party. She was pretty sure the person stalking her would only strike when she was alone.

Jayson had been sleeping at Kelsey's place every night and, as she had thought, her enemy made no move on her as long as Jayson seemed to be living there, too. Jayson's schedule was back to normal including the nights and this meant him spending many hours at the gym and a lot of time for Kelsey to be alone. She no longer felt really frightened in her condo but she couldn't get away from the constant thoughts, wondering how someone could hate her like this and if she had ever really wronged anyone. Kelsey believed so much in justice herself and it irked her to think that some psycho could consider her to be on the wrong side of things and themselves in the right. But this is how the messages seemed to read.

The weekend with Juan's family had gone fine. Afterwards, the two couples had spent some time hanging out on South Beach, taking photos of the restored art deco hotels and walking with the crowds of tourists and party people on Ocean Drive. Kelsey had felt freer than she had in a long time. And it felt good to her to see Miranda laughing from the heart as she swung down the packed street hand in hand with Juan, a man Kelsey knew could be good for her friend.

Just the next Saturday, though, Kelsey was hearing the craziest news. Jayson told her that Miranda might be talking to Marshall, Joe's ex- partner.

"Remember that little fucker you talked to on the phone?" Jayson asked her, "the one with the filthy mouth who sold cellular service? Well, your friend's thinking about dating him or working for him or something. She just used my phone to call the guy before I realized who it was she was calling."

Kelsey felt shocked, like she had the air knocked out of her. Jayson was calling from the gym where Miranda must be also. She had expected him to be back at the condo by now. He had promised. They had agreed to be at Kelsey's lawyer's office to pick up copies of the papers on the closing sometime before one-o'clock today, which is when the lawyer closed his office for the weekend.

Kelsey had said that she thought Jayson trying to squeeze in a workout in the morning would be trying to put too much into the day now that they had the meeting scheduled with the lawyer. But Jayson didn't want to postpone the workout, and lose out on the special afternoon they had planned, lunch on Hollywood Beach and then a four o'clock matinee at a nearby theater. Jayson got up very early to go to the gym and promised to be back at her place by noon, which would give them just enough time to get to the lawyer's office before it closed.

Now it was almost noon and Jayson was asking Kelsey to talk to Miranda, who she could hear talking wildly in the background. Why did Miranda always have to have her crises on someone else's time?

Kelsey could hear the ugly snap of impatience in her own voice but she couldn't help it.

"Tell her I'll call her when we leave the lawyer's. Not that we're going to make it, anyway! Do you know what time it is? Maybe I should just go by myself."

Her voice dripped with bitterness and she was aware of how out-of-proportion her annoyance might seem to Jayson. But she felt justified. She had warned him that the timing wouldn't work.

"No, don't do that," he said. "Give me ten minutes and I'll be there. I can do a lot with my bike in traffic."

Kelsey was waiting for him downstairs in her car with the passenger door unlocked and wide open. She started out all huffy but then Jayson captured her in a deep, sensual kiss, working on her mouth like it was a more intimate part of her body. Kelsey became lost in it, forgetting and forgiving everything.

When Jayson pulled away he looked into her face and said to her, "You're my life, Kelsey, you know that?"

Her body tingled and her mind replayed what he had told her as she drove toward I-95.

She had to pull her hand out of his to grasp the wheel with both hands as she made her merger onto the highway. Glancing into the mirror, she noticed cars and trucks packed in with no gaps. The people today seemed like nasty drivers, no one wanting to let them in, as usual. Kelsey made a swift move to take her place in traffic, just as she did every day commuting. Now she brought her speed up, and joined with the stream of traffic at about seventy-five miles an hour, staying alert and attentive because, every so often, all three full lanes would abruptly hit their brakes. Delays were almost as frequent now on Saturdays as on workdays.

Kelsey scanned the rear-view mirror occasionally, watchful for the creeps who would dart between you and the vehicle in front of you before there was even a full car length open. This, combined with the sudden application of brakes up front, could lead to an accident if you were daydreaming. Kelsey had seen enough of it on her way to work every day on the clogged highway. An auto accident was one thing she did not need. Kelsey had a clear driving record and low insurance, despite her newer car. She despised this road and the sprawl that led to it and she didn't intend to let it mess with her.

"What are you thinking?" Jayson asked her.

"Just that they planned this all so badly," she said. "Florida was so brand new. It could have been a model for the rest of the country. Instead, they let the developers' greed run wild."

"It's everybody, though," Jayson said. "It's the average person, everyone driving here today. They're the ones who let the developers do what they do."

Probably Jayson was right. Kelsey looked at all the cars and sport utility vehicles jumping from lane to lane, all in a hurry. The drivers' anger and dissatisfaction were apparent in how they drove. Many of the drivers were hiding behind tinted glass and others had faces set in stony masks. All these cars looked brand new, although this could be deceptive as Florida weather tended to preserve auto finishes. Meanwhile, large trucks belched out smoke and hovered aggressively behind Kelsey's small car.

"I hate this," she said.

She noticed how Jayson was sprawled in his seat, legs spread, with his magnificent leg muscles bulging against his faded jeans, while the hard-on he had from their kiss slowly faded.

Almost flirtatiously, Kelsey requested, "Could you put on your seat belt?"

Jayson grinned back at her. "You're not Miranda. I don't think I need to worry."

But it was Kelsey's way to worry. She was sandwiched between trucks. The small truck in front, which came from a Spanish food market, seemed to be burning oil. The eighteen-wheeler in back, a furniture truck, weaved impatiently but was unable to get into the other lane to pass because of the traffic. Kelsey was gnawing her lip, holding the wheel tightly.

"Just do it for me," she said. "I've got these two trucks here and I've got thirty minutes to make a forty-minute drive!"

Jayson put on the seat belt, responding to the unmistakable premenstrual tension that Kelsey could hear in her own voice.

"Might as well pass the guy in front," Jayson suggested.

"I will," she said, through gritted teeth, "if I get the space."

Now Kelsey saw the space open up and made her move into the middle lane. She was gratified that the spot was too small for the mean trucker in the furniture truck to follow her for now.

Jayson seemed amused. "You're so aware of every other car. That's good, although it must drive your girlfriend nuts."

"You know," Kelsey said. "Miranda is really starting to scare me. I'm spending all my time with you and it's like she's going totally out of control. I don't know if I can carry the responsibility for her right now."

Jayson began talking about Miranda but Kelsey was distracted. Something felt wrong under her; something was grating, possibly in her engine.

"Jayson!" she said, "there's a noise, something in the engine. Something's wrong."

He looked at her blankly. "Are you sure?"

The noise of the truck behind them was so loud now that it drowned out any sound from inside the car. The trucker was back on their tail. But how so suddenly?

They had to be losing speed. Kelsey pushed harder on the gas. It went down spongily and there was none of the thrumming response she was used to from the engine. Instead, a deep shuddering came from the very bowels of the car. The speedometer showed seventy dropping to sixty.

"My God," Kelsey breathed. A choked sob came out of her throat. "The car is dying."

Jayson swung around to check traffic behind them. Kelsey had already checked it in her mirrors. She was boxed in completely in both lanes.

She knew Jayson was thinking, trying to think of something to help them. But there was no time. The car they were in was now dead completely, in an instant. She had no electrical power at all and the power steering was gone. The brakes could just get them killed unless she could first get the car onto the shoulder, and then stop it.

The truck behind them was going to hit them. Kelsey knew this. If it did, they would spin out of control into the other lanes of traffic. And they would die.

Kelsey stayed very calm, her lip clenched between her teeth, her hands tight on the wheel, deliberately breathing in extra oxygen. She saw Jayson in the corner of her eye, the man she loved. The decision was hers.

They were down to fifty miles an hour now; any slower and there would be no chance.

Kelsey anticipated a hole between a cream-colored Lincoln and a green Chevy Blazer that would open for her in the inside lane in one second if she kept losing speed at the rate she was. They were by the Broward Boulevard exit. Kelsey remembered a wide area at this exit, where the shoulder mixed with on and off ramps on an overpass. It was not a good place to do this. But she had to go.

She experienced the light color of the Lincoln flitting past. Then Kelsey jerked the wheel hard to the right. The horn of the furniture truck blared, like a horrible noise exploding from out of her own insides.

Something jerked them. Kelsey hung fast to the wheel as the car spun. Then there was a screeching sound of metal as something was torn from her car. The green Chevy Blazer was right up by Jayson's window. Kelsey pulled the wheel to the left, straightening her car. For a moment their nose pointed forward. She lost more speed and saw the Blazer pass them on the left, weaving crazily down the road. Kelsey's Avenger was still sliding, with the rear of the car leading now.

"God!" Kelsey said, "the exit lanes."

They were dancing through the exit lanes, led by the back of the car. Cars swerved around them, horns blaring. Kelsey saw the glare of sunlight off the cars. Another car sideswiped them. Now they went into a total spin.

"I'm not dying," Kelsey said.

She clung harder to the wheel, trying to get any control, deliberately getting rid of more speed by completing the spin. They hit the guardrail glancingly with Kelsey's front quarter panel, which folded up like it was made of paper. Then the car finished with her door against the guardrail. Something burst out of the wheel, hitting Kelsey in the face and chest and hurting her. For a second she thought it was part of the accident, then she realized it was the air bag. She tried to push around it to see Jayson.

He was already out of his seat belt on his knees, reaching for her. "Kelsey, are you hurt? I need to get you out of the car!"

"I'm fine," she said and she helped him to wrestle her out his side of the car. She was overwhelmed by the noise of traffic as they got out of the car and stepped onto the road. Her car was facing backwards, facing the traffic entering the road from the ramp. Cars whizzed by within inches of them, blaring their horns as Jayson pulled Kelsey further from her car and toward the guardrail.

He shielded her from the noise and confusion with his body and he stroked her hair, as he watched the car, maybe to see if it was going to blow up. Kelsey gave a sob as she glanced out of the corner of her eye. It didn't matter. Her beautiful red car was now an ugly wreckage anyway.

"I can't believe this happened," Kelsey said. "This isn't right!"

"Kelsey," Jayson said, pulling her face up to look into her eyes. "You saved our lives. That's all that matters."

He kept stroking her and checked on the bruised left side of her body. He called 911 on his cellular while the one million indifferent drivers slashed by them. It was very hot. Kelsey pulled away from Jayson and insisted on walking back to the car alone to get her purse.

It was amazing how things could change so quickly. This car had symbolized her energy for the past two years. Now it was curled at the side of the road, with part of its hood arched in what looked like a sneer, its rear bumper torn off, deep dents where several cars had hit it and a big white blob in the driver's seat. Kelsey's leather purse lay between the seats, undisturbed. She grabbed it and pulled registration and insurance cards from the glove compartment.

At times like this Kelsey tended to stay unemotional.

"What do you think happened?" her boyfriend asked her when she got back to him.

"It's the stalker," she said with conviction. "He did something to my car."

"Well," Jayson said, "then you are not going back to that job!"

His voice raised and he took a step back from her. He looked furious. "I am not going to stand by and watch you get killed for that fucking job!"

Kelsey started to cry. She knew that he was right.

Now Jayson paced, yelling at the cars on the Interstate. "If you're out there you fucker, leave her alone! Come for me! Why don't you come for me!"

He screamed until he was hoarse, then held he her close again. "I just feel bad," he said. "I feel like I'm powerless against this."

Kelsey felt afraid, too, because this time she could have died and her enemy would have killed Jayson also. If anything had been different, if she had handled the car any differently, the eighteen-wheeler would have taken them instead of just the bumper. If she hadn't told Jayson to put on his seat belt...

It had suddenly gotten cloudy. A damp smoggy breeze blew and Jayson faced into it, towards the approaching police car.

"Baby," Kelsey said, leaning her head against him. "I'm sorry for all of this. I really do love you."

The two police officers that arrived on the scene insisted that they tow the car off the highway. Kelsey began to feel lightheaded in the two hours it took to get her car towed to a garage one block off the exit. The garage charged her an outrageous eighty-five dollars just for the tow, and they insisted on cash, so that Jayson had to pay for it. Then the head mechanic took them aside, right before closing. There was no doubt the car was totaled but Kelsey had demanded that the garage search for the engine problem that caused the accident.

The mechanic, a man in his thirties with wet dark hair, looked at Kelsey's thighs in her short skirt as he spoke. Then he looked up into her face like she was crazy, or tainted in some way.

"That engine's blown. You had no oil in that car. Looks like somebody drained it out the pan, then disconnected part of your electrical so you'd have no idiot light. Does somebody have it in for you?"

He looked at Jayson, obviously noting the muscles and the striking good looks and probably thinking that he and Kelsey were having some torrid sexual affair.

"Has she got a jealous ex boyfriend or something?" the mechanic asked Jayson, all the while leering at Kelsey as though he could understand how a girl like her could get a guy in trouble.

Back at the condo, Kelsey went immediately into the bathroom, put the water in the shower on and then sat down on the toilet seat. This had been the longest damn day and she had the feeling that they were only going to get harder. Nothing was certain anymore. She would no longer have a job to go to after tomorrow morning because what happened today would leave her no option but to quit. She no longer had a car. Tomorrow morning when she woke up she would have no direction. Sure, Jayson was with her but he could leave any time he chose to. She had never felt so at sea.

Kelsey started talking to herself. "I can't believe I bought this condo now. What am I going to do? I can't believe I put myself in a situation like this. That damn road! It finally got me. That damn I-95! It finally won!"

She leaned over her legs and, shielded by the noise of the water, she dissolved into huge sobs that shook her body. She could not deal with the feeling of helplessness. It was even worse than the fact that someone was stalking her and maybe wanting to kill her.

"I can't do this," she cried. "I can't do this anymore..."

Kelsey's face was wet with tears and her body slick with condensation from the steam. Her empty stomach heaved with her sobs. A while later Jayson opened the bathroom door.

"Do you really need to do this alone?" he asked her.

It took a while for Kelsey to go into his arms.

Late at night, instead of sleeping, they made love. Jayson stroked her face gently in the semi-darkness and Kelsey reached for him with her lips and her fingers.

"Don't worry, sweetheart," he said. "Don't even think about the problems tonight. Just make love to me."

He cupped Kelsey's back with one strong hand, pulling her closer to him and moving her in languorous circles on his body. His thrusts were in rhythm with his kisses. It was so easy to become lost in the sensations of making love to him. The feelings that she shared with him were so beautiful. They were nothing like those edgy feelings she used to have in bed with other guys when she'd strive so hard for orgasms that never came. Now Kelsey felt connected to all of nature and the universe. Jayson said that when she gave him a blowjob he felt he was floating in the ocean. That's how he made her feel. Like she was right now floating in that nighttime ocean and there was no danger anywhere.

"I love you," she said.

Jayson looked deeply into her eyes and took turns kissing her upper and lower lips. His penis was deep inside her now. It brought feelings that she never could have imagined.

"It's just us, Kelsey," he said. "We're together now. Just you and me."

She had tears at the corners of her eyes and imagined maybe that he did too. They had been locked together like this for two hours. The way Jayson moved, the slow trance-like way, meant that he could make love to her all night long. It was ironic how different this was from the quickie in the locker room that first day.

Kelsey brushed her hands over Jayson's hard butt cheeks as he worked inside her. It was a perfect rear end, the cups molded in steely muscle, moving powerfully and gracefully. Feeling her gorgeous lover's ass brought up an excitement in Kelsey so that she felt like she was going to climax.

Jayson was singing to her under his breath, some rock song sung like a lullaby, while he kissed and nibbled at her neck.

Suddenly, the image came to her of her little car huddled by the side of the road. Someone else's deliberate action had ruined something that was so beautiful to her. She hadn't even realized how much she had cared about it.

"My car!" she cried, but quietly, trying to muffle it by biting against Jayson's shoulder muscle. And she really felt lost then because her orgasm came, dark and delicious and transporting her away. It was mixed with her tremendous sobs of despair.

Jayson finally went to sleep. He had a long day to face tomorrow. He would take Kelsey to her office to clean out her desk, then to the gym where he planned to leave her for part of the day while he ran to meet a client at his office. It was as though he had to baby-sit her every moment now to keep her safe.

Jayson slept so peacefully, with his muscles in repose, the blanket pulled almost completely over him. He had the face, with the white blond hair, of one of those little boys in the posters, the kind they show saying their nightly prayers. He breathed softly, just ruffling the edge of the covers. The gentle curve of his features, which embodied innocence and tranquillity, were so at odds with the imposing bulk of his body that lay hidden under the covers. She loved this man so much. At the moment, Jayson was her only assurance that the world was still a good place.

Kelsey had pulled her limbs out of his. There was no way she was going to sleep tonight. In fact, she could never remember having a night of truly untroubled sleep. Her nerves always got the better of her, sometimes for no apparent reason. And now her weariness didn't matter. The strain on her nerves could only get worse, with the ordeal she was involved in. She wished she could be like Jayson, worrying about the problems of each day only, living in the present. She wished that she could sleep deeply one night like he did.

147

It was three in the morning when Kelsey realized that she had forgotten Miranda.

"Shit!" she said out loud, angry with herself. She leaned over to kiss Jayson on the shoulder. Then she crawled out of bed to go in the other room so she wouldn't disturb him with her call.

"Miranda!" She felt like crying when the other girl answered, wide-awake. "I'm sorry I forgot to call," she said.

There was silence.

"Miranda, someone tried to kill me today," she said bluntly.

"What!"

"We were on I-95," Kelsey said. "Someone tried to sabotage my car. That damn, horrible highway..."

She started to sob again, this time making no effort to hide it. The thought of that road was somehow her breaking point. It symbolized all that she feared in South Florida, the impersonality, the impermanence- and the constant danger.

"Miranda, I feel so terrible now, like I so deeply did the wrong thing buying this condo. How can I ever live here?"

"You poor girl," Miranda said. Kelsey could hear that her friend spoke from the heart. For the moment, with her boyfriend there in bed and her friend here on the other end of the phone, she felt like she really could be safe.

The next day Kelsey was going to go into Confidential Investigations, clean out her desk, tell Mr. Lester that she quit and walk out forever. Miranda was very happy to hear this and she told her friend that she was definitely doing the right thing. Miranda could be practical when she had to and so she suggested that she spend the day with Kelsey after the desk was cleaned out, so that she could keep an eye on her in case the stalker showed up. She could stay at the condo rather than Kelsey having to sit at the gym all day and she could help her friend make plans.

"It is a good idea," Kelsey said. She appealed to Jayson the next day. "You can do what you have to do. I'll be safe with Miranda."

After all, Miranda was no longer a suspect in Kelsey's mind. She wasn't exactly the type to fool with a car. Kelsey felt ashamed for even thinking Miranda could have done any of the other things.

Jayson kissed her and winked at her, agreeing with her idea about letting Miranda come over so she would be safe. "Whatever you want," he said. "Today's your day."

"You know what my idea is," Miranda said when she got to Kelsey's place. "Instead of getting another job investigating, you can work with me. I'll get you a job at the department store."

She was trying to sound really bright and upbeat, but when they embraced Kelsey could feel her best friend trembling. And Miranda felt so frighteningly thin. Kelsey hadn't realized how much her friend had been changing.

"Florida's really done a number on us, hasn't it?" Kelsey said.

Miranda laughed and embraced the smaller girl again, seeming more lighthearted. "You're lucky to have Jayson," she said. "He really cares about you."

"I know," Kelsey said, "and I'm trying to learn to accept that, even with all that's happening. Now what's this with you?" she asked. "About Marshall? I thought we agreed that those guys were borderline criminals."

Miranda went to the doorway to smoke and Mr. Cooper skittered out of her way.

"I wouldn't worry about Marshall," she said. "I was just talking to him. I wanted to leave my options open on the job front. And he's not that bad once you learn how to get past all his manipulating. Now, why not talk about something more interesting? Like your sex life with Jayson."

Kelsey folded herself onto the couch. She realized that she felt willowy and sensual, wearing cutoff shorts and the camisole that Jayson had given her at Christmas. She rubbed at her own throat as if remembering his touch.

"It's wonderful, Miranda," she said. "I'm not the same person that I was. I feel as though I have more patience with the whole world now that I see the kind of bliss a person can experience. Do you know at all what I mean?"

Miranda smiled wearily, yet indulgently, as she gazed down at the parking lot, which was now all cream and white and gold vehicles, minus Kelsey's standout red car.

"I could understand it, I guess," Miranda said. "It's what we all dream about, to feel like that. Even I do, even though I'm so cynical. I can come my brains out with any guy off the street. But to have time stand still for me like that, the way it does for you with Jayson, I've never been there."

"Jayson really is the best," Kelsey said. "It's like his looks don't even say anything about him, compared to what he's like in bed. He knows it and he's not ashamed of it. He's not boastful. It's just like he's deliberately forced me to feel sexuality in the intense way he does."

"I could tell that about him, I guess, that he was really good in bed," Miranda said thoughtfully.

And Kelsey suddenly thought about it. Miranda still didn't know about the time in the locker room. So she would still think that she had been the first of the two friends to get close to Jayson. And there was too much water under the bridge for Kelsey to explain all that now.

"I'm sorry," she told Miranda. "Possibly it could have been you."

Miranda shook her head. "Not like that," she said. "I can see what you two mean to each other. I think that you really do belong together. It's obvious that he loves you."

Miranda's words echoed in her head and Kelsey felt the memory of Jayson inside her last night and she blushed with happiness. Suddenly, and at such an odd time in her life considering the physical threats being made against her, Kelsey felt that all was right with the world.

"I really do want to live," Kelsey said and she described in detail the incident with her car as Miranda slid down the doorframe, her bellbottoms filling half the doorway. Miranda listened seriously and was silent for a while even after Kelsey finished talking.

"Get back here!" Kelsey yelled suddenly, as Mr. Cooper had made an uncharacteristic run for the open air. At Kelsey's reprimand, he slunk back toward the bedroom. "He senses my troubles, I think," Kelsey said.

Miranda looked up at her. "I would think that the stalking would stop now. The guy scared you off your job and now you're not able to testify about any of the evidence in court. I personally think that it was your job that led to this stalking. I know Jerry agrees. He said after the thing with the milk that you should have gotten out. Even he's looking for another job. If anything else happens, though, even the slightest thing, take a vacation up to New York. The kind of creeps from here are not gonna follow you up there."

"I thought of it," Kelsey said.

But going back to New York and selling the condo would mean giving up on the Nova University grad program. She knew she could always apply to another college somewhere up North. The real problem was Jayson, a man who swam in the ocean three hundred and sixty-five days a year and who got orgasmic basking in the Florida sun, a man who often shivered when she left the window open on a sixty-degree night. The payoff for Kelsey would be that she would finally feel safe. But she knew Jayson would never agree to move to New York. She didn't even know if right now she wanted to herself.

"I can't decide yet," she told her friend. "I'm so confused with what I want."

Kelsey licked her lips because an idea was starting to form in her mind, an idea with good energy. "You know," she said, "I've got all this free time right now..."

Instead of filling her with dread, the concept of being jobless for the first time since she was fifteen years-old filled her with energy now, so that she squirmed on the couch and Miranda came over to sit by her.

"Well, what are you so crazed about?" her friend asked.

"I've got the time," Kelsey said. "I could go home on a visit. I could even bring Jayson."

Something felt so right, like this visit had been so overdue, and fate was letting it happen, like things were coming full circle, her boyfriend, her family, her friends, everything together. Like as a kid you know the adult things you'll have in life, but not who the principles would be. Now she was seeing the circle, those people who might forever represent her life. It was a warm feeling.

Kelsey grinned and Miranda replied cynically. "I guess it would be a way to call your Mom and tell her you just lost your job and have her be blissfully happy instead of getting mad at you."

They laughed together like conspirators.

Chapter 13

The Watcher thought about Kelsey. By avoiding the car accident, she had escaped an end that could have been the most merciful. Thoughts of her were in one corner of his mind, while the rest of it waited, resting and taking in the sounds of the night outside.

There was the brassy laughter of the tourist girls, along with that of their mothers and grandmothers, the generations mingling. The revelers went about the patterns of their lives while the wind carried away the sounds of their voices. He did not concern himself with them.

So many things had to be given up in this quest. He understood that it was unusual to be able to see both the beginning and the ending of one's own life, with both connecting to a particular space in the middle where things had gone awry. One single night, one prideful human being had deliberately messed with the scheme of things.

Kelsey Reed had stepped up when she shouldn't have, where she shouldn't have, and had altered fate itself. She had upset the delicate balance of how things were supposed to go in the world. The Watcher knew this.

Just as the God of the Hebrews was a vengeful and unforgiving one, so the Watcher was unforgiving. Justice was his only purpose now.

He sat on his bed, as he had so many nights in prison, thinking. Only here, there was no one to spy on expressions of emotion that might pass over his face just as an afternoon thunderstorm would blow in through the summer day.

He took out the photograph that was getting ragged. He noted this, but didn't worry, because the time that would end his needing it was soon approaching.

The girl in his photo was blond, big boned and gorgeously plump, her smile exploding off the paper. Sunlight mixed in her windblown messy hair, shimmering in it like the purest gold he remembered.

Her love for him and for life itself seemed to burst forth, with no self-consciousness. She had been so happy that day. Behind her in the photo there was a banner for the South Florida Fair and a crowd of people in their merry-making. He could still remember everything.

The woman was laughing; her shirt pulled partly aside as she reached to catch the big red stuffed dog he had thrown to her just before he snapped the picture. The tops of her full breasts were spilling partway out of her loose cotton shirt, looking so plump and ready and full of life.

With one hand the Watcher stroked his lover's blond hair in the picture and, with the other, he reached down and touched himself, stroking himself to an erection. Slowly, he caressed himself, bringing forth the excitement, as he concentrated hard on the woman's eyes.

As he came, in huge violent bursts, two large tears squeezed out of the watcher's tightly closed eyes.

Chapter 14

They were on their way to New York State and Kelsey felt immediately better as their flight rose up into the air. It had been almost a month since the last incident with the stalker, and nothing had happened since, but Kelsey felt physically better getting away. There was this feeling that whoever had targeted her was somehow linked to Florida and would not ever follow her back home to New York.

"I can't wait to see my parents." Kelsey spoke enthusiastically. "They're really the most wonderful people. You're going to love them."

"Then why are you so nervous?" Jayson asked. He rubbed her arm and looked at her from under lowered lashes.

They took a rental car for the four-hour trip to Endicott and Jayson drove the entire trip. Along the way, the state highway wound through farmland and hills covered with snow and crossed several rushing icy rivers. The pavement was dry today, although at other times it could be snowy and treacherous. Kelsey knew she should really be the one driving the winding highway but, since the wreck of her car, she'd felt better letting others do her driving for her.

Jayson looked so confident; with his massive legs in tight jeans sprawled comfortably as he maneuvered the dark green luxury sedan. She wondered what it would be like to still be with him when they would both be forty years old. She got the feeling he would be just as commanding, still taking care of her like he was doing now. As he drove he glanced up at the unfamiliar hills inquisitively, he asked her questions about her past and they spent the hours long drive talking about her experiences growing up.

Kelsey's home was on the Susquehanna River- a stately, old three-story farmhouse on several well-trimmed acres with the wide river flowing behind it. Kelsey perked up at the sweet familiar smell of the property. She could smell the thaw in the breeze, almost like the coming of spring.

"This is impressive, very peaceful," Jayson said, warming himself in the first beam of sunlight that had broken through that day, obviously enjoying the view and in no hurry to move from his corner of the car.

"That river is moving fast," he commented.

He was right. The normally sluggish and mellow river was moving hurriedly, looking abnormally swollen in its banks.

"It's the thaw," Kelsey said. "We usually don't see it like this until spring."

She stepped out of the car and squinted at the river, appraising. It felt good to be able to read nature the way she could with the river. She had learned its every mood and nuance since she was four years old and her family had first moved into the house.

Kelsey and Jayson now saw the two young children coming down the front stairs, holding hands, helping each other. She hadn't remembered how small and vulnerable her niece and nephew were, with their unzipped jackets hanging over layers of bulky sweaters and gathered wool caps on their heads. They looked so serious. The older Melissa would not hurry forward until her smaller brother, Cody, had safely made it down the final step.

Then they approached the adults cautiously, not freely as she'd expected. She saw her sister come out of the front door, pulling her Navajo patterned blanket coat around her. When the children got near Kelsey, they broke their grip with each other and they ran towards her, now the same eager kids she remembered.

Melissa broke into a big smile, showing new white teeth that had replaced the baby ones. "Auntie Kelsey! You're here!"

Her wild strands of reddish hair blew around them as Kelsey bent. Melissa grabbed her around the neck in a bear hug and Kelsey lifted her up.

The shyer Cody came to Kelsey and hugged her around the knees. He turned his face up to glance at her as she pushed his silly hat off and ruffled his silky hair. Kelsey noticed how the hair was long and needed a cut. She had missed these children so much.

Melissa cuddled against Kelsey, charming her into agreeing that she and Jayson would take the children to the carousel at the zoo and to the mall. Then she looked over at Jayson.

"Why are you shivering?" she asked him.

He was visibly shivering in his leather jacket; and he had his hands tucked into his jeans' pocket for warmth. He laughed at the child's question, exaggerating the shakes to make the kids laugh.

"I'm from Florida, hon; this is all new to me."

Kelsey set her niece down and Melissa went closer to Jayson and looked up at him with a squint. "You never seen snow before?"

"Na- Uh." Jayson shook his head, looking miserably around him so that even Kelsey laughed out loud.

Sarah had stalked up to them. She laid an arm over Kelsey's leather coat, fingering the material, while blowing smoke in the other direction so it wouldn't get in Kelsey's face.

To Jayson she must look so much like Miranda. The only difference was that Sarah's hair, cut in long wild layers, was light brown rather then red and it was straight rather than curly. Kelsey's sister was tall and lanky. Her abrupt movements and high cheekbones made her look snippy and pissed off.

Sarah was just like Miranda except for the hair, and the red hair had shown up in her kids. But the children didn't share their mother's keen expression. They had wide placid faces inherited from their father.

"I'll show you how to make a snowman," Melissa offered Jayson.

But Cody interrupted, looking up at Kelsey's boyfriend like a little cherub and saying, "My mom says Auntie Kelsey always dates losers. Are you a loser?"

Jayson smiled from ear to ear, bent and brought both children into a spontaneous hug. Then he looked up at Kelsey while he staged-whispered to them, "Your aunt loves me for only one thing. It's the special way I tickle her. I give no mercy!"

He backed up and then he lunged at Kelsey, grabbed her around the waist, and wrestled with her as she laughed uncontrollably. Then he made a show of just noticing the giggling children.

"Now I'm going to get you guys!"

Jayson loped around the big trees in the yard, making a fool of himself chasing the kids, who were flushed and laughing and who started throwing snowballs at him.

"Ooooo, owww!" he yelled when their missiles connected.

Kelsey's Dad came lumbering up from the back yard, wearing a hunting coat and a red cap with flaps over the ears. He was shaking his head at the foolishness going on. Kelsey could see from a distance how drastically he had aged, even though he had not lost any of his bulk.

"He's *not* still working outdoors?" Kelsey asked her sister.

"If he doesn't, he sits inside and drinks," Sarah said. "What are we supposed to do?"

Kelsey shook her head helplessly. When her dad got there he took her in a bear hug. He swung her around off her feet before she could stop him.

"How's my little girl?" he asked, heartily. "Still taking up with the losers, I see." He indicated Jayson, who was rolling on the snow with the two little children beating on him.

But her father's broad face was lit up with delight. She could see the cares lifting from him. And she noticed her sister smirk, evidence of a jealousy that was many years old.

"So, are you staying home this time, Kelsey?" her father asked. "Your mother and I pray every night that you'll come home to us. It's not the same without you here. Your Mom's heart is broken..."

"It's true," Sarah said bitterly. "All they do is obsess about you."

Jayson had dusted himself off and he stepped up, smiling brightly, to shake Kelsey's father's hand. The older man locked eyes with Jayson as they shook. He was the taller, but Jayson had the slightly broader build. Kelsey could sense the feeling of a contest between the two of them.

Her Dad narrowed his eyes in a show of disdain for the sculptured muscles that showed through the gap in Jayson's open jacket.

"We had a saying for guys that liked to build their bodies like that in the army," he drawled. "Somethin' don't seem quite natural, a man wants to build up his muscles like that just to look pretty..."

It was a tense, silent moment as their hands fell out of each other's and they stood there glaring. Kelsey was afraid Jayson would throw a punch and her father's heart would kill him in the subsequent fight. Instead, Jayson knitted his brow thoughtfully, then gave a little laugh.

"You're right," he said. "My Pop taught me the value of a day's hard work. You got something needs done around here, point me at it."

Then he stood up tall, totally unashamed of his massive body, as though he was standing before his own father.

She sensed her Dad connect with Jayson's sincerity. He whacked her boyfriend on the shoulder before heading inside to tell her Mom they were there.

"Oh, I got plenty for you to do!" he said.   And the big man laughed to himself until he wheezed, as he walked away.

While Jayson watched Kelsey's retreating father, Sarah was watching him.

"I'd sell my soul for a piece of that," she said to Kelsey, leaning over to speak in Kelsey's ear and indicating Jayson. "It just shows up how hopeless things are between me and Todd."

"Are you really going to get divorced?" Kelsey asked.

"It looks that way. Maybe me and the kids can come visit you down in Florida for a while," Sarah said.

"Sure," Kelsey told her.

Her sister prowled over to Jayson and she looked over the swelling muscles under his shirt, and then down at the crotch of his faded jeans.

"Are you for real?" she asked.

"I'm not sure how you mean that," Jayson said calmly.

Sarah tossed her hair and stuck out a hip. "If you're not sure, then you must not be," she said.

Jayson let just the slightest bit of sexuality darken his eyes. When he acted this way, it was about anger, Kelsey knew.

"Well, if you need to ask me, then I guess you're not for real either," he said and he smirked in Sarah's face, rejecting her.

Sarah stomped off, calling her kids and Jayson walked toward the house with his arm around Kelsey. "I'm sorry about my family," she said to him.

"I don't mind your Dad. He just wants me to prove myself. Nobody's good enough for his little girl. But I can't believe your sister."

"She does it with all my men since junior high," Kelsey said. "It's no big deal."

Kelsey's mother met them at the door, wiping her hands on a dishtowel. She grabbed Kelsey in a crushing hug and Kelsey felt months and years worth of tension slip out of her mother's petite body as the older woman choked back sobs.

"You're home, my angel, you're finally home!" Then she stepped back to look at Kelsey, who was wiping away her own tears. "You're different," her mom said. "You've grown up. You must really be in love this time."

She let go of Kelsey's hands to take Jayson's. "You really love her, don't you?" she asked.

"She's my life," Jayson said. Her mother caught him in a hug and then jumped away. "You're soaked! And freezing. You poor boy. Go upstairs and get changed. We gave you the guestroom. I'll get you an old coat of Edward's for later. When you get down, we'll have some coffee and cake."

"It's your Valentine's cake, Kelsey. Me and Cody frosted it!" Melissa said. She and her brother each took Kelsey by one hand and pulled her toward the kitchen.

Her father already had an assignment for Jayson. He wanted help cutting a tree apart that had fallen at the river's edge.

"It's the big oak that fell," he told Kelsey. "It's lying halfway across the damn back yard. That tree that you used to fish off of when you were a little girl."

Kelsey lingered with the other women over coffee and the heart shaped cake. She watched her father through the back windows, as he strode towards the tree. Jayson followed wearing a light colored plaid jacket that belonged to her father and both men were carrying chain saws.

Mary Reed looked pretty in a new peach colored dress. Her hair was freshly dyed and cut into a stylish bob. She was not usually a high maintenance woman and it was obvious she had done this for Kelsey's and Jayson's benefit.

Before the men went outside, her Mom had embarrassed Kelsey by telling Jayson what was on the menu for dinner. "I made a pork tenderloin, scalloped potatoes and regular baked. I didn't know if you ate meat, Jayson, so I also made a nice macaroni and cheese casserole, just in case..."

Kelsey knew how her family must look to Jayson, like some caricature out of the nineteen-fifties. But it was really like that in her home. The meal her mother had made for tonight was not that different from everyday, and her family really did try to live by traditional values. The only dark cloud had been her father's tenancy to drink too much, and the resultant damage to his health. There had been a bad time when she was six years old. Sarah was in the hospital, her father lost a job and they almost lost the house. But, as they did with everything else, they had come through that hard time together.

Kelsey's father had been in for several bypass surgeries in the past four years and his medical bills had depleted a lifetime of savings. But the family still had the house and each other and Kelsey was confident they'd come through this like they did everything else.

Kelsey's mother stood at the window, with her eyes moist and tired in her otherwise bright appearance. "I worry about your father," she said, "when he does work like this."

"Don't worry," Kelsey said. "I talked to Jayson. He knows not to let Dad really do anything, just to make sure he feels useful. Jayson's looking out for him," she said, proudly.

"Jayson reminds me of your Dad when he was younger," her mother said. "Edward used to be handsome like that also. Are you going to marry him, Kelsey?"

Kelsey's jaw dropped. Her mother's intuition was so amazing. She had known Jayson for an hour and was already sure of the depth of Kelsey's feelings towards him. But marriage? Kelsey had always expected to do it someday, but she hadn't expected it to be to someone like Jayson. She had never even known someone like Jayson. And how could she think about marriage when her whole life was falling apart?

She hadn't told her parents about the attacks on her, or even that the car was gone. All she had told them was about having to leave her job. But it was as though her Mom sensed the facts in this, too.

As Mary Reed cleared the table, she bent to look into her daughter's eyes. "Stay with us, Kelsey. There's nothing for you in Florida. You can go back to college up here in New York. And if you're that serious about Jayson, he can stay here too. We'd work something out..."

Her mother's plea overcame Kelsey with emotion. It did feel so safe and right here. Maybe Jayson could even be persuaded to stay for awhile.

"Mom, I don't know," Kelsey said. "I'd have to think about it. I couldn't do anything until I sold the condo. You'll have to give me some time on this."

This seemed to satisfy her Mom who said, "I think this is a time when we all need to pull together as a family."

Jayson chuckled at Kelsey's frilly white bedroom, where the walls were a shrine of old cheerleading photos, as he stopped in to say goodnight on his way to the guest room. After he left, Kelsey put on a new nightshirt her mother had bought for and her and then she curled up with her favorite stuffed animals, trying to get to sleep. She listened to the rush of the river and watched the moonlit shadows on the wall. These were all things that used to comfort her as a girl, yet she felt nervous and afraid. Her breathing was so shallow that she had to keep taking extra breaths.

She must have gotten to sleep around two or three in the morning because there was a nightmare. The stalker had come to find her here. He was a big man and he was standing in her bedroom.

Kelsey heard screams. Next thing, she saw her mother and Jayson standing in the doorway asking her what was wrong. She explained that it must have been a nightmare. Her Mom gave her a light kiss on the forehead and whispered, "It's all right if Jayson stays with you. Just don't let your father know." Then she went back down the hall, calling to

Kelsey's grumbling Dad. "It's okay, Kelsey was only having a nightmare."

"It seems like an old drill," Jayson said, checking on the swaying trees out the window. "Did you always have nightmares like this?"

"Sarah used to wet the bed. When she was four they found out it was a serious bladder condition and she had to have a series of operations. She was in a hospital in New York City for a few months and my Mom had to stay away with her most of the time, and I guess I had problems with the separation. Sarah finally got better, but then I started with the nightmares. So my parents went from one thing keeping them up all night to another."

Jayson tried to curl his body around Kelsey's in the daybed, but she jumped at his touch. "This isn't going to work, Baby," she said. "I'm just too jumpy in this room. I think I need to be alone."

The next day, while they enjoyed the unseasonably warm weather at the zoo, Kelsey caught Jayson checking on her oddly as though making sure that she was okay. The children were elated to see all the native animals that were out during the winter, but mostly, Kelsey thought, they were happy to be with their aunt and her new boyfriend. Even with Sarah hanging on her and complaining about marital problems, Kelsey still felt like all was right with the world, just being with family like this.

Later, the group went to the mall and Kelsey spent more then she should have on the children, buying them toys, clothing and books. Then they all played video games at the arcade. Sarah's husband, Todd, a mostly out-of-work roofer, had been busy today because of the sudden thaw. He joined them later at Kelsey's parents' house for dinner and to watch the movie Jurassic Park on video. The kids were thrilled.

For another night Kelsey did not sleep. The draft from the old windows left her shivering although the room was not really that cold.

They spent a week at Kelsey's parents'. The second day there, Kelsey walked down by the riverbank with Jayson and her Dad to see the work they had done on the tree.

Her father said, "We ought to have it all cleared out of here by the time you guys leave, if this boy doesn't sissy out on me before then."

Jayson rubbed his lower back dramatically and winked at Kelsey.

"I'll help you guys," Kelsey said, gathering up some of the cut logs.

She and her father started to reminisce about how she used to be a tomboy and, as well as hunting and fishing with him, she would always help with tasks around the property.

Mid week, they were unloading groceries and Jayson hurried out of the house to stand beside Kelsey at the back of her parents GMC Jimmy.

"What is it about all the women in your life, Kelsey? They all offer to give me blow jobs," he said with a laugh.

"Who, Sarah?" Kelsey asked.

"Who else?" he said. "She tried to corner me in the pantry just now."

Instead of getting upset and asking which other women he was talking about, Kelsey just laughed. "At least it wasn't my mom!" she said.

"Your Mom is a good Catholic woman. I don't think she would even think of having sex for recreational purposes." Jayson smiled and gave Kelsey a hug.

When her sister came to her later in the week and asked if she and the kids might come down to the condo in a few weeks, Kelsey was enthusiastic. She held no grudge against her sister for being the way that she was, and she had complete trust that Jayson would have no interest in Sarah's advances. It made her feel wonderful that the kids would be visiting her in her home and she was already planning the things she could do for them.

The last night of Kelsey and Jayson's visit everyone sat around the formal living room. The group included a fat great-aunt and some adult cousins who lived in the area.

Everyone was relatively somnolent after an enormous dinner that Kelsey's Mom had prepared. They were now drinking after-dinner liqueurs and nibbling on chunks of cheese and fruit that her Mom was passing around. Everyone was in a jovial and loose kind of mood. Her Dad drank Scotch and told old army stories and stories about when Kelsey was a girl. Her Mom looked radiant, a little giddy from the liquor.

Melissa was curled up sleeping in Kelsey's lap. She whined when Kelsey finally took her upstairs to bed at one-o'clock.

When Kelsey came downstairs the group was talking and laughing about the subject of her and Jayson and marriage.

"I think marriage sucks," Sarah said.

"I couldn't disagree with you more," Jayson told her. "I think it would be an honorable beautiful thing, especially with Kelsey."

He was sitting on the yellow loveseat patterned with roses. This was Kelsey's own favorite place in the room to sit. She went to sit beside him, under his arm, while her mother beamed at her.

"What?" Kelsey asked her Mom.

"It's just that the whole family is so impressed by the relationship you two have. We'd back you up whatever you decided to do. Isn't that right, Ed?"

Kelsey's father cleared his throat, obviously having trouble saying something emotional. He looked into his daughter's face. "I care about Kelsey more than anything in the world and I want only the best for her. Jayson, you've acted like a son to me this short time that I've known you. And I'd be proud to have you as part of this family."

Why did everybody seem to think that she and Jayson were getting married?

Jayson straightened up, he took Kelsey rather formally by the hand and he took a deep breath, looking directly into the older man's eyes. There was something in her boyfriend's posture that she did not like.

"Mr. Reed," Jayson said, managing to say the words firmly. "Mr. Reed, you've given me reasons to respect you but I would be ashamed to call you my father. Because you've already betrayed the sacred trust that goes with that word."

The room already had that silence of two in the morning, with the deep snow falling gently outside. But now all Kelsey could hear was the flow of blood in her own temples as she watched her father's ruddy face blanche, until she seemed to be able to see the bones underneath the excess flesh. His whole body began a trembling that looked like it would never stop.

Her Dad's eyes looked empty. It terrorized Kelsey what she was seeing. But still Jayson would not lower his gaze or let go of her hand. Her boyfriend quickly glanced at the others in the room.

"I used to wonder why this beautiful confident girl would be terrified whenever a man touched her. And now I've had to watch the nightmares she has whenever she sleeps upstairs in that bedroom."

Kelsey could see tears already flowing out of her mom's eyes. Her sister, sloppy drunk, was starting to hiccup with sobs.

Jayson turned to Kelsey, looking into her eyes with his compassionate ones.

He said softly, "I think you're ready to remember, Baby. What happened to you that Christmas when you were six and your Mom went away to the hospital with Sarah? Do you remember?"

He was implying that her father had sexually abused her. Kelsey's bowels and bladder reacted first, trying to gush panicked liquid all over the couch. Kelsey's first reaction was to fight to keep control of her body. Then she was tumbling down into the fear and darkness of that time in the past. Her father *had* molested her. His mouth had been all over her, stinking of liquor. He had cried to her that he was going to lose the house. He had cried that baby Sarah might die because he hadn't gotten her to a doctor sooner. He had gone to Kelsey for comfort in the nights because he loved and trusted her the most. He had used her little girl's body like a woman's. Just that one season, it had gone on, but it had tainted Kelsey for life.

"I do remember," Kelsey said, facing her family.

Kelsey's mom had her hand at her throat. "Please don't do this," she begged, "your father's heart... You'll kill him."

Kelsey glanced to Jayson. "You have to," he said.

"Daddy," she said, meeting the tear-filled eyes of the only man she had ever trusted, the only man she shouldn't have. "I remember how you hurt me now. It's haunted my whole life but I couldn't remember what it was. You raped me, didn't you? It's true, isn't it?"

Her father's body was bent like nothing else, not even the heart condition or the years of drinking, had ever been able to do to him. He lifted his tear-filled eyes to her, his whole body shaking violently.

"It's true, Kelsey," he said. "I did those awful things to you. I sinned against you and against God..."

He broke down, sobbing and coughing.

Kelsey's mother jumped to her feet to go help him but she gave Kelsey one last unforgiving look. "Why did you have to do this *now*?" she asked her. "Even if it's true, you know it will kill him!"

Numbly, Kelsey surveyed the wreckage of her family. Her mom and sister rubbed her father's broad back as he breathed in wheezes, struggling for air. They were trying to get him to take his medicine but he seemed not to care.

"You're not wanted here," Kelsey heard her mother say to her.

The distant cousins, and the fat great-aunt who got up to try to comfort Kelsey, were all staying the night. But she was being put out into the snowstorm.

Jayson held Kelsey up as she lost footing several time in the six inches of fresh snow outside. He tried to hold a coat around her to protect her from the wind-driven sleet that tore at the whole front of her body and she felt she was in a dark and burning hell now, hopelessly lost.

"I'll take you back to Florida," Jayson said, shielding her from the brutal wind with the bulk of his body. "I'll take you back home."

Chapter 15

"It's a classic example of blaming the victim," Jerry said to Kelsey. She had told him the story of what had happened with her parents and about what happened to her in the past as they ate lunch on stylish Las Olas Boulevard, a few doors down from the art gallery where Jerry now worked. Someone was always with her now. Either Jerry or Miranda was always hovering over her whenever Jayson was away, like she was fragile and might shatter.

"At least I don't seem to have the stalker after me anymore. No evil eye, that is"

"Oh, Kelsey," Jerry said, "that stalker had to be somebody from the job. I'm so glad that you got out of there. And I'm so glad I got out!"

"Yeah," she said. "Now all I have to do is worry about making a living. I was so sure that my parents would help me out if I ever needed help with the mortgage. Now they're totally out of my life." She tried to laugh but it didn't sound right. "I've like, got nothing left."

Jerry rubbed her arm in encouragement. "You've got me," Jerry said, "even though I'm poorer than you are since I left Confidential. And you've got your health. Just joking, but seriously, you look totally radiant lately. Something's changed."

Kelsey basked in the compliment. She had noticed the change herself, especially since she and Jayson had come back from New York. She couldn't avoid noticing her own energy when she looked in the mirror.

"Now you can claim your sexuality," her handsome boyfriend had joked with her days later when she had stopped hiding in the bathroom and crying and finally started talking again. "You can do all the dirty things you always wanted to do," Jayson said. "You can get totally depraved."

Then he had flung her down into the bed more roughly than usual. "You're going to take all of me inside you, and today you're going to beg for it!"

Kelsey had laughed throatily and responded by capturing him between her slim strong legs, laughing as she gazed up tantalizingly into his flirting eyes.

"You're right," she said. "The fears about making love are starting to go away. How did you know that just knowing the truth about the abuse could do that for me?"

"Because that's what you're like. Knowing the facts means everything to you. Not knowing drives you nuts. Like when you didn't know if I had noticed you at the gym. Or, with that guy that was stalking you, the thing that bothered you most was not knowing who it was."

Jayson was right, as usual. Now Kelsey had an insight into why she had always been such a control freak. But losing the family that meant more to her than anything in the world also meant that she regained truth and power over her life.

Jayson spent days in bed with Kelsey, making love to her for hours. He examined every curve of her body in the mellow afternoon light, as though memorizing it, and he reassured her that her family would someday come back to her. But it was just a kind gesture on his part. Kelsey understood why her mother had turned on her like she did. The horrible truth that had finally come to light was the one that would kill her father. He wanted to die now. He had no will left to live.

And, no matter how Kelsey's mother loved her daughters, her husband was her life. He had occupied her every thought since she had met him when she was sixteen years old. He had been her prince, and the center of her world. Without him, she would not know how to live. Now she had to resent the daughter who had signed his death warrant.

Kelsey understood. She loved her father very much, too, and she could understand how her Mom must feel. Being Edward Reed's daughter, being hard and a fighter, Kelsey would no more be able to say the words "I forgive you," than her father would be able to ask her to say them. It was her dear mother that she more regretted losing.

The worst came when Kelsey got up one afternoon slick and panting from sex with Jayson to answer her insistently ringing telephone. Her sister began screaming at her over the phone. Kelsey walked naked into the kitchen, cradling the phone against her ear. Then she walked back into the bedroom, fifteen minutes later, dazed and with her face drenched with tears that she didn't even bother to try to cover.

"Sarah says she won't let me see the kids, Jayson. She says she doesn't want to talk to me anymore. This means I won't even know how Dad is doing. I won't even know if he dies. And to take Melissa and Cody away from me- it's not fair. She knows how I love them. Sometimes I feel like I love them more than she does. And they're hurting so much with this divorce thing. Who's gonna be there for them? She says she'll get a restraining order if I try to come around them. Isn't that insane? It's like *I'm* the abuser..."

"No," Jayson said, "she is. Didn't you notice how shy and frightened those children were? Either she or her husband is doing something to them."

"No!" Kelsey wailed, and she sank down onto the rug. "Why did I leave? Maybe I could have noticed it and done something. Maybe if she came down here she would have let the kids stay with me for a while."

Jayson lifted Kelsey up, walked her over to the mirror and tilted her chin up so that she was forced to look at her ragged hair and tanned, only slightly curvy, young woman's body, with the dark hair now growing back in at her bush. Like Miranda called it, this was a teenager's body. What could Jayson, who was so sophisticated, see in this awkward, unformed thing? Ironic, that she had just learned what had happened in her childhood, and instead of being able to fight it out with her parents, with just a few words, she had ended the rest of their lives.

The rest of the drama was now hers. Why did Jayson even bother with this hesitant body, a body that hated itself and yet, even so, demanded pleasure and satisfaction? She caught his eyes in the mirror.

"Look at this girl," he said. "This is my little girl, who I have to worry about first. How are you going to help your niece and nephew when you're still a little girl who needs taken care of? You do that first, you come to terms with Kelsey first, and, I promise you, all the rest will fall into place."

He nuzzled her under her hair. "Okay?"

"Yeah," she said. "Okay. How about you, though? What can I do for you?"

Her gorgeous man crushed her in his arms, licking and kissing all over her face and hair, then brought her finally onto his lap on the side of the bed to make love to him. "You're already doing it," he said as he moved inside her. "You're doing it perfectly."

Kelsey became more and more languid with him each day, concentrating on the moods of her own body like Jayson wanted her to. She wandered around dreamily, half naked, experiencing the sensations of objects brushing against her skin. She was so preoccupied with her own internal workings that she basically forgot the external clock.

Eventually, she had to think about getting a job. She had no savings left and the only way she was paying her mortgage was by getting cash advances on her credit cards. This was the first time in Kelsey's memory that she did not have any savings. Ironically, it was buying the condo itself that had put her in this position. If things had gone as they were supposed to, in a few months some of the savings would have been replenished. Now, between buying the condo, and the costs the stalker had left her with, the savings were gone. She had paid the hospital bill, paid for new tires, towing and mechanic for a car that was gone. The insurance had barely given her enough to pay off the car.

At any other time in life, Kelsey would have been totally destroyed by her financial crises and the uncertainty of her life. Now she was just so grateful for every hour that she lived. The stalker hadn't taken her life and he was gone now. That was the important thing. For the first time, Kelsey saw life not as a daily challenge, but as a mysterious gift, to be slowly unwrapped.

She talked to the realtor and had her condo put back on the market. The realtor was fairly optimistic that she could get most of her money back on it. The problem was timing. Tourist season was already well into it's second half and there was a glut of places such as hers on the market. To make matters worse, a few of the features that had appealed to Kelsey would make the place harder to sell to others. One was the fact that it was relatively close in. Many young working people liked the newer developments further out west, places with all kinds of amenities and other young tenants. And lots of seniors were flocking to Palm Beach County now, to avoid the higher crime rate and the greater crowding here in Broward County. This still might have been no problem, except Kelsey's condo was not exclusively fifty-five plus, which was what almost all of the seniors buying in her price range preferred. Kelsey had liked the fact that her development had a mix of ages. But in terms of selling, she had boxed herself in.

"What are you telling me?" she asked the lady from the realty. "Should I drop the price way down?"

"Just be patient," the agent told her. "If you drop the price, it'll look like something's wrong, and, to tell you the truth, I don't think I could get you a buyer right this minute even at a lower price."

Kelsey examined herself in the mirror. She had put on a little weight and her muscles had smoothed out because she had been ignoring the gym even though she had nowhere better to go. Her eyes looked sleepy and dumb, but kinder than they ever had before. Her chestnut hair had natural highlights. Her skin was sun and wind burned from riding Jayson's motorcycle on errands.

Kelsey hated the bike for herself even though it looked so sexy when her boyfriend rode it. Jayson promised that he would sell it and get a car that she could drive to job interviews. He offered to pay for a car for her but Kelsey did not much like the thought of herself as someone's paid bimbo. It was ironic for her to even be in the position. She had always been the world's biggest workaholic and the person most responsible with money and she was the last person to have to take money from someone else. She did bend her principles enough to agree to let Jayson buy a car but she wouldn't let him put it in her name.

Kelsey didn't care much about getting rid of the condo. Even though it would be safest to unload it now, in case she didn't get another secure job, selling it would mean she'd have nowhere to think of as home. Nova University had rejected her; in fact, she'd gotten the rejection letter immediately after she returned from New York. It would have been nice if the timing had been different. Now that she had no longer had the reason to stay in Florida, she also had no way of going back home to New York.

Kelsey's mortgage was one thousand dollars a month. She'd find some way of paying it, if she ever got around to sitting down with a budget. She laughed and flashed her white teeth at herself in the mirror.

Kelsey finally let Miranda get her a job. She was now depending on the least responsible person she knew in relation to practical matters for her career. Kelsey started working for seven dollars an hour, part time, in the lingerie section at the department store where Miranda worked. Kelsey's immediate supervisor in the department, Jane, was a forty-year-old bitch who wore black turtlenecks with an inappropriately pointy bra underneath, a helmet of hairspray and bifocals on a chain.

Kelsey and Miranda spent much time joking about this woman, who seemed straight out of the early sixties, and Kelsey felt not the least bit intimidated by her. Kelsey did decent work here, just like at any of her previous jobs. The difference was, work was no longer a priority for her. Now it was not a challenge or part of her personal identity. Now it was just a time-clock and a paycheck, just somewhere to go in the morning.

Since Miranda could not leave her post, Kelsey was always the one to come visit at the cosmetics counter. She'd watch Miranda, in flowing pink robes, give expert cosmetic makeovers, talking crooningly to the women the whole time she applied cosmetics to their faces. Or Kelsey would stand there gossiping with her friend when no one was around, and Jane would find her there and scold her and then walk her back to the underwear department.

Kelsey hoped that at other times her supervisor didn't notice the two bodybuilders lurking behind racks of expensive bras and panties. Jayson and Juan would hold the delicate lingerie up in front of their big chests and dance around laughing, waiting for Miranda and Kelsey to come and join them for lunch.

In the middle of April, Kelsey had only worked at the department store for three weeks and she was fired. She protested because she thought it was about all the little stuff, like the gossiping with Miranda or the guys hanging around. But those things had nothing to do with it.

Her boss's boss was there when they met in the conference room, and maybe Kelsey should have realized this was a little out of the ordinary.

"You're just lucky we don't call for some kind of criminal investigation." Kelsey's supervisor, Jane, said.

"What are you talking about?" Kelsey raised her voice. These women were crazy.

"We're talking about cocaine, selling cocaine on store premises, exchanging drugs in the parking garage," the store manager said, looking at Kelsey like she was less than human. "We have surveillance video of you and your friend. Now, Miranda Meriwether has been with us two years and we never had a problem until recently..."

It hit Kelsey with a shock to her gut that Miranda probably was using drugs at work. The best thing that they could do was just get out of here without fighting with anyone or else Miranda could be in some very deep trouble. So if the store didn't want to bring the police in, no problem. Kelsey wasn't going to stand here and argue, no matter what the hurt to her own pride.

"Is Miranda okay?" she asked them.

"Funny," the store manager said as she escorted Kelsey to a security guard who waited for her at the elevator, "she kept asking the same thing about you."

Kelsey wanted to search for her friend in the parking garage, but the security guard strongly suggested that she get a cab immediately. In fact, he called her one from the house phone in the security office.

Kelsey missed her old job and her old life. She used to be working diligently at this time of day, rather than being sent home to get naked and take a bath and watch Oprah while she waited on the couch for her lover to come home. Jayson would be all sweaty from the gym, carrying takeout and responding with a hard-on when he saw her breasts naked under her camisole. She and Cooper, always lying on the couch, bathing in the air from the ceiling fan because she needed to save electricity. FPL was already threatening a shut-off.

Jayson loved her like this. He said she was in her dark night of the soul and he brought her some new age books on the topic. Kelsey already knew what it was, this dark night of the soul. She had always sensed that it was just around the corner. That was part of why she had always kept herself so uptight. Now, in losing everything, the theory was that she could find herself.

The fan, the TV, the damp couch beckoned. But Kelsey needed to look for her friend after what happened at the department store. Miranda would be running now, not only from her own trouble, but from the harm she had caused Kelsey. There was no answer when Kelsey called the Davie apartment. She knew there wouldn't be. Cooper screamed angrily for food while Kelsey made her calls; he had fallen so easily into the habit of having all her attention. Then she had to cut Jayson off when she called him on his cellular. "Just let me speak to Juan!" she said, harshly.

Her being secretive about why she had to speak to Miranda left both Juan and Jayson pissed at her. She hung up, pacing. If she had a car, she could try some of the bars where they often hung out at happy hour. She called Jerry, begging him to get out here before Jayson did, so he could take her searching for their friend. Jerry picked Kelsey up and they cruised around the bars on the Intracoastal Waterway. Finally he brought Kelsey back to her condo.

Jayson reached her there by telephone and said he'd already been over and read the note she'd left on the door. "Why don't you just tell me what's wrong with Miranda?" he asked.

"It's me she needs now," Kelsey said. "Please. I'll call later when I know that she's okay."

Kelsey knew who she would have to call. With disgust she punched out the numbers. Cutting off the perky intro she said, "Marshall, this is Kelsey. I just need to know if you've seen Miranda." Marshall Sawyer had seen Miranda. In fact, he told Kelsey that Miranda had called him when she was let go, they had gone out together and he had just brought her girlfriend back to the apartment in Davie. Kelsey thanked him grudgingly and immediately set out to see her friend.

Later, lying on Miranda's bed on top of an old and slightly dirty spread, Kelsey asked Miranda what had happened.

"I had no money for rent. It was a simple thing, just handing over some coke to Marshall that I got from Lou. It just went horribly wrong. I'm sorry, Kelsey"

"Why didn't you ask me for the money?" Kelsey asked.

Miranda stared at her. "News flash," she said, "you don't have it. That's why I had to get you the job."

A few days later, Jayson showed up with a car. It stood out in Kelsey's parking lot, not like hers had, as the hippest and brightest thing there, but instead as the plainest. Odd person that Jayson was, he seemed proud of the black 1990 Escort and of the fact that he had been able to buy it all in cash. With the problems Kelsey had been having lately with her own finances, she was in no position to criticize her boyfriend for being conservative.

The inside of the car was functional and depressing. But Kelsey curled into the passenger side gratefully and Jayson began driving her all over Broward County for job interviews.

There was one clerical job in an attorney's office. Kelsey had gone to the interview in a slightly inappropriate outfit, a pastel lavender sweater, a painted satin miniskirt and metallic lavender leather platforms. But they actually liked her. She was giddy in the car, twisting around while telling Jayson the story of how well the interview had gone.

Back in Deerfield, she jogged up her outside stairs ahead of him, balancing the paper sack of groceries he had bought while waiting for her. Jayson, a few steps behind her, laughed at her energy.

Kelsey stepped inside the condo breathless but, before plopping down the groceries, she made a quick check around, a habit she had picked up since the poisoning. All was normal except the red light blinking on her answering machine. She played the message and it was the lawyer's office, asking her to call first thing Monday to talk about when she could start.

She ran to Jayson. "I've got the job!" she yelled. "I've really got the job."

She flung her arms around his neck and they swung around the kitchen, dizzily.

Jayson rubbed the silky material on her hips, as she took out the last of the groceries. This was a can of cat food that she quickly opened over the sink.

"Stop!" she whined, playfully, pushing Jayson's nuzzling face off her neck so she could call the cat.

"Cooper!"

He wouldn't come.

Jayson was getting her all hot and bothered and she wanted to call Miranda and Jerry with the news about the job offer. She plopped the whole can of food into the cat's dish and stood there with her hands on her hips, talking in a stern voice that usually worked with her cat when he was being stubborn.

"Cooper, just get out here and eat! I know you don't want me going back to work. But I've got to pay the bills... Come on, you know you get sick when you don't eat..."

Jayson had folded the grocery bag and put it away in the closet. "That's some way to talk to your cat," he said.

"Well, I told you he plays these head games. I'm surprised; he hasn't done it in a while. He's probably under the bed."

"I'll find him," Jayson said.

He left and she heard the thump when he went down on his knees and heard his muffled calling under the bed. At first she smiled, but then, as she called Miranda's and left a message, she was starting to get a chill on the back of her neck.

Jayson came back to the room. "I can't find him," he told her.

"That's crazy," she snapped. "He's hiding!"

She stomped off to search the rooms herself. Kelsey moved rapidly, something telling her she had to. In the bathroom, she ripped aside the shower curtain, then checked behind the toilet, shutting the door behind her, closing the room off in case the cat was here and doubled back. The linen closet took two seconds. She left towels strewn all over the floor.

"Jayson," she called out testily, "check all of the kitchen cabinets and under the sink. And do it quickly!"

Kelsey checked behind the bureaus and under the bed again, then slowed down to methodically check the bedroom closet. There were so many items to get behind. Luckily, she kept everything very organized, so a search was even possible.

She did the living room closet while Jayson moved aside the couches. He tried to take her by the shoulders to calm her for a moment, but she pulled away.

"He's not here, Jayson, he's not in the house. We've got to check the balcony."

She ran out there. It was a gray day and the air was damp. There was no sign of Mr. Cooper on the balcony or down in the courtyard.

"Maybe Miranda came and picked him up for some reason. Is that possible?" Jayson was asking.

Kelsey just shook him off, thinking how it was rush hour traffic right now, how the normally quiet streets in the neighborhood would be busy, and envisioning what the six-lane Hillsboro Boulevard would be like.

"No," she said, "I've got to change my shoes..."

It took Kelsey only seconds to get her tennis shoes on, then she was outside knocking on doors. Meanwhile Jayson walked the complex, checking behind shubbery and under cars in the parking lot and, all the while, maddeningly calling.

Kelsey's heart was racing so painfully. The twisting, sickening fear was so much greater now than at any other time. Cooper was her responsibility, and she had let this happen.

"Have you seen my cat?" she asked the old people, swallowing so as not to cry. "The gray one that always sits in my window."

"No, dearie, we'll tell you if we do..."

Everybody was home basically. They all offered to help, and wanted to sympathize with her, while she kept looking down over the rail to check on Jayson.

Kelsey was impatient. She knew, logically, that she had to check the complex first, but it was that road out there, that raging East to West road where her animal might be dying right now.

She ran down the steps and joined Jayson in the parking lot. "We've got to check the roads now. He could be dying out there."

Jayson tried to hand her car keys. "Why don't you take the car and go in widening circles, and I'll go on foot."

"No," Kelsey said, "I'll go on foot. I have to. You take the car. Please."

Thankfully, Jayson was not going to stand there arguing. He seemed to understand, like she did, that every second might matter.

Kelsey ran past the condos and apartment complexes in her neighborhood, where people were pulling groceries and briefcases out of their cars.

"Have you seen a gray cat?" she would call to them; then she'd go back to jogging and calling, "Cooper! Cooper! Please, where are you?"

All time came down to running the neighborhood, her throat scorched, her calves ripped by thorns and cactus plants as she ran into decorative shubbery. Yet her body knew it could do this forever if she had to. She darted back and forth across the streets, narrowly missing cars. She flagged a few of them down and asked about the cat.

Jayson passed her occasionally in the car and she took just the briefest of seconds to tell him that she was okay. His stops became less frequent as his circles went wider. She knew that he would finally be going onto I-95, which, after all, wasn't more than a few miles away. But if Cooper was there, he was also dead.

Kelsey found herself wishing for an instant that she would find him dead, so at least she could assure herself that the death was sudden, rather than him lying hidden somewhere, slowly suffering. Then she tried to push the morbid thought out of her mind and replace it with optimism. The convenience store sat on the corner of Hillsboro, and she couldn't face the roaring busy road yet, she just couldn't. Her breath would hardly come now. She bent to get some air in, then went inside the store and asked the manager if he had seen a cat. He shook his head.

This was crazy and she knew it. No one else losing a cat where she did would even come out here, the area was just too busy. But she wasn't going to let Florida and her own carelessness take everything away from her. She had checked the window in the bedroom, the one she always left cracked open for him for fresh air, and the screen had been loose. She had never checked because Mr. Cooper had never shown any inclination to roam and the window was secured with a lock that kept it from rising more than a few inches. It was all her fault.

Kelsey ran onto Hillsboro Boulevard with drizzle now coating her hair and clothes. The traffic fumes were choking her and the noise was maddening. Cars and sport utility vehicles were practically bumper to bumper. She always thought of this section of road as going very slow when she was impatient to get home. Now she realized how fast the traffic was actually traveling. The air from the cars' passage flared her short satin skirt as she ran along the narrow shoulder. She almost fell off balance, some of the cars got so close.

Kelsey couldn't see the other side of the road. Her cat could possibly be lying on the shoulder there. The shoulder and all of the yards on this side of the road were clear. It was no use calling. Her voice couldn't be heard much above the traffic. Kelsey ran about a half mile on the north side of Hillsboro; then she steeled herself to run across to the south. She clenched her eyes shut while the car horns screamed at her as she darted through them at a moment when they had slowed. She could not wait for a break in traffic because she knew there wouldn't be one until seven-o'clock tonight.

Oh, Cooper, why are you out here in this horrible world, she thought. Why did I buy the condo thinking it could be home? She panted as she ran down the south side of the road. Maybe if he didn't die, they could leave, move to somewhere like North Carolina, where the weather was good but people still lived in communities rather than this damned unlivable sprawl.

There was a gray, ragged shape by the side of the road a ways up. Kelsey stopped. She did not want to see. From here it did not look large enough to be her cat. She approached it at a slower jog, then sidlingly, then she stood over it while the traffic whizzed past. The gray fur was the elongate remains of a crushed squirrel, its black eyes still gleaming, its head intact.

Kelsey pushed at her hair, too sad and appalled to even cry. Jayson found her there, sitting on the curb, near the dead animal with her exposed legs sticking all the way out of the skirt and her not even caring.

Kelsey's voice was gone from all the screaming. Back at the condo, she put some tea on for them and Jayson reassured her.

"We'll go out again later," he said, "and walk the neighborhood. But we need to wait for the rest of the people to come home."

Meanwhile he made the calls to Miranda and the building manager, just to make sure that no one had come in with a key and taken Mr. Cooper out.

Kelsey went into the kitchen to get her tea and she stopped to look at her cat's yellow bowl on his Garfield placemat, remembering how he ate so messily and how it had always made her laugh.

"Oh, My God!" she cried, sobbing loudly and openly for the first time since all this trouble had started, maybe the first time ever. "He's really gone."

Jayson didn't interfere in her grief. He went out to take one more turn around the building. They ordered in a pizza and then spent most of the evening knocking on doors and searching.

"Let's go back and watch some television," Jayson said, when it was already after ten o'clock. "This way we can be up early to check the shelters tomorrow." The idea of the animal shelters didn't really hold out much hope for Kelsey, but she agreed.

She had gone into the bedroom to change and to run her hand once more over the rip in the screen. She came out quietly and she found Jayson sitting on the couch, bent over, fiddling with a little golden wire ball with a bell inside, the last toy ever bought for Cooper. It was one Jayson had picked out for him when they were going to leave him with Miranda when they went up North.

Softly, Jayson cried. She saw how his body heaved as he sniffed the tears back in. When he looked at her, his eyes were rimmed in red. "I loved him, too," he said.

Chapter 16

The next afternoon Kelsey was out on the walkway outside her condo, drinking a beer and pacing. She'd pause to examine the torn bedroom window, and then she'd pace again, thinking. Jayson came to the doorway of her apartment and watched her squatting there, with one finger stuck under the screening and her brow furrowed.

It was a clean cut, a straight line that followed the frame. It was a slash. There was no way her cat could have done this. Someone had cut her screen deliberately. Her body washed over with chills.

Kelsey looked up at Jayson. "Somebody cut this," she said. "I think it's the same person who was stalking me."

Jayson came over and bent with her to look at the screen. "It's possible," he said finally, tiredly. "I don't know if it's something you could..." he started to say and then trailed off.

"I know," Kelsey said. "It's not something you could prove. But I know. And that's what this person is intending. That I know." Her eyes narrowed and she downed the rest of the beer in an angry gesture. "Let's get out of here," she said. "I don't even want to be here right now."

They headed to Jayson's place. Kelsey disliked being at her condo with Mr. Cooper gone. She was pretty buzzed by the time they approached the small row of efficiencies on Hollywood Beach. She had been drinking since coming back from an animal shelter that morning and Jayson was now carrying another six pack of beer, which she had asked him to buy.

When they stepped into the courtyard there were three rough-looking men and a blond woman sitting outside of one of the other efficiencies. Their room had been left open and loud classic rock music and garlicky cooking odors spilled out of the open door. One of the men was still eating. He had pulled out a kitchen chair and had a bowl of spaghetti and sausage in his lap. The other two men had taken chairs off their neighbor's small patios. The woman was sprawled in a chaise lounge, wearing a bikini despite the cool sunset breeze.

The group had empty beer bottles lined up all over the sandy lawn. The men, with their all black clothing and muscular tattooed arms, struck Kelsey as bikers. She looked around and, sure enough, three Harleys were taking up two of the six parking spaces alongside the building.

"Jayson, what you been doing?"

The leanest of the men, the one who looked to Kelsey to be a sort of leader, lurched drunkenly to his feet and grasped Jayson by the forearm, in a kind of handshake like they were old friends. He had dark stubble covering a knife scar, flashing black eyes, and a red bandanna tied over his hair. He was a dangerous looking kind of guy, similar to some of the crime suspects that Kelsey had seen in her job at the State Attorney's three years ago.

"Lend me some money, man," he said to Jayson and it sounded much like a demand.

Jayson just laughed. "Get a job," he replied.

The biker took it in good humor and then he looked up and down Kelsey, who was wearing a big shirt over bike shorts. Meanwhile, his woman squirmed in her chair like a big cat trying to find the sun, although there was no sun out. She murmured to herself while sucking on a beer with her eyes closed.

"Stay out here and drink with us," the biker said. "Lee, get them some chairs."

The youngest man, the one wearing a Harley T-shirt, jumped up to steal them two chairs from one of the other patios.

Kelsey and Jayson sat down and cracked open beers and Kelsey watched the French Canadian tourists lazily strolling up and down the Broadwalk. She didn't care that she was sitting with these rough people or question the fact that her boyfriend, who worked in a professional job, could blend so comfortably with these men and not be at all intimidated by them. Kelsey was used to Jayson being adaptable in all things.

She was busy brooding about her stalker, desperately questioning his identity in her mind. It was as if, with this final thing he had taken from her, there had been a connection established and she should be able to know who he was now.

"My name's Rick," the dark-haired biker said, disturbing her reverie, and he shook hands with Kelsey, and then, again, with Jayson. He then introduced the youthful Lee and the gray haired Bo as his "brothers" although Kelsey doubted there was any blood relation.

Rick called to the blond woman in the chair. She stretched and looked at Kelsey with blue cat's eyes rimmed in black, which were sleepy but unfriendly.

"This is my woman, Tina," Rick said. "Why don't you be sociable?" he asked her.

"Where's the fucking sun?" Tina complained in a whiskey voice and then crawled onto her stomach, giving them a view of her rounded ass cheeks with just a yellow thong between them.

She was darkly tanned, in her late thirties but looking older because of her leathery skin and the lines in her face from smoking. But her body was all curves, spilling out of a swimsuit that would be small on Kelsey, even though she was thirty pounds lighter. And Tina had D-cup silicone-enhanced breasts proudly spilling out of the string tied bra. She was just the type of white trash that Kelsey disliked. Usually they didn't come to this beach until the room rates dropped drastically in summer.

But, right now, it didn't bother Kelsey; she just drank her beer, thoughtfully.

"Something on your mind?" Rick asked Kelsey.

"Just some problems about work," Jayson answered for her.

"Let me tell you about work," Rick said. "I come all the way from Oklahoma for this construction job in North Miami and then the fucking boss says he don't have no money to pay us..."

"That's Florida," Jayson said. "It seduces you like a whore and then takes your wallet, if you know what I'm saying."

The group all laughed and Kelsey thought "Amen to that".

Night fell and they continued to listen to music with the same songs playing over and over again. They all got up and started singing and dancing around. Jayson's voice was so amazing. Even though he was just kidding around, his talent stood out. It wasn't hard for Kelsey to picture him working as a singer. She noticed that he was still nursing his first beer while she was going though them at a pace with Rick and his brothers.

Someone had put on a slow song by Elvis Presley and Jayson pulled Kelsey to him, dancing and singing it to her earnestly, with all the words perfectly memorized.

Then there was a lull, with only the sound of the ocean, while they all got their breath. The slutty Tina pulled herself out of Rick's arms and went over to Jayson, who had flung himself down on a chair. Tina stood over Jayson with her back to Kelsey and her legs slightly spread. Kelsey thought she was going try to get Jayson to dance with her.

Instead, she reached behind her for the strings of her bikini top.

"When was the last time you saw some real titties?" she asked. She flung the top away, shoving her tits toward Jayson's face.

Kelsey saw only a red haze of fury. She threw her beer bottle against the little wall that separated the rooms from the beach so hard that it shattered. Then she ran at the other woman, crashed into her with one shoulder and, roaring like an animal, she knocked her to the ground.

The bigger woman yelled and grunted, trying to scream and fight. But Kelsey got on top of Tina's back and used her strong legs, one at a time, to control Tina's arms. Tina's face scraped in the dirt. Kelsey brought one of the blonde's arms all the way up and behind her back, as she had learned in self-defense classes, so that now Tina began to tremble and cry. Kelsey knew that what she was doing was very painful, but she didn't care. She brought the arm up a little further.

"You stay away from my man! You hear, bitch?" Kelsey yelled. "Stay away from my man!"

Tina fought at the dirt with her legs. Out of the corner of her eye, Kelsey saw Rick try to come to his girlfriend's aid. Jayson restrained him. He did the same thing with Bo, who also tried to interfere.

"Kelsey," Jayson called to her. "It's okay."

Finally she listened to him and let him help her up, while the filthy and crying Tina scrambled toward her boyfriend's waiting arms.

Jayson led Kelsey towards his door. "It ain't a party 'til something gets broke," she heard him say to the other men.

The bikers started laughing, amused at the whole catfight. They were so drunk that they would probably remember none of this in the morning.

Kelsey couldn't really believe what she had done to Tina. But she was still drunk and confused and fuming angry. She pounded at Jayson's chest as he pushed her inside his room. She didn't know what she wanted.

"You're so tough, aren't you?" he said, laughing, and she could feel his erection against her.

He started licking and kissing her face and upper body. "You took her down just like a cop," he teased. "Didn't you? You hated her so much, you wanted to kill her."

He brought Kelsey to the bed, while still she fought him, trying to get her legs behind his to trip him. Jayson cupped her butt, threw her down and got on top. All she felt was his panting lips on hers in the darkness and his incredible muscles pushing against her own strong body.

"You're so tough, Kelsey, aren't you? But you're not tougher than I am. Are you?" he insisted.

He pulled her hands over her head, slowly, so that she was aware of what he was doing. She could squirm and fight all she wanted until she had to subside and let him do what he wanted.

Jayson pulled his shorts down and shoved his hard-on into her, grunting with the thrill of it. And Kelsey gasped. She felt thrilled too, as he thrust into her saying, "You're so tough Kelsey. You're so bad. I knew you had it in you, the way you fucked her up."

Kelsey passed out from the drinking while Jayson was still pounding her.

In the middle of the night, she woke up and she saw Jayson in silhouette at the dinette table, looking out the window at the empty Broadwalk and the dark ocean.

He said softly, "I wanted to watch you. You just passed out."

Kelsey was not worried. She had seen her father pass out many times. It was in her blood to be able to handle alcohol. Instead she was impatient. There was something very important she had to say.

Her voice came out, roughened by the drinking and fighting. "I think I know who's stalking me!"

This was the thought that had woken Kelsey from the deep, stuporous sleep with her heart raggedly pounding. She had awakened feeling she knew the identity of her stalker. And now she felt totally sure.

"I know who it is." She struggled up in the bed. "It's Dave Daniels."

Jayson turned to her, "And who's that?"

"It's that guy from the Everglades, near Naples." Kelsey said, "the one who stole all the credit card numbers and I was there for the raid on his trailer."

Now all the details were rushing back to her, all the sights and sounds and smells. It began with the first time she had argued with Daniels over the phone several months before over a few non-sufficient funds checks drawn on his own account that their office had agreed not to prosecute. There had been something in his cleverness and egoism that had fascinated her and she had ended up talking to him for an hour, even though it should have only taken minutes to get his agreement to repay the checks. Then there was the shock of sitting alone in her cubicle at work after she had connected him to the larger string of crimes. She stared at his driver's license photo, that she was seeing for the first time blown up to full screen on her computer, and wondered how the ugly young guy hidden in those layers of fat could be the same man who sounded so self-assured on the telephone.

Then she had seen him in the flesh that disturbing night in the trailer. She had seen his hatred and the alabaster rolls of his body fat, felt the feeling of sex disturbed in that bedroom and the way Daniels had showed no fear.

"It's personal, Kelsey," he had said.

Kelsey tried to explain to Jayson why she was so sure that Daniels was the one stalking her now and doing all these terrible things to her. At first Jayson tried to argue, saying it might be a mistake to discount the drug dealer who lived in Fort Lauderdale and who the police thought was the most likely suspect.

"No," Kelsey said, pushing away a glass of water her boyfriend offered. "I'm totally sure of this. This guy, Daniels, was really bright. I don't doubt that he could figure out ways to get into my computer at work and my car. Or that he'd make me lose Mr. Cooper. It's just his style, the kind of things Dave Daniels would do."

As she ruminated, running the scene in the trailer over and over again in her mind and trying to recall exactly how Daniels looked, Jayson broke in and asked, "But why? Why after three years?"

"I don't know," Kelsey said. "Everyone seemed to think that he would just want to go back to his family, that revenge wouldn't be worth it to someone like him, that his family came first."

She remembered that moment when the young man's body brushed up against hers after he had been handcuffed. It was a body that was at least one hundred pounds overweight and fat people usually stank, but Daniels did not. Unlike everyone else in the room that night, he gave off no acrid smell of fear. All he showed was a cold inquisitiveness. He had wanted to look into Kelsey's face, as if committing it to memory.

Suddenly, Kelsey felt fear, a bad cold fear that she could not shake. "Jayson," she asked, "is the window still open? Could you close it?" Her teeth were chattering.

"Kelsey," Jayson said, "it isn't like you to be afraid. If it is Daniels doing these things to you, then we can find him and do something about him. But you've got to get control of this fear. It's scaring me. And I don't think you should be drinking like you are."

"He could kill me!" Kelsey said. "He hates me."

Jayson paced and punched a wall in frustration. Kelsey knew he just wanted to get at the guy that was hurting her but he could do nothing until Daniels chose to show himself. Or until they tracked him down. She felt tired and very deeply shaken.

"Baby," she said, quietly, "just come and hold me for a while."

The next morning Kelsey sipped at her black coffee, watching tiny grains of sand get blown against the window by a strong easterly wind. She was impatiently waiting to use the phone. Jayson juggled the cell-phone in the bathroom, arguing business while toweling off from his shower.

"I've got to go to Tampa on Wednesday," he told her when he completed his call. "Maybe you could stay with Miranda."

Kelsey had other plans. The first thing she did was to make a call to check with the lawyer who was supposed to hire her. She was told the oddest thing. The lawyer told Kelsey she couldn't start work until he had the money to pay her, and that might be several weeks. At any other time this would have made Kelsey crazy but this time it fit in with what she wanted to do.

"Could you drive me home, Jayson, before you go to work?" she asked.

Her boyfriend was reluctant to let her go back to her condo alone. He felt that she was safer at his place, even with the three bikers two rooms down. But Kelsey wanted to get home where she could use her own phone for long distance. "Those guys," she said, referring to Rick and his buddies. "Don't you worry about living with people like that?"

"They're just little bitches," Jayson said. "You don't need to worry about them."

Kelsey shook her head. The three bikers had looked pretty real to her and she had dealt with criminals in the past in her line of work. Did Jayson get the idea he could take on these guys just because he was big? He didn't understand there were other kinds of dangerous.

"What does this Daniels look like, anyway?" Jayson asked. "Possibly I would see him if he really was hanging around you."

"He's fat!" Kelsey snapped. "Grossly fat. Trailer trash, real young. He has a nice face, I guess. But the weight is the main thing. You can't miss it."

"So, you're telling me that some fat fuck is your stalker?" he asked, incredulously.

"Forget about that!" Kelsey raised her voice.

She didn't like the implied insult, that a joke of a man like Daniels could make her run scared. She knew Jayson hadn't meant anything like that but the thought bothered her, so she changed the subject.

"I want to know about Tina, and all the others like her. Did women hit on you all the time when you were with your ex-girlfriend?"

"She was the one who got all the attention," Jayson said. "I was just a nobody."

"Your gorgeous ex-girlfriend. It really makes me feel wonderful to know that she was better looking than you are," Kelsey said, sarcastically. "I wonder how I compare. I'm surprised you don't go with all these girls that throw themselves at you. Or maybe you do." She spat it at him, angrily.

The big man sat down with his tea and muffin and egg white omelet. He was trying to eat and she knew she was disturbing a calm ritual that was important for him. Jayson always had to eat a big breakfast for his bodybuilding. Finally, he threw down the food and stepped up to her, his light brown eyes lit by anger.

"I am so faithful, Kelsey! You wouldn't even know what it means to me."

Acting offended, he drove her home in silence. In a way Kelsey had wanted to push him away. She felt she needed time alone to sort things out about Daniels. But Jayson finally broke the silence and called to her when she got out of the car at her place.

"I don't like you being here alone," he said.

Kelsey went to him and took his hand, forgiving him and accepting what he had said about being faithful.

"Don't worry about Daniels," she said. "I think I recognize his timing. And I know that you're faithful to me," she said more gently. "I just don't know why you won't say you love me."

Jayson rubbed at his eyes and his face and he looked up at her sadly, seemingly at a loss for words.

"It's your old girlfriend, isn't it?" she asked. "You still have feelings for her."

"Kelsey," Jayson said, "she's not coming back to me. And I'm with you. It's just, I made a promise once about not saying the words to anyone else, and I guess that's holding me back."

"That doesn't make sense, Jayson. She left you," Kelsey said, "and I'm here."

"You are here," he said, reaching out to stroke her face. "And you're the only thing in this world that means anything to me." Jayson's eyes were so earnest that Kelsey knew that he was telling the truth.

He gave her a deep kiss before driving away. "Call me if you even think there's a problem today," he said.

Kelsey called the Lee County Sheriff's Office as soon as she got upstairs. One of the deputies remembered her from three years ago and she was able to sweet talk him into giving her Deputy Ryan's home phone number. Ryan had retired three years ago when the Task Force had broken up. The last time she had heard from him was when he had called her over a year ago to let her know that Dave Daniels had been set free.

Now when he answered the phone, the confident voice with the slight Florida accent brought back to her vivid memories of that night in Daniels' trailer, when Ryan was almost killed by the suspect but left laughing about it.

"Frank Ryan here."

"This is Kelsey Reed. I used to work with the Fraud Task Force."

"I remember. How's Fort Lauderdale treating you?"

"Not so well, actually. I need some information about Dave Daniels. Would you know where he is right now?"

"Well," Ryan paused to think. Kelsey enjoyed the strong down-home sound Deputy Ryan's voice. She missed working with these men.

"Like I told you," he drawled, slowly, "Daniels got out of prison over a year ago when I called you. That was a minimum- security prison near Lake Okeechobee. And he got out on an appeal, so that means he's a free man. Nobody's tracking him in any way."

"I understand that," Kelsey said. "I thought he was somewhere else though, a different prison."

"He was. The first one was a much tougher facility in the center of the state. That prison is called Redbrook. After less than six months Daniels was transferred from there to the minimum-security at his request."

Something sounded tense in Ryan's voice. "What are you not telling me?" Kelsey asked.

"It's just that Daniels was a local boy and we all thought the punishment was kinda harsh. They sent him to that federal prison with murderers and terrorists and I don't think he needed something like that. A lot of people talk about prejudice because of race but I think that boy ended up where he did because of social class. Because he was white trash."

Ryan sighed. "Kelsey," he said, "Dave Daniels almost shot me. But for awhile there, my partner and I weren't sleeping nights because we were responsible for that young man getting taken away from his family and getting sent where he did. I'm no lawyer, but I was a cop for twenty-five years and if there was ever a case that called for probation, that was the one."

Kelsey sensed that he was subtly vilifying her. But she hadn't chosen Daniels' punishment- a judge and jury had. She had only supplied them with facts. "So you're not sure where he is now? Or if he's back with Allison Hart?"

"Well, I haven't heard anything about him here in town. But I spend most of my time out on the lake, fishing. I try to avoid cops as much as possible." He chuckled to himself. "If you're worried, Kelsey, I can talk to some people and track him down for you."

"Would you do that?" she asked. "Please."

"No problem," the retired police officer said, dryly. "Give me a few days."

Kelsey's heart was beating faster when she got off the phone. She sensed trouble around this whole case. She felt that she was on the right track to finding her stalker. But there was fear, also. She did not really want to face Daniels.

She took a deep breath, then dug an atlas out of her bedroom closet. The small town of Redbrook where the prison was located wasn't that far from Tampa, less than a two-hour drive. She knew Jayson wouldn't want her going to the prison but maybe she could just borrow his car and not let him know where she was taking it. With his misplaced bravado, he wouldn't be able to understand the seriousness of the situation, that Daniels might possibly be capable of killing both of them, if Kelsey did not stop him first.

She called Jayson at work. "Baby," she asked, "could I come to Tampa with you on Wednesday?"

"Sure," he said. "I'd love it if you did. I'll get us a nice hotel. The only problem is, the day we're there I might be working until ten at night. That's what happens every time I go there."

Kelsey said it was no problem. For her purposes, having the whole day free would work out perfectly.

After they hung up, Kelsey made her next call, to get directions to the prison. She did not see hiding the fact that she planned to go there as deceiving her boyfriend, but rather as protecting him.

Jayson chose to take a whole day to drive them to Tampa. He wanted Kelsey, who had never been farther north in a car than her exit in Deerfield, to see some of the coast.

"You'll love A1A," he told her, rolling down his window so that they could breathe the fresh air.

Highway A1A was the low-speed scenic route that went up the coast all the way from Miami to Jacksonville. Kelsey had only been on A1A right at Fort Lauderdale Beach and Hollywood Beach and may have crossed, but not noticed it, once or twice going to her own beach in Deerfield. She'd also seen it once at Miami Beach with Jayson and Juan, and once after the unfortunate experience with Joe, when she was in Pompano. There were always time constraints that forced her to take I-95 whenever she drove and so she never got to see the scenic route. Driving on A1A meant traffic lights, and many areas where the speed limit was thirty miles an-hour, and pedestrians carrying beach gear darted across the road. But today Jayson had made the time so that he could introduce his girlfriend to something new.

Right after Fort Lauderdale, on the coastal road, were the expensive high-rises at Galt Ocean Mile and then came Lauderdale by the Sea, with its variety of two-story hotels. These hotels had bright paint and cute names and they looked interesting, but a bit primitive. As they continued north into Pompano Beach, there were more and more of the high-rise condominium and time-share buildings, wedged in beside each other and blocking the view of the ocean.

Then the road wound, they passed the small lighthouse at the Lighthouse Point Inlet, and the big condos suddenly gave way to single-family luxury homes. Some of the houses were right on the ocean with impressively landscaped entrances that made it hard to catch a glimpse of the mansion-sized residences behind the greenery. Other homes were on the Intracoastal Waterway, which was on the other side of A1A, and there was no obstruction to the gorgeous view. Many of these beautiful houses had sizable yachts tied up to their docks, boats Kelsey assumed were mainly for show. She and Jayson drove through the towns of Manalapan, Gulfstream and Ocean Ridge. Kelsey had heard about these areas before because they were known to be wealthy. But now she truly enjoyed seeing the graciousness of this lifestyle that seemed so different from that on the other side of the Intracoastal that you could truly imagine all the traffic and the chain stores and auto lots didn't exist.

They bought lunch at a deli, then ate at the public beach at Boynton where the shelters were built on a steep hill, overlooking the dark blue ocean. This was also different for Kelsey. She hadn't ever seen a beach in Florida where there was a drop to the ocean. After lunch they got back on A1A, traveling through another exclusive area on their way to Palm Beach. The landscaping around the rich people's houses was striking, with broad symmetrical royal palm trees and stunning red hibiscus flowers. In some places trees formed a shady arch over the road.

"This is all so exciting," Kelsey said, feeling the thrill rise up in her chest. "How did you know about all this?" she asked.

"You just have to keep your eyes open," Jayson said.

Jayson gave her two choices when they reached Palm Beach. They could either wander famous Worth Avenue to browse in the ritzy shops, or they could go inland and stop at the Dreyer Park Zoo.

Kelsey chose the zoo and she was pleasantly surprised by how park-like and charming the small zoo was. She and her handsome boyfriend walked with arms around each other, laughing at the antics of the animals. She was so happy to be here. She never knew that South Florida had places like this. She had been too busy with work and too afraid to leave her familiar spaces. She hadn't looked around, even though she had been dissatisfied with what she knew.

Jayson showed Kelsey another beach in Jupiter, in northern Palm Beach County, and they strolled on a jogging trail on a high bluff above the sea. Kelsey marveled at the pure colors of sea and sky and how deserted this beach was, except for a few people running their dogs and some white sailboats in the distance. Then Jayson drove Kelsey past the Jupiter Lighthouse, painted an unexpected brick red, and he explained that, even though A1A appeared to vanish, it actually just changed name. They followed this deserted, tree-shaded road through the exclusive community of Jupiter Island, ten miles of exquisitely landscaped million dollar homes, half of them right on the ocean. The drive was peaceful and mesmerizing and Kelsey sat in the passenger seat fantasizing about them living in one of these mansion-sized homes, and waking every morning to look out at their own private beach.

Kelsey and Jayson continued to follow A1A north, breathing the fresh air and looking out at the ocean wherever it was revealed. They also stopped at several souvenir stands where they bought postcards and mesh bags full of Indian River Citrus. They ate a seafood dinner at a small restaurant in Cocoa Beach and then spent a half hour at the famous Ron Jon Surf Shop, where Kelsey bought herself and Jayson bags full of clothing. The colors of the ocean sunset bathed them as they walked back to the car and Jayson pulled Kelsey into a hug, wrapping her in his massive arms.

"Well, that's some of the East Coast of Florida," he said. "I've been all around the state and I'd love to show it all to you."

Kelsey slept for much of the ride to Tampa, awakening once for dark, calm highway. Another time she briefly opened her eyes and found that they were on a major road, lost in the glare of a thousand headlights. When they got to their hotel, a big new Radisson on the outskirts of Tampa, Jayson insisted that Kelsey go swimming with him even though it was so late at night.

The closed pool was theirs alone, with the area around it darkened except for the streetlights on the paths. Sinking into the chilly water felt exciting, like sinking into liquid metal. They glided separately for awhile and then came together in the middle of the pool, rippling the water as they turned in lazy circles. Jayson graced Kelsey with his touch, dropping silver water droplets over her as he reached to slick back her hair. Then he put his hot mouth over hers and they made love in the cool water in the middle of the sleeping courtyard. Afterwards, he carried her to their room wrapped in a beach towel as she gazed at the stars and yawned on the sultry air.

"This is perfect," Kelsey murmured. "Nothing could ever be like this."

The next morning she left Jayson at his firm's new office in downtown Tampa. She took his car, telling him she was going to a shopping mall and would be away all day. As soon as she was on the road, she took out her maps.

The drive to Redbrook Prison made Kelsey impatient. First, she was caught in stop and go traffic on the outskirts of the city. Then, on the back roads, amidst the ugly rural scenery, she kept noticing how she was accelerating faster and faster. Each time, she'd slow down again; thinking that the last thing she needed was a speeding ticket, then she'd find herself going faster again, lost in her thoughts.

At the prison, Kelsey showed her private investigator's license and told the corrections officers that she was on official business. The guards allowed her into a private office where they were drinking coffee and preparing for a shift change. She was still in the administration area and nowhere near where the inmates were housed.

When the supervisor on duty heard that Kelsey wanted to see David Daniels' file, he just looked at her incredulously.

"What you're asking for, girlie, is impossible," he said. "This guy got out on appeal. He's like any other citizen now. The only way you're going to get those records is if a police agency is asking, and then, only with a warrant."

Kelsey complained, "But, I've come all the way from Fort Lauderdale." She hoped they'd give her something, even unofficially.

She had noticed one of the guards eyeing her intently. He was a man in his forties with a belly hanging over his belt and a fringe of reddish hair. In appearance, he was not that dissimilar to the way she remembered Dave Daniels. As Kelsey belted her leather trench over her black miniskirt, this guard said to his boss, "I'm taking off a few minutes early," and he followed her out, helping her through the various security gates.

She and the guard then stood in the parking lot by Kelsey's car. She noticed the convicts in an exercise yard behind two layers of fence and razor wire. The place was crowded and the men were noisy. She could hear them from here.

"So, why do you want to know about Daniels?" the guard asked her. "I hope that you're not an enemy."

"Not really," she said, "But why do you ask that?"

"Because I consider myself a friend of his. I wouldn't want anything happening that could hurt him."

"But something could be worked out where you'd give me information?" she asked.

"Yeah," he said, glancing back at the prison building, "but it would have to be back at my apartment."

They drove to his apartment, Kelsey following in her car. The prison guard lived in a duplex in a crowded neighborhood. Not much sun got past the shrubbery in front of his windows and his apartment was dim. They sat down together at the kitchen table and the prison guard, whose name was Bob Walker, brought Kelsey Scotch on the rocks in a not very clean cup. They raised their cups to each other and then he commented, "You're a very pretty girl. I've always preferred brunettes."

"I'm not going to whore myself for information!" Kelsey said, angrily, "if that's what you thought." She pulled two crumbled fifties out of her jacket pocket and reached them towards him. "But I am ready to pay," she said

"I don't want your money," he said and he reached out and gently touched the side of Kelsey's face. Though it felt strange, she allowed it. Walker looked intently into her eyes. "I'd just like to look at you, because you're so pretty. All I can say is, I hope you're a friend of Dave Daniels', and not one of the people who sent him to jail."

Kelsey finished her drink, got out of her coat and hung it on her chair. "Why?" she asked, "what is it that happened in prison?"

The man stretched and sighed, and rubbed his belly. "Well, I prayed for him when he came in here. I liked the boy immediately. He had that fat body and that baby face but he acted like a man, not sniveling or anything like some of them do, even though he knew what was going to happen to him…

"When I walked him down the block, with two tiers of guys yelling at us, even I didn't feel too safe. They were all chanting, 'Fat Boy, Fat Boy' and he said to me and it made me laugh, 'I'm a dead man walking here, aren't I?' I hated to say it 'cause I respected the guy, but I told him his best bet was to try to hook up with some con who would protect him, but he'd never do that; I never really thought he would.

"Things quieted down when this one inmate named Crash came out of his cell and looked at Daniels. It was like they were all waiting to follow his lead. Everybody was afraid of Crash, even the CO's. Outside he was a high-level drug dealer and inside he was leader of the most powerful gang in the prison. I myself knew of Crash stabbing an inmate, and the guy died even though it could never be officially proved that Crash was the one who did it. Then there were two other suspicious deaths in the three years he was at our facility. The grapevine said that Crash had those deaths ordered.

"Usually Crash didn't bother with new guys, that sort of shit wasn't his style. But he just immediately started hating Daniels. Maybe it was because the Fat Boy stared him in the eye and didn't look down.

"Crash yelled at him, 'you're mine, Fat Boy. You ain't gonna live beyond tonight'. And that was the last thing that was said before we took Daniels to his cell."

"So, Crash attacked Daniels?" Kelsey asked.

"The whole fucking cell block did," the guard said, rubbing at his eyes. "Led by Crash. As many as twenty guys beat the boy and a couple of them raped him. It was the worst beating I ever saw, and I've worked in the system for more than eight years. I guess the Fat Boy just wouldn't stop fighting and that made the guys crazier."

Kelsey just stared, open mouthed, realizing that she had been responsible for this. She had known, of course, the stereotype that young guys in prison got raped. But maybe she had thought of it as a joke of sorts, something they deserved. She hadn't pictured it to be like this, or even pictured it as something that would really happen to Daniels.

Bob Walker went on speaking, like the memory of the scene was cut into a groove in his brain and he wanted to keep repeating it.

"Crash was bending over the Fat Boy when some of us CO's came and we heard what Daniels said.

"He said to Crash, 'You better finish it now, because I'm coming for you.' I thought that Crash was stupid not to take Daniels' threat seriously. Other cons who talked like that were usually serious about taking some kind of revenge.

"But Crash just laughed at Daniels and said, 'When you come out of the infirmary, Fat Boy, you're gonna be my fat bitch.'

"There was so much blood; I remember it because I was covered in Daniels' blood, literally covered. We weren't supposed to let that happen, 'cause of HIV, but I figured that he was pretty safe because he was a family man and all. And, anyway, he was dying. It took three of us CO's to carry him because he was so fat, and we had to get him outside the wall for the helicopter. The warden said later that he was surprised the three of us went into those showers to save him. We could have been killed or beaten ourselves, but it was like we were looking at the face of evil inside that room. We had to do something or we'd carry that evil inside us, you know what I mean?"

"What happened to Daniels?" Kelsey asked, feeling sick herself, wishing in a way that he had died then, to have brought him some peace and dignity. Any thought now that he had quietly gone back to his family was gone. He would want revenge for what had happened to him. She would also if she had been in his place.

"You got to understand, Kelsey," Bob Walker said and he looked her in the eye like he suspected who she was. "It was the system that did this to Daniels. A man like him belonged in a minimum-security facility; he never belonged here. I don't care what the charges against him were, someone got something wrong."

Kelsey was watching him, quizzically.

The guard continued. "Daniels was in a coma for a while. The worst of his injuries was a ruptured spleen, and his chances of surviving that were small."

"But he did?" she asked.

"Yes. He spent two months at the county hospital, then three months back at the prison infirmary. Warden tried to get his transfer immediately, but nobody listened. When Fat Boy came back into the population, there was something so frightening in his eyes that you couldn't look at him. Some of the cons would look down and they didn't care who thought they were pussy, they just didn't want him near them. I guess they were all afraid because of whatever part they had in that beating. But he never did nothing to any of them.

"A few days after coming back, Daniels went after Crash in the gym. I guess he'd stolen some surgical tools in the hospital and read some medical books. What he did was so carefully executed and so horrible that we all still talk about it. He cornered Crash in front of a mirror. The same twenty or so guys were there, but no one went to help Crash once Daniels started on him. First, the Fat Boy used a scalpel to cut the tendons in Crash's legs and this six-foot-two, massive guy just fell to the floor, screaming and twisting around, because he couldn't walk any more. Then Daniels dragged him right up to the mirror and he cut tendons in Crash's arms so that the bigger guy went totally limp and had to watch everything that was being done to him.

"Fat Boy raped Crash in front of the mirror. At the same time he cut into Crash's voice box so he couldn't scream, and he kept saying to him, 'Now you're *my* bitch'. And then he cut his throat. The scalpel that was used was never found. And, even though we know the whole cellblock was there, no one would talk about it. The inmates got punished for not talking, but they still stayed quiet. They say a couple of CO's might have been there too, but supposedly nobody saw nothing. In the end, one of the other guys that was a known enemy of Crash's confessed to the killing, a guy who had a few life-sentences anyway. So that ended the investigation.

"They gave Fat Boy some time in solitary for the fighting part of it, which was all they could prove against him. And he didn't mind that, because it gave him time to plot his legal defense and plan the rest of his revenge.

"I always knew Fat Boy was planning revenge on somebody else, somebody other than Crash. In fact, the thing with Crash was probably very small compared to what his larger plan was. I used to hang outside Daniels' cell and I was basically his only friend here. He trusted me because I saved his life when we took him out of the showers that day. We'd talk about wives and kids; that was before I was divorced, and anything that was going on in the world, but he never told me who it was he planned on hitting when he got out.

"They finally transferred Dave Daniels to the minimum security prison in the Everglades when he was already a murderer."

Walker stretched and he looked over Kelsey, who had already shared several glasses of Scotch with him.

"Fat Boy has already prayed for his immortal soul," he said. "And I'm sure he'd be the best friend in the world to anyone that gave him half a chance. But all I can suggest is that the person he's looking for pray for theirs."

He took Kelsey's hand, and held it for way too long.

"He hasn't contacted me, by the way," he said. "I think he knew that people would come around looking and that if I knew where he was, I'd have to talk..."

When Kelsey got outside, and was climbing into her car, Walker called after her. "Be careful driving, with all that liquor in you..."

Kelsey weaved as she drove the car back to Tampa consistently speeding without even being aware of it. Among other things, Walker had told her that Daniels had suffered some permanent physical damage from the attack, including the loss of much of the vision in one eye and chronic crippling pains from an injured disc in his neck. The constant physical pain was just another reason Daniels would never be able to forget what had happened to him in the attack.

Kelsey got onto the wrong roads several times outside the city. She kept playing Jayson's alternative tapes over and over, blasting the music and trying to empty her mind. She tried to keep herself from crying for Daniels because she didn't feel she had the right.

It was already starting to get dark when she arrived back at Jayson's investment firm's offices in a brand new smoky glass building in the heart of downtown Tampa. Everything here was such a contrast to where she had been. The close smells of the guard, Bob's, apartment still clung to her.

Jayson was very cheerful when she met him at his makeshift command central in an impressively large unfinished office, but he did stop to ask Kelsey if something was wrong. When she said things were fine, he seemed to accept this and he proceeded to take her around the building to meet people. He happily showed her off to his nice-looking associates and to the architect who was working on the building. Jayson was supervising the gutting and remodeling of the entire building for the opening of the company's new Tampa office. Meanwhile, he was talking to clients from South Florida on his cell phone. He wore a close-fitting, dark gray designer suit and a high-end platinum wristwatch, and he looked so perfect doing what he did so proudly that it intoxicated Kelsey and almost made her forget her troubles.

It was only when they came back to the hotel, very late, and Kelsey curled on the bed in fetal position, after throwing her soiled clothes roughly into a corner, that she had to confess where she had been.

"Did you screw somebody today, Kelsey?" Jayson asked quietly when she had stayed in that same position, refusing to get up to eat or take a shower, for over an hour.

"No," she said, "I went to Dave Daniels' prison."

.

Chapter 17

Kelsey sat up and pulled a satin nightshirt around her shoulders. She hit the mute button on the television remote.

"Jayson," she said, "this is not going to be easy. At the beginning you asked me if I loved you, and I waited to tell you until I was sure. I knew that I wanted you from the minute I saw you, but wanting or needing someone are not the same thing as loving. The bottom line is, I care about your safety, and I think that you might be in danger..."

"From this Daniels?" he asked.

Kelsey nodded. "When I went to the prison I found out that some horrible things happened to him there. I know for a fact now that it's Daniels who's after me. I have no doubt about it. A bunch of guys raped him. They almost killed him."

Jayson wrinkled up his brow. "But that type of thing happens, doesn't it? Wouldn't someone like Daniels know the consequences that might happen?"

"No," Kelsey said.

She felt like crying in anger and frustration because she had no way of explaining that neither she nor Daniels could have anticipated what actually happened.

"It was brutal, really horrible. The whole cellblock attacked him. I wouldn't have wished that to happen to anyone. And especially not to Daniels. The irony is that all the cops and CO's loved this guy. They all say he was the nicest person they ever met. I can't personally be sure of that. I disliked him because I saw this egotistical quality in him and it antagonized me. But I'm sure he wasn't a really bad person. I mean, he took good care of his family. He was only nineteen years old, for God's sake..."

"It's our society," Jayson said. "It gives somebody like that every incentive to be a criminal. But still, if he's doing these things to you, Kelsey, if he's stalking you, I don't know how you can feel sorry for him. We need to do something about him."

"Jayson, I wish I could pray for him and that it would help anything," Kelsey said. He turned into a monster in prison."

She held back tears for herself, which were just the very surface of her icy fear.

"He killed the man who was responsible for the attack. Daniels spent months in a coma, and then he took his revenge. And I'm going to be next..."

Jayson tried to talk but she cut him off, only now putting into words what had been articulated in her mind.

"He's going to try to kill me." She took a deep, steadying breath. "And if you're in the way, Jayson, he'll kill you too."

Now she couldn't help but cry; she wasn't good at being a hero, it tore her apart knowing what she should do to protect her boyfriend.

"I'd like us to split up," she told Jayson, "at least for a while. I walked into this problem with my eyes open and now I don't want your blood to be on my hands, too."

Jayson stared at her incredulously and he asked her, coldly, "And what do you intend to do about Daniels?"

"I can't sit and wait for him to come." she said. "I'm going to have to find him before he comes for me. Then I have to hope that I can catch him doing something illegal so I can get him back behind bars. Otherwise, it might come to a situation where I'd have to face him, where I'd have to fight."

Jayson, who had been calmly sitting there in his favorite striped briefs, listening to Kelsey tell him that she was leaving him, suddenly moved. It was like nothing she had ever experienced. There was no pain, but the suddenness tore the breath out of her. Jayson grabbed her by the face, cutting off her scream, and he pinned her arms by her sides. He pulled her towards the dresser, then, in one movement, abruptly rolled her up in the bedspread so that she couldn't see or breathe.

And then she felt the icy cold pressure at the top of her head, the tip of her own .32 semi automatic pressed into her hair, along with the enormous weight of his body.

"This is what you were going to do to Daniels, right, shoot him?"

She heard Jayson's muffled voice as she struggled for breath. Then he let her up and gently handed her back the gun, minus the clip, as she panted and glared at him.

Jayson told her, "The problem is, he would do what I just did. He could kill you in a second before you could do anything to him. And you think I would *leave* you to that? I don't know whether I should be flattered that you care about me, or if I should beat the shit out of you for thinking that I'm such a pussy that I can't take on this guy just because he's an ex-con...

"News flash, Kelsey, I don't know what you think loyalty means, but you're my woman. I'm gonna be there for you forever. And maybe I'll be the one to kill Daniels, if that's how it has to be. Now, Baby, come here."

Trembling, she went to him. He had made his point. In a way she was glad that Jayson would be with her although instinct told her that, in the end, she'd be the one facing Dave Daniels. She would just have to be more careful, as her boyfriend had graphically showed her. There was not even an option of backing down from Daniels in fear, because there was nowhere to hide.

She went to Jayson and he stroked the side of her face and cuddled her against his massive chest. Then he guided her in between his legs at the side of the bed.

"Don't worry about any bad things right now, Kelsey, just do it, give me a blowjob, make it like we're floating in the ocean together."

She did what Jayson said. And, for the moment, she was able to escape from the morning's talk about the prison and killings, and lose herself in those feelings that Jayson wanted her to feel with him.

Kelsey teased Jayson until he moaned with pleasure and comfort. Then she pulled away, looked up at him and asked in a purring, enticing voice, "Is it true that you've never seen snow before this year?"

"Never before, Baby," he murmured. "I'm just a warm weather kind of guy."

They headed back to Fort Lauderdale the next day, driving through the center of the state this time. Kelsey felt much freer in a way now that she knew what she would have to do. She would have to track down Dave Daniels and finally confront him, whatever might happen. She didn't mind if Jayson helped her but, either way, she knew a meeting with Daniels would be inevitable. She preferred to be the one to initiate that meeting, rather than having Daniels take her by surprise.

Kelsey let her leg hang out the open car window as she dreamily watched the scenery. She and Jayson drove past fields of grazing Brahman cows and the animals' tan skin and hanging jowls made her giggle. It felt refreshing to her to see countryside like this in Florida, like she was getting some kind of reprieve.

"You never see cows in this state," she said, "at least not in Broward County."

"Only one place," Jayson said with a grin, "a field out there by University Avenue, sort of near Miranda's neck of the woods. There's a herd of black and white cows, and traffic whizzes by them on all sides."

"Really?" Kelsey asked.

"A few years ago, most of the development you see past Highway 441 used to all be farmland," Jayson told her.

"How do you know all this?" she asked.

"I'm curious," he said. "I don't tend to take things at their face value. I like to know what makes things the way they are. So I read all the time, and I ask people a lot of questions."

"You're the perfect guy for me," Kelsey said. "I so much relate to the way you think."

"I'm going with you when you look for Daniels," Jayson said. "You do understand that, right?" He looked towards her and they cracked smiles and then grinned at each other warmly.

Houses they saw on these back roads looked so cute, set back from the road on secluded little ranchettes. Jayson told Kelsey that these places could be had for between sixty and eighty thousand dollars. A good modular home in this area could be bought for less than thirty. Kelsey looked at him long and quizzically.

"We should do it. We should buy one of these houses," she said. "It's not like I have a job tying me anywhere."

She almost meant it, about moving. She had some idea how to run a family farm and she missed the simplicity of rural living. As for the commitment it would mean for her and Jayson, that was the part that put it all in the realm of dreaming.

"I would do it," Jayson said, "but I thought you liked the city."

"Not hardly," she said. "Not anymore. You'd be the one to get bored first."

"Try me," he said.

But then they both started laughing and let the subject go. As the day wore on, they drove through orange groves, and over rolling hills, and the landscape looked nothing like the Florida Kelsey knew.

They had a big, rich dinner at a truck stop. Then, in darkness, they finished the final leg of the journey. They drove through an unspectacular small town, which Jayson told Kelsey was called Belle Glade and was known for the harvesting of sugar cane. The town was on the shores of Lake Okeechobee, although you couldn't see the lake from the road. Then there was the eerily silent drive down State Road 27, a two-lane road which had nothing on either side for what seemed like fifty or sixty miles. There was nothing at all, no lights or houses or gas stations, just the hiss of the tall sugar cane and the moon suspended up in the sky.

Coming back home felt like such a jolt. It was even worse because, as soon as they got to Hollywood Beach, Jayson left Kelsey at his room, running out to catch the second half of his evening college class. Kelsey stepped out to call Miranda from a pay phone on the breezy Broadwalk. It felt odd when her girlfriend commiserated about the loss of her cat, Mr. Cooper, because that loss seemed like it had taken place a million years ago.

When Kelsey got back home the next day there were several messages on her machine from Deputy Frank Ryan. Before calling back, she wanted to do her routine- water the plants, go through mail and make herself a smoothie, a routine that was now missing Mr. Cooper, the most vital part.

Kelsey had one sip of her strawberry smoothie when the phone rang at precisely nine-o-clock. She knew this must be Deputy Ryan waiting for a decent hour. She did not want to answer; she knew that his insistence in trying to reach her probably spoke of something that was not good.

But nothing prepared her for what Ryan had called to say.

"Hello, Kelsey," he said, "I've got your information." He sounded enormously tired, not like she had ever heard him. Then he went silent, just repeatedly coughing with a dry cough.

"Why won't you tell me?" she demanded. He was still quiet. Finally she filled him in on her trip to the prison at Redbrook. "I know that Daniels is after me," she said, "if that was what you were going to tell me."

In a stony voice, Ryan said, "Allison Hart is dead. She shot herself a few weeks after Davie went into prison."

Kelsey's silence joined Ryan's in the static of the phone. He made a growling sound, maybe clearing his throat.

"I never meant this..." Kelsey said, accepting it like it was all her fault. She felt shock all through her body. She had never liked Daniels, and she had liked even less his fleshy bleached blond wife. But now she felt devastated and empty.

Ryan brusquely contradicted her. "You weren't the State Attorney who tried the case," he said, dismissing her like she was no one.

"What happened to the kid, Brandon was his name, wasn't it?" Kelsey asked, hoping against hope that there was something good that Ryan could tell her.

"The boy is gone, into adoption, sealed records. Not even our police department can get into those records. Daniels tried, for three years; he tried every legal avenue available to him. They think he was responsible for some illegal stuff, too, as soon as he got out of prison, but it didn't help, he couldn't find the boy. The adoption was juggled between several states and several different agencies and somebody lost paperwork along the way."

"But doesn't Daniels have a right to his son? He's a free man."

Ryan sighed. "Brandon wasn't legally his son any more than Allison was legally his wife."

"I don't get it," Kelsey said. She had been sure Brandon was Daniels' own son.

Ryan seemed impatient with Kelsey. "If he had acknowledged Brandon as his son, then Allison would have gone to jail for statutory rape. Davie was only fifteen when Brandon was conceived. They lived in their own little community as a family, and everything was okay until the whole house of cards came down."

Kelsey shuddered. "Oh, my God..." she said, as the import of everything came to her.

As someone whose own family had been such a great priority, she understood what it would be like to be that crazed animal out there somewhere, wandering without wife or child, when apparently, since he had been a child himself, that family was all he had ever known and treasured. Daniels had come back, basically from the dead, only to find that there was nothing to come back to.

The former cop spoke to her sternly. "Kelsey, my partner Pierce and I were on the force for twenty five years, and we were basically going to leave it with a clear conscience, without any of those ethical dilemmas where you could never really know if you did right. Now, Pierce and I have talked after I found out your information and we find that, after all, we left the force on this kind of note. Doug feels the same way that I do. Not quite right, an unrest that may never go away.

"I'm standing on my deck right now, looking out at my lake, and I'm holding a rifle which I keep with me all the time now, a hunting rifle that I keep by me in case Daniels comes my way. That boy spared my life that night in the trailer when he could have taken it, but now I only wish that I'm the one he comes to and I can end this mercifully and quickly."

202

So, Ryan was also completely sure Daniels was intent on bloody revenge. "Don't worry," Kelsey said in a voice roughened by sudden emotional pain, brushing off the cop's implied accusations against her. "You're not the one he has the grudge against." She was certain she understood Daniels' twisted notion of justice. "It's me he's coming for," she said. And she hung up.

Kelsey thought very deeply about David Daniels. She replayed the images of the man in her mind. She didn't know what she had expected him to be that day when she had first spoken to him on the telephone; he had seemed very cynical and powerful. Something about arguing with him had brought up energy in herself; there was something electric. He had repaid his own bad checks just in time to avoid being prosecuted, showing his intuition into, and his disdain for, the rules of the criminal justice system. Because of his egoism, she had almost wanted him to be the one responsible when she found out someone was doing the large-scale credit card scam.

And then she had found out the rest of the facts about Daniels- that he was a nineteen-year-old Florida cracker, with an elementary school education, and that he was grossly fat.

She remembered his ugliness that night in the trailer. Dave Daniels was not a cuddly fat person. He had been watchful, an attitude unbecoming to his kind of body. She remembered how his family had reached for him, how Allison kept telling him she loved him, how the two of them had leaned their foreheads into each other's and how Davie had made a promise that he couldn't keep, that he would take care of everything. Now Allison was dead. It was all the fat man's arrogance that had brought it about.

Kelsey remembered the light sheen of sweat over Daniels' rolls of fat skin, the only sign of his discomfort at being surprised in his bed in the middle of the night, having his family and his freedom taken away. Kelsey wished that she had looked at his eyes then, instead of avoiding them. Maybe she could understand something more now.

She wondered where he might be at the moment. He was in one of two places, she was sure, either back in the Naples area, or else right in her own back yard, able to watch her every step she took, yet smart enough not to let her see him. He would live and breathe every moment for watching her, Kelsey was sure, and for his revenge.

Her intuition had been right about Daniels several times before; the first when she had made the unlikely connection between a string of credit card crimes and a guy that had owed a few bad checks for under a hundred dollars six months earlier.

The second time had been about the guns, and the fact that Daniels *had* been capable of committing murder. He had committed murder, after all. He had killed the inmate named Crash in prison.

Now Kelsey's instincts told her that Daniels was linked to her. She knew that, in a way, she had brought this on herself. Even if she won in the final showdown, which she expected would be coming soon, her life would never be the same. Right now there was very little left in her life. She herself had changed also, with a very different idea of right and wrong and no more seeing in black and white.

Kelsey could go on with a life with Jayson but her family was gone. And she acknowledged to herself today as she sat on her wicker couch that she would never return to a career in law or criminal justice. She despised herself for her own part in that system and, worse, she was getting a glimpse of a dark side of herself, a part of herself that had possibly gone after Dave Daniels the way she had for reasons other than professional ones.

She sat on her couch all that day and she let darkness fall without even going into the shower. She made a few calls- to the hospital that had taken Allison's body, and to the State Attorney's office in Lee County to ask for information on Dave Daniels' family. She called in a few favors there and one of her former coworkers gave her information that led her to foster parents in La Belle, near Fort Myers. Kelsey called this couple and they agreed to talk to her about Daniels if she could drive across the state tomorrow to see them. Then there was nothing more to do as the light faded, but to sit and think.

Daniels could have come at any minute but he did not. Kelsey wondered if he had some way of knowing that she was finally onto him. She assumed that once she left for the West Coast tomorrow, then he would know. He was probably wondering what had taken her so long.

Later on, Jayson came in singing to himself, carrying containers of Thai takeout and dancing in circles, high after his workout. He stopped and stared at Kelsey when she retreated to her darkened couch after letting him in.

"Daniels may be out there," she whispered roughly. And then she started to cry, and wipe at her messy nose as her boyfriend wisely left her sitting there. It was the guilt that was the greater pain, not the fear for herself.

"Jayson," she said, through her tears, like she was crying for Daniels, "he's got nobody anymore. His wife is dead..." Kelsey choked on the tears. "...She killed herself. And his little boy is gone. Daniels came out of a coma and found this out, that there was no one left. He loved her so much. I can't take it..."

Jayson leaned on a stool, looking at her oddly. "I don't understand," he said. "Are you saying that you feel sorry for this guy? I thought you hated him."

"I'm saying I'm responsible," she said.

And then she clammed up, angry at herself and at Daniels for the fact that she was now in a place emotionally where even Jayson couldn't go.

The couple left for the West Coast of Florida the next day. Jayson was going to miss another day of college but he wouldn't let his girlfriend go alone.

"Don't worry," he said, "school will be done in a few weeks; and then we'll have more time together."

Kelsey had thought they would drive Alligator Alley, a monotonous fast highway that slashed straight through the southern portion of the state. Instead, Jayson introduced Kelsey to the scenic two-lane Tamiami Trail, which passed through marsh and Indian Reservation on the way from Miami to Naples. There were canals on both sides of the relatively narrow road. Battered pickup trucks were pulled over near the water and men sat on the banks of the canals, fishing with long cane poles. Then there were the signs advertising 'gator tail and airboat rides and she saw some of the tall airboats tied up in the canals, waiting. Kelsey had always thought that it would be fun to ride in one. But she had never done it had because Miranda and Jerry had both said it was stupid and refused to come out here. The same went for going fishing, something else she used to love to do.

"You know," Kelsey said, "one of these days I'd like to go fishing."

"Sure," Jayson said, distractedly, but gently. "We'll do that."

There were spots of bright white in the sawgrass, elegant white egrets wading or gliding from one side of the road to the other. It felt odd that on a beautifully sunny day like today, Kelsey would need to be thinking in terms of her own mortality, that in order to protect her life, she might need to take Daniels'. And there was that tight fear in her gut that maybe he was faster and more clever than she was and that this day, or any other, could be her last. These beautiful sights could be the last ones she would see. She curled against Jayson's arm, glad that he had chosen the scenic route.

Near Naples they saw the first signs of trees knocked down for residential development and houses under construction in large subdivisions where the earth was still raw and red. On both sides of the road were compact strip plazas so new most of the storefronts were still for rent and supersized convenience marts with twice the gas pumps as older stores. South Florida on the East Coast had many more millions of people than this area did, yet it had obviously started growing around here, too. And Kelsey knew from her experience with the megalopolis on the other coast that, whenever they built, people would quickly come.

Jayson was finally off his cellular phone. "May I use it?" Kelsey asked, "to call the prison, the one out by Lake Okeechobee?"

Jayson shrugged as he navigated traffic and he handed her the telephone. He stopped at one of the brand new convenience stores to get gas, while Kelsey argued with various officials and was repeatedly put on hold. Finally, she got the guard that Bob Walker had promised to talk to for her. This man, who sounded much crisper than his alcoholic friend, made sure to start out by telling Kelsey that she was very wrong to be requesting the information and she was only getting it as a personal favor.

The guard gave her details and dates she already knew. "My friend told me why you want information, but there's not much helpful I can tell you," he said. He explained he had never met Daniels and was just looking at his old file.

"Here's something interesting," he said. "When Dave Daniels came to us, no one wanted to be in a cell with him; there was some rumor about him and some violence with another inmate at Redbrook, so most of the men were afraid of him. We had this one guy though- Nick Constantine- real big player in Vegas and the West Coast as far as white collar crime, he was staying in a private cell and he offered to take the boy in, said he wasn't scared of anybody.

"I don't know if you might have heard of Nick Constantine ever on the news, but he was old, in his late sixties, and he had some powerful friends in his day. Constantine made billions of dollars in land developing and other businesses and he never paid any taxes. But he started out as a dirt poor two-bit con man like Daniels and he could relate to him. I guess he sort of adopted the boy, because they became good friends.

"Constantine was only in for a short stint on a plea. After he was released he used to fly back out here every now and then to see his buddy. Daniels had a powerful friend there. And if there was anything the boy didn't know about white collar crime, I'm sure he learned it from his mentor..."

"Computer hacking or finding out personal information about somebody, surveillance?" Kelsey asked. "Would he be good at that kind of thing?"

"You couldn't get a better education if you went to school for it" the guard told her. "In fact, let me mention something else. You know that Daniels was a jailhouse lawyer, don't you, and that he got himself off of that twenty-year sentence on appeal? That's like every con's wet dream, you know? While he was in here, he helped some of the other inmates with their cases, too..."

Kelsey sighed, watching the wind tug at Jayson's crisp shirt as he pumped the gas, and wondering how bad this could get before it was over.

"The man could barely read before he got here," the self-righteous guard went on, "except for having the Bible memorized. But he got himself an education here. He earned his GED and most of the credits for a college degree. The only reason he didn't leave here with his bachelor degree was that inmates are only allowed to progress at a certain speed. But he probably got the bachelor's as soon as he got outside... he might have even gone farther."

"And what was the degree?" Kelsey asked, with a scratchy discomfort forming in her throat.

"Criminal Law, what else?" The guard laughed, obviously another Dave Daniels cheerleader, although this one only knew him from his records.

Kelsey thanked him, and she was about to get off the phone, when the guard added, "One other thing, possibly you knew this, but it's interesting to me. Psychiatrists tested Daniels and they found out he was brilliant- basically a genius. The guy might have come out of a trailer park, but he's a lot smarter than you or me..."

Kelsey shut off the phone. It was troubling to accept that someone who wasted his life living like white trash and not bothering to take any care of his pathetic body could have been born so smart. Yet every day Dave Daniels demonstrated his IQ the way he stalked her.

"Let me ask you something, Kelse," Jayson questioned her when she got back behind the wheel and she gave him the latest installment. "What's the point of getting all this background information about what kind of person Daniels is when this stuff can upset you more? Don't we just have to find Daniels and get the police on him?"

"Yes," Kelsey said, "but I need to know him like he knows me. To know my enemy, I feel I need to see his home ground... And there are things I may be able to understand..."

"No one is ever going to tell you that you did wrong, Kelsey. You were just doing your job."

"But I need to know if I *did* do wrong," she said, "before I can go on."

Jayson drove through the growing Florida West Coast city of Naples with assurance, just like he did in all the other unfamiliar cities she had seen him in. And then he took a back road in the direction of the larger neighboring city of Fort Myers where the regional trauma hospital was located. They stopped at a Wendy's for lunch and ate from the salad bar, and then made the mistake of going straight to the hospital from there, with their stomachs overly full of greasy chili they had eaten along with the lighter food. Kelsey hurried down the glassy hospital corridors with heels clicking and Jayson following with his head bowed, looking uncomfortable and unhappy to be there, just like she felt.

At the emergency desk, Kelsey was told that the nurse she needed to speak to was on lunch break and could be found in the cafeteria. Kelsey had expected the nurse to be on lunch. And she had planned it this way because she knew that she'd be asking for confidential information that the emergency room nurse, who'd acted friendly over the phone, might be reluctant to share in front of her supervisor.

The nurse, whose name was Darlene Bennett, was thirtyish with long red hair loose down her back and a worn hair scrunchi stretched on her wrist. Like her uniform and hair tie, her face also looked tired. A scent of fresh cigarette smoke clung to her uniform when she greeted them. They sat down at her table after introducing themselves and she gave only the slightest second glance at Jayson's looks, barely interrupting her weary body language.

"I thought you might not come here," she said to Kelsey, taking a sip of hot coffee from a styrofoam cup. "All this talk about the girl that killed herself got me real disturbed."

"I'm sorry," Kelsey said, and she suddenly felt gooseflesh come up on her arms. "I met Allison only once. It's her husband I'm looking for now. I need to know what he might have heard and how it affected him."

"I feel like it's my fault!" the nurse said, her voice crackling with emotion.

"Why?" Kelsey asked. "I thought Allison was dead at the scene. Wasn't she miles out in the countryside when she shot herself?"

Kelsey's voice sounded crisp and businesslike. She had done her research before coming here. She hoped Jayson and the RN didn't take her as callous. She would grieve for Allison in time, but now there was information that needed to be obtained.

"The same girl was here a week before," Darlene Bennett said and she raised her reddened eyes to Kelsey and Jayson.

The nurse was thin and rangy. She reminded Kelsey of local trailer trash herself, as she wiped her nose on a crumpled napkin. Kelsey wondered where the woman had her tattoos- a rose over the breast, perhaps, or maybe at the ankle.

"She came in after a sexual assault," the nurse continued. "A couple of guys who were staying at the hotel where she worked tried to burglarize the office. Allison walked in on them, trying to stop them, and they beat her up real badly. I guess they thought it was a joke to sexually assault her, as well. A girl like that, that type of girl, wouldn't usually come in here, anyway. She'd just figure it as a consequence of where she was working and go on with her life."

The nurse sniffled again and gulped more coffee. "Allison Hart was pregnant," she said. "The low-life fuckers made her lose her baby!"

She looked at the two of them, as though for sympathy. Kelsey stared at her, feeling dazed at hearing this news. Jayson looked away and turned to look out at the people eating lunch in the sun on the other side of the plate glass. He was obviously also disturbed.

"She lost the baby?" Kelsey asked, her mouth hanging open in surprise.

"I have kids of my own," Darlene said. "This girl would have been strong. She told me her husband was away dying in some prison hospital, which, I guess you're saying he lived, but she didn't think so at the time. She didn't even let herself cry. It was an extremely high-risk pregnancy and she didn't want to risk anything to stress the baby. Of course, what those punks did to her had already killed it. There was nothing we could do to save it."

Jayson sighed and got up. He touched Kelsey on the shoulder. "I'm getting some tea," he said. Kelsey knew Jayson well enough to see that he was tense and he needed a break to hide it. She herself felt her insides turning over with tension and emotional pain.

In privacy with another woman, the nurse let herself cry openly. When Jayson returned with his tea, she wiped her face again with the napkin and resumed her story.

"When Allison found out the baby was dead, she went crazy. She had nowhere to go. That baby was everything to her. She had been living for that unborn little girl. It was obvious. I asked the doctor that night to admit her to the psych unit after they got done with her physical problems. I just had a real bad feeling. But she wasn't making any definite suicidal threats and she had no health insurance.

"But her eyes were just dead, you know, after she stopped crying. And I just knew. They admitted Allison overnight to treat her for the injuries from the attack and to abort the dead baby. Then the next night I found out that they turned her back out on the street. Or back to that sleazy hotel where she worked."

The nurse started to sob while she talked now, not seeming to care who heard. "They brought her back to the emergency room a week later with a bullet in her head. I was there, on the team trying to revive her. I recognized her hair first thing. That real bright blond hair..."

Kelsey hadn't showed emotion when they talked, and she thanked the nurse with a cool handshake, seeming in a hurry to get away. But, as she and Jayson left the hospital, she started to tremble and her legs began to feel watery. Her words came out in gasps and she held onto Jayson's arm for support.

"I didn't mean," she said, "for something horrible like this to happen. I can't believe there was a baby too, an unborn baby."

She laughed, but painfully, not with mirth.

"No wonder Daniels hates me. His entire life is gone because of me. And if he loved that family like I suspect he did..."

Standing outside between two manicured rows of deep green foliage and red and orange hibiscus flowers glowing in the hot sun, Kelsey violently shook with chill. What kind of love must Allison Hart have felt for her husband and his child, to take her life in such an appallingly brutal way when she thought she had lost them?

Jayson took Kelsey by the shoulders, trying to hold her attention. "Baby, I don't think this is good for you. Maybe we ought to go home."

She looked past his pleading eyes to the car keys gathered in his hand. "No," she said, and she pulled the keys away from him, shaking in her attempts to unlock the driver's door. "I need to see that hotel where Allison worked!"

Jayson tried to talk her out of going but Kelsey paid little attention as she drove as fast as possible up route 41, to the industrial section of Fort Myers where the hotel was located. She turned over in her mind thoughts of what had driven Allison to come to the hotel, to exchange maid work for a place to sleep. Allison would have known that the hard physical work would have endangered the pregnancy. Was working at the hotel the only way she thought she could get her son Brandon back from the Department of Children and Families? How desperate had she been?

Kelsey rattled the undercarriage of Jayson's car taking it over railroad tracks too fast. The motel was just on the other side. She could see white curtains billowing out the opened windows from the far side of the tracks.

The motel was called Tranquility. An angled fifties style logo on the sign was crossed by the word "pool" and, in small black plastic letters on a white board, someone had formed the phrase "lowest rates- weekly, monthly". The pool was cemented in, with broken outdoor furniture piled on its deck, and the hotel formed an L-shape around it, with the railroad tracks in back and an abandoned factory facing the courtyard. The whole area was deserted and gray and it had an ancient feeling that was unusual in Southern Florida, where even so many of the tawdry things were brand new. It felt good to have Jayson with her because the place felt frightening.

Theirs was the only car as Kelsey pulled into the shadowed area in front of the office. Quietly, they stepped out of the car and walked the cement walkway in front of the rooms, looking into each empty room. Kelsey had never seen a place like this, with mismatched covers on the sagging beds and cracked mirrors. A mildew smell wafted out of the rooms carried on the breeze from in back.

Thinking about staying in a place like this, like Allison had in her final days, made Kelsey shudder. Surely a place like this was the very end of the road.

Kelsey looked up at Jayson quizzically, but there was nothing he could say, he had no answers. Without speaking further, she let go of his hand and stepped into a room by herself. She walked back into the bathroom where she could smell years-old piss that seemed to have gotten into the rotted floorboards, then she stood in the dim kitchenette where, even in daylight, a large cockroach hurried across the stainless steel cooktop.

Of course Allison had found a way to go to the Everglades to die. After this, she would have so badly wanted to see green and beautiful things around her at the end.

Kelsey came back out to Jayson. She shuddered, drawing in her breath, "I can't talk to anyone here," she said.

He started to lead her away when an older Indian lady in traditional dress stepped out of a room adjacent to the office. She looked very tired and bleary eyed and she limped toward them deferentially, squinting.

"Can I help you?" she asked, quietly, almost in a whisper, looking at Kelsey.

Bitter, unshed tears swam in Kelsey's eyes.

"No, no, you can't," Kelsey said, barely loud enough to be heard.

Jayson didn't seem able to speak either. He hurried her to the passenger side of the car and then rubbed at his eyes and face as he took the wheel and drove away. On I-75, heading back south to Naples where they planned to stay overnight, he opened the windows and drove very fast so that the clean air rushed around them. They stayed silent for a while.

Jayson spoke first. "When we get back to Naples, why don't we go somewhere nice?" He shouted to be heard over the wind. "Let's go to the beach and then to a really nice hotel."

Kelsey looked towards her boyfriend, who looked hurt and miserable, despite his upbeat words.

"You blame me, don't you?" she asked. "You can't look at what I've done in all of this and not despise me. How are you ever going to touch me again, knowing that I've been involved in this?"

They had pulled up to a meter by a beach walkover and, as they stepped out. Kelsey could already feel the refreshing sea breeze. Jayson looked at her oddly over the top of the car, not answering about whether he blamed her. He just grinned and opened his dress shirt and stripped it off. He took off his pants, not seeming to care who saw, and then he grabbed a towel from the back seat to cover his waist while he stripped off his underwear and pulled on swim trunks. Then he looked into Kelsey's eyes amusedly.

"Aren't you losing focus, here?" he asked her. "We're here to try to save your life. But now Daniels has you doing his job for him, the way you're feeling guilty. That's not the Kelsey that I know."

He urged her to follow him onto the small, relatively secluded beach. Although there were a number of tourists, chattering in many languages, the only buildings bordering this beach were private homes.

Kelsey followed Jayson into the cool, shallow and very calm water of the Gulf. But even though she had worn her swimsuit under her clothes at his urging, she was unable to go further than waist high.

Jayson looked at her inquiringly. She couldn't swim right now. There was too much on her mind. She shook her head and tried to smile. "Go ahead," she told him.

Jayson arched his broad sculpted back in a dive and then slipped through the water. She watched him swim farther and farther out, with the silver water breaking over his straining muscles as he left her in the shallows like Miranda always did. She could sense his pleasure as he worked his body against and with Nature. It was good that he could find such a sure relief this way.

Kelsey dunked her hair in the shallow water, and then she went to sit on the beach amongst a litter of shells. It had become cloudy but the sea air felt good drying the salt water on her body. She felt in a saner place in her mind. It had been a good idea on her boyfriend's part to come to the ocean, she thought. Jayson, who was so far out now she had to strain to identify him, had saved her just in time.

It was true she was not here to do Daniels' work for him, but rather to stop him, so no one else got hurt. There was no way she could do anything to undo the past. All she could do was to stop the violence now. She could preserve her own life, which, as much as Daniels' life, was worth something. She would be strong enough to do that. She would fight brutally for her life if she had to. She knew it was the right thing to do.

It took a long time for Jayson to return from swimming. When he did, he drove them further down the coast to a highrise hotel that he had selected. This luxury resort was so different from the place that they had seen today that it would not bring up memories. But the whole drive there, rather than relaxing, Kelsey kept checking the side mirror to see who was riding behind them and checking every face on the street, in case Daniels was following them. Even as they checked into a twelve-story beachfront luxury motel, she had the very strong feeling that someone was monitoring their every move.

Chapter 18

With interest, Dave Daniels watched Kelsey Reed conduct her investigation. She was right in his backyard now, sticking her nose into his life. This morning she wore a new dress in soft pink cotton that clung to the vee between her firm thighs. He watched her as she waited impatiently for the valet to bring the car from the parking garage.

Although Daniels hated Kelsey, he was also compelled to stay near her, because she was the only link he had left to his past. If not for her and her desperate interest, the truth was that on a gorgeous bright day like today the past that he dwelt in was totally swept away. Except to him, and to Kelsey Reed. These were all the same places, but no remnant of that past was any longer visible.

Although this was a sunny day, Daniels was brought back vividly to the memory of a cloudy stormy one. It had been late summer, a few months after Allison had discovered she was pregnant with Brandon and they were weathering a storm in Allison's old apartment above the Citgo station. It was a tropical storm coming in from the Gulf that was being watched as a possible hurricane.

The insufficient old windowpanes rattled furiously. The wind howled. Palmettos were uprooted and tossed around the parking lot under the drenching rain and a metal cigarette sign danced on its chain, clanging.

Davie cuddled Allison against him. A storm that at other times might have thrilled her was today bringing fear.

"You don't have to raise this child, Davie," she'd said. "No one would blame you if you didn't."

He realized the doubts were probably coming from some primal source of fear, a mother afraid she could not provide for her baby. But he also knew that they had been over this. She knew that he had promised to devote his life to her and their family.

He stroked her silky hair and kissed down over her belly that was just now starting to show. Allison was so warm. He shielded her warm body from the draft and the noise of the storm with his own. "I want to be a father," he said. And he would never forget the warmth of the moment, as he held his family then, his wife and his unborn son. "I want so badly to have a little boy. We'll call him Brandon, like you want, after Brandon on the TV show. And I'll raise him up good, like my Daddy did me. Only this son is going to have all the advantages that we never had. I want so badly to do this."

He remembered another evening, when his golden-haired child, held up in his wife's arms, attempted to turn patties on the barbecue grill. Brandon had a look of intense concentration, trying to take Daddy's place while Davie ran to the store. That evening, with the sun filtering through the trees and the relative cool of autumn coming on, had been a blessing to him. Davie had taken the short trip to the convenience store down the country road and he had experienced an odd sudden loneliness. And then, within a few minutes, he was back with his family and they were happily continuing what they had been doing before he left.

It was toward the end, because Davie had been driving the brand new metallic beige Tahoe. He pulled in and Allison and Brandon glanced up at him, and their faces lit up even though he was only bringing home soda. He got out of the truck and started toward them and his wife and child met him halfway. Brandon reached one arm around his father's neck.

"I helped," he said. "I'm making the hamburgers the way you do."

Allison smiled and laughed, shaking hair out of her face. "Brandon's better at this than I am," she said. "I hope we didn't ruin anything."

Davie looked over the sizzling overcooked food, which smelled so good. The smell of their burgers drifted in the humid air, while a weak evening breeze made caressing noises in the willows that hung near overhead.

The last rays of evening sun lit Allison and Brandon's flushed and expectant faces, both so blond and beautiful and both his. Davie gripped them both in a bear hug, spinning them slowly around, while the cat twined gracefully between the adults' legs.

"Everything's perfect," he had murmured. "Everything's perfect."

Chapter 19

Kelsey wore a pink cotton dress that came to just above the knee. It was significantly longer than the trendy styles she usually wore but she had chosen this relatively conservative dress in order to make the best impression. With it, she wore light-colored espadrilles laced up the ankle. She carried a brown briefcase, empty, because she planned to impersonate a worker from the State Attorney's office.

When she saw Jayson come downstairs carrying their bags, she was afraid that the subdued effect of her wardrobe would be lost. His clothing looked very slick, as usual. To the locals he would look just like the typical South Florida hotshot entrepreneur. He wore tan jeans-style pants that were tight on his sculpted quad muscles, fancy, off-white lizard cowboy boots and a tailored shirt open at the throat. The gold loop earrings were absent today and Kelsey could swear that his dyed yellow hair looked a little toned down, just making him look more handsome, like a model out of GQ. His reflectorized Revo sunglasses and his ubiquitous metallic-colored cellular phone completed the picture- so sharp that it took your breath away. Definitely not something people would approve of around here.

"Couldn't you have worn jeans and a flannel shirt or something?" Kelsey chided.

Jayson just laughed as he tucked his phone into his chin to make a call. "I'll stay in the car," he said.

What had seemed like such a tremendously long drive that night three years ago now went by quickly. They overshot the entrance to the Three Pines Trailer Court at first. It seemed like such a small place hidden in the trees and tall grasses. It was difficult to pick out, although for years it had loomed so large in Kelsey's mind as the epitome of how white trash people lived, the closest she had ever come to seeing it.

Now the trailer park seemed innocuous and very quiet. The sound of the wind over the marsh predominated. Most of the vehicles were gone, with everybody away at work and they had to get out of the car to search for the manager. She was a young tanned woman that they found lying asleep on a chaise lounge between two junked RV's. The woman looked like the type they often saw on Hollywood Beach, women who were leathery and harsh, even though they had trim bodies.

This woman squinted up at them with a friendly smile. Kelsey noticed how her face was somewhat asymmetrical.

"Can I help you?" the manager asked, then exclaimed, "holy shit!" as her sun was blocked by out Jayson's silhouette. "Sorry," she said, noticing Kelsey's proprietary reaction. She wiped her body with a towel and then threw a big T-shirt over her bikini. "You must be the lady from the State Attorney's office."

"Kelsey Reed." Kelsey extended her hand. "We'd like to see number 181," she said, while starting for the direction where she remembered the cul-de-sac. Jayson and the manager followed her. The whole park seemed smaller than she remembered. It took them only a minute to get to the faux wood-trimmed trailer that had made such an impression on her that night.

Kelsey stopped dead in front of it, just breathing the air. Her pulse took off in her chest. There was such a strong feeling that she wished she had never set foot in this trailer, wished she had just left Daniels in there alone.

Everything was different now than it was three years ago. Even the faint smell that came from the trailer was a sour neglected smell, different from before. The toys were gone and the outside of the trailer was in disrepair now.

"The current tenants, they're not involved in any way with Dave Daniels or his wife Allison Hart, are they?" Kelsey asked.

The manager shook her head. "No. After that night that November, that was the last anybody saw of them, when you guys took Davie off to jail."

Kelsey was looking for hatefulness against Daniels in the woman's face, but she didn't see any. "I take it you don't think he should have been arrested?"

The woman kicked at some debris on the lawn. "It's hard to see what purpose something like that would serve. They were good people, especially Allison. She would have given someone the shirt off her back. They were wonderful parents and nobody in this park ever had a bad word to say about them."

Kelsey rolled her eyes at Jayson. She had already told him how everyone put Daniels on a pedestal and cast herself as the bad guy. The only piece that never fit was why, if Daniels was as good a person as everybody said he was, he committed the crimes he did.

She decided to ask the manager straight out. The woman seemed like she had been a good friend of the couple's.

"It seems to me," Kelsey said, "like everyone portrays Dave Daniels as such a wonderful person. Then why do you suppose he stole from people like he did?"

The manager paused in raking the garbage together with her feet, looked at Kelsey very directly and sighed.

"This is only speculation," she said. "They were always poor and lots of times they were late with the mortgage. Dave used to pick up some odd jobs, working with animals, mostly, and Allison would find work cleaning or fill in at the convenience store sometime. Wasn't like there weren't plenty of lean times when they were almost on the street. But this time Davie got scared. I think it was because of the baby..."

"Brandon?"

"The new baby." The woman smiled warmly. "They weren't ready for it. Allison had to leave work as soon as she got pregnant. Basically she was supposed to stay in bed for six months, and possibly she was going to have to be admitted to the hospital for the last weeks of the pregnancy, if there was any chance for her to carry the baby to term. It was a girl, by the way; they saw her on the ultrasound, and that was going to be the last baby Allison could have. They were very excited about it. But, like I say, I think Davie was scared.

"They were about to lose their trailer, their income from Allison's work was gone, and suddenly Davie pays up the balance of their mortgage in cash. We knew that something was up. But, you know, more power to them. They said they were gonna resell the trailer and buy a little place up in Northern Florida with some acreage. Davie would make a living like he used to, hunting and fishing and they planned on farming for their food. The irony is, a few good offers came in for their trailer after it was already seized, after he was in jail."

Kelsey was exasperated. Something was being missed by all the people she was talking to. "Okay, I see what you're saying. They were good people who had troubles. But couldn't the Department of Children and Families have helped a family like that? Isn't that what social service agencies are for?"

"You really don't understand, do you, Miss Reed? People like you just can't understand."

The park manager narrowed her eyes at Kelsey, after first glancing at Jayson, who had picked the worst moment to take a call on his cellular phone. The woman went on. "These people were Florida natives, Florida crackers, that had nothing to do with the cities that grew up around them. Dave Daniels lived most of his life right back there, in the Everglades; he knew how to hunt and how to wrestle 'gators. Your social services system isn't made for people like that. People like them take care of their own, you understand?"

There was a lengthy silence, broken only by Jayson arguing a big money business deal on the telephone. When he was done, the three headed back to the office and the manager yelled at a child wandering in their path, "Go find your mama, and tell her to put some shoes on you!"

Kelsey had just one more question for the woman, but she decided that to get a truthful answer, she'd have to be totally truthful herself and appeal to the woman's strong sense of right and wrong.

"Ma'am," she said, "I need to find Dave Daniels. I know you wouldn't want any harm to come to him, but I need to know if he's been here or if you know where he is. There have been threats made against me. I think it's him and I think I'm in danger."

The woman sighed, looked over Kelsey and took a while to answer. Finally she did. "He called here," she said, "when he first got out of prison. He wanted to see if I or anybody else from the park heard anything about Brandon. We didn't. That was the last I heard from him."

Kelsey and Jayson got into the car. The manager leaned in Kelsey's window and spoke to her privately, so close that Kelsey breathed in her cigarette scented breath. The woman rolled her eyes to indicate Jayson.

"If you're doing him," she said, in a Florida-drawly stage-whisper, "then you're the luckiest girl in the world. That one is good- and he knows it, too!"

Kelsey blushed for Jayson who was already starting to chuckle as they rode off. He was so used to women shamelessly hitting on him that he was able to laugh about it.

Before they could leave the yard, the manager tapped on the rear of the car, and she jogged forward so Kelsey could hear her. "If it *is* Dave Daniels after you," she said, "don't bother to hide. He made his living tracking things." And then she scowled with resignation as the city people drove off.

"Don't worry about what she said," Jayson told Kelsey, pulling her toward him on the seat and rubbing her arm as he turned back onto the country road. "It doesn't matter if she says this guy was a hunter.

You're the investigator; it's your talent. Don't forget that. Now let's get to La Belle."

Jayson spread the map on the steering wheel and Kelsey helped him to navigate back to route 80 and the small town of La Belle. The whole time, she brooded on what the trailer park manager meant by making a living by hunting and fishing. This was a side of Dave Daniels that Kelsey had never known about. She hoped that the foster parents could illuminate it further because she sensed that it was important.

"This is pretty," Kelsey said, as they passed under a canopy of trees approaching one side of the small town, which seemed not much bigger than a bank, a hardware store and an old-fashioned Citgo gas station with a large sign for Bait and Tackle.

"You're such a small town girl," Jayson said warmly. "But I can see the appeal, it's very peaceful."

They had no trouble finding Daniels' old foster home on one of the side streets in the small residential section of the town. The map Jayson had bought at a Seminole owned store on Tamiami Trail was hand drawn and showed all the local roads and trails, as well as topographical features of the swamp. At the address Kelsey had been given, they pulled in under the shade of old pine trees and saw no one at first. There were multiple buildings on the large property but they all seemed in disrepair and uninhabitable. Finally the door cracked open on a small travel trailer.

First, two children ran out and started chasing lizards that they spotted basking in the palmettos. The kids were followed out of the trailer by a darkly tanned old man who wore rough clothes and a baseball cap. Slowly, he helped a heavy woman down the steps. She was old, with opaque granny glasses and enormously swollen ankles. It took a painfully long time for the man to get the woman down the stairs and lower her into a lawn chair.

Jayson rubbed at his eyes under the glasses. "Guess you can do this one on your own. They don't appear very dangerous."

Glancing at the impression he made contrasted with the pathetic old people by the trailer, Kelsey supposed it was best for her to go without him. She gave her boyfriend a quick kiss and hurried across the loamy ground to the couple.

"Mr. and Mrs. Smythe, I'm Kelsey Reed, from the State Attorney's office," she said and extended her hand to shake with both of the older folks. "Thank you for agreeing to speak to me."

The old man tried to offer her something to drink. His voice trembled. His wife, blinking behind the glasses, heaved for breath. The trip down the stairs seemed to have been too much for them.

"You used to be foster parents? For Dave Daniels?" Kelsey asked.

Indicating the two young children, the trembling old man said in his native Florida drawl. "Yup, we did, but now all we do is take in some day care. David Daniels was with us for a while when he was eight years old and then, again, when he was fifteen. What is it you need to know?"

He eyed Kelsey suspiciously from behind his bifocals while his wife fought patiently for breath.

"I need to find out where he is," she said. "Has he been back to see you or contacted you recently?"

Mr. Smythe shook his head. "Last I knew, him and his wife were living at Three Pines. Then I heard there was some trouble with the law."

The old man's glance grew darker, looking her over as if intuition told him that she was the one who put his foster son away. Then Smythe began to laugh until he was wheezing and then he straightened up and held Kelsey's gaze directly. "If he doesn't want you to find him, Missy, you won't."

She was suddenly uncomfortable with Mr. Smythe's gaze. For reassurance, she glanced back at Jayson, who seemed to be napping in the car while the kids ran in circles around it.

Kelsey stood up straighter. "Why wouldn't I be able to find him, Mr. Smythe?"

The man swung his arms wide, indicating all the dense woods that bordered his property. "Because this all is his home!"

The old man, Smythe, watched Kelsey to see if she understood, then he sighed.

"Dave lived back there in the swamps with his daddy, Bill. His momma was a Seminole Indian. They didn't have no formal education 'cept for the Bible; Bill Daniels was real big on that, preaching to anybody that would listen.

"Nobody knows exactly how the family was able to make a living. They hunted, and Bill sold 'gator skins when it was still legal, and they got by. They didn't need much.

"But bad luck used to hang over that Daniels family. The wife got real sick, with cancer of some sort, and Bill went wild, taking her to all sorts of fancy doctors in Miami. That was the first time we had Dave. He was here with us for three weeks or so." Smythe rubbed his wife's swollen hand. "Remember that, honey?" he asked and his wife nodded enthusiastically, the first sign that she was aware of her surroundings.

The old man went on, "Dave was a good boy, real quiet. He always helped out around the place. We sent him to school those three weeks, but he was nothing like the other kids. His momma died then and his daddy came back to get him.

"Dave had to grow up fast. I know he was working with Bill even then. And, at eight years old, the boy knew all there was to know about the woods. He started doing alligator wrestling shows with his Daddy at County Fairs and at the Zoological Park."

Kelsey was having a hard time absorbing what she was hearing. She and her friends had watched an alligator show at the Native American Tribal Gathering in western Hollywood last year and it had thrilled Kelsey. Now she tried to imagine Dave Daniels' thick body slipping into the swamp water, entwining itself with the alligators and struggling violently.

"You're sure?" she asked.

"Oh, yeah," the old man said, caressing his wifes hand. "Those Daniels boys worked with snakes, too. Venomous snakes, also. Learned from the Indians, they said. Rumors were that they lived with those rattlesnakes back at their cabin in the swamp. Hell, I believed it. Wasn't nobody gonna check."

He started laughing and it took him a while to settle down. "Next time Dave came to us he was basically a full grown man, and he stayed with us just a few months. Dave's Daddy was dying in the VA hospital then, some old head wound from Vietnam. Maybe that's why Bill was always so crazy. But he raised the boy good. When Dave met Allison we were all for their relationship. My wife and I been together forty-eight years and we could see what those two had together. The law had it so they couldn't get married because of Dave's age. But they had our blessing. And the Lord's, I'm sure. Is Dave in any trouble with the law now, Miss Reed? Is that why you came here?" he inquired.

The couple both had their eyes on her. Kelsey felt no need to tell them anything that would hurt them. She shook her head and talked through a lump in her throat. "He's not in trouble," she said. "I just need to talk to him. Is there any chance he'd be at that old cabin you mentioned?"

Kelsey felt nervous asking. She didn't really feel prepared to go there and confront Daniels on his own turf.

Mr. Smythe concentrated for a while. "It's possible," he said. "I didn't really know Dave well enough to tell you."

With her chest tightening, but with her body language still confident, Kelsey asked, "How would I find this cabin?"

"It's in the area of the Corkscrew Swamp Sanctuary," the old man said, "back in the swamp, in a place called Rattlesnake Slough. How to find it, I don't know. You'd have to get one of the locals to take you there."

Kelsey thanked the old couple for their time, too preoccupied to worry about how they were capable of taking care of day care kids when they could hardly walk.

"He's an alligator wrestler and rattlesnake charmer!" she said to Jayson when she returned to the car and plopped down in her seat, laughing at the gothic turn her life was taking.

"You're serious?" he asked, tipping his sunglasses so she could see the concern in his eyes.

Kelsey let the story rush out, letting him know finally that she intended to look for her enemy at the cabin in the swamp if she could find it.

"Let me be the one to go there, Kelsey," Jayson said. He pulled the car to the side of the road and brought out the map. "Let me do this myself. I can take your gun. This is the Corkscrew Sanctuary and there's a place called Joe's Fish Camp a few miles away. I could rent a boat there and they could give me directions."

Kelsey touched her boyfriend's soft handsome face, which had become so incredibly dear to her. She understood that Jayson's life would mean nothing to Daniels. In his mind, Kelsey had taken his lover, so he'd probably consider it an Eye for an Eye to kill this young man. And Jayson thought he had to risk his life just because he was sleeping with Kelsey.

"You can drive to the fish camp," she said, "but you're not going in alone. We'll both go," she insisted.

The man who met them in the fish camp parking area was of indeterminate age and very stocky. His body odor wafted to them on the breeze, with the smell of fish guts and infrequently washed clothing. He shifted a toothpick from side to side in his mouth, while giving them a bad look.

"Don't figure you guys are in the right place," he drawled.

The day was mild, with a slight cloud cover. The man in his many layers of clothes, with the gray sky behind him, looked somewhat ominous to Kelsey.

"Let me handle this," Jayson said to Kelsey, passing the cell phone to her and removing the silver sunglasses. He took a few steps forward and extended his hand to the man, who wiped his hands on his pants and reluctantly shook with him.

"We need a bass boat with a small engine and some oars," Jayson said, "and whatever directions you can give us to get to Rattlesnake Slough."

The grizzled owner eyed the bodybuilder blankly, chewing the toothpick and darting cynical looks at the pink purity of Kelsey's outfit.

Jayson spoke up, touching the man on the shoulder to get him moving. "But what we really need right now is some food!"

"Well, this ain't no restaurant," the fish camp owner said. "You got cooking facilities in the cabins. But I was frying up some catfish for myself. You all are welcome to share it," he told them with a wicked grin and then he shuffled toward the fish camp office. Kelsey rolled her eyes. But Jayson was already hurrying ahead with his newfound friend.

They ate what might be Kelsey's last meal, if she did encounter Daniels. This meal consisted of greasy portions of fried local catfish, eaten off foam plates on the counter, where Polaroids of men holding fish were slipped under the Plexiglass and a stuffed boar's head presided over all.

When Kelsey inquired again about directions to Daniels' old cabin, Joe, the owner, answered with his mouth full of the Cajun spiced fish. "That stuff about those boys keeping rattlers with them might be just a rumor. I been here few years myself and I never seen no cabin. Could be there, though. You just have to keep going north."

He hunched over their topographical map with them, marking it with his grease stained fingers. "There's an old observation tower out that way. Pass it, and the Slough should be to your north. That's the most I know."

Then he looked up at them suspiciously. "Some good bass fishing out there too, in case you're interested..."

As Joe helped them off the office dock, Jayson said to him, "Why don't you hand us in some poles and some bait?" When Joe ran to get the supplies and Kelsey looked at her boyfriend like he was nuts, he just looked at her with this boyish expression. "Well," he said, "if we don't find Daniels today, we can get in some fishing."

Jayson looked so innocent, sitting there in the front of the boat. He navigated the channels through the swamp with his map, while Kelsey controlled the engine, steering to match his lefts and rights. Jayson had changed into a white T-shirt and jeans, the most casual clothing she had ever seen him in, while she had changed out of the dress into comfortable chinos and tank top. Kelsey looked around at the wooded hammocks that were draped with ferns, vines and exotic wildflowers. She gazed into the black water where she could just make out the forms of soft-shelled turtles swimming around the boat. She lifted her head, looking up to follow the flight of large wading birds that were crossing to another part of the swamp. The white egrets and hefty blue herons flew so close overhead at times that you could feel the fanning of their wings. This was all new to Kelsey and she found it truly exciting. She glanced over at Jayson and he also looked exhilarated being here. Kelsey smiled. She felt happy here in a unique way. She actually felt more centered than she had in a very long time.

When she spotted the tilted old observation tower a half a mile to their southeast, her mellow mood immediately left and her body went on the alert again. She quickly killed the boat's engine.

Jayson looked back at her and she pointed. "That's the tower," she said. "We'd better stop using the engine here in case Daniels is anywhere around."

They switched places and Jayson took over with the oars while Kelsey directed them through the channels. She couldn't help but feel that there was something magical here. The air had a rich peaty flavor and it tasted alive and life affirming. There were the sounds of the birds and the rustle that the sawgrass made brushing against their boat as they moved slowly through it.

"How deep do you suppose this water is?" Kelsey asked.

"Not deep at all," Jayson said. "The spring rains have just started. Two weeks ago this was probably all dry and the animals would have been looking for water in the gator holes. Even now we'd have no problem walking through here."

Jayson spoke as knowledgeably about the Everglades as he did on most other subjects. She expected the usual answer, that he got the knowledge reading books and asking strangers questions, but she couldn't resist asking anyway, keeping her voice low.

"And how do you know so much about the Florida Everglades?"

"Juan, mostly," Jayson said. "He's of Cuban decent but he was born here in Florida. He and I used to come out to the Everglades all the time to camp and go fishing."

"It's beautiful," Kelsey said, looking around her at the greenery everywhere and the peaceful water. "I could spend time here," she declared, her lungs growing more alive with each breath she drew in. She pulled her hair impatiently into a ponytail and adjusted the pistol in her waistband. "It's a shame," she said, "that it had to take Dave Daniels to finally get me out here. If I had come sooner, possibly I would have done things differently."

Jayson came up behind her, taking her in a gentle embrace. "You're here now," he said, kissing along the nape of her neck and reaching in front of her to tease her erect nipples with his fingers.

Momentarily, Kelsey let her eyes drop shut and she was starting to sigh with pleasure when the noise came. A reverberating bellow, not so much an explosion but more of a roar, the noise seemed to shake the islands and the water itself before fading away.

Kelsey fumbled for the gun, sitting up higher to look in all directions. Jayson held her down. He was laughing.

"It's just a 'gator," he said, "a male. He's probably a few feet from us somewhere."

Kelsey examined the water and the dense foliage but saw nothing. The alligator could be anywhere. "Is he hungry?" she asked.

"No, he's horny." He laughed. "It's the start of mating season. He's calling for a female."

Jayson continued touching Kelsey, more insistently now.

Hours later, Kelsey was first to spot the rowboat. She signaled Jayson to stop and then she ducked lower in the boat as they proceeded slowly, trying to make the sound of their oars like the natural lapping of the water. When they got closer she saw how old the boat was. Its entire floor was rotted into the muck. She would not have made the connection between the boat and the cabin except that Jayson pointed the structure out to her. It was a wood and thatch shanty built high on stilts and sitting up toward the middle of the large hammock. The cabin was so engulfed in trees and vines that it blended with the foliage.

Kelsey directed Jayson to pull the boat under a leafy mangrove and they sat there, totally still. "Let's just listen," Kelsey said, "and watch for a while."

There was no sign of life as they waited. If they hoped to complete trip before nightfall, they would have to do something now. Kelsey told Jayson of her plan to creep around the cabin. She had planned a path through the underbrush where she would not be seen.

Jayson put a firm hand over hers. "Give me the gun, Kelsey. I'll be the one to go," he said.

"No," Kelsey hissed, "this isn't your fight!"

"But you're my woman!" he hissed back in her ear. He slipped the gun out of her fingers and into his own firm grasp, climbed out of the boat and began his stealthful progress up the island.

Kelsey took up a fishing knife from the tackle box for her own protection and she scanned up and down the channel, aware of the possibility that Daniels might not be on the island now but might be following them by boat.

It didn't take Jayson long to return and he was walking and talking normally now. "There's nothing there," he said. "But I don't know if you want to see this place. It might give you the creeps."

Kelsey climbed out of the boat, oblivious to Jayson's warning. She wanted to know all she could know about Dave Daniels.

Directly in front of the primitive house was a huge fire pit, containing what was probably decades' worth of charred remains. The pit was big enough to cook some large animal like a wild boar. Seeing it brought Kelsey up short.

"This is probably where they did all their cooking," she said, "I doubt there is any kind of kitchen in there."

Jayson smiled at her naiveté. "No toilet either, or electricity. You do realize what you're looking at?" he asked.

The next thing Kelsey saw was snakeskins. The skins hung all around the underside of the home, in the shaded area under the stilts where it appeared the men had done most of their living. She gasped when she almost stepped into the curtain of cured skins, most of them trailing rattles.

"My God," she said, while Jayson fingered a rattle, looking fascinated.

"Be careful," he said, "when you walk. There could still be some live snakes around here."

"You think they lived with them?" Kelsey exclaimed.

"Don't you?" he asked, as they pushed through the curtain of skins to investigate the dim porch area.

This entire outdoor room showed signs of a strange sensibility. Someone had painstakingly created furniture- a table and several chairs and work surfaces. But they didn't realize that, because they had chosen imperfect types of wood from the swamp, the pieces all looked like the works of a lunatic. Gnarled, and twisted, the legs of the furnishings looked like those of some horrific animals, starting to creep forward.

That same person had an interesting sense of humor. They had crafted dozens of wind chimes out of various combinations of fishing lures and animal bones. These played an off key, but strangely lulling, tune in the light breeze.

Kelsey looked around at various implements, including one that looked like a spear and hand-hewn bowls, which were made from hollowed out gourds, she guessed. There was also a fifteen-foot alligator skin tacked to the underside of the floor, one of their kills, she supposed.

Kelsey wondered about the mind of the young man who had thrived in a place like this and the thought of it shook her to her core. Obviously Daniels was now able to function in her world, at least enough to stalk her without getting caught. Would she have been able to function in his?

"What are you thinking?" Jayson asked.

"What it would be like to be him," Kelsey said, getting a sudden vision of the milky rolls of fat on the boy's belly and feeling a closeness, and an immediacy. "...What it would be like at night with all this dark wilderness around you..." She looked around dreamily.

"What do you feel for this guy?" Jayson asked her, a little harshly.

He sounded disturbed, jealous. Kelsey chose not to answer him. She climbed the wooden rungs to get upstairs.

Here, two windows had rusted screens nailed over them. There were two cots; each made up with a different colored Indian blanket, now faded. Another blanket hung between them for privacy. One bed had a side table with a basin on it. There was a faded Bible and an intricately carved hunting knife in the drawer of the primitive bedside table. A big rough- hewn crucifix hung above the bed, which was made up with tight corners, military style.

The other bed also had a cross above it. But Kelsey knew immediately that this one, the one with the orange and red blanket and the bone wind chime hanging above it, had once belonged to Davie.

Kelsey sat down on the bed, staring at an orchid that was growing out of a knothole in the wood right outside the window next to his bed. The flower was the loveliest and lushest purple color she had ever seen, fit for some mysterious rainforest rather than this primitive shanty. She wondered if the young Dave Daniels had placed it there deliberately, to live off the humid air and mist, and to flourish in the years to come no matter what happened to him.

She was so lost in thought that she was surprised Jayson had entered the room and was raising his voice at her. "What are you doing, Kelsey?" he demanded of her.

Coming slightly out of her trance-like state, she told him. "When I first saw Dave Daniels, he was sitting in bed. I guess I always wondered what it would be like to be him. But I can't know that, can I?"

Jayson took her hand and gently pulled her from the bed.

"You wouldn't let yourself live a horrible existence like this," he said. "You'd fight it. Don't forget who you are. Don't let Daniels do that to you or else he will win."

Later Kelsey thought about it all in the stifling kitchen of the cabin they rented at Joe's Fish Camp. She cleaned and fried a fish that Jayson had caught while he was still busy fishing off the dock. Kelsey pushed at her hair that was now long and wild, with all of the highlights grown out. The slight down that had grown back on her upper lip emphasized the darkness and depth of her eyes. Her bikini wax had also gone neglected, she had become more muscular, losing weight around the ribs, and yet the constant sexuality had somehow caused her breasts to swell and become fuller. Many days, like today, she wore casual tops without a bra and it didn't matter because she was starting not to care what people thought of her. Pushing back her sweaty hair, and standing in the doorway to gaze at the magenta sunset and the big human shape of her man sitting by the dark swamp water, Kelsey was very aware of all the physical changes in herself.

She felt loose and careless. She knew, in some ways, she was starting to act like white trash, just like Daniels. But yet she felt roused from some slumber and infinitely more wide-awake than she had ever been.

"Jayson," she called out in a hoarse voice, "dinner!" And she shuddered with gratefulness that, after this day, she was still alive.

Chapter 20

Jayson didn't move from the dock so Kelsey went to him, walking barefoot through the grass. She found that he was no longer fishing, but looking at the sunset and feeding a soft-shelled turtle, whose head broke the water as she approached.

It was now almost dark. Kelsey brushed the tips of her breasts over Jayson's tense back muscles. "Come to dinner," she said, huskily, "there's something I want to tell you."

He came back with her and she sat on his lap in the old-fashioned kitchenette and fed him pieces of breaded fish.

"I'm so happy to see you cooking again," he said warmly.

Kelsey squirmed with pride. "I used supplies from Joe's little general store." She referred to the provisions that Joe sold off a rusty shelf in a corner in the office. "Don't you want to know my news?" she asked brightly.

"What?"

"I'm not going back to work in criminal justice. I can see that it's not right for me. Maybe I'll do something with interior decorating."

She felt so excited about all the clear possibilities that were now opening up. She wanted to make love. And she wanted to be the one to initiate it this time. But Jayson stopped her from lifting his shirt and undoing his jeans.

He nuzzled against her ear. "Let's take a ride in the boat," he suggested. Then led her outside, gently guiding her in the almost total darkness. At the dock, he helped her into their small boat.

As Jayson maneuvered the boat up the silvery black creek, Kelsey realized that their way was illuminated by stars. A sparkling intricate blanket of them overhead sparkled on the water and it was like nothing she had ever seen.

She drew in breaths of the nighttime air quietly while listening to the singing of frogs and the subtle noises of larger animals rustling the sawgrass or sloshing into the water. "This is so wonderful," she said, trembling at the intensity of her reaction to this place. She reached out, letting her fingers trail in the water, wanting to feel its coolness.

"I wouldn't do that, Baby," Jayson said. He came to sit near her in the boat, pulling her hand out of the water and holding her tightly against his body. Then he sang to her, an old blues lullaby that didn't seem silly at all at the moment, just powerfully romantic. A citronella candle burned feebly at the other end of the boat, Jayson had lit it to repel mosquitoes, which were a major problem out here in the 'Glades. If they were getting bitten, though, Kelsey didn't notice. Nothing could have disturbed her much right now.

"Let me show you something," Jayson said. He turned on the flashlight and slowly directed it on the water in all directions around the boat. Kelsey saw what he meant her to see, a hundred brightly glowing gems in the water, round phosphorescent points of light, some of them slowly moving.

"What are they?" she asked. "They're so beautiful!"

Jayson leaned against her and played his hands and mouth gently over her face and hair. "You know what they are, Baby. They're alligators. That's their 'eye shine' you're seeing- the reflection off their irises."

Kelsey was overwhelmed by the intensity of the moment. "I want to make love to you, Jayson. I want to show you everything I've learned. Lay back," she instructed in a whisper which would not disturb the animals, some probably as big as eight or ten feet, that again lurked unseen in the water now that the spotlight was out.

Kelsey assertively opened his jeans and then removed their T-shirts and balled them into a pillow for Jayson's head. Her lover lay back, with his perfectly developed body illuminated by white starlight and his eyes dreamily gazing at Kelsey with the backdrop of stars behind her.

Kelsey climbed carefully on top of him, finding her center of gravity in the boat, and she lowered herself onto his erection. She listened to nature before finding her rhythm to ride him. And then she rode Jayson, moving her body in sync with the drifting of their boat in the currents and the restless rumblings and splashes of the animals around them in the water.

The lovers sighed with the pleasure that seemed to transcend their bodies and to join them for a moment with nature. Then a breeze came up, a strong, titillating breeze, rich with all the smells of the swamp. It lifted their spirits and brought them to climax together. Jayson quietly closed his eyes and gripped Kelsey's hips. A groan erupted from out of Kelsey, a primal declaration of her pleasure that was met by the sounds of the animals and of the night.

Ironically, the first evidence of Dave Daniels did not come until they arrived back in Fort Lauderdale the next day. Jayson had driven Kelsey to an ATM so that she could take a cash advance on her last good credit card in order to make May's mortgage payment. She had climbed across his lap in the car to slip her credit card into the machine and Jayson was teasing her by tugging on her breasts.

"Stop!" she giggled. "These things have cameras!"

Distracted, it took her a moment to realize that the ATM machine had gobbled up her card.

Kelsey's mouth dropped open as she watched the screen flash at her "Overlimit card. Please contact your financial institution."

"It's Daniels," she said, dropping back into her seat. "He's gotten into my credit cards!" She tried to keep the teary edge out of her voice as she said bitterly, "he's done this to let me know that he knows I went to his home."

It was hard for Kelsey to keep control. This latest act seemed so direct and intimate, like he was deliberately closing in on her.

"I can't pay the mortgage," she said in wonderment.

Jayson gripped the steering wheel harder in anger, but he spoke calmly. "He's just playing games. First, talk to your bank. Maybe there's nothing actually wrong. But then, if there still is a problem, I can help you with the mortgage."

When they got back to her condo, Kelsey found that her plants, including the purple flowers on the windowsill, had died. The air was stale and dead. Usually, Miranda would come to take care of Mr. Cooper and would air out the place. Now, there was no need for anyone to come. Kelsey was unused to the emptiness.

While Jayson scoped out the refrigerator, Kelsey checked her messages. The machine was full and all but one of the calls came from Miranda, who sounded progressively bitchier and more worried. "Where are you, Girl? And where is Jayson? This is getting to be crazy. I'm calling the fucking cops if you don't call me back!"

Kelsey and Jayson looked at each other after that last message and started to laugh. They couldn't help it. "She is such a drama queen," Kelsey said, finally releasing some of the tension about the credit card.

The last message was for Jayson from Juan. "Yo, Buddy, I can't reach you on your cellular. It's about that bodybuiding competition in Miami. Are we going, or what?"

Jayson tried to tell her that he was not leaving her, but Kelsey insisted.

"I'll go to Miranda's," she said. "She needs to talk to me, anyway." Jayson willingly agreed to drive her to Miranda's. They had spent barely fifteen minutes at the condo before leaving again.

Miranda greeted Kelsey at the door of her apartment wearing only an unbecoming red crochet bikini. She pulled back abruptly from their hug, wrinkling her nose.

"You smell like a swamp!" she said, and glanced up at Jayson. "You look shitty, too. Where have you guys been?"

Jayson gave Miranda a reassuring kiss on the cheek and looked into her eyes to focus her attention. "Kelsey will tell you all about it. But, Miranda, you need to take care of her. Any sign of some guy hanging around here, some fat guy, you call the police first, then call me."

Jayson kissed Kelsey deeply before he left.

"Daniels is into my credit cards," she immediately told her friend. While Kelsey talked, Miranda led her into the kitchen for a cup of hot tea. She also hung fresh towels in the bathroom for Kelsey to take a shower.

"Don't worry," Miranda said. "Your friends will help you out."

Kelsey summed up their trip for her friend, omitting only some of the more gruesome details about Allison and the baby. Then she made the calls to her credit card company. She discovered that the rest of her line of credit had been used up in topless bars and adult bookstores in Miami and Fort Myers.

"That scum!" she yelled, slamming down the phone.

"I don't understand," Miranda said, leaning back in a big chair with her legs stretched out to rest on the bed. "Is this guy some kind of pervert?"

"No!" Kelsey said, "not at all. He's mocking me. He intends for me to lose my home. But he's rubbing my face in it; trying to tell me I'm a whore!"

Miranda looked seriously concerned for her. "Maybe don't read so much into it... Do you think Jayson might help you with the condo?" she asked. "He's got all kinds of money."

Kelsey sighed, thinking about the compromises she had already made. "He doesn't really have that much. His company deals with high-risk investments, so what he makes is really erratic. Then, he's paying for college and paying eight hundred dollars a month on that creepy little room at the beach. With the way he spends on clothes and meals out, he doesn't have much left. Miranda, I already let him pay this month's mortgage. But I don't know what's next."

She and Miranda looked at each other, sharing the same thought until Kelsey voiced it. "I know that he could move in. It could save so much money. But with all that's been going on, I don't know what it would do to the relationship. And he's all that I have. I can't afford to lose him."

It wasn't until almost one in the morning that Jayson called to say he was on his way up from Miami. Kelsey was already yawning and groggy when Miranda chose to tell her own bit of news. Miranda intended to go to work as a telemarketer for Marshall Sawyer's cellular phone service company.

Kelsey tried to argue with her but Miranda was convincing. She seemed to be more stable and grounded than she had been in a while. She told Kelsey, "It's a legitimate job where I can make some good money and start paying up back rent and other shit. There's no drugs involved. That's ancient history. Don't worry about me."

At this point, Kelsey was too tired to argue. There was a knock at the door and Kelsey felt like a little girl, handed off to Jayson in the dead of night, while he thanked Miranda for staying with her and keeping her safe. Dave Daniels seemed to be taking away her independence as well as everything else.

Kelsey was fearful of bringing up the subject of moving in together to Jayson. Emotional commitment had always been frightening to her. Now fate was bringing Kelsey and Jayson together so quickly. She felt she could not resist the rightness of them getting more and more committed. Yet she felt she was not necessarily standing on solid ground.

When they got back to her condo, she plunged in and said what needed to be said, totally shutting out her fears and doubts for the moment.

"I think it would be a good idea for you to move into the condo," she said. "It's the only way we're going to make it financially. I can't keep taking money from you if you have to pay for that place at the beach."

Jayson lowered himself to sit next to her at the table, gazing at her wonderingly. "Is this about money?" he asked.

She shook her head, swallowing a lump in her throat. "You know I love you. It's just that I'm ready to make the commitment now."

What Jayson said next absolutely shocked Kelsey. With a totally straight face he said, "If we're going to move in, then we need to be married, or at least engaged."

She stared at Jayson for a very long time. From the set of his body, she knew he was serious.

Not that she had ever thought about them marrying. But now there was something that hurt her so deeply. In an outraged whisper, she asked, "How could you marry me when you've never even told me you love me!"

Jayson rubbed at his eyes and said in a small voice, "I show you every day..."

They stared at each other with grief in their faces, knowing that until one of them compromised on this they would not be moving in together.

Finally, Jayson said, "Don't worry about the condo for now. I'll help you with whatever you need."

It was three in the morning. Their day had started at seven-o'clock back on the West Coast of Florida and now they were tired. Leaving the table, they retreated to Kelsey's chilly bed, where they could sleep deeply and worry about their problems at a later time.

The next week Kelsey went to work for the law office on Powerline Drive and she collected one paycheck, which she insisted Jayson take for part of the money he had loaned her. At the time of her next payday, however, there was no more money. Apparently the firm was under some sort of investigation and they were having their assets frozen. Kelsey left the job until they at least could pay her what they already owed her. It was ironic that Miranda was having better luck getting paid telemarketing for that crook, Marshall Sawyer. It was as though life was taking place in slow motion, as though Kelsey was waiting for Daniels to make an appearance, so that she could finally confront him. Anything that she might accomplish at this time could be useless anyway since Dave Daniels could ruin it in a moment.

She and Jayson didn't discuss moving in together for a while, although she knew that it remained on both their minds. He loaned her the June mortgage payment and she found out that he had pawned his platinum dress watch in order to do it. She wondered why she hadn't thought of pawning something herself, rather than letting Jayson sneak out and do it so that she wouldn't have to. She felt troubled and she again brought up the idea of them moving in together.

"Maybe I'll compromise," Jayson said, and he pulled her to him gently. "Just give me some time on this one, Baby."

Kelsey looked deeply into his topaz-colored eyes. "I'd rather have you say the words," she said.

He didn't break the look. "I know that you would," he said.

Even Miranda agreed that the fact Jayson wouldn't say the words "I love you" didn't mean much because the love that he felt for Kelsey was so apparent. And Kelsey felt it herself, a love that was so rich and powerful that it swept her up and engulfed her like the ocean, that dark warm ocean outside of Jayson's room.

This summer, like the last, was incredibly hot. The weather became so hot it made Kelsey's blood feel thick and her mind cloudy. Her senses were filled with nothing but Jayson- the sight of his dear sparkling eyes mesmerizing her, while he lowered his body over her, with his muscles highlighted like some sculpture in the moonlight, his eyes fixed on hers and his body determined with wanting her.

There at Hollywood Beach the moon had an odd way of rising. It would come over the horizon gigantic and yellow orange and swollen, occupying a great portion of the sky. Later, it would rise up and become smaller and silver. Then would come flashes of heat lightening in the distance. Jayson had the patience to sit out there all night and watch all of it, to listen to the intimate whisperings of the palm fronds and the rushing of the waves all night and, from him, Kelsey learned to do this, too.

"My life is completely different since knowing you," she said, sitting beside him one evening in the damp sand. "And I really mean that, not just like any girlfriend would say it to her boyfriend to be romantic. I mean really, my life has taken a completely different path since knowing you. It's frightening in ways, the place I am now, the depth of the love I feel and the depth of all my feelings."

"I know, Kelsey," he said. "I'm right there with you." He pushed her gently down into the sand and he stripped her jeans down and entered her. She watched his eyes, filled with streetlight, glance up briefly at the Broadwalk to make sure no one could see them under the lip of sand.

Every sultry night Jayson would take her down to the beach and have her. He would make love to her in the aquamarine colored ocean during the day. He made love to her in her own swimming pool the nights they stayed at her condo. Kelsey's life consisted of feeling the Florida heat and making love to Jayson Carter, tasting his mouth, responding to the relentless seduction of his tongue, arching herself to join her body to his.

"I'm intoxicated by you, Jayson. I was never a passionate person but now I feel like we've stepped beyond, into somewhere most people don't go."

Jayson grinned, thrusting inside her as they spoke in whispers and then rolled over to laugh at the nighttime sky.

237

"This is special for me, too, Kelsey. I could die making love to you. I could just do this and do this until I die, I'm so incredibly obsessed with you."

They had stepped beyond an ordinary relationship into this drenching consuming passion where there was only each other. Kelsey felt that she experienced Jayson's soul when they made love and she knew that he knew hers. He had understood her better than she understood herself when they first met and now she recognized herself as the person he had seen then.

Kelsey had the knowledge that this was it; this was the man she was meant to be with for the rest of her life. His gorgeous face and body were just extras. It was the way that he made the world itself come alive that was so special to her. She would love this man just as much if he were ugly, maybe more. She was so obsessed with him that she knew she would devour the excitement of his ugliness if he was ugly. She laughed to herself and he wanted to know what was so funny.

"You know, at the very beginning," she said, "you wanted to know if I would love you if you were ugly. Well, I was thinking about that, how my love for you is so desperate and aggressive. I just want to love you for your soul, to get inside every cell in your body. This love has nothing to do with what you look like at all. You could be the most revolting-looking man on the planet and I'd get off being with you... Can you understand that?"

She hoped that he could understand the fury of her love. She sensed that he did. She knew that even Jayson, who was so self-contained, hadn't expected their connection to turn out like it did and he was also being carried away by it.

"You know," he said, playing with her wet pussy lips and spreading them as she lay sprawled out on the sand gasping with the intensity of her feeling for him. Hers was a hunger that could not be satisfied although they were together so many hours of every day, a hunger that still raged when he was inside her.

"You know..." he whispered meanly. He was testing her, testing that the intensity she spoke of was real. "...Every time we make love out here on the beach, your stalker is probably back there somewhere watching you; watching your little hips and your tight ass and the way you let me put my big cock deep inside you. And he's probably thinking what a slut you are and how he'd get off on killing you."

Jayson held his wet penis over her, trembling with restraint. "Do you ever think about that Kelsey? Or are you just too gone when I'm fucking you to realize? Is it really that intense? Do you care more about fucking me than you do your life? Do you care about it more than your pride?" he whispered.

Kelsey knew the greatest intensity in the world was here with Jayson, with his soul so brutal and yet so innocent and gentle. She reached up to kiss him. "I love you so much, Jayson," she said. "I'd fuck you in front of the whole world..." She felt the dirty words catch in her throat. But she would talk this way for him; she'd pass any test he put out for her. She knew that surely now in her own soul. She arched her body to take him snugly inside her and captured his shining eyes with hers.

"I'm terrified for my life, you know that Jayson?" she confessed, telling him and herself the real truth for the first time. "I really believe he's going to kill me, yet the biggest intensity I feel is still being with you. I'll pass any test you want." An image flashed before her of the rolls of creamy white flesh, the crafty eyes, standing in the shadows on the Broadwalk, watching her and hating her. "I'll fuck you in front of Daniels!" she cried and began crazily thrusting. And then she started violently sobbing until it shook her whole body.

Jayson slid out of her, and he cradled her in his arms, kissing her wet face and cleaning sand away from her eyes and mouth and hair. "Kelsey," he soothed, like he was comforting a child. "He's not there. I've been watching every time."

He stroked her forehead and kissed her hair but her sobbing wouldn't stop. She started dry heaving like she was going to throw up. "I was just being a mean motherfucker," Jayson said, apologizing. "It gets me off to play head games, to test you like that. Don't worry about it."

Staggering beside him up to his room and still sobbing like a crazy woman, Kelsey felt for a moment the warm armor of the sexuality stripped away and felt a suddenly cool ocean breeze. And she could feel, with a certainty, the lonely and patient presence that had been there all along, that had been in her life for three years although she didn't know it. She sensed the cold presence and recognized her own fragility in her desperate fear of him, a fear that could do her no good. Daniels could be standing in one of the little alleys between the buildings right now.

After that night, Kelsey pulled slightly away from Jayson emotionally, asking him for some time alone at her condo. Her friend Jerry kept her company and he was also driving her to job interviews at the galleries on Las Olas. She had lied to Jayson and told him that she was sleeping over on a Friday night at Miranda's. In reality, she needed space from Jayson. She felt somehow compromised after what had been said on the beach. And she knew she needed to be alone with her fear, to face it, because she now realized that it had been destroying her.

The worst thing Daniels could do was to kill her. But she needed to make peace with her own soul and its desires. She was leaning on all her pillows, with the gun hidden under her covers, when the phone rang. She leaped in the air; sure that it was Daniels calling because she was finally alone.

After the first few softly spoken words, she was still thinking it was Daniels. Actually, it was Jayson. His call was unexpected.

"You win," Jayson said, simply, "I'll move into your condo in July if you haven't gotten a job yet. We don't have to be engaged, although we can be any time you want to."

Kelsey said not a word. Jayson sounded serious and contrite, not like he expected her to answer. "Kelsey," he said, finally, "please get Miranda or even Jerry over there. I'll go crazy thinking that you're there by yourself."

Chapter 21

Jayson started bringing his things over one bag at a time each night he slept at Kelsey's condo. But something didn't feel right. Maybe it was that he kept expressing doubts about what they were going to do, or maybe it was the empty feeling in the condo without Mr. Cooper there.

Kelsey was seeing Jerry practically every day for her job search. Afterwards, he would take her to lunch and they'd gossip together. Her friend had changed very much in the past few months and she felt privileged to see this newer version of Jerry. His unruly hair was much longer and pulled back into a ponytail, his clothing was very stylish and his whole manner was freer and more relaxed. He said he was very happy that Kelsey had chosen to work in the creative fields. He told her how changing careers had already changed his life for the better. Working at the art gallery gave him an outlet for his imagination and a chance to make other people's lives better.

And Jerry turned out to be right that it might work for Kelsey. That day, which was an unusual ninety-five degree Wednesday, Kelsey came bouncing out of a gallery that specialized in handmade items for the home. She ran up to the driver's side window of Jerry's car.

"I got the job!" she squealed and leaned into the window for Jerry's hug.

And that is when she got the brilliant idea to surprise Jayson with a special gift. She already knew that Jayson was moving into the condo on July first even if she did get a job. He had told her that he wanted to. But Kelsey wanted to do something to address the strange emptiness they were feeling, something that could make their moving in together the special experience it was meant to be. She knew that part of their problem was the loss of Mr. Cooper. Without him, they felt like a family that had lost one of its members.

Kelsey knew how much Jayson loved animals and she remembered him saying once that he used to have a cat when he was younger. Of course, there could be no replacing her cynical, old gray tomcat. But she thought if she bought Jayson a kitten, it could be a sign of hope for both of them.

She wanted it to be the perfect animal for them because they would be spending many years with it. She remembered Jayson telling her that his cat had been big and furry and so that was the kind of cat she determined to get. With Jerry's help, she scanned newspapers spread all over a table in their favorite cafe. And when she saw an ad for Maine Coon Cats, she knew that was the type of cat she would have to buy; that breed of cat was about the biggest and furriest you could get. She hugged her own arms with enthusiasm.

"Jerry, he's gonna love it!" she said.

Paying for the expensive animal would only be possible if Kelsey pawned every piece of jewelry she owned. But it didn't matter; Jayson had already done so much for her. If she could give him back a tiny bit of all the pleasure he had given her, then Kelsey would be happy. There was also the matter of getting Jerry to drive her to the pawnshop in a bad area of Lauderhill, but he agreed to do it.

Jerry said the errand made him feel like a character in a noir detective film but he admired what Kelsey wanted to do for Jayson. He thought that it showed real love. He said that he would have never imagined Kelsey standing in a seedy pawnshop and giving up all her jewelry and smiling about it because she wanted to do something nice for someone else.

"You've turned a corner," he said, jokingly. Maybe he was jealous that he wasn't the man making her act this way. But he didn't show it. He just acted very happy for the positive changes in his old friend.

Jerry drove her back home and gave her a kiss on the cheek as she got out of the car, holding the large kitten she had purchased.

"You're wonderful, Kelsey," Jerry said. "I definitely envy him. Now, you better get upstairs or it won't be a surprise."

Kelsey wanted so badly for Jayson to be happy that she actually felt stage fright when she heard his steps coming upstairs. She trembled, hugging the kitten against her chest and adjusting the red ribbon she had tied around its neck, fluffing out its fur and pulling out stray hairs.

"He's going to love you," she said to the kitten. The young animal also trembled, and it smelled very slightly of pee. The kitten had been nervous since getting here, maybe picking up Kelsey's own apprehension that it would not satisfy Jayson.

Kelsey had paid a thousand dollars for the cat, hoping that she would get it exactly right. The twelve-week old kitten was a purebred Maine Coon Cat, extremely large, fluffy and multicolored, just like he had once described his cat to be.

Jayson stepped through the door, talking on his phone and smiling. His eyes immediately locked on those of the cat she was holding and he disconnected the call without saying good-bye.

He looked very big as he approached them and very displeased. He was imposing in his size. Kelsey felt the large kitten squirm, leaking more urine onto her arm.

"What did you do?" he demanded. The anger in his voice was chilling. She had never seen him like this.

Kelsey held her ground as Jayson stepped around her, looking at the uncomfortable animal from every angle. Tears started forming in her eyes but she didn't want to give him the satisfaction of seeing her break down crying.

His light eyes slanted down, focusing on herself and the frightened kitten like they were one and the same, both frauds, offensive to him. There was something cold and merciless in his voice.

"What exactly is meant here?" he asked her coldly.

It took Kelsey a moment to get her thoughts together. Jayson waited.

"I wanted us to feel like a family," she said. "I don't know why I did this exactly. I pawned everything I own."

She said it with an ironic twist to her mouth, laughing at herself. "It's just, I've been so devastated since losing Cooper. And I remember how you talked about your cat that you used to have. You called him Scruffy, right?"

Jayson reached out to scratch the large kitten under its chin. It was already the size of Mr. Cooper at its young age. "So this is meant to replace Scruffy, then? And your Mr. Cooper? Like they just never existed? And we can just move on?" he persisted in the cruel steely voice.

The kitten started panting, terrified of him. This was the first animal she had ever seen that did not love Jayson. She wondered what it would feel like to have her boyfriend hit her. Because that's what it felt like he wanted to do. And it was all so irrational.

"So, what particular breed is this, anyway?" he asked, while the kitten endured his caresses. "Something expensive, I'd imagine. You'd only want the best for me."

Kelsey held up her head as she answered him. "He's a Maine Coon Cat. They get very large. This one is only twelve weeks old. I was going to call him Fluffy. If you wanted to keep him, that is..."

A very long silence went on. "...If this is not going to ruin your moving in," she said. Kelsey started to tremble as the dark thought really sunk in.

Jayson stepped back and started slowly to pace. "You know," he said, "about moving in. It makes me wonder why, if you love me so much and you're so desperate to have me live with you, why you don't want to marry me. Makes me think you really don't love me like you say you do."

His voice got very quiet as he faced her again, interrogating. "Is it all about the sex, Kelsey? Is your supposed love for me really about how I look?" Suddenly, his voice rose to a bellow that shook the kitchen. "Why the hell won't you marry me!"

Kelsey was stunned at the unfairness. Her voice trembled with anger and hurt as she yelled back at him. "You're the one that's the problem here. I shouldn't even have agreed to move in with you if you won't say you love me. And you expect me to marry you! That's fucking twisted."

Jayson's teeth clenched together in anger. There were blotches of color on his cheeks. "You know why I won't say it. It's a promise I made..."

Kelsey started yelling furiously into Jayson's face, letting out anger and resentment she didn't even know that she had. "I know about your damn promise! Well, I've got a news flash for you. Your girlfriend left you. She didn't care shit for you..."

A roaring sound came out of Jayson and he crossed the space between them, with one hand extended toward Kelsey's throat. It happened so quickly that she could not even move back.

"Don't you *ever* talk about her!" he bellowed.

Jayson tried to stop himself, but the force of his attack was so strong that it carried Kelsey across the kitchen and into the glass doors on the other end of the living room. His arm shook with restraint on her neck while the cat gouged its claws deeply into her exposed chest. She let the cat drop and she glanced down at the hand that was on her throat and then back up into Jayson's eyes. He also looked down at his hand and she could see his horror at what he could have done here.

Gradually, he let his hand slip down and backed off a few steps.

Indignation swelled inside Kelsey and she knew she had to stand by what was right, had to stand by her pride. He had already taken so much pride away from her but, especially now, it was all she had left.

"Say the words, Jayson, or I want you out of here," she said, quietly. "If you don't love me, if you won't say it, then I don't want you in my life."

"You're telling me you want me to leave?" he asked.

Kelsey just nodded. If she spoke, she was going to explode in tears.

Jayson narrowed his eyes at her hatefully. "You want me gone, I'm gone. I'll go back to California. But don't ever expect me to say those three words to you!" He finished yelling at her and turned to walk towards the front door.

"Go then," she screamed hoarsely. "I don't need you!" She lifted a heavy piece of Indian pottery and threw it. The pottery smashed against the front door frame. But Jayson was already gone.

Air from the open door filled the condo and Kelsey just stood there in the darkened living room. The kitten's eyes glowed under the wicker couch where it had hidden. Kelsey stood there for a very long time listening to the sounds of an occasional car in her parking lot, the neighbors' TV's through their open windows and what she thought might be the far off traffic on Hillsboro Boulevard or even I-95.

She had no idea of how much time passed. Time no longer mattered. Jayson was gone. Kelsey's blood flowed, her senses worked, she breathed for Jayson. Being with his body was part of her body now. She felt like she could not even die without her boyfriend. There was no Kelsey without Jayson. Now Jayson was gone.

An hour later or maybe more, a large male silhouette appeared in the open doorway. Kelsey's heart leapt and she ran forward, stopping suddenly when she realized that it was not Jayson.

Her purse with the gun was back in the bedroom. This could be Daniels facing her now.

It wasn't. The man stepped fully into the doorway, with his shoes crackling on the broken pottery. It was Juan Reyes, wearing a tiny tank top over his glistening muscles and looking around, perplexed.

"Kelsey?" he asked softly, "is everything all right?" He sought out her eyes in the shadows.

"Yes," she said, stepping out and blinking in the light.

"What happened to you?" he asked, coming forward and taking her by the arms, and his face knitted up with concern for her. Kelsey glanced down where he was looking at her chest in the skimpy gray camisole. There were several huge welts across her small chest, beaded up with big shiny drops of blood. Blood had soaked parts of the shirt.

"That?" Kelsey asked, dreamily. "The cat got scared and scratched me."

Juan looked troubled staring down at Kelsey. She had never appreciated how attractive Juan actually was with his big, soulful dark eyes, his deeply tanned skin and softly defined features. He was slightly taller and bigger then Jayson.

Juan glanced back at the broken vase suspiciously. "Where's Jayson?" he asked. "He was making plans for me to come over tonight and then we got disconnected or something..."

"He's gone," Kelsey said.

Juan's mouth dropped open. "No," he said, finally. "He wouldn't ever leave you."

"He's going back to California," Kelsey said and laughed hysterically. "You better find yourself a new friend."

"I'll stay with you until we can get Miranda over here," Juan told her. "I don't want this character who's been stalking you coming around."

"Him? I don't care about him!" She started laughing crazily again.

Juan stayed with her while she took a shower and cleaned up the cuts. She changed into a new shirt, throwing the bloody one away. When she came back out to the living area she found the deeply tanned bodybuilder crouched down, cleaning up the last fragments of pottery. He smiled when he saw her, offering her something to drink, soda or a glass of cold water. Kelsey felt that he was humoring her, he was treating her so delicately. She knew that Juan was a good friend and that he cared about her, but seeing that look of genuine concern in his expressive brown eyes truly maddened her. Kelsey could not deal with being an object of pity because his best friend had dumped her.

"Juan," she said, laughing lightly so that she hoped he could see she was now okay, "we can't just sit here staring at each other. I'll be fine. I know Dave Daniels' methods by now. He'll let me suffer with the breakup for a while before doing anything else."

Jayson's friend was looking at her oddly. She had started talking about her stalker like she knew him. She guessed it might seem strange.

"Anyway," she said, gently, "I really want to be alone right now, Juan, I really need to. I'm sure you can understand."

It was Juan's character to always be a gentleman, so he finally agreed to respect her wishes, only after she assured him that she would call the police at the slightest indication of trouble. The big man backed out the doorway, telling her that he would stop by periodically tonight just to check the property. She thought he might have also called Miranda but she wasn't sure.

When Juan was gone, Kelsey got a bottle of good wine from the refrigerator, grabbed a glass and went to sit at the top of the outdoor steps, leaving the door of her condo standing open behind her. She looked out into the night and found its moist black emptiness to be much like what was inside of her.

She raised her first full glass to the darkness in a toast.

"Dave Daniels," she called. "You see that my man's gone. So now you might as well come and get me. It's just you and me now. Come and get me!" she called and she saw some of the old people's lights go on and faces peering out of curtains.

But there was no sign of her stalker. He would want her to feel what it was like to be alone.

Kelsey was awakened the next morning by the sound of the kitten crying to her for food. She lifted her face from the cement and three empty wine bottles rolled away from her. The day was coming to life and emptiness still swept around airily inside of her. She prayed for death.

She went to care for the neglected kitten. Its eyes were glassy and it dragged the pathetic bow. She did not blame the animal. It was Jayson's unrealistic arrogance that was at fault, and her inability to love right or to be loved.

As she went about her chores, Kelsey stared straight ahead. Her motions were mechanical. Without Jayson this was all going to be one never ending day, today and all the days after it.

Someone had sabotaged Kelsey's job opportunity. She took her first shower and ate her first non-alcoholic meal exactly a week after Jayson left, on the day she was supposed to start work at the gallery gift shop. But, as soon as Kelsey reported for work, the female manager turned her away. The woman gave some excuse but, from the odd way she kept looking at her Kelsey, like she was dirt, Kelsey was sure that Daniels had gotten to her and somehow poisoned her mind.

Kelsey wandered out onto the evening street, laughing to herself. Jerry had dropped her off to work the closing shift. It was six-o'clock and now she would have no way home until he came to pick her up at ten.

After that night, and the loss of yet another job, Kelsey spent a great deal of her time drinking. She'd lie in her bed with the lights off and her gun clutched near her and she would hallucinate an image of Jayson's body gently brushing against her and his voice whispering to her. She would have murmured conversations with him even though he was not there.

Juan used to drive by three times a day and circle the parking lot in his shiny green truck. Sometimes he would stop by at her door to see how she was doing. Miranda was there a good deal also. At some times they would talk; at others, Kelsey would ignore her friend and duck back under the ocean print covers to talk to the ghost of Jayson.

Miranda had taken to wearing very dark lipstick and painting her nails in blackish red Chanel Vamp, and she'd straightened her hair so that it hung in strands. The look accentuated her pallor and the unnatural brightest of her eyes and Kelsey wondered what combination of drugs her girlfriend might be on at the moment.

But it wasn't like she could say anything. One day Miranda held Kelsey in her arms, smoothing her messy hair. Kelsey knew she reeked of alcohol; she was totally out of control.

"It's just Jayson's arrogance," Miranda said. "He wants things to be his way. But he'll be back. He loves you."

"No, he won't," Kelsey said, sucking back tears. "When he says he's going to do something, he does it. And he said he wasn't coming back."

"Well," Miranda chuckled, looking at Kelsey with heavily lined cat's eyes. "At least he taught you how to screw. Now you can do it with anyone you want!"

Miranda took her out to bars several times but Kelsey got the feeling her friend was disturbed and concerned by her behavior. Kelsey preferred to go out with Wendy Pedersen, the ditzy young blonde who had stolen her job at Confidential Investigations. Wendy was very reckless, willing to drive anyplace, and hot to pick up guys.

This is what Kelsey wanted. She found herself hanging on guys at last call, not remembering how she got there. But mostly she sloppily gyrated on the dance floor, too drunk to stay with any one man for more then a few moments.

Kelsey would take the cordless phone into her darkened living room, rest it on the glass-topped end table and stare at it, wondering if she had the courage to make the call to Jayson's home in California. Her heart would thump in her chest when she even thought about making the call. And, when she finally tapped out the numbers, she felt her bladder try to give way with nervousness. She had a phone number for Jayson. On one of her old phone bills there was a record of the long distance call he'd made on Christmas Eve, the call to his father's house in California. Now Kelsey called that number.

The gruff suspicious voice of an older man answered the phone. "Yeah?"

"Mr. Carter?" Kelsey asked.

"Who is this?" the man demanded.

"Kelsey Reed. I'm calling for Jayson."

"You're the State Attorney?" Jayson's father asked.

"Sort of," Kelsey said. "I used to work for the State Attorney's Office. Is Jayson there?"

"Young lady," the father said, sounding much older than she had pictured him. He seemed to be getting comfortable in preparation for giving her a lecture. "Now listen carefully and I want you to take everything I'm saying to heart. Jayson is a good boy. But all he's going to do is use you and break your heart. And you're no damn good for him either. I don't want you in his life!"

Kelsey tried to speak but Mr. Carter talked over her protests.

"There's plenty of pretty girls out here and he's doing just fine with them. What you need to do is change your phone number and move on with your life. Do I make myself clear?"

Kelsey had never been spoken to like this. The man's words were brutal, and left her stunned. But Kelsey's reaction was to defend herself. With an attitude, she snapped back, "*Whatever!*" and hung up.

Kelsey felt in shock, not knowing what to make of what had been said to her. It was bad enough Jayson had disrespected her, but now his father, who sounded about a hundred years old, had also done it.

She lurched in the direction of her bedroom, stopping only to shut out lights and snag a wine bottle from the kitchen.

Kelsey no longer had nightmares. These had stopped when she came to terms with the fact she had been sexually abused by her father. Now she slept in a deep dreamless sleep.

But now something was pulling her out of that slumber, something insistent. In the dark, Kelsey fumbled around, disturbing a wine bottle that spilled out its dregs and the gun, in order to reach the cordless phone that was ringing. Then she fumbled with the on switch. It was completely dark in the room except for the glow that now lit the numerals on the receiver.

Kelsey's voice came out sounding fuzzy and slurred. The man's voice on the other end was cruelly mocking. It was Jayson, sounding a million miles distant.

"You called my Dad, Kelsey. Don't you ever do that again!" he said, threateningly. Then, more gently, with a laugh in his voice, he added, "The old guy could've had a stroke or something. If you want to call, you can reach me out here on my cellular. Now, what do you want?"

Kelsey's whole universe was narrowed down to one imaginary spot the size of a pin point, which was Jayson's voice so far away. At this point there was nothing she could say.

"What do *you* want?" she asked him. "Am I really like nothing to you now?"

"I'll come back right now like nothing ever happened if you agree to compromise, if you'll take me back without me saying the words."

"I can't do that," Kelsey said, sadly.

She heard Jayson growing angry, she recognized it in his sarcastic tone. "So, Kelsey, have you been drinking? I know you have. You've probably got a bottle in bed with you right now to take my place."

"And how about screwing around? Have you screwed around on me yet?

"Well, you might as well," he said, " 'cause I've been fucking and sucking my way through all the bimbos I can find out here."

He paused, seeming to enjoy hurting her. "What do you think of that?" he asked.

Kelsey felt like a fire raced through her, an enormous out of control fire of destruction, desperation and rage.

"*Wear yourself out, Jayson,*" she retorted, coldly, and she hung up.

In the dark, Kelsey threw up a stomach full of sour wine all over her bed and it felt like her heart came out of her insides with it. Because she and Jayson were over.

Chapter 22

Several nights after Jayson's call, Kelsey talked Wendy Pedersen into driving her to Hollywood Beach. Instinct kept telling Kelsey to go there. To her, the whole three-mile stretch of the Broadwalk smelled of Jayson. She associated him with the smell of the ocean, the people's strutting bodies in their swimwear and the odors of food wafting out of inexpensive open-air restaurants.

Wendy did not want to leave Kelsey when they got there but Kelsey felt it imperative to get rid of the other girl. She wanted to be alone with the stifling breeze beating against her. She finally talked Wendy into leaving her and then she walked amongst the thousand indifferent individuals passing on the Hollywood Broadwalk; the old tourists, the teens gliding on in-line skates, the overripe young girls in thong bikinis.

Kelsey stood out, crazed as she was with her own desperate thoughts. She bought a cold beer in a large plastic cup and ran with it onto the beach, leaning into the rising ocean breeze so the strong wind slipped and danced in her red satin mini-dress. Kelsey carried matching, bright red high-heeled sandals and her rosebud mouth was glossed with one of Miranda's cast off lipsticks, also in fire-engine red.

As everything faded to shades of bone and gray, and the crowd moving on the Broadwalk seemed to take on a fairy quality, Kelsey in her red satin dress became the brightest spot on the beach.

She was sure that Jayson could somehow see her, that he was somehow in the rising sea and the pulsing air and in the few brightly-lit high clouds which paid no attention to the coming of nightfall. He was inside her still and she trembled with the electricity left by his love.

Even if Jayson hadn't made the horrible statements about sleeping with other women, Kelsey probably would have slept with some man herself if Jayson didn't come back to her. Unlike her ex-boyfriend, she did not see loyalty as something to obsess over, but rather as something practical. She would have stayed faithful to him forever if he had stayed with her.

But, with him gone out of her life, and a madman stalking her, she didn't see how it would matter. One-night-stands were the way Kelsey had always dealt with a broken heart. Now her heart and soul and life were gone. With his comments, Jayson had only added fuel to a crazy self-destructive fire that was already leaping out of control.

Kelsey walked all the way to the shopping mall near the end of the Broadwalk and then turned back. The first hour of night spread a chill over her bare shoulders and had filled her with a feeling of restlessness and she hurried into a small noisy bar to escape the emotions as much as the chill. Some older man with a sun-damaged face and a T-shirt with a picture of a Florida Pompano over a protruding beer belly bought her drinks and a basket of fried clam strips that she ate voraciously. He seemed to find their conversation amusing, although she couldn't remember anything that she had said to him. Kelsey was unsure of how many drinks she'd had or when she left the man, but she ended up back on the Broadwalk.

Deep night had fallen and many of the lights were dimmed and Kelsey found herself walking barefoot through plastic tables and chairs in front of an ice cream parlor. She realized that her shoes were gone and she laughed to herself, thinking that those red high heels had been from the back of her closet and were one of the few items of her clothing Jayson had never seen her wear.

Two young guys wearing damp swim trunks approached Kelsey. They seemed like frat guys of some sort. They had laughing eyes and the start of beer bellies that they pressed against Kelsey, supporting her arms on both sides and getting too familiar, sliding their hands over her. All of them started chuckling.

"Can we do anything for you?" one of the guys asked with a leering grin, and Kelsey spat in his ear, laughing.

"Yeah, I need a few thousand dollars and a personal body guard! You guys wanna do that?"

She shook with her hiccuping laughter as she backed away from them. She wouldn't have cared what they wanted from her, she felt compelled to get back to the bar where she and Jayson had first danced.

It wasn't hard for her to find the bar because many of the patrons were out on the pavement, holding drinks in paper cups and laughing loudly with each other. A different band played tonight and the place was much more crowded. Kelsey pushed herself between bodies on the dance floor, confused and getting knocked around. She tried to dance with a drink in a plastic cup sloshing down her neck and onto her bosom. Two big guys on the edge of the floor came forward and made a sandwich with her, dancing with Kelsey between them. She drank more, whatever the men handed her, and then she reeled off, staggering all over the dance floor.

Another man now held her up as she lurched against him trying to dance- a man with a black motorcycle jacket over a faded tank top, dark hair and coarse stubble on his chin. He seemed very familiar, someone who Kelsey already knew.

Hanging on his shoulders, Kelsey gazed up into his face. "Who are you?" she slurred.

"Rick, from your old man's hotel," he said. He lifted her by her arms, keeping her from falling. "I came out to get cigarettes and I saw you in here. You seem pretty out of control."

She looked at his strong face in the lights they had turned on for last call and she recognized him as the biker who lived next door to Jayson, the one she had been so afraid of. He was smiling at her warmly.

"Get me out of here," she said to him. "Walk me back to the hotel."

They seemed all alone on the Broadwalk, with just the smell of the salt water and leather and cigarettes off his jacket and his roughened hands catching on the satin of her dress each time he tried to steady her.

"You know, Jayson and I used to come out here all the time and make love," she said to him carelessly.

In response Rick pulled her into his arms, rubbing his stubbly face against hers and murmuring in a deep husky voice, "I don't need no trouble from your old man."

Kelsey gazed up at the biker who held her. She had never been this close to this type of man before. Her hair whipped around and she felt the excitement of pinpoints of salt on her lips.

"He's gone," she said. "He's in California and I'm not with him anymore."

Rick's rough face lowered onto hers and possessed her lips. The kiss was oddly soft, tasting powerfully of liquor and cigarettes. She closed her eyes for it and felt his strong tongue dip into her mouth and seek for hers. She could feel every long stringy muscle in his body tensing as he began to lift her off the ground.

Kelsey clamped her legs around Rick's waist, fiercely making out with him right at the wall in front of Jayson's hotel.

Rick seemed lost in it with her until she worked a hand in to get at his fly and tried to loosen his silver belt buckle. Then he pushed her away gently, setting her down on the wall and holding both of her hands still with one of his.

Look, you're damned beautiful," he said. "But you ain't worth dying for."

Kelsey struggled, laughing in his face. "What are you talking about?"

"That man of yours is some mean motherfucker. I ain't seen him or heard about him myself in prison, but my nose tells me the guy's an ex-con."

Kelsey was so drunk that it took her a second to see the amusement in this. She was the one just about to screw a *real* ex-con and he wouldn't even have her. Meanwhile the dark one, Dave Daniels, might be hovering out there right now in the whipping wind viewing all of this, another ex-con.

"Jayson's a damn slacker!" She yelled at the biker and kicked out at him with her feet. "You blew it, you idiot. Jayson talks tough 'cause he's a musician and his band used to play in all kinds of bars. He only talks the way he does because he thinks it's cool. What kind of loser are you to be afraid of him!"

Kelsey struggled against Rick and he gathered her in for one more deep kiss, but then he pulled away and winked at her. "I ain't taking no chances," he said, and he walked back towards the hotel.

There was a salt-pitted pay phone next to the wall. Kelsey fell on it and dialed Jerry Klein's number collect. She pictured her friend answering the phone in his crisp clean bed, with his trim smooth body comfortable in silk boxer shorts like he had worn the night they once slept together, while she was alone out here with nature's fury.

"Jerry," she said, "I'm really fucked up here. I need some help."

She let him find her lying in a pool of yellow light, looking like a puddle of rippling red satin where she was stretched on the concrete while the furious wind caressed her.

To her friend's shadow that blocked the streetlight, she said, "You take me now, Jerry. If it's not you, it's going to be someone else. It's going to be everyone else!" She roared with laughter that was lost in the wind.

Jerry squatted down by her. "I know for a fact that I'm bisexual now. Does that bother you?"

He looked so handsome with his new ponytail. Kelsey got up on her knees and lunged after him, growling like an animal. "I want you!" she said.

Jerry responded by gathering her to him and smoothly slipping a hand between her legs. He whispered to her excitedly, "In that case, I'm going to take you home and do it right."

Kelsey sobered up somewhat riding to her condo in Jerry's Honda Prelude. It felt like a nice safe cocoon in the darkness with the cushiony upholstery and red glow from the CD player. She told Jerry what Jayson had said about sleeping with other women.

"The guy's a prick," Jerry said, softly. "I mean I love him to death and all, but he can be pretty vain about his looks."

Kelsey snuggled up to Jerry in the car and, surprisingly, she felt heat start to build between them, as though Jayson had never been there.

Later, in a nest of covers on her wicker bed, Kelsey straddled Jerry, enjoying the leanness and sliminess of his body as she teasingly brushed her own over it. He was so different from Jayson. Jerry was also without an ounce of fat on him, but he didn't have the enormous bulk of muscles. They moved together easily and gracefully, whipping their bodies around energetically and laughing together.

Jerry's eyes sparkled at her. "You are so good now, Kelsey. He really taught you to love this, didn't he?"

"Whatever," she said tensing her body to achieve a glorious orgasm. Breathless and smiling, they embraced tighter.

"You're my biggest weakness, Kelsey," Jerry said. "I think you always will be." He gently touched her face. "If there's ever any trouble with this Daniels person or if you ever need a man in your life, I'm here."

"Okay," Kelsey whispered, resting her face down on the pillow and falling comfortably to sleep.

She let nothing disturb them that night. A late night call had come when they first got back. Kelsey had the machine set up to keep the voices muted and it took the message without her hearing who called. She had no curiosity about the caller. It had to be Jayson with another mean commentary and she was in no mood to hear it.

Morning came and they forgot about the phone call. They made gentle love again, not afraid to look into each other's eyes. Then Jerry suggested breakfast and Kelsey baked cinnamon rolls and chattered to her friend while she worked, filling him in on all the details of her life that he had missed when she was spending every minute with Jayson.

Jerry took her out to an art and crafts fair on Las Olas Boulevard that day. They had lunch out, then spent part of the evening at his apartment on Bayview before he brought her home.

"I could stay the night," he offered and she knew he meant because of Daniels.

"I've been fine," Kelsey said, reaching up and kissing him half on the mouth and half on the cheek. "I just need to get things straightened out and get some rest. But I'll call you tomorrow, okay?"

Jerry left and Kelsey stood in darkness at her counter retrieving her messages. There was first static, then a woman's voice. This voice was sharp and agitated, insane. It was Miranda speaking but it seemed as though she had finally gone over the edge.

"Are you there, Kelsey?" the crazed panting voice demanded. "You little bitch!"

The voice got higher, with a maniacal excitement. "This is all your fault. Whatever happens, it's because of you!" Her friend let out an odd cross between a screech and a howl before the message ended.

Kelsey went into a cold sweat, pushing at her hair with one hand and stabbing out her girlfriend's number with the other. Listening to the ringing Kelsey whispered impatiently, "Babe, what is wrong with you?"

Miranda didn't answer and Kelsey contemplated what she could do. She could have Jerry drive her to the clubs they usually frequented or even to the apartment in Davie to look for Miranda. But she had a feeling that if her friend didn't want to be found, she wouldn't be. Kelsey didn't think Miranda was unconscious from a dangerous drug overdose. Her friend had sounded more lucid than that.

Maybe Miranda was just mad at her. Kelsey knew, for a fact, that she would have to get her girlfriend off drugs this time, no matter what it took.

Kelsey called Jerry after trying Miranda's number a few more times.

"That was Miranda on the machine last night," she told him. "She's acting really crazy. Would it be all right- I'll keep trying to call her, but if I don't reach her by one or two, could we go out looking for her?"

Kelsey turned on one or two soft lights and made an effort to straighten up her condo. Then she sat on the couch with the cordless phone and found that she had fallen asleep for a few moments. Wearily, she got up and stretched, took a crime novel and brought it into her bed with her. She'd keep trying her calls until one-o'clock and then she'd call Jerry and they could go out looking.

At half past eleven Kelsey's phone rang.

"Yes?" Kelsey said, cautiously.

"Kelsey Reed?" the unfamiliar male voice asked.

"Who is this?"

"This is Deputy Warren at the Broward County Sheriff's Office."

Immediately, Kelsey thought the call must have to do with Dave Daniels. But then the sheriff asked her, "I understand you're a good friend of a Miranda Meriwether, is that correct?"

Kelsey felt her throat tighten with sudden fear. "Why, what happened?" she insisted. She knew it had to be something to do with the drugs, something bad.

"Miss Meriwether is dead," the policeman said.

There was only the sound of Kelsey's heart in the silence, a sound that grew louder and more violent. Her first thought was that she would be next. Right now she seemed to feel the shadow of the wing of the angel of death over her.

This had to be Dave Daniels who had done this. Or it could be the drugs- the more logical explanation.

Kelsey didn't know if she would even choose to live with Miranda gone.

"What happened?" she asked.

"Well," the deputy sighed, "sometime late last night or in the early morning, your friend was driving at high speed on Route 27 and she flipped her car."

Kelsey's mind was working madly. She had seen that road, way out in the country somewhere. What was her friend doing there?

"You're saying it was an accident?" she demanded. She must have sounded odd to the police officer, but time might be of the essence. If Daniels had done it, they needed to go after him now. Kelsey's breath was heaving in her chest.

"It seems that way," the deputy said. "We've already found a good deal of drugs and alcohol in her system. The only other thing we thought about was suicide. That's why I'm calling you. Was she maybe depressed lately or did she talk about taking her life?"

No, Kelsey thought, this cannot be happening. Daniels had to have done it. Miranda couldn't have killed herself. And not in such a desolate place, in such a horrible way. Not because of me. An involuntary sob escaped Kelsey's throat.

"She was mad at me." She sniffed back her tears. "I don't know what it was about. All I could do is give you the tape from my answering machine. There's also this ex-con; his name is Dave Daniels. I have reason to believe he's been stalking me lately. I've already reported it to the local police, but maybe you could check him out in reference to Miranda. There's also her boss, a real sleazy guy. He could have given her the drugs."

257

The deputy sounded bored. "The boss checks out fine. He's the one who identified the body. We'll come over tomorrow to get that tape..."

"Where is she?" Kelsey asked. "Where's Miranda? I'd like to see her."

"She'll be sent back to her parents first thing tomorrow morning," the deputy told her. "And there's nothing you want to see. The crash was pretty brutal."

Kelsey pictured that road again, with the sugar cane on both sides and the smell of muck in the ditches, the endless miles. What was Miranda doing there?

"Officer," Kelsey asked, "Route 27, that's the one that passes by Lake Okeechobee, isn't it? Which direction was she headed?"

He hesitated a moment. "Towards Fort Lauderdale," he said. "She was headed back towards Fort Lauderdale."

The fact that Miranda was headed in that direction made this inexplicable thing even more of a mystery. Kelsey noticed that after she got off the phone with the deputy, she found it hard to breathe, as though there was no air in the room. In her bedside table, Kelsey had a rosary. She knelt with it beside the bed and she prayed for her friend, while her tears drenched her.

She prayed for a very long time, then she called Jerry and passed on the news. "Miranda died last night," she said bluntly.

Jerry came to her that night to stay in her condo in case Daniels had been involved, but he slept on the couch. Jerry was able to see the haunted guilt in Kelsey's eyes. They had been making love while her friend was driving to her death in that bleak landscape.

Maybe it had happened because Miranda was being chased by a madman. Or maybe she was the one who was mad, rushing toward destruction in her hatred for Kelsey.

If one of them had died, Kelsey thought that it should have been her, not her sweet vibrant friend who had never injured anyone in her life. The only thing that Kelsey knew for sure about Miranda's death was that somehow she was responsible for it.

Chapter 23

Miranda's parents told Kelsey they blamed her for their daughter's death, for bringing her down to Florida and for the drugs. Kelsey had called them and begged them to let her come to the funeral in New York and Miranda's mother cried that it would be worse seeing Kelsey there than even having to see their daughter being buried.

Kelsey knew that the woman was a hypocritical blowsy tramp who had mistreated her daughter one way or another every day of Miranda's life, but she swallowed back her protest in her own shame. She was going to go to Miranda's apartment and clean out her things. Kelsey had a key and she knew that if she didn't go everything would just be thrown out. There was nothing of monetary value there and Kelsey knew that the relatives would have no interest in it.

It was going to be Kelsey's last time in the Davie apartment, the apartment that had always seemed to smell of dust and to hold some sad premonition.

Now Kelsey knew what that premonition was; the fact that her friend's life would be ended before she ever had a chance. Miranda used to say that she was a mongrel and that she had no place to fit in this life. Yet Miranda had this quality; she always saw the best in people. That should have been worth something.

There was not much here in the apartment. A small stack of personal papers that her girlfriend had saved were in a bedside drawer. Kelsey was reluctant to read these but neither did she think it would be right to simply throw them away. She put the papers into her purse, to keep with her own mementos at home. The sad thing was that there would be no one else to claim these papers, no current boyfriend; and Miranda's family had always been her enemies. Kelsey had been the only person really close to Miranada in this whole world.

Kelsey checked on the kitchen, not wanting to leave any mess to embarrass her friend. But everything was immaculate; Miranda never even cooked here.

Standing at the dresser, which overflowed with all kinds of cosmetics, Kelsey got all choked up. She couldn't clean this; the landlady would have to. There were such memories- of Miranda's wide, green sparkling eyes that were always cynical and gun shy, yet eager to see the world, and memories of the way her face used to always smell powdery and lightly perfumed from all the makeup.

When they were little girls Miranda used to persuade Kelsey to come with her and raid her mother's and sister's makeup. Then she and Kelsey would giggle as they covered themselves in tacky red lipstick and rouge, false eyelashes and cheap cologne.

Miranda also loved to play pretend, begging Kelsey to do it, although Kelsey preferred tomboy things like playing ball or wading in the river. So Miranda used to always volunteer to play the odd one, the prince who saved the maiden from the tower or the robber to Kelsey's cop. In real life it was ironic how Kelsey had turned out to be the bad one, the one responsible for what had happened.

Kelsey took up one of Miranda's hair scrunchies, a lovely beaded one, and wound it in her own hair. Why had her best friend hated her in the end? It ate endlessly at Kelsey's stomach, causing a deep ache that might never go away. Superficially, the tragedy had helped her to pull her own life more together and cut out the drinking, at least in public.

She still had the sense that Dave Daniels was somehow responsible for what had happened to her friend. And she was ready to put a bullet through that vengeful heart of his the day she could look him in the eye and find out how. The problem was, even if it was Daniels, it was she who brought him into the picture, into her friend's already screwed up, yet innocent life. Or maybe Miranda had thought something so bad of Kelsey that it had either driven her to such despair that she had killed herself, or to such anger that she drank and drugged enough to lose all control.

Kelsey was glad now that her family was out of her life. She would not want anyone to look upon her terrible guilt. And the space inside her would always be there, always deeper and emptier, even if Daniels screwed up and allowed her to live. She was haunted by the laughing words she used to always say to Miranda, "I've got your back, girl". But, when her friend really needed her, she hadn't been there. Kelsey was supposed to be the tough one, yet Miranda had been there for her emotionally every time. Where had she been when her friend was dying?

Jerry was waiting downstairs in the car. She had asked to be alone for this task, and she didn't really want him walking in. There was only the closet, anyway.

Kelsey dragged in a black plastic bag and slid open the doors. She was overwhelmed by the scent of her friend, the remnants of the perfumes, some delicate and others strong and intense. Tears welled in Kelsey's eyes.

"Why did you have to die?" she said out loud.

She brought a sleeve up to her mouth, crying into the velvety fabric, and she moved down the line of clothes, touching and reminiscing over each item. They were clothes that looked straight out of a thrift shop-velvets, crochets and many extreme colors. But they had reflected Miranda's vibrance, the love for life she wasn't even aware of, but which brightened the lives of all those around her, especially the ever conservative Kelsey.

These amazing garments. They were the only things left to reflect the soul of her friend. Kelsey stuffed a handful into the bag. The rest would go when the landlady cleared the place out. But these Kelsey would keep solely for the memories.

Then she pulled a chair over to look for the velvet dress. Jayson had bailed Miranda out when he found out what she had done to get it. He paid for the dress for her, telling Kelsey that it was the least he could do after walking out on her in the middle of the party to go to her best friend. Kelsey had forgotten about that night. It was going to be Miranda's finest hour and instead it turned into another occasion when Kelsey outshone the other girl.

But Kelsey knew that Miranda would desire to have the dress kept. To her, it was a treasure that had been much respected. Kelsey found the blue velvet dress where she thought it would be, on the top shelf, in the original box. She opened the box, smelling the light fresh scent and feeling the delicate glowing fabric that was so out of place in this drab apartment. Kelsey caught something small that rolled from the box. It was the glass ballerina pendant Jayson had given to Miranda that night of the formal party.

Kelsey put the necklace back in the folds of fabric. This is how she would always see her friend, like a delicate ballerina. And Jayson had been able to perceive this quality. Kelsey cried as she climbed down from the chair, crying, this time, for the loss of both of them.

Kelsey had already missed one mortgage payment. She got one offer on the condo but it was low enough that it would mean her losing more money than if she just let the bank foreclose. But she could just not make herself feel imperative about any of this. A man was out there who had targeted her and who was doing these terrible things. She realized how extreme his actions had become and how unfair. Right now she felt a need to be alone with her grief.

She felt a need for a lot of quiet time, sitting in her condo going through her things and thinking, methodically going through the memories of her life, trying to analyze things for what they really were. She had so many photo albums filled with pictures of herself and Miranda. There were only beautiful memories of her friend and they were smiling together in all the pictures. Kelsey couldn't fault the past.

She would sit there in her condo drinking, with the cat curled up beside her chair and the tactile memories of Jayson would come to her, unbidden.

There had only been him. He was her life. He must have known this. They were apart but yet he was still inside her. She breathed his memory and felt languid and peaceful even during her monstrous grief and her fear.

One day she heard a song on the radio and it brought her to attention. She felt the tingle in her blood as she heard the singer's wailing voice, the haunting melody that was like an old Spanish ballad. The song was about a man obsessed with a women, Chris Isaak's "Wicked Game". Kelsey had probably heard it before but now it spoke directly to the longings of her crazed hollow soul, the heart that felt shredded, and yet on fire with her longing, just like in the song.

She wanted for Jayson to hear the song. It didn't matter if he choose to come back; she knew they were bound together anyway.

Kelsey bought a CD with the song on it and brought it home. Her heart thudded strongly with confidence in what she was going to do as she dialed Jayson's cellular number.

"Jayson Carter," he answered.

Kelsey started the song, playing it loud on her stereo and holding the phone up near it so Jayson couldn't miss it. The wailing voice dropped to an inmate roughness as the singer accused the object of his obsession of playing a wicked game by making him need her.

Kelsey was riveted by the song; she began crying but she held the phone away from herself so Jayson would not hear. She could picture him processing the song on his end. His eyes would slant down, his lips would move to the words. But she could not imagine what he would be feeling.

When the song was over, Kelsey disconnected the phone without speaking; she wasn't expecting anything but she had a feeling of thrill in her blood. The song was like a horrible anthem for her feelings.

She had played the song for Jayson during the day. That night she was sitting in the chair in her living room in a small pool of light. A photo album was in her lap but she was basically paying it no attention, just staring ahead into the semi-darkness. She was very mellow from the wine she had drunk.

She felt only minimal interest when she heard the door opening. A man had let himself into the apartment. She heard the cat crying, she could smell a brand new leather jacket and the fresh air that came in off his clothes. California. Jayson. She couldn't remember if she had given him a key or if the door had just been left open.

Kelsey just felt a tremendous weariness, as though all the energy was trickling down out of her into the chair. She didn't budge.

Jayson stepped partly into view, wearing the new brown leather jacket with layers of clothing underneath it. He looked like a stranger, only vaguely familiar.

"What's up, little guy?" he said. He bent to scratch the kitten on its head and ears and it allowed it. Obviously, it did not remember him from the last time.

"Doesn't she feed you, Fluffy?" he asked the animal. Then he straightened up and went to the cabinet. She waited for his comment when he'd find no canned cat food, only dry. Sure enough, he mumbled, "This is it? Okay, then." He shook the dried stars into the bowl and Fluffy began eating, greedily. She had forgotten to feed the cat again.

Kelsey remained perfectly silent, just observing. Jayson went to the bathroom and vigorously washed his face and hands. He also took the time to clean out the cat box, which Kelsey hadn't touched since he left. Then he dropped his jacket and outer shirt in the bedroom and he came to her. Without speaking he knelt beside the ottoman where her legs were still stretched out.

He looked up at her and his eyes were luminous and earnest. With the peroxide gone and his hair now a dark brown color, he looked more serious and respectful.

He slipped a hand between Kelsey's crossed knees, loosening them and gently caressing.

"After you played me the song," he said, "I couldn't stay away. You had the power to bring me back."

He didn't break his gaze from her curious and demanding one. "You know me," he said softly. He started gently kissing the insides of her legs, in apology, in surrender. And then he looked up at her with a genuine pleading in his eyes. "Don't make me say the words, Kelsey," he begged her. "I can't do it. I'll never be able to." He was gazing up at her with this incredible intensity. "But, you know, God can look down on me and maybe he sees I already broke my promise."

Jayson was practically crying. He lowered his head so she wouldn't look at him. Then he softly kissed her legs, like a supplicant, starting with the ankles, while she watched him with the same stoniness. Finally, he looked up at her eyes.

"Say something, Kelsey."

"Miranda is dead," she told him. She showed no emotion yet.

Jayson slid back away from her, with his face registering the shock. "What happened?" he asked her, looking stricken and showing more outward grief than Kelsey did.

Kelsey told him the story of the accident, every so often feeling her own grief break through, like she was going to start crying.

Jayson leaned against the ottoman, with his head resting on his knees. When he lifted his head she could see redness around his eyes. His chest was heaving.

"She was such a beautiful girl," he said, "a beautiful person. She cared about everyone. I'm so sorry!"

He took both of Kelsey's hands and now she broke down crying. "It was my fault," Kelsey said. "Miranda died because of me!"

Jayson pulled her down into his arms, holding her in a crushing embrace, kissing her hair. "You poor thing," he said. "You never should've had to go through this alone."

"Just don't ever leave me again,' Kelsey said in a shaky voice, and he pulled back to look into her eyes.

"I never left you this time," he said.

They cuddled together, being very gentle. When it got late, Jayson led her to the bedroom. It felt odd for her coming in here without a bottle, odd to think of being with her boyfriend again.

Jayson stripped down to a pair of trendy-patterned boxers, preparing for bed in his usual buoyant mood. Casually, he said to Kelsey, "You really didn't go out and sleep around on me, did you?"

Kelsey's silence caused him to stop in his tracks to look at her and his expression darkened. Kelsey forced herself to look in his eyes, not even starting to face the tangle of emotions- the guilt and the disgust he was bringing up.

"It was just one time," she said, "with Jerry. It was only because of you and what you said..." Her words trailed off in pain and confusion.

Jayson drew in a deep breath, seemingly trying to get a hold on his own emotions. Then his voice came out sounding infinitely saddened and broken. "I know it's not your fault. I put you up to it."

Kelsey looked over the silvered curves of Jayson's muscular chest and abdomen, his sexy eyes that looked like an animal's- a lion's or a panther's- might and his perfect nose and lips. Jayson could always get her off balance. Like now, she felt her whole world tipping. "You mean, you didn't cheat on me, that was all a lie?" she asked.

Jayson grinned as he crawled into bed beside her. "Of course I didn't," he laughed. "I just wanted to see what you would do."

Then he centered himself over her, appearing to have totally forgiven her to the point where things were back to normal.

"You don't mind me doing this now, do you?" he asked, amusedly, prior to entering her.

Kelsey shook her head miserably.

Jayson slipped inside her and she felt their souls immediately and powerfully binding, as they always did.

In between teasing kisses, Jayson said to her, "You never have to worry about me cheating, Kelsey. You're my world. And this is all for you. Always."

After their lovemaking Jayson curled up and began peacefully breathing. The warm body next to her felt wonderful and yet Kelsey could not sleep. She kept twisting and turning, keeping him from resting as well.

Jayson rolled over. "Baby," he commented, "it was pretty upsetting seeing you with that wine bottle when I walked in tonight. Can't you stop drinking? Can you do it for me?"

"I guess," she told him. "It's just been so hard with you being gone."

"I'm sorry about that," he said "It was so wrong of me, especially with the fact that madman could be around. I figured that you would stay with your friends. But still... with what happened to Miranda, even if Daniels had nothing to do with it, which he probably didn't, I don't intend to let you out of my sight at all... Are you still going to let me move in?"

"Probably it would be best if you didn't, not right at the moment," Kelsey said. "I had one job set up but it fell through. Now that you're back I'm going to get back out there and start looking."

"Kelsey," Jayson said, "at least let me take care of you. Even if you don't want me to move in, I can still take care of some of the bills. You don't need to do this on your own."

So much of the coldness she had built up was breaking down. Kelsey felt as though her heart and soul were linked to this man's. For the first time, she had some inkling of how he had felt in this relationship all along. She realized everything they possessed was meant to be shared, and that their whole future would be shared together, every day, exactly like this. Jayson's expectation was not the modern concept of a relationship where the man and woman kept their property separate. In his old-fashioned concept she was his property, as well as his full responsibility. But she realized, in her gut, that there was no problem with this, she did love him this way. His love crowded out the whole world, yet at the same time made way for it. His love *was* the world.

"Jayson," she said, "just because you won't say you love me doesn't mean you don't, does it? You love me unbelievably. You're as frightened as I am of it, aren't you?"

Jayson kissed her on the hair and held her close. "There's only you and me, Kelsey. That's all there is. I spend my whole life just knowing you. Every breath I breathe is you. And you know it, 'cause you feel it, too."

"I do. But it's hard," she said. "I was so used to being independent. And this kind of relationship wasn't even what I had in mind for the future. It seems so stupid now, how people get married without even trusting each other or even knowing each other. And we're so far beyond that already."

"So, I guess your loving me is no longer about my awesome muscles or my pretty face," he teased. She could feel him smiling in the darkness. But she knew this was a very serious subject to him. She knew he resented his looks because it took people's attention away from who he really was. She remembered the conversation months ago where he told her that most women ultimately disliked his intensity and his romanticism. She didn't. She was ready to fully love him.

And Kelsey had done a vast amount of thinking since her best friend's death.

"I do have this tendency to judge things by their appearances," she said. "I've realized that lately.

"I guess that your looks were why I first became obsessed with you. I thought you were God, the way you looked, and I would have demeaned myself in any way just to sleep with you... As you saw by what happened in the locker room. But, at the same time, I was already starting to love you. What first caught my eye about you Jayson, was the way you moved, and the way you could be still. That was so powerful. It's all about the way you think. If you looked on the outside like you really are on the inside, you'd probably be a very old man, because you're so heartbreakingly thoughtful and wise. That's what I love about you. I've had to grow up to even be equal to loving you."

Jayson gave a gentle yawn, twining her tightly in his huge arms.

"I can be here for you, Kelsey," he said. "But there's a lot of pain that I have inside, and it's nothing you can fix. Can you even understand that?"

She never thought about what kind of pain Jayson might have known. But of course, only some really serious pain could have shaped him to be as powerful as he was.

"I have my own pain, now," she said brokenly. "And I still want to love you. In a way that's understanding, isn't it?"

"Yes," he said. "I guess it is, Babe."

The next morning, over breakfast, Kelsey said to Jayson, "I still don't know how I feel about having you pay for my apartment."

But she said it in a light joking tone. Any separateness there had been between them was gone now, miraculously, since Jayson had come back.

He grinned at her. "So, how are you going to deal with it when I'm paying for a house for both of us?"

Kelsey waited a few beats, realizing finally that it felt good to be talking to him like this. There was no one else anymore to think that she was wrong. Finally, there was no one else but the two of them. It would be okay to let him be there for her every day, and for him to totally protect her.

She tossed her hair over her shoulder and she teased back, "And how do you know you've even got a job?"

Jayson agreed that Kelsey had a point. He had taken a leave of absence from his job and he would have to show up at the office to see where he stood. And he didn't want her to be alone in the condo, with Daniels possibly around. It was as if, for Kelsey, life had suddenly become brighter again. She didn't have to do this by herself anymore.

"Come to my hotel room," Jayson suggested. "Stay there when I go to work." Kelsey gladly agreed.

After that Kelsey spent a great deal of her time at Hollywood Beach. Jayson preferred that she stay in the room until he got back from work, but Kelsey didn't like to stay inside and she figured that she was completely safe amongst the crowds. There was always the fear that

Daniels was watching. And she knew that he would be gloating over her pain. But she also had the idea that maybe it was all over. If Daniels' goal had been to take away the person that she loved the most, just as he had lost Allison, he had done that by taking Miranda. And it had been unexpected- she had somehow thought he would go after Jayson. Instead he had taken the girl who had been a sister to her and left the guilt and the permanent ache of emptiness in her heart.

In a way, Kelsey had this come and get me attitude. She suspected that even Jayson, who believed Daniels was responsible for some of the other things, did not believe that he caused Miranda's car crash. But Kelsey did. She had a bottomless faith in Dave Daniels. But she could not pull a trigger on him until she was sure. If he had killed her friend, then she could kill him. In a strange way she looked forward to seeing Daniels again, seeing if all that she remembered was wrong. She had never even really looked in his face that night three years ago. She would like to do that now.

Jayson was amazed by the Kelsey that he would now come home to now. She practically lived on the beach and this is where he would often find her, down by the water, wild eyed and coated with sand, this girl who used to hate the gritty sand and the oppressive summer heat.

"What are you doing?" he asked, gently caressing Kelsey's face. On this day she wore a smoke-blue halter and denim cut-offs and she was crouching in the surf.

"I was swimming," she said, "and then I went up to the room. But I just came back down 'cause I was bored."

"You look so incredibly exciting," Jayson told her, running his hands over her damp tight body. "Like a friggin wild woman. You've changed ever since we went to the Everglades. It's as if you're getting ready for some showdown with this Daniels and you're starting to be like him."

Instead of being offended, Kelsey shook her salty hair and laughed.

Jayson grabbed a handful of it. She could see that he was getting excited.

"I remember when I first met you, how you had those two big highlights in your hair," he said. "Now they're gone. And you're so tan, so dark over all with your hair and your eyes and skin, you're so scary this way, Kelsey. Before, you were just dressed up to look like all the other girls. Now this is you, crawling in the surf like this, like some spunky little animal. This makes me hot!"

He flung her down on her back on the wet sand with the water frothing in her hair and pulling it out and he tried to slip his hard-on into the corner of her shorts in broad daylight. Kelsey rolled teasingly away, rolling with the waves, and then she swam away into deeper water. Jayson dived under, and then he came up holding her waist and blinking water out of his eyes.

"Since when do you swim?" he asked. "You used to be so afraid of the water."

"I've got other things to be afraid of now," she said.

Then she ducked under again, with her butt cheeks pointed toward shore, and she led Jayson further out, showing him the ocean as she had learned it.

Jayson didn't mind the fact that Kelsey was still going out with Wendy Pedersen occasionally. It gave him an opportunity to spend some time at the gym by himself, and to come back later at night from his business trips without worrying that Kelsey was all alone. Some of the trips that were supposed to be overnight he was able to make in one day; he'd get back as late as twelve or one or two, but at least Kelsey did not have to sleep alone.

"I've got a girl's night out," she told him about one Friday night, and she was a little nervous because she was deliberately omitting something, the fact that one of the girls was Jerry.

In fact, it was a party at one of the better restaurants in honor of Jerry, because he had bought into the gallery that he worked at and he was now a part owner. Jerry's two roommates were hosting the Hawaiian themed dinner and show at the Mai Kai, something Jerry had said he always wanted to do if he ever had a special occasion to celebrate.

And now he did. His life had changed incredibly in the past six months, almost like Kelsey's had changed in the other direction. Jayson had been completely forgiving of what she had done with Jerry. "He cares about you," he had said. "I can't blame him for that. And, anyway, he's had you for only one night; I'm the one who's going to have you the rest of my life."

Jerry was not as generous. When Kelsey wanted him to ask Jayson to the party, he balked. He looked into her eyes incredulously, like he couldn't believe how insensitive she could be when it came to his feelings for her.

"Jayson's a punk," he said, "I don't care to see his self-satisfied face at my party. Or I'm going to end up punching it, okay?"

He was laughing at himself as he said it, but Kelsey understood. She saw his real pain at losing her again. And she was torn between the two men.

It was easiest just not to go into the whole thing. It wasn't as though with Jayson here she would ever feel sexual desire for any other man on earth, including Jerry.

Of course Jayson didn't suspect anything. He was just glad that his tough week at work was over. "That's cool," he told her when she said she and her friends were going out on the town. "We were going to do a long workout, and then Juan and some of the other guys wanted to go to a sports bar in Boca. I told them I couldn't go out, but if you want, I will go with them. I haven't gotten to spend any time with those guys in a while."

He was grinning as he made his calls to set up his own evening and Kelsey let her guilt go. Instead, she put her mind on what she would wear for the evening that could be something wonderful, that could make her feel like the Kelsey from the old days when she didn't have a care in the world.

Jayson dropped her off at Wendy's parents' house, giving her a long passionate kiss before driving off. Wendy was supposed to sleep over at the condo and Jayson wouldn't see Kelsey again until morning. After he left, Wendy giggled with Kelsey about their intense goodbye kiss and she started confessing how she used to have a crush on Jayson when she had first met him.

Kelsey helped the younger girl to dress in a white shirt that looked sophisticated over a black skirt. Then she realized that her own outfit, a red skin-tight dress was just not suitable; it made her look tough as nails, with her newly muscled calves and long strands of hair.

"Have you got anything I could borrow?" she asked and Wendy offered anything in her closet.

The young blonde's wardrobe tended to look cutesy, but at the moment this appealed to Kelsey. She chose a short dress with layers of flirty gauze and a pattern of a few very large flowers on a pure white background. The layers lifted and bounced when Kelsey walked, the movement of the dress making her smile.

At the restaurant, she greeted the people at the long table warmly, surprised that, other than Jerry's two roommates and their dates, she knew no one here. Jerry's new friends were all from the art gallery; they were older and had an air of stylish sophistication. But it made Kelsey feel good when Jerry pulled her into the seat next to him and introduced her to everyone as "my very best friend in all the world."

Then everyone started talking at once and Kelsey glanced over at Jerry, assessing how he had changed. He looked very urbane and mature tonight, wearing a black shirt with burgundy embroidery, decorated with small round mirrors. He looked the part of a gallery owner, like he really fit in with these people.

"I'm really happy for you," Kelsey said and Jerry seemed to understand just what she meant.

She and Wendy got buzzed on mai-tai cocktails decorated with fresh fruit and they started helplessly laughing when Shane, one of Jerry's roommates, twined bright lais around his waist and got up, trying to imitate the dancers. It wasn't really funny but every time she and Wendy saw the dancing girls after this, they giggled helplessly.

Kelsey got lost in the performance and the atmosphere of the thatched roof, the smoky torches and the wildly shimmering skirts of the dancers. With her pleasantly full belly and mild buzz, and surrounded by nice people, she found it all mesmerizing.

The only one who seemed a little too serious was Jerry. Kelsey asked him what was wrong.

"I guess it's about being alone," he said. He indicated his roommates, who were standing up, pulling out chairs and being perfect gentlemen to their female dates. "I think they're lying to themselves. But I'm no different. I don't know where I fit in."

Kelsey shrugged. She cared about Jerry for what he was but her bias had always been thinking he was straight no matter what he feared he might be- it was just easier for her this way.

"Jerry, listen, Wendy and I are going to Creamsicles after this," she said. "It's just around the corner. And I don't want this evening to end. Why don't you come with us?"

Jerry agreed at first. He said his good-byes to his friends and followed the girls to Creamsicles in his car. But then as he stood with them waiting to get into the club, he got that same absent look in his eyes that he had earlier. It seemed as if his mind was somewhere else.

"I can't do this right now," he said to Kelsey. "I need some air. I think I'll just drive around."

There was this aspect like he had something on his mind that he had to think out and he seemed restless tonight.

Jerry pulled back and Kelsey gradually let go of his hand. "Call us later," she urged. "We'll be at my condo."

Kelsey got exhausted dancing at Creamsicles. She and Wendy kept meeting guys. But she found herself missing Jayson and his formal way of slow dancing that she had come to appreciate. She even thought of calling him but realized that doing that would be totally uncool. She was the one who had lied tonight and he deserved at least one night out with his friends.

Wendy was hanging all over some young guy who had slicked-down side-parted hair and uptight business clothes and who looked straight out of the eighties. This guy, who Kelsey found out worked for another private investigator's office, ended up riding with them and making out with Wendy in the back seat while Kelsey was forced to drive.

Her friend kept leaning forward to whisper in her ear. "I think he may be the one for me. Did you hear what he does? Isn't that an awesome coincidence?"

Kelsey had already heard it enough times and she found something sickening in the way they continued to kiss in her parking lot. She did not want this loser guy staying in her apartment overnight like Wendy wanted him to.

She knew Jayson would be pissed, but she wanted to stay in her apartment alone. She had done it for three weeks when he was gone and no harm had come to her. And tonight she was in such a good mood. She just wanted the good feeling to continue rather than doing something she didn't want to because she was running scared.

"Wendy," she said, getting out of the steamy car. "I think I need to be alone tonight." Her friend looked up, questioning. "I'll be fine," Kelsey said and clicked confidently up the stairs in her high heels.

Kelsey had gotten in the habit of coming home and not bothering to turn on lights for a while. Now she closed the door behind her, set down her purse and keys and she was going to check the apartment but Fluffy was at her feet, screaming insistently and batting her ankles with his paws.

It was creepy. The cat's cries sounded almost like a human voice, trying to tell her something was wrong. Cooper used to do this. Now Kelsey had the feeling to take it very seriously.

She gently pushed the cat away with her foot, listening and sniffing. Although there was no sound at all, Kelsey thought she smelled something odd. A corrupt kind of smell. Something human.

She slipped her gun out of her purse and cocked it, tucking the cordless phone in her jacket pocket. Kelsey could run at this point but it meant avoiding a confrontation that would only come at another time.

In police stance, and moving along the walls, Kelsey advanced into the condo. She could see there was nothing in the living room. Although creepy in the chill darkness, the hallway and bathroom were okay, too.

Whatever it was it had to be in the bedroom. Kelsey felt terror sweep through her as she approached her bedroom doorway. The smell was strong, carried on a breeze from the open window. With her insides churning with fear, Kelsey took the final step to see into the doorway. And then she saw an object hanging, swinging directly over the bed.

Kelsey lifted the gun and almost shot, blinded by her fear. In the dark, she could see that the object was human. There was blood flowing, dripping onto her bed. That was the stench she had smelled.

Her mind was going. She thought an uncontrolled scream would rip out of her.

Quickly she scanned the corners of her bedroom trying to ignore what was in the center of the room, swinging from the ceiling fan.

There didn't seem to be anyone else in the condo, just the body and Kelsey.

"I can't do this," she whispered to herself, but she stepped closer. She had to, on the chance that whoever Daniels had left for her was still alive.

It was a man, with his dark clothes loosened. From the size, she knew it was not Jayson. This was her first relief.

Stepping closer, she saw that the black blood pooled on her light-colored comforter was coming from ragged cuts on the man's exposed stomach, flowing in rivulets down his black jeans. The head was bent so that the chalky face looked downward. Now Kelsey stepped up closer and she saw that she was looking up into the face of her best friend.

She recoiled and took a step back in horror.

"Jerry," she breathed.

It was all so appalling, seeing his face in gentle repose, his neat ponytail and the ruined clothing he had worn earlier tonight.

Jerry was rigged into some kind of horrible harness, with belts of Kelsey's passing across his chest, between his legs and up his back securing him to the fan. It looked like something S&M, except it also included several pairs of Kelsey's leggings, which were stained with Jerry's blood.

She was shaking, filled with a desperate chill, thinking that he was dead. She had to check. Kelsey reached up a trembling hand to her friend's wrist, which was hanging limply and was darkly bruised, as though it had been bound. She felt the wetness of the torn skin as she curled her fingers around the pulse point. Kelsey needed to get her own body under control so that she would be able to feel for that delicate thread of life. She closed her eyes and quieted herself and she was able to feel it, a slow pulse, as though the blood pressure was low but, still, Jerry was alive. She could save him.

"Thank God," Kelsey whispered, opening her eyes.

And she was face to face with the most awful sight she had ever seen. The cuts on Jerry's smooth abdomen were not random. The deep cuts had been gouged into him deliberately; spelling out the word FAGGOT in blood that was still flowing but starting to crust over.

Kelsey backed away, starting to hyperventilate. "My God, oh my God." She was shaking so hard but she had to call for help or her friend would die.

Kelsey fumbled with the phone, hitting memory for Jayson's cellular. When he picked up her voice rose desperately.

"Jerry's hung up in my house! Help me! Please! He's dying!"

She was sobbing, out of control, as Jayson asked if she was home and if she was in any danger. And then he broke the connection.

Jayson was going to call 911 but Kelsey knew it could take a long time for an ambulance to get here this late on a Friday night, when it was prime time for auto accidents.

She inched toward her friend's body, shaking but knowing she had to help him. She slid off her shoes and climbed up on the bed and lost her balance momentarily and fell against Jerry.

He suddenly let out a raw moan and his eyeballs rolled in her direction. Kelsey let out a gasp. Her friend had been turned into a monster.

"Jerry," she said, "It's Kelsey. I'm going to help you. An ambulance is coming."

She tried to get her shaking hands on the tight knot behind his neck, but it was too tight, and she realized that she wasn't strong enough. If she dropped him and his neck or back was broken it could kill him. If she only loosened part of the rig, the other straps might choke him.

"No doctors," Jerry murmured. He was crying. "He did this to me!"

"Who did this?" she demanded, balling up her linen jacket and pressing it on the grisly wounds on his stomach. Kelsey knew that Daniels had done this, but she wanted Jerry to confirm it.

"A big guy in a black sweat jacket. I didn't see his face. I was cruising. I gave him a blowjob."

Jerry began crying more violently and coughing, so that Kelsey felt fresh blood pulsing from under the fabric.

"I never was with a man before," Jerry said. "I can't have anyone know this happened! No doctors, Kelsey, promise me!"

His voice rose to a scream and then he went silent, with his head falling back on his chest.

"Oh no, Jerry, come back!" Kelsey felt again for her friend's pulse, hating Dave Daniels for doing this to Jerry tonight. She pictured the fat man approaching her attractive trusting friend in the darkness and somehow seducing him, destroying Jerry, who was so beautiful, just because he hated her.

Kelsey felt gentle hands on her hips lifting her off the bed. Jayson was here. He gave her the briefest hug and then he climbed up on the bed behind Jerry to try to loosen the belts.

"If he gets jarred at all, his neck might break." Kelsey warned.

"I can lift him," Jayson said.

Gently, Jayson lifted Jerry's limp body until the belt came off of the fan. Then he gradually lowered her friend on to the bed. He was pressing the cover firmly down on the bleeding and checking for other injuries when EMS arrived.

Kelsey answered the two paramedics' questions while they worked on Jerry. She prayed he didn't regain consciousness right now because he would hate her for calling them.

Two police officers also came in but Jayson held them at bay until Jerry was taken out. Then they came to Kelsey, standing a little too close and giving her curious looks.

"We seem to be seeing a lot of you lately, young lady," said the older officer. He was the same man Kelsey had talked to with her complaint about her food being poisoned.

Now he roamed her apartment, looking at her things as though they were somehow tainted. She got the feeling he hadn't liked the word carved on Jerry's belly.

"Aren't you going to take fingerprints!" Kelsey demanded, amazed that they were touching things, destroying evidence. "Have you even checked out Dave Daniels?"

The policeman smirked. "Well, it's obvious that we've got some kind of sicko here..."

There was something off in how the officer said it, like maybe he was forming some kind of twisted suspicion in reference to Kelsey. Her gut told her that these officers would be happy if they could pin something criminal on her. It was ironic, cops used to be Kelsey's friends. Now all the cops she came in contact with seemed to hate her.

Jayson brought Kelsey out to the kitchen while the officers did their thing in her bedroom, pulling her away before she could say anything nasty to them.

She held onto Jayson, crying and shaking him to get his full attention.

"I can't do this anymore," she cried, hiccuping with hysteria. "I can't do this!"

The image of the dark body swinging over her bed, silhouetted against the lighter window, was ingrained behind her eyes. She kept flashing back to it.

"I'll never sleep in that bed again," she said, with her chest heaving for breath. "I can't be in this apartment! Not ever! It's been ruined, Jayson. He's taken everything from me!"

Kelsey stared into the distance, realizing that this was true, her stalker had methodically taken apart her life.

In a while she calmed down, letting her breathing get steadier. Jayson offered her a bottle of flavored water from the refrigerator but Kelsey pushed it away, looking at him directly.

"I'm going to let them foreclose on the condo," she said. "I can't be here anymore."

Just then, Kelsey caught a movement out of the corner of her eye, a striped tail disappearing into a dark doorway. The police had left the door wide open and Fluffy was slipping out into the starry night.

This suddenly brought back an image, a memory of a fat ragged cat slipping out a doorway three years ago. Daniels' cat. Kelsey felt the bile rise in her throat. That night three years ago the cat had been lost as the police officers carelessly left the door open on Daniels' trailer. Kelsey had stood there dumbly and watched it go. This is why Daniels had done what he did to her innocent Mr. Cooper! It was all falling into place.

"Fluffy," she screamed raucously, "get back in here!"

Jayson ran to the doorway and grabbed the cat.

Chapter 24

"Let's look for Daniels!" Kelsey said. "If he just did this to Jerry, then he has to still be out there. And it doesn't seem like the cops are looking very hard. Anyway, I can't sit here anymore."

They went out into what was left of the night and drove circles around their parking lot and the neighborhood, peering into dark shadows in the shrubbery.

"You really think we can find him here?" Jayson asked.

"I know he's here," Kelsey said. "He's gloating over his handiwork." But they didn't find Daniels that night.

Kelsey and Fluffy went to stay at Jayson's place. She wasn't surprised when the police called and told her that they couldn't find any fingerprints or any connection to a Dave Daniels at her condo

She went several times to try to see Jerry in the hospital but he was still very ill and she was told that no visitors other than family were being allowed in. Apparently his parents had flown in from Chicago but had only come to see him once. Kelsey thought something odd was going on.

When she finally did get in to see Jerry they had transferred him to another ward. Kelsey realized when she was buzzed in through a locked door that it was a psychiatric ward.

Jerry was in a private room with a hospital bed. She hardly recognized the gaunt face shadowed with bruises that turned away toward the wall when she walked in. A heavyset blond girl in a patterned nurse's uniform was sitting by his bedside concentrating on reading a worn *Family Circle* magazine.

"Excuse me," Kelsey said and the nurse's assistant looked up with a sullen expression. "What's going on here?"

"Suicide watch. Your friend here is talking about killing himself," the girl said and went back to her reading.

"Jerry," Kelsey pleaded, gently reaching for his shoulder in the hospital gown. He turned on her so suddenly that she stepped back. The angry face that turned on her was feral, with an odd violet hue reflected in the pupils of the familiar brown eyes. With horror, she realized that most of Jerry's teeth were gone, probably knocked out in the violent attack.

He spoke in an exaggerated gay lisp, completely different from how he had ever spoken before. The change in him shocked Kelsey almost as much as the brutal attack that had put him here. Her friend had gone mad.

Laughing to himself, Jerry said, "They say it could be months before they do plastic surgery on my stomach. The wounds are healing badly. Apparently there's a life-threatening infection they have to treat first." He howled with laughter, and then looked up into Kelsey's face.

"Funny isn't it? They all talk about my 'injuries' like they don't notice what it says! Including my parents. They want to take me home, but they won't even look at me anymore. I'm just a fucking faggot to all of them! Not that I'd ever want to touch anyone again in my life. Your buddy Daniels, or whoever, saw to that..."

Kelsey opened her mouth to speak but Jerry cut it off.

"The real irony, the real irony of this is, the man is supposedly after you but it's everybody else getting killed! That figures with you, Kelsey doesn't it?" Kelsey saw that the abused face was staring into hers with blazing anger.

"You're just a bitch, Kelsey," he lisped at her. "A stinking self-serving bitch. I've figured it out. *You're* the enemy here and I never want to see your hypocritical face again!"

Then, violently, Jerry began sobbing. The nurse got to her feet, pushing him back so he wouldn't rip his IV's. "You need to leave!" she said to Kelsey.

Kelsey ran down four flights of stairs, with her eyes clouded by her tears, thinking of Jerry's life, ruined, like hers was, his body violently carved with some blunt object like a screwdriver while he was hooded and gagged, and his sharp good-natured mind gone, probably forever. She thought of Miranda ending her life on a dark road as abandoned as the surface of the moon, driving faster and faster, over a hundred miles an hour, until the engine of the little car probably screamed out in protest. Miranda, who was afraid, above all things of being alone, dying in a place like that. She thought about the superhuman force necessary to drag that screwdriver one and a half inches deep through Jerry's flesh, just grazing the internal organs...

Dave Daniels did have the capacity to kill after all. Kelsey had been so damn brilliant scoping that fact out. The problem was that *she* had been the one whose actions had driven him to kill and to destroy innocent people. The attack on Jerry had been so similar to the rape of Daniels. There was so much violence and bloodshed that she had inadvertently set into motion. She had been the culprit, just like Jerry said. Kelsey heard her own breath echoing in the stairwell as she ran.

All Daniels had wanted was to stay in his warm bed and play with his new toys. Dave Daniels was a fat lazy fuck wanting nothing more than the creature comforts of life. The guns were because he was a goddamn hunter. Kelsey thought she had read him so well, but she hadn't gotten it at all.

He had probably known all this when he looked into her eyes that night in the trailer. She hadn't even bothered to look into his. Daniels had called her a stupid bitch. He had tried to tell them that he was a good guy, not really trying to hurt anyone.

Only now did she believe him. Back then, Dave Daniels had probably been a good guy. Now he was doing what any good guy would do if he had the deaths of his family brought about by someone else's misplaced pride and the fact that she got high on power. Now he would show her exactly what it felt like to be him.

And Kelsey would have no opportunity to tell him that she had been wrong. If it ever came to a time of her finally looking into his eyes, it would be a fight for life and death. And she knew she would be fighting. The truth would never come out. Except that she knew it in her heart.

Kelsey sat down at the bottom of the stairs for a long while before going out to a pay phone and calling Jayson to ask him to pick her up.

It was dark when they got back to his room. He prepared a bodybuilding supplement drink for himself and a cup of tea for Kelsey. They drank in the dark, watching the white skim of waves on the dark water in the distance.

"Jayson," Kelsey said, finally, "there's something I need to explain..."

What she was going to say was extremely difficult for her and she had to go through much soul-searching to get to it. This had been the first time she had ever looked deeply within herself and found something there that she truly did not like, something that wasn't like her as she knew herself to be.

Her listener was quite. Kelsey took a breath, letting out the words carefully and, as she spoke, realizing in her heart the truest reason for why Dave Daniels was doing what he was doing.

"Jayson, I told you that on the day we raided his trailer, Daniels stopped at the very end to look me in the eye and he said 'this is personal, Kelsey'. I think I know the reason why he said that now."

Kelsey sighed, and went on. Jayson's inquisitive eyes in the dimness were making this harder.

"My own feelings about Daniels... I think he was aware of things that I wasn't even aware of at the time, and this is what he hates me for now. Remember I told you that I first knew of him because of bad checks written on his own account?" She took another breath. "I spoke to him on the phone at length. And I was impressed by him. The man was very articulate. You have to understand he has a certain power when he speaks. He and I were enemies but it was like we were totally on the same page when we communicated. I was excited by him in a way. I had never spoken to someone like that before..."

Jayson was oppressively silent and then he asked her, coldly, "You're saying you were attracted to Daniels?"

Kelsey said, in a small voice, "In some way, yes. From the way he talked, I perceived him as a very powerful person. After all, he had been able to make me feel that excitement. Then I had my suspicions that he might be involved in the credit card scam and I pulled up his driver license photo. And he was grossly fat!

"I despise fat, Jayson, I just really have a problem with it. I recoil from it, as though it means some terrible weakness in the person. And I was so angry!"

Kelsey's small frame shook, remembering what it had been like siting alone in her cubicle staring at the bloated face in the picture, a face that had played her so badly, probably laughing at her even as she flirted over the phone.

Not that it had been obvious she was flirting, but Daniels would have known.

"He was fat!" she continued. "A fat nobody. And here I was crediting him this great intensity. I felt intrigued by him! When I saw what he really looked like I felt disgust. I felt anger at him for deceiving me about what he was."

Jayson sipped at his shake and it left a white mustache on his upper lip.

"I bet I know what you're going to say next," he said and she could detect a disapproving quality in his voice.

Kelsey hated what she had to acknowledge but, in a way, it was giving her freedom.

"I think," she said, "that I pursued the case the way I did, not only from a sense of justice, but also because of the personal betrayal I felt. That's what Daniels somehow picked up on, like he could see inside my soul better than I could. That's why I think he's out to kill me now. Because he can see this was all ridiculous. It was all needless."

There was a silence, lasting a very long time. In the time they looked out the window, they saw a few people pass although it was getting late and was getting chilly. With the window shut, there was only the deep quiet, like the quiet of Kelsey's own mind. Both Jayson and Fluffy respected her need to think and feel and be undisturbed. Jayson stood to rinse out glasses; Fluffy was licking down his bush of a tail in the dark cavern under Jayson's bed. Neither approached her for a while.

Then Jayson came up and gently stroked her cheek with the backs of his damp fingers. "You're brave to face this, Kelsey," he said. "I don't suppose what was motivating you was much different from what other people do every day. You just had these horrible challenges thrown at you when he began stalking you and you've chosen to face truth, whatever it is. I admire you for that. I just hope," he said, "that you don't have any kind of feelings for this man now..."

"Different feelings," Kelsey said. "I respect him now, in ways. I see that his lifestyle did have some value, although I didn't realize it then. I'm not so quick to judge people now as I was then. And I have this desperate appreciation for human life. If I were to see Daniels and his family now, I would wish them no ill will. If I were to see Daniels now, I wouldn't be as offended by the fat; I'd want most of all to understand what makes him tick as a person."

Jayson pulled her head to rest against him, so that she could feel the familiar excitement rise in her just from touching the hard stomach muscles under his shirt.

"It seems like whatever Daniels was before," he said, "he's stepped over some line now and he's become lost in madness. You don't want him dragging you down into it."

He took her gently into bed with him. "Now show me how I taught you to make love, make all the troubles go away." Jayson knew that Kelsey liked to keep the lights off whenever possible now, so he left the room dark as they found each other's bodies. They blended their bodies together in the warm cocoon of darkness, until the stuffy enclosed space filled with the smell of their sex.

There was only their love; it was what had brought Kelsey to truth. Now, although she was capable of feeling such fear and regret, she was also so much more alive than she ever had been. She felt very sorry for

Dave Daniels. But, at this point, whatever happened, she was okay with it happening. Kelsey was not hiding from the truth or from herself anymore.

The next day, doing a few quick curls with the big barbell before getting ready for work, Jayson asked her about Jerry. She told him all that had happened, that even if there ever would be any hope of Jerry recovering mentally, it wouldn't do her any good. His parents were taking him back to Chicago and he would never be back in Florida.

"All your ties are gone, your family and your two best friends," Jayson said. "What are you going to do now?" he asked her, his face scrunched up in saddened concern.

"It's just you and me now," Kelsey said.

She knew that her face showed a sad resignation. But she hoped Jayson also saw her sincerity, her belief in the way their love could grow and the desire she had to build a new life together.

"Anytime," Jayson said, "that you want to leave here, we can. I'll look into buying a house like we talked about and we can move to central or northern Florida where Daniels won't be able to find you. Or we could go to California."

Kelsey looked at him oddly, wondering why a young man with a perfect face and an awe-inspiring body like his would want to hook himself to a girl who looked like her. Other than looking spunky and in good shape, there was nothing special about her. Some men would call Kelsey's face cute, others, if they were being mean, would call it impish.

"What is it about me, Jayson?" she asked. "Why did you pick me when I look the way I do? I know that I look okay, maybe I look better than average, but I couldn't possibly be up to your standard."

"You are extraordinary, Kelsey, your intelligence and the power of the desire that you had for me. Never will I forget that, Kelsey, the way that you wanted me."

She knew that Jayson meant it, she could see the intensity blazing in his eyes.

"Okay," she said, gently, "I can try to trust you with whatever you want to do." She sighed. "But we can't be buying a house right now."

She felt herself spinning upward, strangely excited at the thought of them living together in a house and buoyant with hope and expectation. "You don't even have the credit rating for it. And you're not in a particularly strong place with your job right now."

He gave her a kiss on the top of her head. "Minor details," he said, "Trust me with it..." Dressed in his work clothes now, he looked so incredibly sharp and perfect, like he could be trusted with the world.

Jayson started making inquiries about buying houses in other areas, while Kelsey bummed around the beach, often alone with her own thoughts. She was still making phone calls to her old police and investigative connections, trying to get information on Daniels.

Whenever Jayson would bring up the subject of Kelsey's condo, she would ignore it. She had been in touch with the bank and she knew the date of the foreclosure, but she was reluctant to think about what she would do with her things. Any thought of the condo chilled her, she would flash back to it at times, feeling shaken and nauseated. The home that had once held the illusion of all safety now represented the embodiment of all her fears; the condo represented Miranda's death, the obscene disrespect to Jerry's body, and all of the violence that could be done to her.

Kelsey had lavished her love on every item in that apartment but now she thought, if she ever had to see any of her possessions again, she would scream. She knew she would never be able to survive for another minute if she had to do it in her old place. She was only surviving by being here, by distancing herself from the past.

Finally, Jayson cornered her into talking about it. "They're going to take your key soon, Kelsey and you have some valuable things in that condo, things I know mean a lot to you. We could rent a mini-storage and Juan and I could move the furniture, but you'll have to go there and at least to tell me what you want."

"I don't want anything," she said, and she tried to explain what she was feeling.

Jayson looked skeptical and disturbed. "I can understand your fears," he said, "although I can't really imagine what it was like walking in and seeing Jerry like that. But I still know what some of that stuff means to you. It would hurt me to see you turn away from it. Some of that stuff is beautiful, it's a part of you."

"A part that used to be me. The only part of me now is surviving. I'm content with being that way."

"Okay," Jayson agreed, "I'll go there and just pick up the personal stuff, the clothes and important papers all. You tell me what you want."

Kelsey agreed and provided Jayson with a short list of the things she wanted and, as soon as she did, he made a trip to the condo. Alone and fearful in his efficiency, Kelsey was glad when Jayson finally got back. He had taken a very long time at the condo and he had a sentimental far-away look when he came back, like he had just put a dear relative to rest. Kelsey could understand; it was only now that she could feel an emotional distance from the comfortable home that had meant so much to her. She understood the respect that Jayson still felt for her past.

"It was sad to have to do that," he said simply. When Kelsey went out to retrieve her stuff she found Juan's pickup instead of Jayson's car. And, in addition to the black plastic garbage bags she had given him, Jayson had also bought a pretty new set of pink and purple soft-sided luggage and he had packed it tightly with her things. He had retrieved many times more than the amount she had told him to.

She could see Jayson in the lit up picture window, watching her as she dragged stuff out of the truck bed. She wondered how they were going to make it all fit in the little room. She knew her next week would all be spent unpacking and organizing. But she felt good, actually, like she could do this.

Sooner or later one of the properties in the more northern counties would come through, Jayson would complete the transfer at his job and their new life would begin. But right now there seemed no hurry. It was as if all that Kelsey needed was in this truck bed and inside that picture window.

Days later, Kelsey had unpacked her stuff in the room and everything was neat and put away, as if in expectation of something. But still Kelsey did nothing. Outside, the crowds on the Broadwalk thinned out even more as summer wound down to its lowest point, the time when tourism was at its most sluggish. The days were searing hot and Kelsey took to staying inside after her morning swim in the warm glass-calm ocean.

She'd sit at the table and read the newspaper, following any news of a hurricane. The National Weather Service kept warning of one possibly turning this way but, instead, the weather stayed maddeningly sunny. Kelsey's legs were incredibly tan and smooth, in fact, she had never been this dark in her life. She used to stretch her legs out on the vinyl chairs, brush the sand off her calves and paint her toenails outrageous colors.

Carefully, she'd scan Jayson's two different newspapers for any item that might relate to her pursuer. Meanwhile she watched the constant comings and goings on the Broadwalk, alert for that one hulkingly overweight individual who might come at any moment, who might materialize out of the crowd to stare at her through the louvered windows. But she knew that, at this time of day, Daniels wouldn't be able see into the tinted glass and she would be able to catch sight of him first.

On this day, a Tuesday, Kelsey was restless and she felt certain that the hurricane was coming because she could sense the unrest within herself. Jayson usually limited the amount of liquor he kept in the house because of her drinking too much but she knew they had a few ice-cold beers. She padded to the refrigerator and got one out, then flicked on the television that came with the room and tuned to the Weather Channel.

Watching the repetitive programming, Kelsey could hardly keep her body still, her skin felt so sensitive. Maybe her restlessness was sexual. No matter how much Jayson made love to her, it never seemed to be enough. Her body constantly tingled under his touch. She even felt this way when he was not around.

Kelsey got rid of the weatherman and she looked through the other channels to find something sexy that would suit her mood. She got a bit excited to see one of the talk shows that boasted a bunch of fat bimbos with bleached blond hair who seemed to be arguing over the lone man, a sort of nice-looking very muscular guy with an earring and dark five o'clock shadow.

The show was called "My Sister Stole My Man" or something like that and Kelsey sat forward in her seat. She giggled when the mother, who weighed about three hundred pounds and looked totally tawdry, started yelling at her youngest daughter.

"When Jack come out of prison, I told you he was trouble. He just wanted the first woman he could find because he ain't had one in so long..."

The man chuckled to himself, like his mother-in-law was ridiculous. The girl started screaming back, but the bigger woman drowned her out.

"He made you think you was all that. And him acting like he was something special 'cause of how he looked. Well, Jack got those muscles working out in prison, cause that's all those convicts have to do! Yeah, he had plenty of time to lift weights. Well, look at his lazy butt now. He ain't lifted a finger for either of you girls since he got out of prison!"

The girl in the red dress, the one the guy was cheating with, jumped up with her hands on her hips. "He does plenty for me!" she said. The man was up on his feet meanwhile, cursing at the old woman that he was no common criminal, and the first girl ran at her sister, yelling, "Slut!" The two hefty girls met and grabbed handfuls of each other's hair.

Kelsey was laughing, with her thighs pressed together in a weird appreciation, when Jayson walked through the door early, wearing work clothes and with a duffel bag slung over his shoulder. He dropped the bag and glanced at the TV oddly. Kelsey killed it and popped up to her feet to give him a kiss. "I'll make you dinner," she said, "I've got tons of energy."

"That's good," Jayson said, "because I'm beat. It's been a long day."

Kelsey could see from the way he held his body that he was tired. He told her that his company had sent him down to Miami first thing in the morning without notice and he had skipped his usual workout in the afternoon.

Jayson hung his suit jacket in his small space in the closet stuffed with all her things, then dragged into the bathroom for a quick shower. Kelsey yelled to him while she cooked, thinking that she couldn't wait to make love to him, she had been so excited by the sight of his gorgeous body standing in the bathroom doorway.

Kelsey offered him a bite of stir-fry out of the pan when he came to stand by her at the stove. "It's Schezuan," she said, enthusiastically, "and it's hot!"

Jayson looked her directly in the eye as he sampled the food. "You're hot!" he said, and she could see him shrug the weariness off himself as he reached for her. He fed Kelsey a forkful of the food and then he kissed her, with the spices mingling in their mouths. And then he pulled off her shorts and made love to her, balancing her butt cheeks on the very edge of the stove, so that she could feel the heat from the simmering pan lapping at the curve of her back. Jayson drove deeply into her, pushing her flesh closer to the burner while she came, dangerously, but perfectly controlled.

Kelsey was happy. They ate the dinner together ravenously, partly nude and still in the blush of sexuality, still teasing each other. Kelsey then went over and straddled Jayson's lap, hugging her legs around him and looking into his beautiful light colored eyes.

"I love you so much, Jayson. This all comes so naturally," she said. He wrapped her in his embrace.

Kelsey was insatiable, whereas Jayson sounded more like she used to tonight, just wishing to climb into the covers in the dark and caress her affectionately, while complaining about the drivers on I-95. Kelsey kept rubbing her body on him until he responded, a big hard bear being roused from sleep and making love to her three more times, each more vigorously, until he was laughing and grunting with her.

"I love you so much, Jayson," Kelsey said. "I'd die for you."

Jayson let out a big breath after the exertion of having sex; then he propped himself up on an elbow to look into her face, his face illuminated by moonlight, looking as though he was searching there for something.

"I'm glad you're here, Kelsey," he said, "in my home. I'm glad."

Jayson rolled to face the wall, sighing comfortably as he adjusted his large muscles in the soft bed. Moonlight lay across his cheek and his lengthening brown hair. Kelsey listened to his soft breathing.

She wanted sex, her nerves were jumping for it, but she really didn't want to bother Jayson more. All that he had done tonight, making love all those times, had been for her; while he had been craving comfort and sleep.

Instead of waking him, she let her mind wander back to the talk show with the sleazy women pulling at each other's hair and the big ex-con guy who was kind of cute. She flashed the sense of violence and raunchiness back in her mind while rotating her hips subtly and squeezing her legs together. She kept seeing the image of the man's body, which had actually looked pretty sweet. Her body responded now to the remembered image of his creamy tattooed muscles. She knew she could get off on it if she kept thinking about those hard biceps, the big chest and the tight abdominal muscles she could imagine under the tank top.

"...Got those muscles working out in prison. That's all they ever do..." Kelsey remembered the words the mother-in-law had said.

She stopped moving her hips and the excitement faded, changing into something else, something suddenly chilling.

She thought about the stereotype of men in prison, working out with weights, developing their bodies to awesome proportions. Convicts. Working out.

She thought about how the best muscles she had ever seen in her life were right next to her on the massive body curled in semi-fetal position with the handsome face in sweet repose. She had always thought that Jayson, when he went to sleep, looked like one of those little boys in the pictures saying their prayers.

Muscles. The one thing that did it for Kelsey. She would have slept with an ex-convict or a whole line of them if they looked like him; that's the crazy way big muscles turned her on.

Of course, no one could have known that unless they had followed her and watched her crazy one night stands, all big men, or if they were able to get inside her head and know everything that mattered to her. Like Dave Daniels could. Like her boyfriend, Jayson Carter, could.

What stood out most about Dave Daniels was his fat. What stood out most about Jayson Carter were his awesome muscles. Most women wouldn't get past Jayson's perfectly gorgeous body to know the man. But when Kelsey did, she found that Jayson had the most powerful and intuitive personality she had ever known.

He was sleeping so sweetly beside her, with her finally in his bed, in his home like he had said. Kelsey rose up on an elbow to look at her boyfriend and she lightly touched the flesh of a big carved bicep that looked white in the moonlight. She intimately knew the warm soul that lay inside the superhumanly perfect body. She could tell from the way he breathed that Jayson was not sleeping. Somehow, he had sensed her unrest although he still lay completely relaxed, making her want to be drawn down into sleep with him.

But she couldn't.

She knew she wouldn't be able to recognize Dave Daniels' face if she looked into it right now. She had never looked at Daniels carefully enough on that night long ago. It had been a cute face, she supposed, if it weren't for the fat. The grotesque fat that characterized his body. A big man, all fat. Jayson was a big man, all beautiful muscle.

She had been unable to track down Dave Daniels, yet she had the sense that he had been watching her every move, that he had been close. Now she entertained the possibility that he had been right next to her all along, that Daniels had somehow transformed himself into this perfect man, the man she had so easily taken as her lover.

Kelsey's purse was on the floor beside the bed. She could just shoot the muscular man beside her now before he had the time to turn. But she needed to know. At this moment, she needed to know more than anything.

It seemed that the ocean itself went silent as she prepared to speak. Finally, she said the word.

"Davie?"

She watched her lover's back move with his breathing, several breaths.

Then, without turning, he asked, "How sure are you?"

The night trembled around her. She felt for the moment that the two of them were bigger than all of it, but also absurdly small, trapped together in this room. Every breath sounded like a roar and she was compelled to keep her voice as calm as his. Still bound together by their lovemaking, Kelsey knew for a fact that her boyfriend Jayson was Dave Daniels and she respected him for reacting as he did.

"I'm completely sure," she said.

Jayson rolled over to look at her, with his face and body seeming languid and completely exciting to her, like it would be wonderful if they made love together again.

She looked into those extraordinary eyes, so light they were almost the color of the sand. It was a pity she had never looked into those eyes the first time or she would have had to recognize him all along, even without the fat.

Sleepily, but with the frightening eyes still watching her, Jayson said to her, "I'm wanting to sleep tonight. I'm very tried. You've got that gun by your side of the bed. You'd probably get to it before I'd even do anything. It's going to be the last opportunity I give you like that, Kelsey."

He just lay there staring at her, with a look of softness in his face that could be love or, just as easily, deep regret.

Just looking into his face was better than anything Kelsey had ever known in the entire rest of her life. How could she feel this way about Dave Daniels, the man who had disgusted her so much? How could he be here with her?

She knew that he would go to sleep hoping that she would kill him as he slept in order to avoid what would need to come next, just like that day on I-95 he had insisted on riding with her when he expected her to drive to her death. She thought about what he had done to Miranda and Jerry and wished for herself that he would kill her mercifully tonight so she would not have to face tomorrow.

Instead, nothing happened. Soft blackness descended and it brought the sound of the ocean and the warmth of Dave Daniels' body beside her.

Chapter 25

The next morning they woke up where they had been and no one had been hurt. Jayson got up first and prepared breakfast in the sun-drenched kitchen area. Kelsey watched him for a while without letting him know that she was up. The perfection Dave Daniels' body had become was an amazing thing and she looked at it in an odd wonderment. He was so smooth and buffed that his muscles gave off a fuzzy glow in the light. Kelsey examined him from all angles as he moved and he looked utterly seamless. She wondered what the fat man had to do to get this way and what unimaginable dedication had driven him.

Kelsey remembered how he had looked originally. While she did not clearly remember his face, that body was unforgettable, so sloppy the way the fat hung that she had thought it reflected a sloppiness of the soul. It was funny to think that now, because in Jayson's personality there was absolutely no sloppiness; for the entire time that he had been with her absolutely nothing had been done by accident. Not one single thing.

Kelsey began feeling the hate rise up in her as she watched the man she'd been sleeping with gracefully doing his tasks in the kitchen with such assurance. She had never had a goddamn chance against this man from the time that he had come into her life, anymore than he had a chance against her that night in the trailer. It had been her own trusting that had defeated her, her own willingness to finally take a chance on loving someone. And Jayson had been merciless.

What made Kelsey hate him most, though, was the fact that he had victimized her friends. She had been strong and able to take it and he had the pleasure of watching her go nuts as he tore down every piece of her life bit by bit. But why did he have to kill Miranda, as she was sure he had somehow done?

Miranda had been innocent, not even a part of this. Kelsey knew the reason; Daniels family had been innocent victims of it, too. The difference was, she had not gone in and done what she did in cold blood and Jayson had. Miranda had done nothing but trust and care for Jayson and he had killed her.

A hot teardrop burned in the corner of Kelsey's eye. To tear him apart, to rip him apart with gunfire, that would be fitting revenge, to tear apart that beautiful body.

Jayson lifted his eyes to hers questioningly and he bit into his toast in the sun-filled quiet so that she could hear the crunch, just like she heard the mechanical scratching of Fluffy's tongue against his fur somewhere in the room.

"What's up?" Jayson asked. When he got no answer he placed Kelsey's plate on the table. She could see the golden translucent eggs standing up in the sunlight.

"How far are you going to take this?" she asked in a voice that sounded rusty to her.

He knitted his brows and looked at her. "All the way, Kelsey." Then he took a big mouthful of food, and said, as if by explanation, "Allison is dead, so is my unborn baby Tiffani, Brandon is adopted somewhere where I can't find him, maybe being abused like you were as a girl. I thought that you realized that I'm not here about me; I'm here about what's happened to them...'

He seemed to mean that he intended to kill her. Or maybe there was something else in store. Kelsey knew she could stand up to whatever would happen. It felt easier having Daniels here than the constant waiting for him, thinking he was somewhere there outside. Maybe her body had already known for a long time that her boyfriend Jayson was Dave Daniels, although her mind hadn't been ready to accept it.

It was ironic that even if everything ended here, there would still be nowhere for her to go back to. Her condo and all of her things were gone, her family, who had been proven to be abusive themselves, had abandoned her and Miranda and Jerry were gone.

"What did you do with my cat?" Kelsey demanded.

"He was in a shelter in Palm Beach County," Jayson said. "You never thought to check that far north. But he hasn't been there for a few months now."

"You bastard," Kelsey said, in her helpless frustration. "He was an old cat! He isn't there 'cause they probably killed him!" She brushed the hair away from her face, feeling sick inside. "You know how he was about the shelter, how terrified he was about it. How could you do it? You of all people know what it's like to be in jail!"

She was yelling at him and Jayson raised his voice slightly, tensing his muscles into fighting position. "You know, Scruffy never had a chance! My cat Scruffy, you remember him? Just a piece of garbage to you all... It's not like I didn't love Mr. Cooper myself; you know that I did, but he got caught in it. The Lord called out for justice and I had to carry it through. Scruffy never had a chance and you fuckers never even noticed him..."

"I did," Kelsey said, remembering the large multicolored cat that had brushed up against their legs in the trailer. The cat had run out, terrified, into the night when all the personnel crowded the kitchen. "I noticed your cat. I just wasn't thinking right at that time..."

Jayson cut her off. "Come eat your breakfast. We've got nothing but time for all of this."

There was activity going on outside. Kelsey watched at the windows as she ate her breakfast, ignoring her tense companion. Rick and his two biker friends seemed to be tying their stuff onto the sides of their motorcycles preparatory to leaving, like they were moving away.

"They're going," Kelsey said.

Jayson glanced out the window. "Bunch of pricks," he said. "I'm glad they're going."

Kelsey found it amusing, remembering how she had almost fooled around with Rick and what he had told her about Jayson, which she hadn't believed. Rick had sensed that Jayson was an ex-con all along. Only she had been arrogant enough to not notice it.

Jayson got done with his meal and stretched. He looked her over, contemplatively, until she felt forced to talk to him.

"How long have you known that you were going to do this?" she asked.

"The issue skirted around my mind when I was first taken to county jail, to do something to you. I'd think about you and how much I hated you, with your tight little hips in your brand new jeans. You like, dared any man to have you precious pussy, but it showed in the nervous way you stood that you didn't even know how to use it"

Kelsey winced at his cruelty and his perceptiveness. He had been looking at her this way and despising her while she had been looking at his fat body and despising him that night.

"But that was just idle fantasizing," he continued, "I never hurt anything in my life, except the animals that I used to hunt, and even then

I was trained to pray for their souls in the Indian way. I was the last man on earth to ever hurt or kill a person.

"After I woke up from the coma, I asked about Allison and they told me, really bluntly, that she was dead. There was nothing for me to do or say, kind of like the way you must feel now. There was life of endless time in front of me to fill, just a big open question mark.

"Revenge was what I had to do," he said. "My own miserable life was worth nothing compared to those innocent ones that were taken. Kelsey; it's God's will. He's the one who's given me the power to do this."

Jayson gazed at her miserably, as if wanting her understanding.

"So, you blame all this on me?" Kelsey asked.

"Yes, I do. It was personal from the start."

Now, he deeply met her eyes and Kelsey felt herself blush. She had been attracted to Daniels at first, only she had never understood how much. If she had been with him, even with his fat body, it would have been the best sex she ever had; it would have been what she had with Jayson. No wonder the sound of Daniels' voice had gotten her sexually excited when she first talked with him on the phone.

Jayson looked at her like he knew what she was thinking; he looked so very sad. "I know why you did it all, Kelsey. The thing was, maybe it was partly my fault for being a part of it. I know I flirted with you on the phone that day. You have to understand that I am completely faithful to Allison. But I guess I enjoyed the power of toying with you. For a moment, I enjoyed the attention."

"Was I that obvious, that ridiculous?" Kelsey asked.

"You were just very sexually naive," he said. "Maybe in another world you and I could have been partners and it would have been nice. The thing was, you talked to me and you were being blown away by the first hint of a sexual power you were trying to repress and, because you were so self-absorbed, you let your own feelings influence everything. Then bad luck came into play with everything that happened. You couldn't have known that you would have accounted for so many lives. And I made the mistake, in my own pride, of terribly underestimating you."

The day was a beautiful one, free of the oppressive quality that had been in the air the past week. On any other day like this, the couple would have been outside, rolling around in the warm sand and teasing each other. Now there was only agony and life would never be the same. Kelsey realized with fresh surprise that it must have been like this for Jayson every day.

"Davie," she said, "is it all right if I call you that?" He shrugged. "I have to know what happened with Miranda. Would you tell me?"

The big man got up and stretched out his magnificent body. "We might as well go out to the beach and spend our day there," he said. "I'll tell you anything, anything that you want to know."

As he was locking up and guiding Kelsey out the door with two beach towels hanging over his arm, he leaned his mouth in close to her ear. "You could try calling the police, you know, but that wouldn't help. By this point they think you're the psycho. And I've covered my tracks completely this time. I wasn't about to make the same mistake twice dealing with you."

The proximity of him and the sweetness of his breath were so intoxicating that, out of nowhere, Kelsey asked him the most incredible question. "I don't suppose we'll make love anymore?"

Looking at his villainous but indulgent stare made Kelsey tremble. She knew he felt it, too. She could see it. But maybe what she was seeing in him was a desire of hate. The two emotions were similar in how powerful they could be.

"No, hon," he said, "I don't suppose we will make love."

When they reached the water, Jayson swam far out into the glistening ocean and Kelsey thought that the maybe a shark should take him and that would be better for everyone. But maybe he could fight a shark; after all, he had been trained to fight alligators. There wasn't much the man couldn't do.

When Jayson climbed up the little lip from the ocean onto the beach, other girls stared at his magnificence, not even bothering to disguise their awe. Kelsey felt like nothing beside him. He dropped down next to her with the water droplets clinging to his skin.

"Your job," she asked, "how did you get that?"

Jayson laughed and sprawled out on the sand and arched his back so that the annoying teenage girls next to them yelled out, "Oh my God!" and grabbed onto each other and held their hearts.

"You think just because someone has a cellular phone, it makes him a businessman!" He laughed at her. "I knew that would impress somebody like you."

"But I saw your offices," she protested.

"Oh, the job's for real. But my investment company is just a fly-by-night kind of place. Basically, what we do is gamble with our investor's money. They had no trouble hiring a guy like me."

He played in the sand, tracing lines around Kelsey's legs and looking thoughtful. "You know, society is so odd," he said. "Instead of doing the scam you caught me for, I could have gotten the job I have now and had your respect all along. I knew that something like that is what you wanted."

Had she really been that shallow and easy to read that, in a half-hour three years ago, this man could have seen through to the respect she bestowed on people for all the wrong materialistic reasons?

"I'm not like that now," she said.

He nodded. "I know that you're not. I've watched you grow all this time. I wanted to help you grow to the point where you'd be able to see what you did wrong three years ago. But you've done more than that; you've completely changed as a person. I wasn't expecting that to happen."

"You really analyzed my character to that extent?" she asked him. "You tailored everything you did to have some kind of effect on me? How could you understand me so fully, in the space of one half hour, under those circumstances? I should be flattered by that; no one else has paid me that much attention in my entire life."

"It's just my nature to be observant," Jayson said. "And that night, I guess because it was so horrible, because it was the turning point of my life, each detail stuck in my mind and I could call them up later and they'd be precisely right."

"You were right about everything about me?" Kelsey asked.

Jayson rolled around on the sand, displaying all the hugely chiseled parts of his body that she loved so much. The only thing missing was the hard-on in his shorts that was usually there for her when she looked at him this way.

"I was right about how you'd react to things." He grinned at her unpleasantly, obviously proud of himself.

"You know, you're so gorgeous," Kelsey said, in awe.

"This isn't my body," he said. "You saw my body that first night. This is something I did for you."

Jayson went up to one of the food stands to get them lunch while Kelsey stayed on the beach. She could have run, but there was nowhere to run to. Right now, he was the one with all the resources and she was the outcast in society. She had no money; no home, no car, no family or friends and the local police knew her as an irrational alcoholic with paranoid fantasies and a supposed suicide attempt on record. Jayson had seen to that. She had no doubt that wherever she would go; he would follow with his hatred. She felt safer thinking they could finish their conflict here or at least she'd have some time to plan what to do.

Jayson brought her back food, which she didn't touch until he lay down and settled into a catnap next to her. Then Kelsey brooded on things, so sorry that she had done the things in the past to destroy this man whom she had grown to truly love.

When Jayson awoke, blinking his eyes up at the sun, Kelsey said, "It's afternoon, you need to tell me about Miranda."

He sat up and looked truly stricken. "It was the most awful thing I've ever seen in my life," he said. Kelsey saw the genuine tears form in the bottoms of his eyes. "I was following her on my motorcycle. She just kept going faster and faster. There was this whining sound, like a scream; maybe it was the sound of her engine straining. I could hear it over the sound of my bike and over the wind. That night was very windy and clouds kept moving over the moon. One minute, things would be spotlighted and the next it would be totally dark again. The girl didn't know how to drive, you know. She was completely crazy!"

He looked off at the ocean for a while before continuing. "It happened in this area where there was sugar cane on both sides of the road and the canals were drained. Miranda ran off the road. She was going over a hundred miles an hour. Her car went way up in the air and it kept flipping. When it stopped, I tried to go to her. But what was left, you couldn't even tell that there had been a person. It was a horrible accident."

"You're saying it *was* an accident?" Kelsey asked him, her eyes narrowed down intently.

The answer to this mattered so much. If he had killed Miranda, it would be the only one of his acts that she would not, in some way, be able to forgive. Even killing the man in prison could be seen as self-defense; if Crash had been left alone then he would've come after Daniels again.

Jayson seemed different than she had ever seen him, like a part of him had retreated away from her and from himself. Her heart sank, suspecting that he was going to try to justify to himself another murder.

"I didn't make her drive," he said. "She chose to do what she did. I just let her have her keys. I just followed."

She pictured Miranda fleeing in terror, a phantom car in the night being pursued by a dark relentless demon, Jayson on his bike.

"What was she so afraid of and where was she going?" Kelsey demanded, her voice reflecting the hard fury she felt.

Jayson looked at her with his eyes alight with the orangey smolder of the setting sun. "Miranda was trying to save your wretched life," he said comdemningly. "She died trying to save you."

Now Kelsey had another piece falling into place, that Jayson, or Daniels, as she needed to think of him now, had been there that night with Miranda. She wondered about how his mind worked, whether he really was psychotic like some of the doctors in prison had thought. Daniels seemed to believe that he held no guilt for Miranda's death because it was the accident, and not he, that had actually broken her neck. The problem was that it was Daniels who had deliberately led Miranda into the situation; he had set it all up anticipating what she might choose to do.

"I worked Miranda the whole time," Jayson confessed, "I knew she would be my way to get to you. Even when I was dating her, I used her to find out every detail about you."

They had returned from the beach and now Kelsey was sitting on Jayson's bed in the darkened efficiency, hugging to her chest a decorative pillow that Jayson had brought back from her condo. Earlier, when they had come from the beach, Kelsey had asked him where she was supposed to go tonight and he had looked at her strangely and said, "This is your home now, Kelsey. If you tried to go anywhere else, I'd only follow. But in the end it's your choice, I'll just respond to whatever you choose to do."

Kelsey had taken the chance on staying. It was odd that she would even ask, considering who he was and the fact she didn't even know her own feelings, but she had to ask, "Are you saying that things are the same as they were between us?"

Jayson had looked at her and his expression seemed incredulous at the fact that Kelsey could stoop so low with her pride. "It just means that I don't have to pretend," he said. "You're still mine and I'm yours, only in a different way."

Now, in his room, he detailed the story of what had happened that night when Miranda died and it was a horrible story, just like Jayson said it would be, a story it seemed at times to disturb him to tell.

"I played your friend all along, Kelsey. It was a shame because she was a good person; she just hurt a lot inside and that's why she made mistakes. You always seem to think that she was number two and you were number one. I know she felt that way herself, always number two to somebody.

For a while, I enjoyed taking her out and making her feel like number one. But it hurt me, you know..." He ducked his head in charming embarrassment. "...Because I knew I was going the have to sacrifice her at the altar of you."

Now he straightened in his chair, making a more imposing silhouette, and Kelsey could see his eyes glowing darkly, the way she had remembered the menacing look in Dave Daniels' eyes that first night. It was only a trick of the light but she felt it deep in her chest; this time he really was able to scare her. In some ways, this man relished the telling of his stories; he was a merciless combination of Daniels and Jayson. After all, Daniels had never had a mean streak; it was her sexy beautiful Jayson who had aquired that.

"...She wasn't always your friend, Kelsey," he said blandly, "I know you thought she was, but she wasn't. She was out to get you."

Kelsey sat there small and cornered on the bed, but still defiant. "You're lying," she said.

Jayson took a sip of tea and slumped down again. After two days without a workout, he looked even wearier than he had last night, as though his heavy muscles were a burden to him. He had made no effort to go to his job, either. Kelsey suspected that he wouldn't go to work again, the only goal he seemed to have anymore was to finish this with her.

"Miranda betrayed you from the first," he went on, "but that was just her own weakness." Now, he smiled broadly, laughing at the memory. "There wasn't a day, since you pulled that shit on her at the gala, that the girl didn't call me, begging to give me a blowjob or make love to me, telling me she could do me like you never could." He sighed. "She was just letting herself in for hell. She couldn't see what I was, the evil that I've turned into. Maybe she liked me because she sensed in me what I used to be."

Suddenly, he raised his voice to be suddenly harsh and brutal. "But no goddamn woman is gonna make me forget my promise to my wife just because she offers me sex!"

He sat there trembling with rage for a moment and then he spoke again, matter-of-factly. "Between her lusting after me and her mixed up feelings for you, the bitch basically wrote her own death warrant."

"She wasn't a bitch! She was the best woman in the world!" Kelsey screamed.

"You wouldn't have thought so if you knew she screwed me that night," he said. "You would have ripped her heart out yourself! Don't lie!" Then he glared at her with distaste.

Kelsey started panting, and she felt sick. It shouldn't matter to her now, when she knew that the whole relationship had been a betrayal, but still she felt sickened by what Jayson was saying he had done. "You said you didn't cheat on me!"

"I had to do it," he said. "With what was going to happen, she had a right to something..."

"You did kill her?"

"I asked her to come out to the 'Glades with me," Jayson said. "She knew we were out there to cheat on you but she went. She was half out of her mind on coke, anyway. I rented a cabin, just like the one I did with you. I remember it was a very dark night and that cabin was very empty and stark.

"I started pacing and talking and I told Miranda the whole story of who I was and what had happened. I told her the details about Allison blowing her brains out and how our baby was lost, details that you never bothered to tell her.

"Miranda was on my side, Kelsey. She was hurt. She loved you, but she was the first to understand how cavalierly you treated people's lives. She made that call to you on her own. She wanted you to know how much she hated and despised you for what you did to me. After she made love to me, all she could talk about was how she and I could team up and get revenge on you..."

Kelsey felt her insides turn with the pain that in the end her friend had hated her, and maybe that hatred was deserved. But she hadn't heard the real horror yet.

Jayson lifted his head and finished the end of his tea, and then he continued, "The thing was, she thought it was all about me doing things to you like the voodoo doll or emptying your bank account. Then I explained to her about the accident on I-95, how I sabotaged your car and then how I had felt sorry for you so I made sure to go with you, so that you wouldn't have to die alone. And then Miranda lifted her big drug-glazed eyes to mine and it was like she was finally seeing the truth; that I might be willing to let her live, but I was definitely going to kill you."

Jayson shook his head at the memory. Kelsey didn't like the way his eyes now appeared so cold, and his voice so bland as he told the rest of the horrible story.

"It was like Miranda's adrenaline gushed. She jumped up and started running around looking for her car keys. I knew that she was going to make a mad dash to warn you about me. And I had the keys. I was holding them because she was too screwed up to drive."

His voice turned colder. "I held the car keys out to her but I reminded her that I had my motorcycle there, that maybe she shouldn't try to drive, that she was in no shape and there might be an accident..."

Now, his eyes were icy. Kelsey wasn't even sure that she wished to hear the end of the story.

But Jayson continued. "Miranda looked at me and I could see the terror in her eyes. And then she ran. I guess, in the end, warning you was more important to her than saving her own life."

At first, there was silence. Then Kelsey began to cry. The cat put his front paws up on the bed and mewed to try to comfort her.

"He cares about you," Jayson said, "you're finally getting him to come out of his shell."

Jayson's being able to react to her humanly got through to her and Kelsey was able to finally stop crying.

She tried to weigh Jayson's culpability in Miranda's death. Since he had set up the whole situation with an expectation of what would probably happen, it could be considered murder. Yet she could see how, in his strange logic, he would feel since he hadn't actually touched Miranda, he wasn't responsible; that if it hadn't been for Miranda's drunk and drugged condition that night and her terrible driving, she would still be alive. Apparently that was how Daniels liked his revenge; he liked to think of the things he made happen as some sort of fateful justice, rather than as results of his own maneuverings. Just like he had wanted to educate her in her wrongs, Kelsey now wished she could somehow make him see his. He thought that he believed in God, and yet justice was God's alone. What Jayson did, exacting his kind of twisted justice, was the biggest sin there was. She wished he could only see.

"Did you enjoy it when you made love to her?" she asked him, unable to articulate the thing that really mattered.

Jayson came over by her and stripped off his tank top so that she saw all the exquisite moonlight-tinted muscles. Then he balled the shirt up and threw it into the hamper by the corner of the closet. Looking down at Kelsey and Fluffy, he sighed.

"There's only been you, Kelsey, and Allison. Only two lovers in my entire life! The thing with Miranda was nothing. It was sad."

The new brown-haired Jayson was undressing as though he was going to crawl into the bed and Kelsey looked at him curiously. "What is going to happen here?" she asked.

"I need to be true to my beliefs," he said. "We'll talk things out, Kelsey. I need to know what's right before I know what I'll do. I'm not going to kill you in your sleep. I hope you'll do the same for me."

He grinned as he climbed over the top of her just as he had several hundred times before he made love to her. Only this time he didn't let his body touch hers and he rolled down heavily onto his side of the bed.

Kelsey made eye contact with him, hoping he could see that she still saw a chance for him, despite all he had done, if he would only let go of his awful mission now.

"I love you so much," she said. "I can't help but tell you that. I've become an honest person now and that's what I feel."

There were such incredible depths in Jayson's light-colored eyes as he gazed at her, as though he was allowing her to look into his soul. She thought she could see the disgust he felt for himself and all the horrible things that had happened.

"Don't love me, Kelsey," he said. "The best parts of me are already gone. They died three years ago."

She was lost in his pain. She had already begun regretting the whole horrible chain of events, especially since she had gone to the West Coast of Florida and started asking questions. Her heart had already been breaking for Daniels at that time, even as she feared him. The irony was, now that she knew Jayson's character, she knew that he was relentless and that hearing her apologies now would only hurt him more.

Instead, she said something that she hoped he could understand. "I want you to tell me about them, about your family. I assumed so much when I didn't know the facts back then; now I want to know the truth."

"She was nothing like you," Jayson said, and she saw him fill with the energy of remembering, she saw the first truly relaxed smile light up his face, and she understood now that none of the others she had seen in their relationship had been genuine. "Allison was so open with her love, she gave it so freely that it made you think the whole world was full of love; not like you, you're always trying to cover your bets. I had seen so much hardship and unfairness in my life. But when I met Allison, it was like all the promise of goodness and beauty that there was in the world had come true. And, in that first moment seeing her, it was enough to bring me above all the rest forever. All I wanted to do was to make life beautiful for her like she made life beautiful for me."

Kelsey wanted to comfort him, to show him how she was feeling the pain along with him. But she knew he would not accept her touch, he had pushed her gently away earlier when she had tried. So she tried to reach out to him with her words. "You really felt that way about her? Like you had faith that that orchid would bloom?"

Just from the way Jayson looked at her, from the true joy that she saw in his face, she understood that his love with Allison had been extraordinary.

"My wife was like the sun to me," he said, "with her blond hair and big smile. And her beautiful body. She was the most alive person I've ever seen. I didn't have to give up anything to love her. It all came so easily and then we were blessed with Brandon. And the way we loved him was an extension of our love. I wish you could understand, Kelsey. I wish you could imagine..."

She could understand; just looking at the ease and joy in Jayson's face when he spoke about his family showed her the truth. If he loved Allison so much even now, so much more than what he had ever felt with Kelsey; if the memories could light his face up even now; then their love must have truly been something extraordinary.

"You're serious about all of this?" she asked, realizing even more the enormity of the tragedy.

"As a heart attack," he said and winked at her, getting her to smile.

Then Jayson wriggled around on the bed for a while, getting comfortable before finally speaking. "I hated you so much at that time for not understanding and I hated myself for even wanting you to. You killed Allison as surely as if you put the bullet in her yourself because you didn't even have the compassion to understand."

He twisted around some more and she could see that he was fighting not to start crying. Finally he propped up on an arm and looked at her.

"I know what she looked like to you, Kelsey, just some white trash with the roots growing out of her hair. Just like I was some useless piece of lard. And maybe I was. But my wife, Allison, was the most noble person in this world. If you want to understand that, just look at the perfection you see in me now. Anything you find to love, it all comes from her. I learned all the good things I am from her."

Daniels rolled over and pressed his hand against his face. A very long time went by and she knew that he was not sleeping. Kelsey was getting drowsy and slipping into sleep herself when she heard his voice, talking to her so quietly that she had to strain to hear it.

"You make it easier," he said. "Just to have another human being to sleep through the night with. Kelsey, the emptiness is so bad that sometimes I think I'll go crazy. But she's never coming back..."

As his voice trailed away she could almost feel his pain spinning away up to the cosmos. In the black night like this, he was lost. Kelsey could not reach him.

The next morning she watched him as he slept on his back, bathed in white light. His features looked so refined. She contemplated what his face would look like transformed back into that of Daniels. Not that different, she thought, not horribly different. She could stand to wake up to that face every morning. Even the fat body would not be that offensive compared to some of the things she had known in the past few months. She wouldn't be surprised if Jayson was planning on changing back, gaining back all the weight. It wasn't lost on her that he had skipped going to the gym for three day now.

There was a light sheen of sweat over Jayson's body as if he'd had nightmares. When his eyes opened he saw Kelsey staring at him. There was an intimacy there for the briefest of seconds.

"Haven't you felt frustrated with us not having sex anymore?" Kelsey asked him spontaneously.

"It's not what's uppermost in my mind," he said, his menacing tone contradicted by the tired way he coughed and dragged himself to a sitting position.

Kelsey got up and made herself cereal for breakfast. He had only tea, sleepily eyeing her like he didn't know what to do with her.

"It's amazing I could stay in this room and not find anything to let me know that you were Daniels," Kelsey said.

Jayson seemed to perk up, as though he enjoyed nothing more than talking about his own cleverness in deceiving her.

"It was your own honor that kept you from finding things. I had an instinct for how far I could go with you. For example..." he said, and he flipped open his wallet, sliding a Florida driver's license from behind the California one and tossing it to her. "...I thought you'd appreciate this as a souvenir."

Kelsey held the old image of Dave Daniels, the jowly double chin in the driver's license photo touching the top of the fishing logo shirt Allison had been wearing that night in the trailer, the windswept hair unable to hide the riveting eyes. She wondered afresh how she had failed to notice those eyes back then. If she had, then she would have recognized him immediately when he showed up at the gym. There was only one pair of eyes like that and they were looking at her right now, laughing eyes.

Kelsey's eyes flicked to the weight on the license, which was three hundred pounds.

"Quite a change," she said, tightly, and handed it back.

Jayson smiled. He had a way of looking mean when he did that.

"Yeah," he said, "I kept it around, figuring there was the possibility that if you ever got this deep with me, you might refuse to believe that I'm really Dave Daniels. And that would be the cruelest irony of all!"

He laughed, and the unhealthy sounding laughter filled the small room.

Something was dawning on Kelsey, something that made her even more afraid of the man she was with. "So you intended to tell me?" she asked.

"I thought it would be more fitting if you discovered it on your own, you being the detective and all," Jayson said. The sarcasm in his voice made him appear many years older. "The ideal would have been for you to learn to see people in ways other than their appearance suggested. You aren't exactly known for that! But I worked with you, didn't I? And you did get it on your own. What was it that finally told you Kelsey, what made you know for sure?"

"My gut," she said coldly, looking at him with anger for the way he had toyed with her. "But something they said on that lurid TV talk show, about convicts getting big working out in prison, actually opened my mind to it."

"I would have hated to have to tell you," he said, "because it would have meant you had so much faith in love, and so little in survival, that you wouldn't have been the Kelsey I got into this for."

"I should have known sooner," she said to herself.

"It was easy," Jayson said. "My name was changed legally. You would have just had to look backwards from Jayson Carter. Even my bosses know that I've done time. You just never thought to ask."

Kelsey touched the frames of the two photos in the room, the one of Jayson with the other men on the college campus, and the one of the blonde on the beach with her long legs clamped around Jayson's neck. "These photos. Are they bullshit?"

Now he grinned from ear to ear, taking apart one of the frames while he explained.

"I got those when I when out to San Diego to visit my buddy, Nick Constantine. I got a couple of guys together and offered them a six pack of beer in order to get the picture of me and my supposed frat buddies. The girl, who, by the way, was perfect to make you jealous, was a little harder to persuade. She wanted more from me than just beer. I had to let her know that I had a spunky little dark-haired babe in Florida that I was planning on hooking up with..."

"So that was your cellmate, Nick, on the phone, pretending to be your father?" she asked. "And I guess he was tying to warn me off for my own good?"

Jayson nodded to all of it. "He agreed to pretend to be my father if you called. I left that number on your bill deliberately, in case you ever wanted to check up on my past. But warning you off was his own idea;

he said he did it to try to protect both of us and I ended up chewing him out for it."

"Why did you have to be so meticulous?"

"Because it's your nature," Jayson said. "You wouldn't want to be with someone with no background, you would have been suspicious. But I didn't have to do much to satisfy you."

"So all that about you working as a lead singer in a band, was that all bullshit, too?"

Now Jayson gave her a truly warm smile. "Well, that was my vanity. I always fantasized about being a rock star..."

Laughing, he swung open the louvered closet door on the very far left, the one that was usually blocked in by the bed. What it revealed made Kelsey gasp.

"It's just a door," Jayson said. "But I knew you'd never open it."

Behind the door was a row of shelves stacked full of music CD's, hundreds of them. Jayson looked proud, seeing Kelsey's consternation. He started tossing the CD's onto the bed for her to see them. Many of the albums were alternative or classic rock, but the majority of them were unfamiliar to Kelsey, a lot of vintage blues and a full collection of Elvis Presley albums. Kelsey should have known. Jayson had so much knowledge of music. Why hadn't she made the connection to Daniels and his obscenely bloated music collection in the plastic milk crates?

Daniels now met her eyes. "I thought you might possibly remember the thing I had for music. I noticed you checking out my collection that night in the trailer."

He spoke in a hard way but there was also a sense of something else, as though, at that time, he might have liked to be noticed and acknowledged by her.

Standing close to him, Kelsey chose the moment to take her chance; this might be the only chance she might ever have with him.

"Davie," she said, and she knew this caught his attention. He met her eyes and it seemed to be the most real look they had ever shared. "I'm sorry," she said, meaning it. "I'm nothing but sorry."

He held her gaze and reached out with the backs of his fingers to stroke her cheek, the first real touch in days. "I know you are, Kelsey," he said, seriously. "I've known it since Ft. Myers." All there was to be seen in his eyes was the deepest understanding.

It was not freedom that Kelsey wanted from this man but it was important to know she had it, to know if there was any way he could forgive the past enough to start looking toward any kind of future.

She started taking steps backward and ducked to pick up her purse and Jayson made no effort to stop her. Finally she turned and she was working the latch at the louvered glass front door when she felt his breath behind her ear. She hadn't heard his steps.

"Don't move, Kelsey," he breathed, bringing goose bumps of incongruous excitement up on her neck. "I could snap your neck right now. Without a sound, and with absolutely no conscience about it. Just like I fucked you from behind at the gym that first day. This whole year has been about proving that I'm stronger than you are. So don't doubt it now."

Kelsey turned to face him, glaring into a face that held no emotion. It was hard for her to believe that he felt no attraction to her. No one could have been able to fake the chemistry they had together.

"What do you want me to do, Jayson? We know I'm the one in the wrong in all of this. You've already taken everything from me. And taking your love would be the final end of it. I think you sense that too. I'm not that strong, like you say. I'm not strong like I used to think I was."

Now, she heard her own voice sound weary, much like his. "I can't seriously believe that you're going to kill me. Even knowing the things you've done, I don't believe you would do that," she said.

Kelsey also thought that killing her would not suit his plan of revenge, it would mean putting a final end to something that Daniels could never find an end to. Speaking about it seemed to break some unsaid taboo between them.

Jayson sighed. "Just don't try to run, Kelsey. It will mean starting the whole thing afresh. You could be sure that I would find you wherever you went. And it's no longer an equal playing field, you don't have many resources anymore." He gently disentangled the purse from her hand. "Just stay for awhile, Kelsey. It may sound corny to you, but I've been praying a lot these past few days. God should tell me what to do. I think you'd be best accepting His will. That's what I need to do. Is there anything else you wanted me to show you?"

Kelsey shook her head, feeling dazed. What she was in was a living nightmare. She just wanted to open her eyes and have Jayson be himself again, her handsome "Generation X" boyfriend, not this monster she had a part in creating.

Jayson led her back to the center of the room and he handed her a photo that had been hidden in the back of one of the frames. Kelsey was amazed at herself. In other situations, she would have snooped someplace like behind that frame and she would have found out he was really Dave Daniels after the second time they made love. But she had totally trusted this perfect man and she had never snooped in anything in his room. The little bit that she had looked around, trying to figure him out, she had only played into the trap he had set up by setting the stage with fake "clues".

Now he hesitated to let the photo out of his hand to her. "Can you possibly care about this?" he asked. "My family..."

Kelsey nodded with a lump still in her throat from realizing a few minutes ago that this was no longer her boyfriend, but rather a criminal who was holding her prisoner.

"I want to know," she said. "They were special, and I've been very much wanting to know about that, not just the terrible situation of that last night."

"That's good, because you're basically the only one I can talk to about it. You're the only one their existence even matters to, because your own life is hinging on it now."

Kelsey took the large, battered photo. In it, Allison, in T-shirt and jeans, was sleeping on the flowered couch in the trailer and Brandon was snuggled in front of her, also asleep, with his cascade of blond curls and sweetly folded hands giving him an angelic appearance. The giant cat was up on the woman's plump hip, sprawled and sleeping. Only Daniels himself was not in the picture. Kelsey was sure that he had taken it, looking at things from outside, a precursor of things to come.

She was too shaken to say anything coherent. She loved this man so much that his loss was unbearable to her.

Jayson was also unable to speak. Finally, with a sob catching in his throat, he said, "They were my family, my responsibility. It was my pride that caused this."

That was the truth of it. Excess pride had caused the situation, Daniels' and hers. Egoism was the only fault she had ever seen in this man. In sexy Jayson Carter, it only made him more desirable, in Dave Daniels it had proven deadly.

Jayson sniffed back tears that he hadn't shed and he stuck the photo under a magnet on the refrigerator. Then he looked at Kelsey. "You're wondering how the sex was..."

She blushed under her tan and batted her lashes. It was like he could smell it on her, what she was thinking.

"It's not so hard to guess," Jayson said, "I know you're not looking forward to being told she was better. But you'll tear away at the truth, anyway. You always do."

Kelsey knew she would be told that Allison was better, she had probably sensed it that night in the trailer, that the sexual thing the couple had together was something totally out of her reach.

Kelsey opened the closet and she efficiently got dressed in a red ultrasuede bikini with little heart cutouts, showing her naked body as casually as if she was with a woman. Jayson was sprawled in the chair with his genitals showing under cotton shorts, looking much like he had as Daniels that first night. She knew there would be no more hard-ons when he looked at her. That had all been part of the game.

"Why do you even bother knowing me so well?" she asked, as she ripped down clothes, knowing that he despised her pointy breasts that stood out white against her dark tan, and that all his desire for her had been bullshit. "I'm sure Allison was better or you wouldn't have chosen her."

She ripped more clothes down, snagging hangers so they flew over her head. She felt vulnerable under his gaze, probably her sparse tuft of brown pubic hair looked ridiculous to him, too. She remembered how he had first taunted her for getting it waxed, which she didn't do anymore.

"I guess Allison was beautiful," she said. "I couldn't see it under the externals. But a little weight on a woman wouldn't bother you. You see people deep down, immediately. And you would have loved her blond hair and big breasts. Honestly, you prefer big tits, don't you?"

Daniels winked at her. "The bigger the better," he said. Then he let out a long breath and laughed, like she was so ridiculous it made his tension go away. He looked at her with the cotton bikini sagging a bit on her small breasts.

"Allison was beautiful to me like the beach is beautiful. I worshipped every inch of her body."

He got a dreamy smile, obviously remembering, and Kelsey seemed to see years melting away from his face. The innocence she had first seen in Daniels' young face showed through again and it was so much more beautiful than the model-perfect coldness of Jayson's face that she had known. He got up and took Kelsey's hand.

"Allison and I used to spend the whole day in bed together. And she was totally uninhibited loving me. It was because she did love me, she loved me so intensely that her body showed it to me with that kind of power. And, by the way, I'm not the best in bed, Allison was. I was just a fat little shit with a lot of bitterness and a lot of horniness because that's where I put the energy. But the first time she looked into my eyes when we were together, she woke me up, every part of me: my body and my mind. Kelsey, I've told you, I'm just a pale shadow of what she was. I learned it all from my beautiful lover and wife.

"But now I can't turn it off, that feeling of awakeness she gave me. My body is dying for her every second of my life. Those days we'd spend licking and tasting each other on every inch of each other's bodies and we'd do it again and again, memorizing every mark and every bit of muscle and flesh. She would savor all of my fat body with her eyes and with her tongue and her hands and she'd tell me that I was the sexiest man alive."

He smiled, sardonically. "Allison used to say that with my talent for sex, if I lost the weight, I could be the most devastating lover on the planet; that I could make women do anything I wanted. It's ironic, I felt very sexy then, but now I don't feel so hot about myself. Although I definitely did learn from experience that she was right..."

He went on, dreamily. "Allison always was right, she was smart and she was intuitive. She used to be able to see right through people. We used to make love so naturally, like we were bathed in the warmth of the sun. Sometimes now, I'm dreaming and I taste her skin but there's nothing there."

His eyes reflected that blankness although he still held on to Kelsey's hands.

"I love you," Kelsey said, quietly. "Hearing this, it shocks me, although I suppose I could have guessed that you had such intensity with her. I know you've gone out with me to hurt me, but you did make me feel things I've never felt with anyone else. I looked on you like you looked on Allison."

"Davie," she said, and paused after saying the name. "I feel ashamed in a strange way that you brought my soul to such ecstasy. That couldn't have been the intention of your revenge. You just wanted to hook me, then make me feel the drop. But you couldn't have known I felt nothing with any other man before you. I took that from you too, the way I was able to learn to feel ecstasy, and you won't be able to take that away even if you do kill me now."

Kelsey was, in a way, afraid to say this to Dave Daniels but she really wanted to live in truth.

He let go of her hands and rubbed at his growing out hair, with his resemblance starting to shift between that of the two men, Jayson Carter and Dave Daniels. Finally, he reached up and undid did both strings on her bikini top, letting it fall and then looking at her breasts.

"You're a brave girl, Kelsey. Brave to say what you did. I really believe that you do love me. That first night at the trailer Naples, you seemed very shallow. You were a woman with a lot of power and I could see that you abused it on people, like you did with me and my family, to make up for your own weaknesses. At that time your sexuality was all twisted up in you, twisted with anger.

"You used the fact of your tight little butt and tummy and the fact that men wanted you as a way to hurt people. I saw the disgusted way you looked at me and the completely lustful way that you looked at that forty-five year old cop, and you would've rather fucked him than me because he had the good body. And he didn't give a shit for your desire because he was worried about getting his head blown off! And meanwhile, it was my intensity that had turned you on in the first place. I saw all of that and I hated you..."

Kelsey was stunned and she was uncomfortable with the way he looked over her breasts and her slim body. She knew that at any moment he could whip out a knife and do her like he did Crash in prison. She fully believed now in the hatred he had felt for her.

Jayson brought an ice cube out of the freezer and he stepped up to her and slowly brought it over and around the tips of her breasts, watching her responding nipples contemplatively. Kelsey gulped, not wanting to cry; she noticed the way he used the ice to keep his fingers from touching her flesh.

"If you're going to hurt me," she said, "let me put my clothes on. Don't let it happen like this."

"Kelsey," he said to her, with his eyes flashing suddenly on kindness again. "You could have done nothing but used me, for the way my body looked and for the way I made you feel in bed. Instead, you chose to change. With the pressure of someone stalking you, most girls who started out as bitches like you did would have showed an even darker side of their character. But you didn't. You chose to face the truth. And in bed, you never took anything that you didn't try to give back. I respect you, Kelsey. I respect this body."

He flung the ice across the room at the wastebasket and retrieved her top off the floor for her.

She was blown away by what he had said. He had seen the bad side of her character that she had always feared was there, but he had confirmed that she had made a change in it, that she really had become a better person, as she had wanted to.

"Jayson," she asked, "was there ever a time... Did you ever feel anything with me in bed?"

He pulled up a chair so that his legs were open around hers. Then he looked up at her perky breasts and listened for a long while to her breathing. She noticed how when he looked up at her with his darkened hair he was not so stunningly cute anymore, just a fine looking, mature looking young man.

Slowly, he shook his head. "I wish I could say that I did feel something. But I didn't. It was empty, you know. Just motion. I'm still faithful to my wife. I did respect your body, though, Kelsey, and all you were going through, how intense it was for you. In an odd way, I really felt honored being with you while you were making your changes. I never wanted to do anything to hurt you that way."

Kelsey laughed on her tears, saying something only to tease him, because she knew the true answer now. Pitifully, she asked, "Was it hot?"

He gazed up between her breasts to her eyes. "You're hot, Kelsey. You're not Allison but I'm sure you know now that you're fucking hot!"

Then he got up. "I have something more to say, I have to go over something you're going to ask about, about Jerry. But it's not pretty. Let's go down to the beach awhile and live another day."

Chapter 26

He refused to talk about Jerry right away. He said it would be best if they took a swim first and cleared their heads. Kelsey followed him to the ocean for a while, staying near shore where they floated on their backs, and pulled at the water with their arms to maintain their positions. From here they could watch the sunbathers on the beach, the walkers and rollerbladers on the Broadwalk and the swaying fronds of clusters of palm trees.

"Your weight," Kelsey said, "when I first saw you, did you really weigh three hundred pounds?" She felt a sick lump in her throat, thinking that she had slept with a man whose body had been like that. It still felt weird to her.

Children paddled around them. Jayson's eyes narrowed like he knew what she was thinking. "Give or take a pound or two," he said. And then, somewhat meanly, he said, "was there anything else you wanted to know?"

"Just, I guess, were you always heavy like that?"

Jayson sighed, ducked in and out of the water and splashed around. He answered her question in an odd way. "I was surprised at how far back you went into my past. I really was. Going to the cabin and all. I had never expected that."

"I wanted to know who you really were," Kelsey said, "what makes you tick."

"I was grateful," Jayson said. "It was something I had put back into a compartment of my mind lately. But you're right that it influences me." Now, he went back to answering her questioning. "My Mom was a Seminole Indian. She was a heavy woman, and she fed the family in the traditional way. My father was big, but all muscle. I tended to be that way myself when I was working with him, doing the 'gator shows. But then when I got into town that all changed."

313

He came closer to Kelsey in the water so that, as the waves rocked them, they barely kept from touching. "I think you can figure out my problem," Jayson said, and she noticed the particular lushness of his lips, wet now with seawater- Dave Daniels' lips, it was easy to recognize them now.

"It's not very hard to understand. I lived a rough life in the 'Glades, having to hunt and fish for everything I ate. When I got to town I got greedy. It was just so easy to pay a few dollars and open a package and have the food right there. I wanted it all at once..."

He came even closer to her until she saw the agony in his sunlit eyes. "It wasn't just the food. It was everything. I thought that with a lot of material things, I could be the perfect provider for my family. Instead, my greed ended up getting them killed or as good as dead!"

He twisted away from her abruptly and went under the water. When he next surfaced he was already very far away from her.

The day wore on and the tide rushed in to its highest point as a breeze built in the East. Kelsey was forced to come to shore when a considerable shore break built. She lay, shivering, on one of Jayson's hotel towels and no one stopped to talk to her. She wondered how much Jayson must have hated himself for just being human. He wasn't the first person to think they needed the comfort of material things. The devil had just brought her into his life to see that he would be punished and now she was being punished, too.

He finally came out of the water at about four thirty, when the light was already starting to change. There were red welts all across his pectoral muscles and he was white and shaking. Kelsey did not know enough about Florida to know what it might have been that hurt him, a scratch on coral or maybe a jellyfish.

"Are you all right?" she asked.

He tapped the center of his chest. "What you need to do is to shoot me right here for being the stupid little shit who did what I did. I'm too good a swimmer to die out there; or anywhere else, for that matter. I'd need a whole gang of 'gators if it was fresh water, sharks if it's the ocean. And it wasn't happening today."

"Do you really want to die, Jayson?"

She found it hard to believe that he did. He was so filled with life, whether he recognized it or not.

"My wife is dead. My unborn baby daughter is dead. And my son is going to be raised by people who, at best, won't understand him or at worst, will abuse him. And he's going to think, for the rest of his life, that his father abandoned him deliberately... You think I fucking want to live!"

His voice was raised so loud that people packing up their gear on the beach turned their heads to look at them.

"Tearing you down was the only thing that kept me alive. The thought of having my revenge on you."

He glared at her, as if daring her to ask if that mission was now about to end. If she were no longer alive, then he would have no reason to be either.

She looked his body over, she had to, and she saw no changes yet. "What do you weigh now?" she asked, without display of emotion.

He answered her just as coolly. "Two hundred and twenty pounds, four point nine percent body fat, about as close to perfect as a human being can get."

Kelsey uncurled her arms and legs and stepped to her feet, getting up into his face. "And it looks like you're trying to get back to what you were! Not going to the gym, you think I haven't noticed that?"

He cocked his head to look at her oddly. "What makes you think that it's Jayson Carter who I am? That it would be such a tragedy to lose Jayson? With my old body I got to be with Allison, with this one all I've gotten is to screw with you!"

"You must hate me so much," she said, scrabbling up the beach on the cooling sand, facing in the direction of the pretty, two-story pastel-colored buildings and feeling at a loss in the world.

Jayson caught her by the arm on the Broadwalk. She could tell by the smell of his breath that he was hungry and starving, like what he was doing didn't agree with him.

"There's no sense trying to sort out my exact feelings for you when I can't even be sure of them myself," he said.

He glanced around at all of the other people, many of them pretty girls in Spandex, with their lush bodies gliding by him on rollerblades and their surgically enhanced breasts glistening with sweat and suntan oil.

"I got way too close to you, Kelsey, just like you did to Dave Daniels when you were investigating my past. Trying to get to know you to hurt you, I found parts of you I liked. Now you're my only real friend in this world. I hate you for what you did, Kelsey, not for who you are. Unfortunately, it's the Good Lord who said 'if thy right eye offends you, pluck it out'. And this is all about following His Will."

A plump family of five were annoying Kelsey with the spray from a beach shower as they washed off their kids' plastic beach toys.

"You're insane," she said to Jayson, trembling. "Maybe you weren't that night in the trailer, but you are now."

"And you're insane, too, now," he said. "You know that I've twice taken a human life and you know how incredibly little value I put on yours. And yet you stand here. Wouldn't you rather run down this Broadwalk and just keep running, and at least *try* to defend yourself if I decide to take your life, like you planned to do if it had been Daniels? How can you stand there and look me in the eye and watch it?"

Kelsey stood up taller. "I don't think that we're going to go on, either of us, alone. If you do this, Jayson, I'm going to face you when you do it. I'm choosing not to live without you. So I'll take it to the end. Just like you will. I'm not crazy."

Kelsey had once wanted to be a hero and she had doubted she had it in her. Now she saw that stubbornness and the willingness to give your life for a cause were not that different. Unfortunately, this looked like it was going to be the cause.

Jayson looked at her for a long while, long enough to see that she was serious. Then he turned and slouched back towards the room. She felt like the strong one at the moment with truth out in the open.

"Jayson," she said, "let's get some clothes on and then go have some dinner. You can't go on not eating. And anyway, you promised that you were going to tell me the truth about what you did to Jerry. I need to know!"

"It may turn your stomach," he said, with his broad back toward her. "Let's eat first."

They had many open air restaurants to choose from. The places were crowded, with hostesses calling to passersby, and they gave off a festive atmosphere. Kelsey remembered that when there were four of them-herself and Jayson, Miranda and Juan, they had said eventually they would try out all of these places.

She and her companion now chose a table at a restaurant that offered a $9.99 lobster special and the waitress set plastic cups of beer in front of them.

"Remember when there were four of us?" Kelsey asked. "What is going to happen with your friendship with Juan now?"

"He was just window dressing for you," Jayson said, taking a gulp of beer and then licking the foam off his upper lip. "He's definitely a good guy. I met him over a year ago when I first got out of prison and tracked you to Fort Lauderdale. I had to get close to him to be sure he would change gyms with me when the time came; you hadn't yet joined a gym, but I knew you would. It was a long time being best friends with a guy, especially a loyal guy like Juan, and not telling him anything true about myself."

"He used to tell me he thought you were in love with me..." Kelsey said

Jayson smacked his lips on the last of his beer. "Goes to show, he's the kind of guy who always looked for the best in people."

"Why did you do what you did to my friend, Jerry?"

"Anyone who suffered, they did because they were close to you," Jayson said. "Jerry was just your toy, to use when you saw fit. When you cheated on me with him, you probably enjoyed it, but you wouldn't even acknowledge that. The only reason he was out there in that park that night was because of you and the way you dropped him."

"That's not true!" Kelsey protested. "That area where he went is known as a gay pick-up spot! I didn't make him go there."

"Oh yes, you did," he said softly and there seemed to be a demonic gleam in his eye. "Remember, I was there. I saw his face in the streetlight and his eyes were so empty. You have the capacity to do that to people, Kelsey... You know, he actually told me that you were the reason he was going to try to be with a man."

The lobsters arrived, whole and brilliant red. Jayson pulled off a little leg and started sucking at the sweet flesh while Kelsey eyed him, feeling suspicious of what he was telling her. He looked up, half smiling, with juice on his lips.

"He talked to me, Kelsey and he was completely out of it, like he just swallowed a bottle of booze in the car to make himself numb. It was pathetic. I came up out of the shadows with the hood of my sweat jacket covering up most of my face and he didn't know who I was. He just started talking, whimpering incoherently about this girl he was in love with who kept screwing up his life, and I knew it was you, Kelsey. You can be so fucking heartless. He kept begging me to let him give me a blowjob. It was disgusting what you brought Jerry to! He never even saw my face or my body. Any stranger could have done anything to him."

Kelsey was shaking; there was no way she could break into the body of her lobster. "I don't understand how you think," she said to him. "It's like you're blaming me, as though you're not the one who beat him and cut him."

Jayson worked on his food, seeming to relish it, before speaking, even though he kept his eyes averted.

"I didn't enjoy having the little faggot blow me. I could have gouged his fucking eyes out for that! But I needed to show him the error of his ways- for sinning against God with sodomy- and for putting so much faith in you, Kelsey. But he learned," he said. "After the blowjob, he sat down on the ground crying and thanking me and trying to hold onto my legs. That's when I kicked him in the teeth."

Kelsey got the grisly image of them standing behind the dirty cement wall of the park restrooms and of the bigger man mercilessly kicking her friend.

"I pushed his face down into the dirt and he didn't even fight back, not at all."

"He never saw your face?"

"I wrapped a beach towel around his head when I drove him to your place in his car. Then I did the cutting on your bed." Jayson's eyes had this unearthly gleam as he delicately worked on his meal, making her notice how he savored it. But his hands holding the utensils shook.

Kelsey, whose own hands lay limp at the side of her plate, asked him, "How can you bear to talk about this and eat at the same time?"

"You find that a person can do anything. Each of us can be brought to anything," he said.

He lifted a big chunk of lobster, dipped it in the cooling butter and brought it to Kelsey's lips, firmly working it between them. Her head was swimming with images of her friend after the attack and yet her lips and tongue responded to the dripping food, instinctively licking at the butter and finally sucking in the meat and chewing and swallowing it. The lobster tasted sweet. Jayson nodded his head watching her and then he went back to his own meal.

It seemed like there was nothing Kelsey could say to make him feel he should be sorry. Obviously he was still haunted by the attack on him in prison, and she couldn't make him see there was no connection between that violence and her friend Jerry's weak and misguided efforts to search for love. But none of it would have happened if not for her.

They finished eating in silence, then Kelsey began getting drunk on beer after beer and their conversation drifted to other subjects. They seemed not that different from the other diners if a casual observer had been looking.

Several more days went by in the odd limbo before Jayson told Kelsey anything definite about what he was going to do. They were having a light dinner in the room after an exhausting day of heat. August had just turned to September and it seemed to be the hottest and muggiest part of the season. Jayson told Kelsey that the next day he wanted to take her with him to the Everglades and that's where he expected things to end, one way or another.

318

Kelsey just stared at him but he said nothing more. She agreed with him that anything she did to run from him would only prolong things; he would find her anywhere and this would only start again.

But there was a reluctance to just calmly let her life be taken away without Jayson hardly seeming to care.

Kelsey had an idea of someplace she could go where even Daniels would have a hard time finding her, although she would still be at his mercy when she walked out the door. This was a club so big and crowded that she knew she could blend in, resistant to even his tracking abilities. This would maybe buy her some time. The further he got from his own anger, the more reluctant he might be to do violence. She still had the hope that something could break and his mission of revenge could end now, he could start living a life as Jayson, maybe with her. But she felt she had to get away before tomorrow's trip to the Everglades.

The nightclub was several blocks from the beach in Fort Lauderdale, an enormous space favored by the highly drunken collage crowd. The space included three separate bars and girls in string bikinis selling beers out of tubs full of ice. Bodies got so packed in here, especially near the dance floor, that you could hardly move or breathe. They held all kinds of contests, wet T-shirt and best buns, with people prancing around on the stages half-naked and rolls of toilet paper flying like confetti.

The only time she and Miranda ever went there, they had been roughly groped by a hundred men who didn't even look at their faces. The girls despised the scene and had never gone back again. Other people, like Kelsey's friend Wendy, said they loved the club. If Jayson found that she had run away, he would probably search for her at the bus station or the airport, and the middle of a crowded bar should be the last place he would look.

That night, Kelsey waited until her enemy went to sleep, seeming not as peaceful as he usually was. He was having difficulty breathing the overheated air and he yet still refused to use the air condition rather than the windows. But he was always a deep sleeper. Kelsey waited a while to be sure he was lost in dreams, then she went to the closet, choosing jeans and T-shirt as the most versatile outfit she could think of.

She walked the half block from the beach to highway A1A and it was still early enough to pick up a local bus. The bus drove to Fort Lauderdale and dropped her off near the plaza where the nightclub was located and Kelsey joined with the large crowd ascending the stairs. Once inside, she glanced around her just to make sure but there was no sign of Daniels. The nightclub was oppressive inside, filled with sweaty staggering bodies. Kelsey deftly threaded her way through them, moving towards the very center of the large space and feeling safer with each body she put between herself and the door.

She found herself standing in a group of pretty girls who were thin like she was, but a lot younger and totally drunk and stoned. Kelsey and one other girl, a blonde who looked disheveled, like she had just gotten through having sex in some corner of the bar, took turns getting each other drinks because just moving from dance floor to bar was a twenty minute ordeal. Kelsey used the time to think, oblivious to the gyrating bodies on the stage above her. The alcohol she was consuming only made her mind sharper.

There wasn't much she could do. Daniels had made it clear that he had covered his tracks completely and there was no crime the police could pick him up for now, no evidence. She was the one who now had the dubious reputation. She had a doctor who suspected her of poisoning herself and who would have put her in the psycho ward if it weren't for Jayson. The police suspected her of filing false reports and for somehow being involved in what happened to Miranda and Jerry. There was one job she had left under bad circumstances and then she was fired from another job, accused of dealing drugs. Unable to keep or find any other job, she'd had her condo foreclosed on and her credit ruined. Her family and friends hated her and would not talk to her. And Jayson had nurtured her weakness until now she was a full-blown alcoholic, unable to get through even part of a day without drinking uncontrollably.

She supposed he had seen the promise of it all that first night, that the tables could be easily turned on someone like her. Now she would not be welcomed anywhere in this world, she would be seen as trash, as a crazy woman while Jayson, with his designer clothes and history working as a stockbroker, would be welcomed anywhere. People like the police would probably hand her right to him.

She wondered how many years he might persist in tormenting her and, of course, she realized it could be until one or both of them died. What had happened to his family would never go away and he seemed unable to feel forgiveness. Before she knew that Daniels was the same person as Jayson, she thought she might have been able to pull a trigger on him or get him thrown in jail. Now she could not do either, she loved him too much. The best hope she had was to put as much space as possible between now and the past and to let him feel his own compassion for her as a human being. She would hope that he would decide not to kill her and then she was confident that they could spend the rest of their lives working something out from there.

In effect, her best bet would be to sidestep him, communicate with him when she could, back off when it became too threatening, a kind of game of cat and mouse, sort of like what it had been up to now but, of course, different. She thought she might be able to do it.

Some of the men on the bar's stages were dancing so close to her that she could feel their sweat flying off onto her. She ignored them and the women with them, some of whom were lifting their tops and engaging in obscene dances. At least this was a place where Kelsey could safely think and she had to decide her next move from here.

"Holy shit!" the girl next to Kelsey squealed. She grabbed Kelsey by the shoulder to get her attention and she started to jump with her boobs bouncing in her halter, trying to get above people's heads to see one of the distant stages.

The spotlight loved the body there- a gracefully muscled man, undulating with a girl with bleached blond hair, with her D-cup breasts spilling out of the top half of her thong bikini. The dance was sensual, as the man moved his hips possessively over the blonde the way he had learned to do it imitating Jerry. The girl started to lower herself between his legs, while Jayson methodically scanned the teeming crowd.

"Oh my God," Kelsey breathed and she took a step back.

"He's so awesome," the girl next to her was saying. "He's the most awesome man I've ever seen. I wish it was me doing what she's doing. I want to get up there!"

The drunken girl started to move forward, just as Daniels' gaze fixed in Kelsey's direction, even as the slut on stage reached for his fly.

Kelsey grabbed the other girl's arm. "Don't go near him!" she said. "He's a cold blooded killer! He's already killed two people and now he's after me!"

The girl looked at her, appalled. "Get off of me, bitch!" she said. She shook Kelsey off her arm. "You're crazy or on drugs or something!"

Kelsey spun around. It was she, not the other girl, who was in danger since he had spotted her. He would be very angry that she had left.

Kelsey aimed for an exit but she knew it was far. Wearing sneakers meant that she lost much of her natural height advantage to some of the other girls who were in heels and who blocked her way. All of the guys were big, with their shoulders blocking her view front and back. And they wouldn't move. Kelsey pushed and pounded against chests as she tried to run, becoming more and more panicked.

The guys' faces looked slack. She couldn't stand the smell of their breath or of their sweat. Some of them deliberately blocked her, grabbing at her chest and she elbowed them off violently. She couldn't breathe and couldn't see to get out. She cursed herself for her cream colored T-shirt, knowing it showed out, making it easy for Jayson to spot her. When she had first glanced back, she saw that he was off the stage; now she had no idea where he was, except that he was somewhere in the crowd, probably gaining on her.

She remembered the serrated tool the police said was used to rip into her friend, Jerry's, belly, a tool that never been found. She pictured it now, ripping up the middle of her back.

Someone touched her and she lashed out, banging into male flesh. "Get off of me!" she yelled. "Get the fuck off of me!"

She hit the drunken young men in their jaws and in their throats while wildly working her hips to get through the crowd.

Finally, she broke through into the air, standing at the top of the stairs and staring out for a moment at the stars. Then she ran. Jayson would follow but she had been faster, after all, and maybe her luck would hold. She could get in the cover of the buildings and head down toward the beach, which was about a mile away. She'd lie down in the sand and then maybe cover herself with it and she would be hard to pick out until morning. Maybe then she could catch a local bus and, from there, another bus out of town.

Right now, she had a few minutes lead. She liked the taste of the night air and the fact that Daniels could not hold her. She was free. Kelsey made the walk down the darkened street, hugging the shadows of buildings, and then she sprinted across the dimly lit highway A1A.

She sat down by the water's edge on Fort Lauderdale Beach. It was solemnly quite at this time of night, although some traffic still passed on A1A. Kelsey was in the area farthest from the hotels and shops. She stared out to sea at a brilliantly lit ship, maybe a cruise liner that sat far out on the velvety ocean.

There was nothing to alert her that she was being watched. The amused voice seemed to come out of nowhere. When she craned her neck around she saw him standing just feet behind her, kicking at the sand.

"You always head for the beach, don't you, Kelsey, when you want to run away?"

Jayson sounded nostalgic, drawing in big comfortable breaths of air that she could hear filling his nostrils. "Last October, you had that one-night stand with that bodybuilder freak. I watched you on the beach that day. Back then, you weren't wearing Gap Dream yet. Now I can track you just by your smell. I remember the first day you bought that perfume at the Sunrise Mall, you were so lost then."

"You followed me all that time?" she asked, starting to tremble, sitting there on the damp sand.

He paced. A sliver of the moonlight lit the side of his body and half of his face.

"I watched you for longer than that. Basically since I came out of prison. It took me only about a month to wrap things up out in California and Lee County and then I came out here. There was this incredible adrenaline when I first saw you." She saw the whiteness of his smile as he remembered. "The thing was, I could never get that close to you. If you had seen me, the game would have been totally up."

Kelsey got up and approached to stand next to him, and the white foam of the gentle shorebreak rolled onto her sneakers and cuffs. She felt that what she wanted to ask him was very intimate. "Jayson, what actually happened in prison, how were you able to change yourself?"

Jayson expanded his lungs and ran his hands over his hair and then he finally looked at her.

"I didn't actually have a plan of revenge at first. Oh, I would have liked for something to hurt you after you got me arrested and I was sitting in county jail. Then they arrested Allison on some bogus charges that she was conspiring with me and they put Brandon in foster care temporarily.

"Then I got really pissed. I used to think about the tight jeans you were wearing that night and how you thought you were so hot. I would have loved to be the one to knock you down to size. But, like you used to think before you found out the truth, I also thought my nightmare would soon be over. I had seen flaws in the case and, even after I was convicted, I thought I had a good chance of winning my own appeal. Allison's charges were ridiculous, and it wouldn't take long to prove it and have them dropped. I figured that, as soon as she did that and got a permanent place to live, she'd get Brandon back.

"Even when those guys were doing what they did to me at Redbrook, I didn't even seriously consider revenge against you then, just somehow living so I could get back to my family."

He stepped up to Kelsey and took her by the shoulders, gazing intently into her eyes.

"Then I woke up and I asked for Allison and they told me she and my baby were dead, that Allison had killed herself. The next thing I thought about was you, Kelsey. The Lord brought me a vision of your face at that moment and that vision filled my mind and my whole awareness, as I lay there for months recovering. There was no pain and I didn't know sleep from waking; I didn't even feel my grief. There was only your face. I remembered details I didn't even know I'd seen- like the small hairs you had on your upper lip at that time, the orange light deep inside your eyes, the way your breath smelled like strawberries and your pussy smelled like you hadn't had sex in a very long time..."

Kelsey looked at him, appalled. He was trying to make it sound like his knowledge of her was supernatural. And in ways it was- the things he was telling her about herself that night were all true.

"So, that's when you began planing your revenge against me?" she asked.

"The Lord kept showing me your face and finally, when I realized what I had to do, He backed that vision off a little, giving me space to think and plan. Yet I could still call up the vision of your face at will to recall the power of my hatred for you. I had to kill Crash first- to prove to myself that I really could take a human life and to make sure he didn't stop me from getting out and coming after you.

"After that, everything became about the meeting I would someday have with you, Kelsey. It was important that I get out of prison soon because I preferred to start on your life when you were still young, not ten or twenty years down the road, so my appeal had to work. But before I could even be an adequate jailhouse lawyer, I first needed to become fully literate. That's why I started by going for my GED."

He let go of her and began to wander around again. "Three years or twenty years, though, it didn't really make a difference to me. I learned from my cellmate, Nick Constantine, how to track anybody's whereabouts. I learned about computers and banking and anything else he was willing to teach me. What I wanted to do, Kelsey, was to infiltrate myself into your life. To learn it from the inside and then tear apart everything you cared for and everything you thought you knew about yourself, until you'd feel as helpless and as sick at your own evils as you made me feel. I wanted to make your life absolutely as worthless as mine had become because of you.

"There were two ways I could do this- one was by stalking you and doing things like the doll or sabotaging your car or hurting Jerry. The other was to go inside and be your friend, make you love the very thing you despised and make you despise yourself more."

He stopped and he held Kelsey's cheeks, caressing with his fingers.

"The real challenge was to become your lover."

Kelsey just stared at him and he stared back. Finally, he broke into a slow smile that she echoed with her own. Doing this felt refreshing and Kelsey was able to look around her at the fairy-like setting they were in, the strings of lights on the ocean liner, the warm thick breeze and the white surf in the blackness.

"How could you be so sure?" Kelsey asked.

"I didn't leave a lot to chance," Jayson said. "I *had* to have it happen so I worked on every variable that I could. My first impressions of you that night gave me a direction to go in. I knew that someone like you had to like money so I learned from Nick ways to make it. I learned about designer clothes and how to act like a snob. And how did you like that touch of the cellular phone? That was so Jayson, right?"

Kelsey narrowed her eyes at him in anger as he smirked at her. She really had been fooled by the phone. It, alone, had been something that had impressed her.

She lashed out at him now, feeling good to be able to do it. "So, all of that Generation X shit, that was all made up, too? Because I always disliked that about you. You were such the quintessential slacker..."

Jayson crouched down, digging out shells. He was chuckling.

"Yeah, right, I'm such an 'Xer'; my favorite things are listening to Elvis and alligator wrestling... Dave Daniels was just a good 'ole boy, sweetie. All of that slacker shit was for you. I learned it all for you. I learned it mainly from TV and magazines; you don't see many slacker dudes in prison. Even my education, going for my college degree, was something I knew you'd be impressed by. A girl with career ambition like you would be blown away by education."

"I guess I should say thank you for thinking of me," Kelsey joked, coming over to stand by him.

Jayson grinned. "No prob," he said and then he looked up at her, waiting.

Kelsey rubbed her hands nervously over her damp jeans. Finally she spoke, tackling the thing she was most uncomfortable with.

"Davie what about your looks, how did you get to look like this?"

"That first night, in the trailer, there was a small thing that I noticed about you, but later everything hung on it. I noticed that you loved muscles and I saw how much you were turned on by them. You couldn't even hide it. Remember when that cop, Ryan, had his gun on my throat and I had the automatic rifle on his stomach?

"You were there looking at his *muscles*, Kelsey! You were turned on by his body even though he was about to die! I noticed that; I saw the way you looked at him with some kind of lust at that moment and I was sickened by it. But it was the surest thing that I knew about you, that your weakness was a man with muscles."

He reached for her hand and pulled her down next to him.

"So, I transformed myself. The strength of my will transformed me. The power of my need for revenge against you, that's what created this body."

Kelsey trembled under the intensity of his gaze. He still held her tightly by the hand, putting uncomfortable pressure on the bones.

"I didn't even know if I could be like this. It frightens me sometimes." He sighed and played with her fingers. "The first twenty or so pounds went while I was in the coma and on IV. When I realized what I wanted to do to you, I knew that I had to change my body and make it the most awesome thing. I had to make myself someone that you, with your shallow heart, would love for just the way I looked. Just like you hated me before for just the way I looked. How you killed my family because of it!"

Jayson ducked his head and he started to cry. It was the first time Kelsey had seen him really cry openly and, even with his size, he seemed a small forlorn thing in the wide-open night.

She offered strange comfort, touching him on the shoulder and starting to cry herself. "I did love you for it, Jayson. And I did hate you for the way you were before. You were right."

Jayson let her wrap her arms partially around him and he leaned into her as she attempted to comfort him for what she had done. Then he composed himself, pulled himself away and looked out to sea.

"It was funny really, a sick fat guy like me, unable to even get off his back for four months, making a determination like that, that I'd have the perfect body, massive, with no fat, a body that would make people helpless before me. But I determined that I would. And then I worked. I had to take care of Crash first. Then I devoted my time to working my body.

"They had lots of old bodybuilding magazines in prison and I read and memorized every one. I learned the routines the professional bodybuilders used and I structured my own routine so I could get to look like them. Whatever equipment wasn't available there in prison, I improvised. And I was patient; I rotated the days I worked on each body part, I started out with smaller weights and eventually built up to the heaviest ones. And I even cleaned up my diet."

His voice roughened. "I thought of you every minute that I worked out. I hated every bit of fat as I worked it off my body. And I found ways to work, in some way, practically every moment- in my cell, in the exercise yard. On days I needed to rest, I read more about bodybuilding. The whole idea of bodybuilding, Kelsey, is that a person can transform their body to be anything, it's all a matter of discipline and the force of the will as well as the physical work.

"So, I visualized the changes I wanted. I worked dispassionately, just looking at this changing body as an object, an object I would use to someday conquer you. I pictured the muscles that were forming working on you, Kelsey. And I guess that part's done now."

He shrugged his big sculptured arms, looking oddly amused and bewildered.

Kelsey breathed out her words quietly. "You frighten me, Davie. But I admire you for the ways you were able to change yourself. Not for Jayson, but for Davie who, though his determination, created yourself this way. I could follow you to the ends of the earth for that quality. I love you so much as Davie that it's frightening."

He turned on her. "Don't you even understand that I did this out of hate for you!" Looking exasperated, he pushed her roughly into the sand so that she rolled down into the water.

"Of course I understand," she said, sitting up and blinking salt out of her eyes. "But it doesn't matter why, just that you're someone who could change yourself like that. That's what I love you for."

"I don't even know who I am," he said. "How can you?"

He offered his hand to lift her to her feet.

"Jayson," Kelsey said, "has it ever occurred to you that over time you really did change? That some of the changes you made are part of you now and that you can be proud of some of the qualities Jayson has because those are your qualities, too?"

He looked all around as if he was not sure where to look or what to do.

"I guess so. In a way." His voice sounded so world weary. "You know," he said, looking into her eyes, "I wish in some ways that I could have been someone like Jayson. Life for him has been so easy, so unencumbered. After all, I was only a kid then and I was trying to raise a family. All the cards were stacked against me and I was too naive to even know it. This charade has given me the opportunity to reclaim my youth. It's like," he laughed, "nobody's here and I can just have fun. That's like my only goal in life and you accept me that way. It's ironic."

"So, can you actually see that parts of Jayson are you? If what happened didn't, then you might have grown up into this?"

He smiled ironically, looking down over his body and at the brand new long tank top and youthful baggy jeans that now looked the worse for rolling around on the beach. His look was as if to say- this, this is me?

"Possibly Jayson is better in some ways than what David Daniels would have been," he said. "But that me was so much purer and this me has grown out of so much suffering and evil. How could you possibly say that you love it? I thought that you've learned some of the difference between right and wrong."

Kelsey took his hand and they held each other from a distance.

"You don't understand, Davie, it's not like it's two separate people," Kelsey said to this man, who now had longish brown hair like he used to back then. "It's all inside you, good and bad. And maybe you can grow into something else entirely in the future. I want to be there with you. Is there any chance that you might be able to go on, to accept yourself and live, whether I'm involved or not?"

There was stillness for a very long time and then he said to her, quietly, "I really don't know..."

They listened to the water for a while. The ship had left its spot on the horizon. It would have felt so good to just be together at a time like this, to be able to hold each other and then go home against the chill of the night. But now Kelsey was understanding the emptiness that Jayson always felt.

For a moment, she craved again to run away like she had done earlier tonight. There was just such an enormity in what she was facing in her life. She had always wanted to be a hero. Now she was facing up to a man who wanted to kill her, who could kill her tomorrow with nobody knowing it, and she wasn't even leaving. She wondered if her Mom might think any differently about her if she knew that Kelsey might be dying tomorrow out in the Everglades. But it seemed too late for Kelsey to even try to contact anyone, to try to reach out. She just needed to do this.

But she had to know one thing, whether what she had felt between them had been entirely false. Because their passion had felt so powerful, so unearthly powerful. If what she had felt wasn't real, then nothing she ever knew in this world was.

"Davie," she said in a small voice, "how was the sex for you? What was that?"

They were still holding hands, Kelsey chilled to the bone and shaking from getting wet. Jayson played with her hand, lifting it up and down. "You were the absolutely most revolting thing in the world to me, Kelsey. How would you feel about sleeping with the person responsible for the deaths of your family? But I had determined that it was the one thing I could do to truly break you. And I knew I would do it, that I could do anything to you that I had to.

"The thought of doing you was so horrible, I used to remember your scent, which I hated and your square white teeth and the flirty pointed tip of your tongue…"

His description was so extreme that Kelsey relaxed a little and laughed. "You're crazy," she said.

Jayson gave a tight smile in response. "I knew every inch of you and I hated every inch. I was afraid to try and be with you. And then I came to Fort Lauderdale and I followed you every day and I came to hate and despise you even more. I broke into your apartment and I smelled your things, I followed you at the mall and the bars and on all of your one-night stands. I understood you and I hated you. The only saving grace was that cat in your apartment, Mr. Cooper. I used to play with him when I was in there by myself."

Kelsey was chilled at what he was saying. At the same time there was an odd excitement as she empathized with his feelings.

"I never wanted to sleep with you," he said. Now he let go of her hands and he looked like he might start crying again or go into a rage.

"That first time," he spat out, "I really didn't think I could go through with it. But I did. I got up and fucked you. I fucked your tight, angry, hypocritical little pussy and pounded myself against your tight little ass, just like I imagined doing. And you begged me to do it!"

They stared at each other with anger, and a unique closeness, blending in their faces.

"I did what I had to do," he said. "And then I went into the guy's locker room and threw up. It got easier each time after that."

Kelsey didn't know if he was telling her this to hurt her. It seemed more that he was asking for her sympathy- that was how twisted this had all become.

"So, you're saying, each time you fooled around with me, it disgusted you?" she asked, still not totally believing him. She was sure that the reason she was still alive now was something special he felt for her, whether he wanted to admit it or not.

Jayson shook his head to clear it, looking out to sea. "Sometimes I would feel sickened like that, when I remembered what you had done. Other times, I actually enjoyed it, teaching you how to make love. For me, making love had been something natural and good. For you, when you met me, it was a game to be played for power and I guess guys often hurt you with it. I liked the way you put your complete trust in me to learn."

Kelsey swallowed around a lump in her throat, disturbed and happy at the small amount of true tenderness that Jayson was showing.

"There was one thing," he said roughly, still avoiding looking directly at her, just watching the water. "One thing that was special..."

Suddenly Kelsey felt the unmistakable heat start building between them as he spoke. There was absolutely no way it could be denied. Whatever Jayson felt, he was only human, whether he understood it or not.

"The one thing was, when you used to give me a blowjob..."

His voice really roughened now, she recognized the excitement; she knew him well enough.

"That was like a special thing between you and me," he said, "how you used to be so afraid to do it, so nervous, and then I taught you how to and we used to pretend we were floating in the ocean. Remember?"

Kelsey smiled and blinked stinging tears off of her eyes. "Sure I do," she said quietly. Oddly, she felt herself blush. It was like he was a forbidden stranger that she'd had something intimate with. Now he was looking at her.

"How did that go again?" he asked, and he removed his shirt so that she could see the tense glory of his large chest in the moonlight. He unzipped the baggy jeans and then stood totally still. So did Kelsey. Jayson then reached his hand across to her and pulled her gently to him. He lifted his hand with hers to her cheek and then he gently pushed down so that she went to her knees before him.

Kelsey looked up at him with her eyes wide. "Are you sure you want to do this?" she asked.

Jayson smiled down at her. From this angle she observed the slight jowl that seemed to be forming under his chin and the tenderness in his eyes.

"That was my line, the first day, right after I asked you what you wanted... Go ahead," he said to her. "Let's try." He put his hand behind her head into her hair, comfortably and gently and she knew he wasn't going to hurt her.

Jayson had a hard-on and his body smelled clean and neutral like it usually did, but it felt terribly strange for Kelsey to be approaching him this way. She didn't know how she could complete this without crying, with the heartbreaking nostalgia of remembering how the other times had been. She hesitated.

Then Jayson suddenly crushed her face up against his belly, stopping her. "I can't do this, Baby," he said. "I have a lot of true affection for you, but I can't. I'm sorry."

His sentiments for her were so strange and horrible. And so true. It was amazing to her that he would be so true about everything, no matter how it hurt him.

Jayson pulled her to her feet and crushed her against him in a desperate hug. Kelsey pulled back to look at him, sensing that this might be the last such embrace.

"What do you mean by true affection?" she asked.

He looked at her tenderly. "I admire how you handled all that I've done to you this past year. Most people would have cracked and turned evil. But it brought out the best in you. I like you now, Kelsey, I truly do. What true affection means is that maybe, even though neither one of us was each other's type, maybe in some alternate world we could have made it, we could have really worked together."

They embraced tenderly for a very long time, with Jayson caressing the back of Kelsey's head and neck.

"I'm taking you to the Everglades tomorrow, Kelsey," he said. "I'm sorry for whatever…"

He kissed her all over her hair and she melted with it. For her, this moment right now was the most beautiful one in the world.

Chapter 27

It was the day they were supposed to go to the swamp together. They rose early and shared a light breakfast and Jayson's first words to Kelsey were a weather report. "It'll be a good day today, partly cloudy and a lot cooler."

Kelsey gave him a shy smile feeling like nothing now could break the closeness of last night.

Jayson worked around her, packing hot dogs from the freezer into the cooler. "For our buddies," he said, when he caught her looking, and then added, "don't sweat it." He rubbed his hand reassuringly on her back.

Jayson took the photo of his family off the refrigerator and he folded it into his back pocket. Kelsey did not like the gesture. She debated with herself whether she should carry her handbag with the loaded gun in it. But this was all about fate and it felt more right at the moment to take it, so she did. She set her purse down next to the cooler.

Jayson looked over her choice of outfit, a braless camisole top, the one he had given her, and khaki carpenter style jeans. "Is that going to be okay for you out there?" he asked.

Kelsey showed him the hiking shoes she was going to wear. "These are all I'm really going to need."

A few moments later they stepped outside and Kelsey felt the first delicate rays of morning sun on her bare shoulders. Jayson paused before stepping out the doorway.

"Kelsey," he said, "I think maybe we should get Fluffy. In case we're gone too long. I'd like to just leave him with my landlady, if that's okay."

Kelsey nodded, silently, as he scooped up the unresisting cat. Now she felt the full weight of everything lay down on her heart. This was for real. This was it. Now she knew it.

Jayson gave her the key to lock up with while he knocked at the landlady's door, cradling Fluffy in his arms. Kelsey watched in horrified awe, as the woman opened her door and spoke to Jayson with a heavy French accent and the woman's other cats stepped outside, mewing. Jayson explained that they were going away for several days and the landlady smiled at him and reached forward to take the large kitten into her own arms. "He's a beauty, isn't he?" she said, kissing Fluffy on his furry head. "You people have a nice trip," she called after them before shutting the door.

Jayson thanked the woman again and then sighed, "Well, that's taken care of," before getting into the car.

They rolled down windows and breathed the particularly sweet morning air. "Two choices," Jayson said, "Tamiami Trail and we double back like last time, or Alligator Alley, which would be more direct."

"I'd rather go on the two lane road," Kelsey said. "It was so beautiful last time. I'd like to see it again."

They drove west on Tamiami Trail past the sawgrass, the canals and the Native American settlements. This morning especially the light made everything look more defined- the shadows on each blade of sawgrass, the ripples in the water where each of the long-legged white egrets stepped in to wade. And there was that wonderful smell of the marsh again.

"You taught me to appreciate all of this," she told Jayson. "I could find nothing to love in Florida until I saw this."

Jayson's shirt was open and, as he slouched in the seat, it revealed the very slightest sag in the enormous pectoral muscles, one of the first hints that the rock hard body might be changing. Kelsey found it touching and, for some reason, incredibly sexually exciting.

Jayson's eyes were narrowed lazily, without sunglasses and he, too, seemed to be savoring the sun and the breeze.

"You might not like it so much if you had to get a living from it the way the Indians have to these days," he said. "It's still heartbreakingly beautiful but it's brutal, you know. That was how I grew up. Not that I'd change it."

He looked over at her. "What I want to do," he told her, "is to take you back to the old cabin with me. There are things I think have to be examined. I'd like to know what it was in my old life that got me craving the material things so badly that I would take that kind of risk to get them."

Kelsey was comforted in a way that they were going to the old cabin on Rattlesnake Slough. She had the image of the place many times in her mind since she had seen it and she felt there was a sense of unfinished business there.

She felt odd asking her next question. It sounded absurd but her life depended on what he would answer. "Has God spoken to you yet about what you're going to do with me?"

Jayson nodded. "Yes, He has."

Around this time the sky began to darken and they lost the sunlight. Jayson glanced up at the clouds as he pulled into a little gas station on the road to the Corkscrew Swamp Sanctuary, the reservation and his father's old cabin.

"It looks like it will just be a sprinkle. There probably won't be any real rain until tonight. This will be your last bathroom break in civilization, if you need it."

Kelsey used the filthy gas station rest room, bought a snack cake and ate it on the way back to the car. It was odd, how the old man at the counter didn't even seem to notice her. He wouldn't remember her, or the muscle-bound man who had purposely parked around the side of the building, should anything happen.

"I told you it would stop," Jayson said and, for a moment, Kelsey didn't get that he was talking about the rain.

On the road, she tried to look for landmarks, but everything here looked basically the same to her, all trees and marsh. When Jayson pulled to the side of the road into a shallow parking spot she realized that, wherever they were, they had not yet passed Joe's Fish Camp; she would have recognized the place if they had.

Jayson led her over a rise and Kelsey made it through the brush with no problem. Then they were at the water again, at what appeared to be a man-made canal. Waiting, partially hidden in a clump of palmetto fronds, was a bass boat, just like the one they had used at the fish camp, only this one didn't have "Joe's" painted on it in red letters. Obviously, Jayson had put this boat here, waiting for this or some similar occasion.

"Get in," he urged and he bent to hold the boat steady for her.

The man-made canal gave way to a maze of natural streams and marshes. None of this area looked similar to Kelsey to where they had traveled the last time. She wondered if they really were near the cabin. If they were they must be approaching it roundabout, from another direction. They navigated using the outboard motor for a long time, and

Kelsey judged that they had gone a good distance, quite a bit farther than on the last visit.

This area seemed quieter also, even farther from civilization, if that was possible. The rustling of the wind was pleasant and, as Jayson had predicted, the temperature was not too hot. Because of the overcast skies and the slightly strong breeze, everything took on an eerie, expectant quality. Kelsey heard animals creeping through the shrubbery and she heard every little splash of the animals in the water. At one point a school of good-sized fish started leaping out of the water all around them and splashing back in, as though doing a little dance of joy.

"Wow!" Kelsey said.

"Too bad we didn't bring fishing gear," Jayson commented, making the trip to Kelsey's execution sound just like another day in the country.

"Are any of your alligator friends around?" Kelsey asked.

"Yes, they are, you just need to have a certain eye to be able to notice them." He pointed to what appeared to be the very top of a grayish brown log submerged in the water. "See, there's a big guy, over six foot. This time of year, you need to be especially careful. A lot of the females have their hatchlings around and they're very protective."

"I'll keep that in mind," Kelsey said, only half kidding. Then she said what she had been thinking about for a while. "You know, I'm really intrigued by this life. It fascinated me when I was learning about your past. You were supposedly thinking of us buying a house up in Northern Florida in one of the undeveloped areas. If you ever allow us to get past this, I'm sure that's what I'd like to do. You could teach me about the wilderness, all the stuff that you know. Maybe we could get most of our living from the land and out of the woods and I would be willing to do that. I sense that your heart never really left these woods and I would like to know that part of you."

He smiled at her and he looked amazingly innocent because a big yellow swallow-tailed butterfly had landed on his shoulder and sat there gently pumping its wings without him realizing it.

"You're a crazy girl, you know that?" he said. "You want to settle down in the wilderness with a man who's responsible for the death and injury of two of your best friends, who took your family away from you and who has committed his entire life to destroying yours."

Kelsey looked down into the water at a lovely soft-shelled turtle that paced their boat and at the yellow blossoms that floated in the water. "I'll never forgive you for Miranda," she said, "but I won't forgive myself either because I had a part in it, letting her get involved in the drugs and making her so jealous of me that she'd want to go with you to hurt me.

But we can't bring Miranda back. I know you think that one, or probably both of us, should die. But that would only be two more lives gone and I can't see the purpose in that. Wouldn't it be better to do something with the lives we have?"

Jayson captured her eyes in a very direct, challenging way and leaned one arm up on the engine, which he had cut. "So what would you do if I started gaining weight?" He smiled at her meanly.

Kelsey had thought about it. What she needed in Jayson was his soul.

"I'm assuming you *will* gain back the weight," she said. "If for no other reason than out of spite, to make me suffer. I don't care. You're the only man for me in this world and you're the key to me knowing this world. I wouldn't have come this far with you if I weren't totally committed to being with you. I know what I risk by going up there with you..."

"Do you?" Jayson asked and he leaned back a little and tipped the engine off the boat and into the water.

Kelsey pulled in her breath, trying to stay calm. She did not do anything about the challenging glance Jayson was giving her. After waiting there a while, with Kelsey still saying nothing, just the sound of the wind and the bird song and the animals splashing down off the banks and into the water, he decided to move. He picked up the oars and pulled strongly on them.

"You want to know the woods, Kelsey. I guess, then, you won't mind knowing them on their terms."

Kelsey tried to follow which direction they were going by the position of the sun in the sky, but it was difficult. Sometimes the trees and overhanging vegetation blocked the sun out. When she could use the sun to determine their direction, it didn't matter anyway because all they were doing was twisting and turning, following untold little tributaries that were all part of the same marsh.

All Kelsey actually knew was that there was no civilization for twenty or thirty miles in three directions, but if you went south, the road would have to be there and then she would need to head west to get to the nearest town.

There was a very strong gut feeling that Jayson was not planning on leaving the swamp today. Kelsey would stay with him, she knew that she would, but she also did not like the idea of being totally helpless. If he tried to do something crazy, she wished that she could at least get the both of them safely out of here. She did not plan to stand by silently and let him execute her either. If it came to something like that, she would do what she had to stop him, attempting to hurt him as little as possible in the process of protecting herself. She still felt there was hope.

Jayson's back became wet with sweat as he pulled on the oars. Although the water was still choked with weeds here, Kelsey noticed that it was quite deep; she couldn't see the bottom but dead logs in the water at an angle went down five or six feet that she could see.

"It's deeper here," she mentioned to Jayson.

"That's very observant," he said, "it is. I'm not sure of the geographical reason why. If you look at some of the hammocks here, you'll notice that they're also on a lot higher ground, and they're more sizable."

Kelsey looked around at the resplendent vegetation on the islands, the tall trees hung with ferns and bromeliads, the delicate orchids in splendid colors. She breathed in the wonder and the peace of it all. Daniels was unable to scare her with this place; she loved it too much.

He pulled the boat up beside the biggest island that they had seen today and indicated for her to get out. "Watch your step," he said quietly.

Kelsey checked down by her feet while he got the boat pulled up. She didn't like the sound of what he had said.

Jayson came to stand up on shore beside her, taking in a big lungful of the air. "Oh, this brings back memories," he said. "We used to call it Snake Island." He looked at her strangely, just as she noticed that the boat was drifting away very slowly with the mild current because he had never tied it.

"I hope you don't mind," he said, with a crooked smile, indicating the boat he had deliberately let go.

"That one area is the only one that's really deep anywhere around here," he commented. "Of course, we just got out of rainy season so most places are really wet but, aside from right here, we would still be able to stand up in any of them. You know, I could walk out of here with my eyes closed, to the road or back to the cabin. For you, Kelsey, I guess it would depend on if you were for real or full of shit."

He gave her a mean glance. "Then, there would always be the possibility of building a boat. The materials are here; it would just take you more than a day and you'd want to sleep off the ground at night, for your safety. And you'd have to do something about the mosquitoes…"

His telling her these things did not seem like something very good.

Kelsey glanced around herself relatively calmly. Was this what Daniels was going to do to her? Some absurd game of survival? Kelsey's heart was pounding but she felt that she could be up to it. She was already assessing her options. She knew that there was no way she was stepping directly into that water with those alligators; now that Jayson had shown her how to spot them, she could pick out four from where she was standing. Because of the mosquitoes, she berated herself for not wearing long sleeves.

Kelsey brushed her hands down the sides of her pants and faced him. "Is this what God told you to do?" she asked defiantly, "to leave me out here in the Everglades and see if I could survive?"

"God told me to kill you!" he said.

He wouldn't look at her. Keeping his head averted, he started kicking logs and brush violently out of his way in the clearing.

Kelsey looked at him, stunned, and instinctively she clutched her purse with the loaded gun closer to her body.

In one quick furious motion, Jayson was on her. He flung the purse to the side while he knocked Kelsey to the ground, with her face in the dirt and his two hundred and twenty-five-pound weight on top of her back and neck. She could hardly breathe under him and a little groaning sound slipped out of her. It seemed he had already won but she didn't want to die like this. If she had to, she wanted to face him.

"Jayson," she pleaded.

"Don't you ever try to use that gun against me!" he yelled.

She felt him shifting around and she felt him slip the gun into his waistband, between his body and hers. Still, he didn't move off of her.

"Oh my God, oh my God," Kelsey whispered to herself, thinking that he was going to shoot her in the back of the head.

But he was silent for a long time, just breathing.

Something told Kelsey to lift her eyes in front of her and that is when she saw the beautiful bronze pattern of a snake inches from her face. It shifted and then she noticed the arrowhead shape of its head. A rattler.

Jayson whispered in her ear, sounding proud, "You see him? Isn't he beautiful? That's an old granddaddy."

The snake had now coiled into an S, staring her straight in the face and ticking its rattle. "What you want to do," Jayson said, "is to back off slowly when I get off of you, then stand quietly in the clearing."

Gracefully, he slid his weight off of her and she did as she was told, inching slowly back to the dirt clearing.

Jayson stayed on the ground and he reached out his hand toward the snake and spoke to it confidently. "What's the matter, Pops? Nobody wants to hurt you. I know Kelsey can get annoying sometimes but you don't want to bite her. Come on now boy, it's been a real long time."

He held his hand out steadily and Kelsey watched in horror and fascination as the snake relaxed its coils and stretched out its blunt head toward his hand. Gradually, the snake came closer until finally it rested its chin in Jayson's palm.

Then the eight-foot snake began twining up the arm of Jayson's white dress shirt. Jayson smiled and then gracefully, mesmerizingly, he rose to his feet, so that she could see the glory of him with the snake creeping over his body.

"You jumped the gun, Kelsey," he said. "I didn't say that just because God told me to kill you, that's what I'd do. I wanted to tell you about this hammock, but you didn't give me a chance. My Dad and I called it Snake Island because there's a colony of rattlers here, which we used for our shows. When my father died I let the ones we had at home loose here. Some of the snakes that are here, like this guy, are basically tame. Others I couldn't vouch for, the younger ones."

There was something glowing in his eyes as he stood there with the enormous serpent stretching over his wildly defined muscles, something mystical, and she thought that he must know it. With his still gaze leveled on her, he said, "This is me, Kelsey, Dave Daniels. Do you like what you see?"

At this moment he represented to her all the power in the world that a single person could have, he represented the character that she wished she could have. What she wanted in life was to continue to learn from him and for them, together, to seek truth.

"You have more dignity and integrity than anyone I could ever imagine," she said. "All I want to do is be with you, Dave Daniels."

He sighed and gently tossed the rattler a few feet away. "Good hunting, old man," he said and he turned back to Kelsey. His voice was weary again, that ancient weariness in him that was so familiar.

"The Lord told me to kill you," he said, "but I have enough blood on my hands already. And, you see, that's not the worst thing I could do to you."

He stepped forward so that she was able to see the light sheen of sweat that had broken out on his chest and neck while holding the snake.

"Davie," she pleaded.

He drowned her out. "I believe you now, Kelsey, about how much you love me. You're willing to come here and die on my whim even though you're the biggest survivor I've ever known. But you'd do that out of love. Kelsey, the very worst thing I could do to you at this point wouldn't be to kill you- it would be to kill myself."

"No," Kelsey breathed, taking a step forward.

Jayson pulled out the gun and leveled it at the water. He fired three shots at the boat and the high powered ammunition tore into it, making it leap two inches off the water and then it settled back in, gradually sinking.

"You can't do this," Kelsey said. "I can't live without you. The pain every day would be unbearable." She was shaking. "There would just be this black emptiness, forever." Kelsey started shaking her head, hysterically.

"That's the point," Jayson said, narrowing his eyes at her and starting to wander the small beach. "Then you'll get some idea of how I feel every day about Allison and Brandon. And the pain won't ever go away."

She came to stand at his shoulder while he did something strange. He opened the bags of now thawed hot dogs and he began making an odd grunting sound in his throat.

Kelsey saw the first large alligator come splashing off the opposite bank. Jayson threw a hot dog, which bounced off the 'gator's scaly snout and then the alligator twisted its snout, showing her its teeth, and swallowed the hot dog. Now the other 'gators began paddling into place and it looked to Kelsey like some crazed 'gator farm at feeding time.

Jayson looked hysterical, with his face blotchy and tearstained as he recklessly tossed hot dogs at 'gators.

But this must be like with the snake; he must know what he was doing.

"What's going on?" she asked him, crying also, filled with helpless dread at the thought of losing him. She must stop it.

Sucking back his tears, and cleaning his hands from the last of the meat, he regained his calm and composure.

"It's a little deeper here," he told her, "so I was able to practice underwater wrestling the alligators for our shows. I started wrestling 'gators when I was six years old. There are worse things."

The area became quiet again, the 'gators slipping back into the water after their snack. Now there was only bird song and the other sounds of the 'Glades. Kelsey waited for Jayson to look at her.

"You can't do this," she told him, firmly. "If you have to, kill me but don't kill yourself."

Jayson smiled at her and reached the gun forward, extending it towards her.

"I'm not going to do it," he said. "You are. You're finally going to get to use this gun to kill Dave Daniels, just like you always wanted to."

Kelsey felt like she was choking on her own sobs. "I can't, Davie," she said. "I never could. Pursuing you for the wrong reasons like I did and destroying your life was the worst thing I've ever done. It put me in hell for the rest of my life because of the guilt. Maybe I sensed, even then, that you were the man I would love. But you can't deny that love now."

She could feel her eyes and skin blazing, on fire with the energy of what she was saying.

"Davie," she said, "whatever love you still feel for Allison, you can't deny the love that I feel for you. It's so powerful. We can both feel it. I love you more than Allison ever did, can't you see that?"

Jayson lunged for her throat.

He started squeezing with one powerful hand, while the beautiful light-colored eyes that she had loved so much glimmered inches from hers.

"You're a liar!" he said, through clenched teeth. "Allison died for me! They told her I wasn't coming out of the coma and she killed herself because she didn't want to be without me."

He let his hand slip down because he was crying and Kelsey stepped towards him and got into his face, forcing him to see her eyes.

"She died for you. But I would have *lived* for you, Davie, just like I would live for you now! I would've kept myself alive for you!"

Jayson let out a bellow of agonized rage. Then he flung Kelsey down on the ground and she felt a piece of wood ram into her back, hurting her.

"I hate you!" Jayson screamed. "I hate you!"

He aimed the gun, held out in two shaking hands. Kelsey did not believe what she was seeing. He was really going to end it, after all.

She cringed back into the ground as time slowed and she watched the gun drift down her body, first on her head, then her neck, breast, belly and, finally, on her right leg.

"See what it's like to survive!" he said and then there was an explosion.

Kelsey's right calf jumped as a gigantic weight slammed into it, knocking it away from her other leg. Then she saw blood, huge flowers of red blood growing on her pant leg and then on the ground.

She glanced up at Jayson's hard face before the pain started. He was starting to back away from her towards the edge of the island. And then the pain from her leg began, growing and exploding inside her head and her guts so that she screamed and arched her back with it. It was unimaginable pain. It felt like the end of the world. And it would not stop. She knew she had to find the wound on her leg and do something, but she was swimming in the overpowering pain.

Kelsey's vision and the picture of Jayson and the island were starting to fade. She remembered she had to do something- for some reason she had to stay alive. She could still see Jayson watching her from afar and his expression was curious, like he was waiting to see what she would do. She cried to him but her voice didn't come out right and, anyway, he didn't respond. He continued standing there, stonily, as the image of him swam in and out of her vision.

Kelsey was able to put her hands on her leg, trembling as she touched it and bringing up more swells of pain, each one almost causing her to black out. She could feel where the bullet had entered, apparently shattering a part of the bone. She could feel blood moving, still pulsing out of the wound. Jayson was still not responding to her whimpering.

She knew she'd have to do something fast because she was losing so much blood. She took a deep breath, thinking how she'd seen this done in movies. She needed a tourniquet to stop the bleeding, she thought. As she had seen it done, she tore off a piece from the bottom of her pants and, grunting with pain, she slipped it under her leg. She glanced up again at Jayson, who stood now at the very edge of the water, watching her but not helping.

Grimly, Kelsey went back to work on herself. She twisted the fabric tightly, just above the wound, meanwhile dabbing away the older blood so she could see what was going on. She wasn't aware of how much time went by but, gradually, she was able to maintain some mastery over the pain and she saw that the tourniquet was drastically slowing the blood flow. If she could continue with the tourniquet for a while longer, and then use some fabric to wrap the wound, she didn't think she would die of loss of blood. There was also the fact that the bone was broken.

Some time passed and there was still no reaction from her lover, who she could still see pacing by the water, so Kelsey began feeling around her for suitable sticks, something she could use as a splint for the broken bone. This way, at least she'd be able to stand up. She found a small piece of wood of the right length and she held it up to the agonizingly painful leg to get it tied on correctly.

The danger would be infection, gangrene, losing part of her leg. But none of these things would happen if she could get back to civilization in time.

She glanced up at Jayson, one last questioning look.

He seemed to understand. He said to her, "You'll be fine, Kelsey. You're a survivor."

He looked so golden standing there by the water with a fresh ray of sunlight shimmering off his hair and eyelashes and dots of brilliance in the water behind him, warm sunny spots on the backs of the 'gators. Then Jayson turned and dove into the water.

Next, there was a churning, as some of the large alligators leaped at the spot where he had submerged.

Kelsey sprang to her feet and then she banged back down to the ground in agony. Although the splint had held, she had nothing to hold her up.

"No! Jayson!" she screamed.

Then she scrambled back up on her good knee, frantically searching for something that would help her stand up, and still keeping an eye on the water. She saw the black tails of the animals thrashing around, enormous tails, at least four large 'gators that she could see. The animals were thrashing around something in the water.

There was no way Jayson could survive and yet Kelsey had to believe that he could. She had to somehow get to him.

She found the log that she had earlier fallen on. She pulled it loose from the vines and it was the perfect height. Kelsey pulled herself up with the log and used it to lean on to limp down to the edge of the water.

There she screamed at the gators. "Let him go! Get away from him!"

There were no rocks, so Kelsey threw sticks and pieces of wood. If she swam in, they would kill her, too, and she couldn't even see where Jayson was. Two of the alligators had gone, a third one backed off and there was only the one enormous one. And it was swimming quickly upstream, dragging something white.

"Nooooooo!" Kelsey screamed, her throat seeming to rip out with her anguish.

She needed something, anything. If she had the boat, she could follow. But the boat was out of sight, sunk. The gun! She checked the beach and clearing for it. But it must have gone into the water with Jayson.

Kelsey waded a few painful steps into the water and she saw her wound start to seep blood. Then she looked up and saw the snout of one of the 'gators turning back in her direction and coming quickly towards her.

Jayson's words echoed in her mind, "You're a survivor." And Kelsey staggered back a few steps in the water, almost loosing her balance. She steadied herself with the makeshift crutch and got onshore, where the 'gator turned away from her.

This is when Kelsey saw that the center of the stream area was filled with blood, a giant patch of bright red blood, melting into the muddy water.

"No!" she moaned to herself, crying for her lover, even as pain began pulsing unbearably in her injured leg.

He had set this all up, making his death the most horrible one possible, something that would haunt Kelsey's mind every minute for the rest of her life, if she survived today.

And even if she didn't want to live, it wouldn't be as simple as shooting herself. She'd have to stay here and die a horrible death of infection, dehydration or having the animals kill her- either rattlesnakes or gators. Otherwise she'd have to try and save herself. And, of course, Jayson had been right. No matter how devastating living with the memories of him would be, Kelsey would have to save herself; she would have to meet this challenge.

Kelsey stood in the middle of the island, looking around her and trying to plan, even as the waves of pain brought her close to fainting. She knew time was of the essence. The longer it took her to get to medical help, the greater the chance that her leg could not be properly repaired. But there was no sense thinking or worrying about that now, except to get out of here quicker.

There were still three or four hours until sunset and Kelsey did not plan to stay on this hammock overnight. Jayson's warnings stuck with her. In the state she was in, she could not withstand the mosquitoes and there were also the rattlesnakes on this particular piece of ground. Jayson had talked about walking out of here, mentioning in particular that, while the pool at the south side of this landmass was deep, all the other areas were shallow.

There had to be a point to his saying this. It was all a test, after all. Jayson had constructed the whole thing from beginning to end and had made it always just at the reach of her abilities. There was no reason to believe that this final test would be any different or that it would be beyond her to complete. Her guess was that the way to go was on the north side of the island. There was another hammock about twenty feet away and the chain of islands seemed to stretch steadily north, with no very large breaks between them that Kelsey could see.

Seeing what the alligators had done to Jayson, there was no way Kelsey was going to spend time wading through this water the miles and miles it would take to get back to the road, especially with her leg seeping blood.

She would have to find, or build, a boat. Kelsey could guess at her position here. Based on landmarks they had passed on the road, she knew they were almost as far east as Joe's Fish Camp. Today they had traveled what seemed like a farther distance than the distance to get to the

Daniels' old cabin. But there had been more twists and turns in today's journey. Kelsey judged that they were probably very near the cabin; this must be the point of leaving her in this particular spot.

Daniels would want her to feel what he felt, to feel like him. If she was to survive, she needed to get to that cabin. She remembered the old rowboat there. It had looked like something that she could possibly fix, and there were plenty of tools at the cabin that she could work with, including that harpoon-like object which she could use to fight off gators if she had to.

And there was the screen over the bedroom window that would keep out mosquitos. She could sleep safely at the cabin and leave at first light. She imagined that, by then, her leg would be pretty bad. But it was a fairly straight route from the cabin to the fish camp and she was sure she could do it even if she was quite ill.

Jayson, you intended this, didn't you? For me to be like you and to think like you, Kelsey thought, as she looked into the water where the color of blood had now dispersed. Could you still be alive, she wondered, narrowing her eyes at the spot where he went under, and wobbling on the crutch. He had been a 'gator wrestler after all.

Kelsey knew that the biggest of these animals was twice the size of the ones used in shows and there were the others, too, at least four in all. Kelsey had seen the blood and had seen the alligator grasp Jayson's shirt in the water. But, still, she hadn't seen any actual pieces of his body float to the surface. Possibly, no matter how much he had wanted to die, when he hit the water and the creatures attacked him, instinct had made him fight for his life. Maybe he had been able to swim underwater and get away. And maybe he had crawled to shore and was alive out there somewhere, and he'd come back following her again, if she ever survived this. Kelsey tucked that possibility away in a corner of her mind.

She could look for Jayson as she traveled. If he was injured, once she had the boat, she could get him to a hospital. And, even if she didn't find him right away, and he was in these swamps alive but wounded, she could get park rangers to find him once she reached civilization. There was always a chance. But she knew she had to work on this problem first because she couldn't do anyone any good dying on this island tonight.

Kelsey's best guess was that the Daniels' old cabin was northeast of here. If she could find the old observation tower, it would be a landmark and it had to be very near here if her figurings were correct. She had just enough diffused sunlight to navigate by, but she knew she'd have to get going if she was to make it to the cabin by sundown.

Kelsey slung her purse across her chest, thinking some of the things she had with her might prove useful. And then she took the lid from the Styrofoam cooler and carried it to the edge of the water on the north side. She intended to float partly on the lid, holding her wounded leg out of the water while using the crutch to pole herself and to fight off 'gators. She would have to repeat this each time she changed islands. Hopefully, the cabin would be very near. But what she couldn't do was sit here and wait. She understood this.

Kelsey lowered herself as silently as possible into the warm sticky water while she felt fear tighten her chest. It was shallow enough here that her good leg touched the mucky bottom, but leaning on the Styrofoam made her go faster. She directed her eyes on a clear spot on the opposite shore and poled herself, ignoring the sickening pain in her leg, breathing hard, but trying to make as little disturbance in the water as possible. No animals approached her.

She reached the shallow muck on the other side unharmed. She crawled onto the sand, using the trunk of a bush to pull herself to her feet, and she checked briefly around herself for snakes.

Kelsey looked back at the island she had come from and she smiled because she had gotten across this portion of water successfully. She knew she might have three more hours of this ahead of her before she reached the cabin, but she knew she could do it. She knew she could make it.

The End

About the Author

Emma "Freeway" Lincoln writes sexy Florida suspense with underlying philosophical meaning. *Florida Justice* is the first in a three book series of passion and vengeance against the backdrop of all that's breathtaking- and twisted- in South Florida. Emma and her husband- and soulmate- Ray are independent-minded, wide-ranging travelers who like to spend most of their time on the Florida beaches.

Other Books by Emma "Freeway" Lincoln:

Fearless in Florida

&
Coming soon:
Two more books in the "Florida Justice" series: